ONE DARK FUTURE

ONE DARK FUTURE

OPUS X™ BOOK EIGHT

MICHAEL ANDERLE

DISRUPTIVE IMAGINATION®

Copyright © 2021 Michael Anderle
Cover by Gene Mollica Studios
Cover copyright © LMBPN Publishing
This book is a Michael Anderle Production

LMBPN Publishing
PMB 196, 2540 South Maryland Pkwy
Las Vegas, NV 89109

First US edition, August 2020
Version 1.01, January 2021
eBook ISBN: 978-1-64202-772-3
Print ISBN: 978-1-64202-773-0

THE ONE DARK FUTURE TEAM

Thanks to the JIT Readers

Kelly O'Donnell
Jeff Eaton
Dave Hicks
John Ashmore
James Caplan
Deb Mader
Dorothy Lloyd
Peter Manis
Jeff Goode
Paul Westman
Larry Omans

If I've missed anyone, please let me know!

Editor
Lynne Stiegler

To Family, Friends and
Those Who Love
to Read.
May We All Enjoy Grace
to Live the Life We Are
Called.

CHAPTER ONE

April 1, 2230, Low Earth Orbit, Llewellyn Observatory

The horde of data windows and augmented reality overlays in Tony's smart lenses didn't do much to dull the excruciating pain of sorting through the piles of data.

So, he made up stupid questions in the middle of an almost incapacitatingly boring data review. His latest was how many years of his life would he be willing to give up to be the person or persons responsible for a great discovery?

Of course, everything depended on the prize. If it was significant enough, he had decided that twenty years would be the maximum. With the ability to prolong life, that wasn't too much to rake off the end. With a large enough prize, he would be able to afford it.

Maybe six months for something mundane.

Tony had been excited when he was selected for the Vand Foundation Fellowship to Llewellyn Observatory. Not having to hustle for grants to support his graduate work in astronomy meant he should be able to concentrate on the science like he'd always dreamed. It wasn't the foundation's fault his dream wasn't living up to reality.

Even as an undergraduate, he'd quickly understood science was five percent glorious discovery and ninety-five percent hard work.

Or was that ninety-nine percent perspiration, one percent inspiration?

Understanding the less impressive parts of academic research didn't mean he held his patrons in great regard. Tony used to be impressed with charitable groups like the Vand Foundation, but he'd convinced himself they were mostly tax dodges and PR.

It didn't mean he disliked them, but other than *pro forma* letters of thanks, he wasn't about to go overboard.

Still, he didn't mind for the moment. The grant was helping him, and he'd shake Sophia Vand's hand if he ever ran into her, which wasn't likely.

From what he'd heard on the news, she was keeping a low profile, to the point she'd disappeared from the public eye.

He couldn't blame her, given some of the recent terrorist incidents. Someone like her was more likely to be targeted than a random graduate student like him. That didn't stop his jealousy, especially when he concluded she probably didn't even have anything to do with her family foundation other than the occasional news conference.

"If only I could be rich and do what I want and hide when people get annoying." Tony let his head loll back as he let out a long groan. "This isn't what I signed up for. I don't care what they say about that second- and third-year itch!"

Arda, the other graduate student on the station, looked at him with a frown. Tony didn't want to piss him off.

With only three people on the observatory, including the supervising professor, any personal problems would be painful, and Tony wasn't scheduled to leave for two months. Despite his whining, he understood the path to a more stimulating future of concentrating on the big picture while having grad students do the grunt work included his current predicament.

He was the stepping stone at this point in his life.

"What did you sign up for, then?" Arda asked. Something about his accent always made it hard for Tony to figure out if he was being sarcastic. He pointed at a graph. "You're confirming the system analysis with spot checks. That seems to me like it's exactly what you signed up for. What did you think you were going to do?"

"We can let the system analyze all the comet data." Tony gestured toward his wall of data windows. "We waste a bunch of our time doing manual spot checks when we should be spending more time doing low-level analysis on candidates of interest, but Professor Lal's blocking us. He's using us as the world's least efficient error-checking routines." He slapped his palm against his forehead. "It's not even like he doesn't believe the system. You heard him the other day. We're doing this on the *off*-chance we're missing something! That's what he said. I could have done this on Earth. What's the point of even being up here?"

Arda stared at Tony, disapproval building on his face. "I *thought* you wanted to do your thesis project on long-period comets." He tapped at a virtual keyboard and brought up a close-up of a dense comet with a long, wispy tail. "It's not insane that you would be assigned to do data analysis on Solar System comets."

"You're missing the point." Tony lifted his arm and swept away half his data windows. "Look, I'm not trying to be a jerk. I *want* to do analysis work. However, I don't want to do glorified error-checking for stupid algorithms. I'm supposed to be training to be a scientist."

"And *this* is part of science." Arda stared at the comet image. "It's funny when you think about it."

"How is it funny? You find our valuable time being wasted amusing? I'm sure the Vand Foundation doesn't throw around academic grants for graduate students to do pointless busywork."

Arda shook his head, turning away from the picture with a smile. "No, not this work. You and me, being here. That's what's funny."

Tony sighed, doing his best not to show his annoyance to the other student. "I have no idea what you're talking about. Care to explain?"

"Think about it." Arda brought up a three-dimensional image of a long-period comet with an elliptical orbit that had it spending thousands of years away from anything in the inner Solar System at a time. "See this one?"

"C/1822 N1," Tony read off the image's legend. "Judging by the data, still on its way out, with its next closet run around the seventh millennium." He smirked. "I think I'll be done with my data analysis by then."

Arda gave his head a weary shake, his eyes betraying his disdain for Tony's thought process. "When it was last closest to Earth, we'd barely begun mastering electricity. Coal trains were the epitome of transportation technology." He stood and gestured broadly. "In the few centuries on its way out, we've gone from mastering the land to the skies and even space. We've left our home planet and system. We've spread across the stars and run into aliens."

"Yeah? So?" Tony shrugged. "Technology and humanity march on. That's why we run Earth and not penguins or those little bastard koala bears."

"That's just it." Arda sank back into his seat. "We have colonies fifty light-years away, but in our home system, we've never sent a person farther than Sedna. Of all these comets you're complaining about, what percentage have we even sent probes to?"

Tony blinked as he thought about the implications. "You're right, but that's why I wanted to do something with long-period comets. I know all the sexy research is exosystem work, let alone the ton of people trying to do remote analysis work on alien systems. But here, the mystery's still waiting for us, even if Lal's got us wasting time being pointless..." He narrowed his eyes as he focused on his screen. "What the hell? That's not right."

"Excuse me? There's no reason to talk that way to me."

"Not you, Arda." Tony licked his lips and pointed at one of his remaining data windows. It was nothing but columns and numbers, but both knew how to interpret time-series comet orbital data.

"Then what?"

"That's not right!" Tony shouted, his eyes bulging. He summoned three new data windows, all filled with more specific data on a particular comet. His eyes darted back and forth as he continued entering commands. It couldn't be what he thought.

"What's going on?" Arda asked.

"Give me a minute. I'm trying to figure something out."

Arda rolled his eyes and folded his arms. Tony might have annoyed the other student, but if what he was seeing in front of him was accurate, he'd have a far more exciting thesis subject. There was one minor problem with his plan for scientific glory.

"Oh, damn it," Tony moaned. "I'm going to have to admit to Professor Lal that he was right to make me do this."

Arda leaned closer to the screen. "What are you seeing?"

Tony jabbed his finger at a data window. "Don't you get it? One-hundred-thousand-year period on this baby. It's not super-close at about 1000 AUs out from us right now, about twice as far as Sedna, but you see this?" He pointed to several numbers. "These aren't just orbit variations. These are orbital changes from the basic expected orbit, all within the last couple of months."

"That's impossible. Comets just don't abruptly *change* course." Arda shrugged, the disbelief clear on his face.

"Yeah, it's weird." Tony shook his head. "I've seen tracking data on this comet before, and I didn't see these numbers."

"Then it's just some sort of data transmission error." Arda glanced at him. "You're getting yourself worked up over nothing."

"Nope, I just crosschecked," Tony replied. "This is legit data. If anything, there are some problems with the check-sums on the original data, but who cares? There's something making this comet *change course*, Arda, and that's the mystery. Maybe all those old theories about a close brown dwarf star out there are true?"

Arda scoffed. "People have been looking for a brown dwarf close to the Solar System for centuries now, and they've turned up nothing. And suddenly, you think you've found Nemesis in some random data check? Don't you know how unlikely that is?"

"Unlikely isn't the same thing as wrong." Tony gestured at another data window, depicting multiple overlapping orbits of different objects. "But I don't think I've found Nemesis. I think I've found something else."

Arda waited for a moment. "What?"

"This...thing." Tony pointed to another dot on the window. "This makes it even weirder."

"What's that?" Arda tilted his head and squinted. "That's really small."

"Super-small," Tony turned slowly to face the other student. "The historical data from the last couple of weeks has caught a few brief periods of intense thermal activity. If I didn't know better, I'd say it's a ship."

"A ship?" Arda shook his head. "A ship twice as far out as the farthest human settlement in the Solar System? Why would anyone bother flying out that far? A ship way past the HTP?"

"Yes." Tony looked down for a moment and nodded as he worked through the possibilities. "If they'd done most of their primary burns before getting there, it'd be very hard to spot them that far out. It's like you said; they're well past anything with a lot of sensors. It's easy to get lost out there."

"But what...why?" Arda rubbed his temples. "Getting

that far out might take a year or two, and that's one way." He pointed to another dot on the orbital graph. "Sedna's not even in a good position relative to your phantom ship, so it's not like they could top off their supplies. And why travel for potentially years just to land on a comet? Why not just wait until one came in closer and then land like people have done tons of times? This comet might be a super long-period, but it's not special."

"Except for the mysterious course changes." Tony took a deep breath and held his hands in front of his chest. "Now, hear me out before you say I'm crazy."

Arda groaned. "This is going to be painful, isn't it?"

"There are no unusual emissions or readings in any of the spectra with the comet, but those changes don't look like reactions to a star or a black hole." Tony lowered his voice to a near-whisper. "It looks more like a ship doing course corrections."

Arda looked at a calendar on his screen. "It's April 1st." He turned to Tony, narrowing his eyes. "Is this another stupid American April's Fool prank?"

"This isn't a prank." Tony stood, his gaze locked on the orbital path display. "This is a huge scientific discovery. I bet you it is a ship!"

"But according to this data, this comet's been tracked for almost two hundred years."

Tony nodded. "Yeah. So? This is the first time it's demonstrated any movements like that."

"How could it be a ship then? It's coming toward Earth, not away, and the spectral analysis suggests a comet."

"I don't know. It's got to be alien," Tony snapped. "Probably the Leems. Maybe they crashed into a comet or some-

8

thing and they died, but the automated system is still providing some thrust. Even if we don't rewrite the first contact story, we can contribute to history."

Arda chuckled. "You should have majored in history, not astronomy."

"Oh, crap." Tony's eyes widened. "I didn't even think through the implications."

Arda glanced at the data, his brow furrowing in concern. "What implications?"

"The other ship," Tony replied. He gestured widely.

"Let's pretend there's a mysterious ship flying out to an even more mysterious alien ship. What about it?"

"Don't you get it? *Somebody already knows.*" Tony slapped his forehead. "It's a ship or a probe." He brought up another virtual keyboard and didn't speak for a minute while he typed intensely. "Great. Just great."

A new data window appeared, displaying the motion of the comet and the smaller object. According to the simulation, without additional course changes, the smaller object would intercept the larger object in under two months.

"Wait." Arda shook a finger. "Somebody already knows about it? And they knew long enough ago to send a ship or a probe out a year or two in advance?"

"I don't know. Maybe?" Tony grimaced. "But I haven't heard anything about it. Why wouldn't they want this all over the literature? Why isn't it on the news?"

"Because they're worried about being wrong," Arda concluded. "If it's not a ship, and they talked about it being a ship, and then their probe got there and it's just another comet, they'd look like idiots."

"You know what? Let's hit the literature, but don't ask

around on the net. We don't want someone to poach our discovery. If whoever is flying out there didn't publish, that's their own fault."

"You sure?" Arda asked. "We can't even be sure ourselves."

"So what?" Tony replied. "We could also be sitting on a major scientific discovery that will rewrite the history books."

"I don't know about that." Arda sighed, and his shoulders slumped in defeat. "If somebody else already has a probe out there—"

"It's not a probe," Tony insisted.

"How can you be so sure?"

"Because the size and spectra are off. This isn't the first time I've had to filter out ships or probes from observation data. It's just the first time I've had to deal with one that far out."

Arda nodded, thinking it through. "Fine, so it's a ship, but then somebody had the money to send an entire crewed ship out there."

"That means it's all the more likely there is some old Leem ship with a busted hyperspace drive sitting there." Tony made a fist. "It doesn't matter if they're there first. They don't want to publish, right? If we collect enough information, we can publish first. We'll get the credit for the discovery. If it's not published in a journal, it might as well not exist."

He eyed the data, chuckling over the irony of his earlier complaints. "Thanks, Sophia Vand. I hope you're having a good time wherever you are. If it wasn't for you, I wouldn't be here right now, about to change history."

CHAPTER TWO

With a smile, Erik dipped his karaage into his small dish containing a flecked brown sauce. He loved the fried chicken dish well enough, but the sauce sent it to the level of purely delicious.

If there was one great advantage humanity held over every other intelligent species, it was its ability to produce wondrous and glorious variations of fried chicken. Granted, not all the Local Neighborhood races ate meat, and they probably didn't have chickens on their planets, but that didn't make Erik ignore humanity's chicken-based culinary superiority.

Too bad Jia, sitting across from him, wasn't doing her part to enjoy humanity's core advantages. When a woman didn't enjoy chicken, she was letting the aliens win.

Erik took a bite of the sauce-covered chicken, enjoying the spicy notes playing across his tongue. "This is great.

You should have had some, instead of that." He nodded toward the bowl of boring white rice. "Aren't you hungry for protein?"

Jia set her chopsticks down and shrugged. "I'm still full from breakfast. But what's with you? You had a huge breakfast, yet you are stuffing that karaage down like you're starving to death." She looked him up and down. "Is there a *yaoguai* tapeworm in you?"

"Huh? What can I say?" Erik offered her a merry grin before taking another bite of karaage. "I'm a growing boy. And this sauce is probably spiked to make it addictive."

Erik would appreciate the small pleasures while he could.

It should have been a relaxing couple of weeks since the Ascended Brotherhood's attempted sinking of Parvati on Venus and Erik and Jia's showdown with Sophia Vand, but rumors had leaked of their presence on Parvati, and local reporters had been relentless. Emma was screening all calls now and claimed she could identify a reporter with ninety-eight percent accuracy based on their first two sentences.

"No," Jia replied. "You having an appetite isn't a big deal. That's not what I'm talking about. It's just *everything* is spicy for you lately." She pointed at this plate. "Don't think I didn't see you eyeing the hot sauce when you were eating your beignets at breakfast." She grimaced. "I didn't say anything since you didn't go through with that taste atrocity. That's so nasty, I'm sure some purist association would show up to protest."

"I don't know." Erik gave a light shrug. "Ever since we got back from Venus, I've had a thing for spicy foods.

Something about the flavors stuck with me. Can't a man satisfy some cravings?"

"Oh, is that why we've been hitting Blessings of Hyderabad so much?" Jia chuckled. "And this place? Because of their spicy karaage?"

"It's damned good, plus." He looked around before finishing his thought. "It's spicy."

"You could have just said so." Jia offered him a soft smile.

"Hey, you asked where I wanted to eat, and I named a place. No reason for this to get complicated…" Erik's voice trailed off with a frown, then he continued, "and worry too much about unimportant crap."

An auburn-haired woman sitting at a table directly behind them was staring at him with a huge smile. Expectation filled her face, but she didn't say anything.

Something about her short haircut and dark suit suggested corporate manager to Erik's first instincts, but there was a hunger in her eyes that pointed elsewhere. Another fan, possibly. He was beginning to think wearing a disguise in public even when he wasn't working a job for Alina might be a good idea.

Fame had proven more annoying than he'd anticipated.

"Can I help you?" Erik asked, trying to sound only half as gruff as normal. Jia glanced toward the woman with more curiosity than hostility.

The woman stood and strolled over to the table, her cup of green tea in hand. "I'm sorry. I didn't mean to eavesdrop, not totally, at least, but I overheard you talking about Venus." She clasped her hands together under the cup and parted her lips in excitement. "I've been thinking about taking a trip there. Packages are really cheap right now because everyone's scared about what happened on Parvati."

"That's not an unreasonable position to hold," Jia replied.

"Please note that this woman is a freelance reporter," Emma transmitted directly to their ears. "Melanie O'Shay. I've matched her face to pictures on multiple articles sold to a variety of news organizations. Her specialty appears to be, in her own words, quirky human-interest stories. I've found some low-level crime articles, but they are well below the scope you are typically involved in."

Jia nodded at the woman, then looked at Erik, a question in her eyes. Erik swallowed another bite of karaage and gestured to an empty chair. Reporters were like wolves. Sometimes you needed to stand and fight. Running only encouraged them to chase you down. Ripping into her was premature.

Not every reporter was a dick like Lance Onassis, just most of them. He wanted to probe first.

Melanie sat and rubbed her hands together. "Thanks for being willing to share. I've never left Neo SoCal, let alone Earth, but once I read about how you can get some of these vacation packages for half off, I thought to myself, 'You have to do that.'" She stuck out her hand. "Melanie."

"Erik." He shook her hand, not using too tight a grip.

Jia leaned over to follow up and offered her name plus a quick shake. She settled back, a knowing look in her eyes.

"Oh, wait." Melanie gasped. "Aren't you those famous cops? The Obsidian Detective and Lady Justice?"

"Ex-cops." Erik grabbed another piece of karaage. "We work in the private sector now. And we're just Erik and Jia."

"That's right. I vaguely remember reading about that, but I heard that you were on Venus when all that stuff happened? Massive terrorist incident, military and police response." Melanie took on a conspiratorial grin. "You two aren't the kind of people who go running from that sort of thing. Come on, tell me the truth. You were there helping out the cops, weren't you? They probably asked you to help."

Since Erik was still munching on his food, Jia answered, mockery in her tone. "Tell the truth? Shouldn't you start by telling the truth?"

So much for a careful probe. Erik didn't laugh. He didn't care about offending Melanie, but he didn't want to spit out any of his food.

Melanie blinked. "Huh? What are you talking about?"

"Melanie O'Shay." Jia smiled and reached down to her PNIU. After a couple quick taps, a professional headshot of the reporter winked into existence in the center of the table. "It's a striking resemblance, wouldn't you say? Same name and everything."

Her mouth opened, shut, and then did that a couple more times.

With a sheepish smile, the reporter sighed and rubbed the back of her neck. "You can't blame a woman for trying. I got lucky that you came back to this place. My background research indicated that you like to hit the same places, and I've been staking out different restaurants you're known to frequent for a week now, and nothing.

This was a long shot as is. Then you strolled on in here, and I'm like, 'Jackpot!'"

Erik shrugged. "We're changing things up."

"It's not like I lied to you. I gave you my real name."

Erik smirked. "Oh, you're going on vacation to Venus soon?"

"Okay." Melanie groaned. "I did lie about wanting to go on vacation, but I never said I wasn't a reporter. And it's not like I'm trying to out you for doing something awful. Everyone knows you helped take down terrorists on Venus. I don't get why you wouldn't want the whole UTC to know." Her eyes gained that glint of hope. "I could help with that."

They couldn't even go for lunch without someone spotting them. That was reason enough for Neo SoCal, let alone the rest of the UTC, not knowing how integral they were to the defeat of the Ascended Brotherhood's plot on Venus. Erik clung to the one truth he'd learned since his time back on Earth. Wrap a lie up in truth, and it became easy to swallow. People almost wanted others to lie to them.

"Even *if* we got involved in anything," Erik replied, "we're fully licensed private security contractors who happened to be authorized to use a variety of heavy weapons. We might have also happened to be on Parvati for a vacation when the incident occurred. The local police had military forces mobilized to deal with it, but let's say we were involved and shot a gun or two, and I'm not saying we did. Even if we did, we only did it because it's not like we're going to sit around while innocent people got gunned down. There was no special trip or us helping anyone. Hypothetically."

Melanie bobbed her head. "Of course. Hypothetically." She raised an eyebrow. "You're saying that you might have hypothetically happened to be there for vacation at the time of a major terrorist incident? You don't think that's a mighty convenient coincidence?"

"Sometimes the Lady is with you, and sometimes she's against you," Erik finished with a shrug.

"The Lady?" Melanie's face scrunched in confusion. "What Lady? Lady Justice? Isn't that you?"

"Lady Luck," Jia clarified with a smile. "I wish I were her. That would be more useful."

"I see. I didn't realize that Mr. Blackwell was so superstitious." Melanie licked her lips, uncertainty openly playing across her face. "And you're saying you also had nothing to do with the raid on that zoo of non-clone rare exotic animals in Oklahoma that turned out to be filled with *yaoguai*? I know it wouldn't have been *just* you two, but maybe you led the team?"

Erik and Jia exchanged looks. He hadn't been to Oklahoma for decades, let alone to any zoo filled with *yaoguai*. It wouldn't be a surprise if such a place existed. It wouldn't even be much of a surprise if they ended up raiding it.

"Oh, I remember reading about that," Jia offered with a chuckle. At least someone knew what the reporter was talking about. "I think calling them *yaoguai* was a bit much. They were just slightly tweaked clones. Sure, the guy running things was strange, and that's an understatement, but he's in prison now for trafficking in illegally modified animals and safety violations."

"And what about the incident in Lagos?" Melanie pressed. "You telling me you had nothing to do with that?"

"What incident in Lagos?" Erik asked, keeping his smile natural and forcing himself to not look at Jia. For a low-end reporter who allegedly focused on fluff, she was sniffing close to the truth.

"There was an attack on the Sky Garden," Melanie offered in a breathless voice.

Erik nodded. "Oh, yeah, sure. I read about it. But what does that have to do with us?"

Melanie narrowed her eyes. "You're saying you weren't involved in that?"

"Why? Is someone saying we were?" Erik laughed. "I'd love to be the guy who saved the Sky Garden, but we spend most of our time doing pretty boring and standard corporate security gigs these days, and we've not been hired by anyone in Nigeria. You do a job in Nigeria that you didn't tell me about, Jia?"

"Not that I can recall," she answered with a smile. She grabbed her chopsticks and collected some rice, her gaze never leaving Melanie. "And I think I'd remember something like that."

"And what about the syndicate wars on Mars? There are rumors that someone weakened the Dome Society before the other syndicates took them out." Melanie asked. "Or the recent takedown of the Infinity Syndicate in Thessalonica? Information out there suggests a small highly-skilled team was involved in infiltrating their headquarters before the CID push. And you're going to tell me you two had absolutely nothing to do with the disruption of the Grayhead plot in Sydney?"

For all the heavy incidents he and Jia were involved in, it seemed like there were plenty of others across the planet and Solar System keeping other people busy. Erik let out a low chuckle that built to a huge laugh. Other patrons looked his way and murmured among themselves. Melanie's brow furrowed in frustration.

"What's so funny?" she asked with a huff.

"There are billions of people in the Solar System," Erik replied. "And somehow you think that every single spectacular incident involving terrorists or criminals involves two people?"

Melanie averted her eyes. "I'm not saying that *every* incident does, but you can't deny you were on Venus. That's a matter of public record."

Jia finished swallowing some rice. "We didn't deny we were on Venus. We admitted we were on Venus, and we might have been incidentally involved in the incident, but you can't spin that into us being involved in every major showdown with criminals or terrorists that have occurred in the last few months." She shook her chopsticks at the reporter. "The universe doesn't revolve around us. There are millions of good police officers, CID agents, and soldiers out there doing their jobs to protect people. Why don't you go ask the people involved in these incidents instead of making up ridiculous conspiracy theories where somehow we're the only two people in the UTC stopping anything bad from happening? It's insulting to everyone else's efforts."

Melanie gasped and put a hand over her mouth. Her pale cheeks grew scarlet. "I-I just…thought…"

"You thought that you could get away from having to

do human interest stories with some big story concerning crime and terrorism?" Erik suggested.

Melanie sighed and let her head fall forward. "Did you know I did an interview with Rena Winston only two months before you two got involved with her? It was all about her songwriting process, and then boom, it turns out she's a changeling. And I didn't have a clue. I was as shocked as anyone." She ran her hands through her hair. "And I was thinking, 'If I'd just dug a little deeper, I could have had a major scoop.' What about... Never mind."

"Sorry." Erik shrugged. "We're boring now. There's no big story here to be uncovered. We both decided we'd put in our time and dues because of all the high-profile cases. It was getting difficult to live a normal life, so we decided to clock out and do something a little more high-paying and less dangerous. It's not that we never have to shoot at people, but our days of epic showdowns are over."

Melanie gave a feeble nod. "You really didn't have anything to do with all those incidents?"

"We've read about them."

Melanie stood with another long sigh. "I'm sorry to have bothered you." She headed toward the door, her head hung low.

Jia leaned close to whisper to Erik. "I'll give her credit. That wasn't total garbage."

"It was mostly garbage. Just assuming we're involved in anything big isn't an example of great investigative journalism."

"We were involved in a disproportionate number of the incidents she mentioned."

Erik snickered. "Yeah, living the life. Always fun." He grabbed another piece of karaage. "Let's finish up and get out of here before another reporter ambushes us."

CHAPTER THREE

Fifteen minutes later, Jia and Erik sat in the MX 60 on their way back to Erik's apartment. Their flitter was safely cocooned in the standard afternoon metal swarm that was Neo SoCal traffic.

Jia incessantly checked the sensors and cameras, a firm suspicion now lodged deep in her mind. Erik didn't appear to notice as he rambled on about the relative merits of karaage versus different styles of American fried chicken and a fried chicken masala dish he'd had a couple of times in the last week.

"I'm saying the spices make a bigger difference than I thought," Erik explained. "I don't know. I spent so many years out on the frontier, let alone stuffing my face with rations, that I kind of trained myself not to care as much as I should. I've really learned to appreciate food since coming back to Earth. It's not a bad thing. I'm not claiming I can always tell ingredient quality, but I know what I like."

"There is no one following us, Jia," Emma interrupted. "So stop it."

Jia grimaced, both startled and embarrassed by the comment. She'd thought she wasn't being that obvious. Erik hadn't commented, but it was hard to avoid the attention of Emma when she could see so many different ways. Even after their time together, it was easy to forget that sitting inside the MX 60 meant sitting inside Emma's body.

Erik frowned, and his gaze dipped to the dashboard and console displays. "Huh?" He turned toward Jia. "You think someone is following us? I doubt Melanie O'Shay's going to come after us again after that embarrassment. Given how obvious she is, she'd probably be weaving in and out of her lanes, trying to fly stealthily."

"Jia's paid a much higher than average amount of attention to the sensor and camera displays," Emma explained. "I thought it was a temporary situation, but it might be better to bring it out in the open. Particularly since it is annoying me."

"The reporter got me thinking about some stuff, and I think it tripped my paranoia." Jia sighed. "We screwed up, and you're talking about your new fried chicken and spice obsessions. Somebody's got to worry about it."

Erik looked her way, keeping a firm hand on the control yoke. "I'm not saying that I think my life's a waste because I haven't been seeking the best fried chicken across the UTC. I'm just saying I've let myself get too comfortable, mostly eating the same kind of thing. But what does this have to do with being followed? You really think that reporter is still after us?"

"Forget about the chicken." Jia looked down at a camera display. "And no, it's not that I think she's still after us. It's that she knew too much. She mentioned incidents we were involved in."

"What? You're still stuck on that?" Erik scoffed. "She didn't know crap. She just was hoping we had something to do with all that. You heard her. She mentioned things we did, but she also mentioned a bunch of things we had nothing to do with. I hadn't even read about half the stuff she mentioned." He shook his head with a faint smirk. "If she's a secret conspiracy spy, I'll give up all forms of fried chicken forever. Shit. I'll do you one better. I'll give up beignets and fried chicken, all forms, all cuisines."

"Your beignets and chicken are safe. It's not that I think she's a spy. That's not what I'm getting at." Jia lay her head back on the seat. "She's just some low-end reporter, but what about someone with better resources? What about actual investigators working for the conspiracy? We left a big trail."

"So they can trace us to Venus. Big deal. We weren't as open about the other places, and it's not like the conspiracy doesn't already know about us. That's why we use disguises and fake registrations so much. It's not like we're walking into a place and bellowing, 'Erik and Jia are here to kick your ass!'"

"I'm still wondering if we screwed up on Venus."

"How? By saving thousands of lives? By ending a bunch of insane cyborgs and some half-alien freak?" Erik grunted in irritation. "This isn't like you."

"No, no." Jia shook her head. "I should be clearer."

"It'd help," Erik replied. "I don't think anyone's invented a mind-reading implant yet."

"On Venus, we used our reputation to bait the Brotherhood. We basically did walk in there and yell, 'We're here to kick your ass!'"

Erik nodded slowly. "Yeah. I suppose we did, but in the end, it worked, didn't it? That was the best plan we had given the time constraints, and if we'd spent time trying to investigate everything without using ourselves as bait, the Brotherhood might have been able to pull off their plan, and a lot of people would be dead. Any plan that ends with a lot of dead terrorists and fewer dead people is okay by me."

"But don't you see?" Jia frowned and gestured around her. "I'm not complaining about saving people and taking down the Brotherhood, but I am worried we've traded short-term victories for long-term pain. Every time we do something like that, we feed into our already larger-than-life reputation, and we're not cops anymore."

"What does us being cops have to do with it?"

"Because our reputation used to be an advantage when we were cops." Jia saw another bright MX 60 in a nearby lane. Sometimes she forgot Erik wasn't the only owner of the model. "It used to be we'd walk into a room and have a good chance of some low-level criminal giving up because it was us. Not always, but enough to make it worthwhile, but the situation's different now. Attracting extra attention isn't going to make people surrender. It's just going to raise the chance of trouble, and that won't always end with us taking down the remnants of some arm of the conspiracy. We've got no guarantee that next time it won't cause us more trouble."

"Sure, but that goes along with everything we've done. That's not the first hard call we've had to make, and it won't be the last while we're investigating the conspiracy." Erik brought the MX 60 into a lower lane. "But I get what you're saying, and I'll make you an important promise now. I'm never going to get behind a call that cost a bunch of innocent people's lives no matter what. I'm doing this to get revenge for the Knights Errant, but I'm not going to turn myself into some bastard who doesn't give a shit about who he kills. The only people dying in this are the people who have it coming. That's the way I've always been, and that's the way I'll keep going."

Jia winced, now worried about his misunderstanding. "I know you would never do something like that. You don't have to make that promise to me." She let out a pained chuckle. "If anything, it's the opposite. You're the one who had to pull me back when I was getting out of hand. I'm always going to be grateful for that."

"I just wanted to make sure that's clear."

"I suppose I'm trying to be the perfect Lady Justice again, the woman who always knows the right thing to do, but that's not going to happen. It can't happen if we want results. We left the police force because there was no way we could take down the rest of Sophia Vand's friends without taking risks. If that means the occasional stupid reporter bothers us, it's a small price to pay." Jia shook her head. "And we're beginning to win. That's something."

Erik looked into the distance, his hands loose on the control yoke. He didn't speak for a long while, concentrating on the flow of the traffic. Emma could take control at any time, so Jia could only assume her words had loosened more thoughts than her partner was comfortable with.

"While we're talking about all this," Erik began, "I wanted to ask you something."

"Go ahead," Jia replied. "You know I'll always be honest with you."

"You don't think she was it?" Erik asked. "You don't think that Vand was the only real member of the conspiracy, right?"

"Of course not." Ji shook her head. "If she was, I think the ID would have already seen some indication, and operational disruptions would probably show up. Besides, nobody runs a conspiracy that wide without a lot of people near the top. This isn't just a bad corporation or even a corrupt politician. Even if she's the head, she has to have a lot of assistants. No one woman could run something like this."

"Good. I agree, just was curious if we were on the same page. Vand mentioned someone else, a woman. The way she talked before the end was like she thought that woman had set her up. I half-wondered if she meant Alina, but I don't think Alina's even on their radar. I'm not sure if that means there is someone else out there hunting the conspiracy, or if someone else in the conspiracy decided to screw her over. I figure it works out for us either way."

"I'm glad the ID at least has Vand's name to follow up on because just knowing another woman might be involved doesn't help much." Jia laughed. "Now we only have ten billion suspects across the UTC. It might take a while for us to investigate them all, even if the Defense Directorate does end up turning over the jumpship. This might be one slow revenge quest."

Erik grinned. "Hey, I've got hundreds of millions of

years to spend." His grin faded slowly. "You don't think they'll hand it over? Alina seemed to think it was a done deal, and Raphael was pretty enthusiastic about working with us. He's kind of annoying that way, but not too bad."

"I don't know. I think it's a powerful piece of technology to effectively hand over to another directorate's contractors, but it's an expensive doorstop without Emma, and the DD gets that there's no way they can just snatch Emma."

"And I don't intend to volunteer to work for them anytime soon," the AI offered. "It'd be to their advantage to perform whatever tests they need with your help."

Jia managed a small smile. "I'll believe it when they hand it over. Until then, it's just a bunch of promises from the government, and I'm not a person who reflexively trusts everything the government says."

"Now you sound like some sort of insurrectionist." Erik grinned.

"I'd punch you, but you're flying." Jia rolled her eyes. "Once you lose your innocence, it's hard to trust anyone."

"Don't I know it." Erik slowed the flitter to flow better with the surrounding traffic. "But as long as we've got each other, we'll do okay. And we've got Emma, Malcolm, Alina, and the others helping."

Jia looked down at a stream of flitters outside the window, most of her earlier paranoia absent. The enemy would continue to come, and they might be years away from completing the investigation, but with Erik at her side, they would triumph. She held her onto her fantasies of what that might bring, but they depended on how Erik handled things.

"Will it be enough if other people do it?" Jia asked.

"Do what?"

"Right now, the ID is doing everything they can to find all of Sophia Vand's friends," Jia replied. "They're helping us because we're good at taking care of trouble, but what if they find twenty people spread out over the UTC and the ID sends their own people to clean it up? What if you don't get to be the one to take them down? What if one day Alina shows up and tells you they've dismantled the conspiracy and it's all over?"

Erik pondered the question in silence for a long moment. "It doesn't matter. I've been honest that this is about revenge from the beginning, but if I'm certain the people responsible are out, I'll be able to sleep better at night. I want the people who took down my unit to pay, but I'm not going to whine if a ghost makes them pay instead of me."

"Good to know." Jia took a deep breath and slowly let it out, an eerie calm spreading through her. "I keep telling myself that it might take years, but a big fish has already fallen, and now the ID has leads. This could all be over pretty quickly."

She wanted to push into what that would mean for their relationship, but it wasn't the right time. She'd joined Erik out of a sense of justice and outrage at the depths of corruption the conspiracy represented, but that didn't change the strong pull she felt toward the man.

"Quick is relative." Erik scratched his eyelid. "But I'm not going to cry if we get lucky and it turns out all the leaders of the conspiracy are meeting in the apartment across the hall."

Jia smirked. "I somehow doubt that we'll get *that* lucky."

"Hey, did you ever think we'd run into a half-Leem mutant?" Erik's brow lifted in challenge.

"No, I can't say I did." Jia snickered. "Expect the unexpected?"

"Yeah. And shoot it when it shows up." Erik drummed his fingers on the control yoke. "Oh, that reminds me. I was going to stop by tomorrow and check in with Malcolm. He said he was going to the hangar to work on some stuff. I'm afraid if I leave him alone with Lanara for too long, she might grind him up as spare oil. You want to come?"

Jia laughed. "I'm good. Have fun. Make sure she doesn't grind *you* up."

"I'll try my best."

CHAPTER FOUR

Erik lifted his head and took in the full majesty of the *Argo*. Everything about the ship, from its sleek curves to its weaponry, separated it from the tiny, pathetic transport he'd been using to help out Alina. He finally had a ship worthy of his mission—one worthy of him.

He nodded in satisfaction. Since Erik's time back on Earth, he'd learned to accept that having some nice toys didn't hurt nor say anything bad about a man. He might have purchased his MX 60 mostly as a disguise, but there was no shame in flying around a luxury flitter, and the capabilities of the vehicle, both factory-ready and post-modification, had helped him countless times. A good soldier needed the proper tools to do his job.

Half the reason we lost on Molino was that those merc bastards had better equipment, Erik thought. *I like being on the other side of the equation.*

As with the MX 60, the upgrade from the *Pegasus* to the *Argo* wasn't just an exercise in style. The weapons and maneuverability of the ship had saved them during their confrontation with Sophia Vand. He tried to imagine how they could have captured or taken her down in the *Pegasus* but decided it would have ended with the entire crew dead and floating through space in plasma-scorched debris. They would be filed as a flight accident and buried by the Intelligence Directorate to cover its tracks.

Erik understood superior gear alone wouldn't be enough to secure a victory. Dealing with the conspiracy would require a combination of equipment, savvy, and force. If it were as simple as blasting open a door and slapping on binding ties, the Criminal Investigations Directorate and the Intelligence Directorate would have sniffed out Sophia Vand and her friends long before Erik arrived back home.

Someone growled behind Erik, low and threatening. Recognizing the sound, he didn't go for his gun despite the risk. It might not be a *yaoguai* behind him, but that didn't mean he was safe. A man always needed to be careful in territory controlled by someone else.

"Just because it looks patched up from the outside doesn't mean it's fixed, Blackwell," snarled Lanara. She stomped in front of him and poked him in the chest, which required her to reach up. "Just because it has decent self-repair, it doesn't mean it can fix everything when you blow holes in it. It's not magic."

Erik chuckled and raised his hands in mock surrender. "I know. I was on the ship with you when we flew back, and you kept cursing at me and telling me that. In my defense, I didn't blow holes in it, Sophia Vand did. Technically, I imagine her crew did, but you know…"

"Don't feed me that crap." Lanara shook her fist, her eyes narrowed. "You should have solved that shit in Parvati, so we didn't end up in a shootout in space."

Erik suppressed a laugh. The engineer was trying to intimidate him, but her size made it like a Chihuahua barking at a Doberman. Even Jia could do a decent job looming over Lanara. Sheer personality let the engineer bully Malcolm.

"It wasn't like we were dragging our feet," Erik replied. "And she was a big fish. We couldn't let her get away."

"Couldn't you have just reported her?" Lanara huffed and folded her arms. "Then you could have had a bunch of ghosts waiting to pick her up somewhere."

"That would have been nice, but we had no idea where she was going." Erik frowned. "And somebody with her kind of pull could have burned hard for the HTP and bluffed or bribed her way through, assuming she didn't switch to a different ship and use fake identification. If we hadn't chased her down right then and there, she could have ended up halfway across the galaxy before we could begin to track her. We might not have been able to capture and interrogate her, but when you're fighting a war and the enemy general parades out in the open, you take the shot. That's the only way you win."

"That's what this is to you? A war?"

Erik shrugged. "I'm not going to spew out a bunch of crap about how this is all for the good of the UTC, because honestly, I don't care as much as Jia about that. I want the Knights Errant avenged. It just so happens doing that involves cleaning out trash as well. So, yeah, it's a war of bloody damned vengeance, one I'm not quitting until either I'm dead or the enemy is taken out."

Lanara squinted. "You crazy bastard. Just try to be more careful next time." She rolled her eyes, her fingers tightening around her arms. "No reason to continue bitching about it now, even though I've had to waste all my time doing repairs. That said, since I had to go in and fix a bunch of stuff anyway, I decided to work on improving internal power transmission and rearranging the grav field emitters." Her speech sped up, and the anger drained from her face. "I was thinking last week about how if you don't rely on a standard Yau Manifold for emitting patterns, you could potentially tweak efficiency as much as point-two percent in most of the emitters. And then—"

"Okay," Erik interrupted, waving a hand. "You do whatever you need to do. Neither Jia nor I knows shit about this sort of thing. Okay, maybe Jia does, but not more than you. We both trust you to do what you need to get the best of the ship, and as good as we are at wasting scum, you're that good at tweaking this ship."

The engineer leaned forward, her eyes narrowed and her lips pursed in suspicion. "Good. It's important to let the experts handle things. You stick to killing bad guys, and I'll stick to fixing the ship when you don't kill the bad guys quickly enough that they blow holes in it."

"About that." Erik inclined his head toward the *Argo*. "I'm good at what I do, but I can do a better job with better tools."

"What are you getting at, Blackwell?"

"If we had more or better guns, we could take out enemy ships a lot faster." Erik offered her a pleasant smile. "The faster we do that, the fewer holes end up in the *Argo*. Simple logic, right?"

"Alina's not going to give you everything you want just because you ask." Lanara pointed with her thumb toward the ship. "That's already a hefty investment, even before you count the jump drive. You might be her favorite pets at the moment, but you're not the only ones in the galaxy sniffing around for the conspiracy, and you've already been given a lot of toys. I'm sure every ID ghost out there wishes they had a ship bristling with top-of-the-line weapons and the UTC's only self-aware AI."

Erik shrugged. "So what if she doesn't want to fund it? I'm sure you have some spare parts lying around, or you could tear apart a cargo flitter and turn it into a laser cannon. Alina's not going to complain if you don't send in a huge wish list but do something impressive with what you have available."

"I don't know." Lanara cupped her chin. "I'm not saying I *do* have that kind of thing lying around, and I'm also not saying I couldn't do it even if I don't. But if I'm spending time juicing the weapons, I'm not doing other things. Winning a fight in space isn't just about the biggest guns, Blackwell."

"Sure, but if you don't want holes in the ship, you need to give us the tools to make sure we end up with none and the other guy ends up with a ton. Your grav shield assist last time was nice, but we wouldn't have needed it if we could have blown those bastards away in one quick attack."

"I'll look into it, but it's not anything I can do soon. Just getting everything back to where we need to be is still going to take some time. The *Argo*'s ready to fly, but I'd prefer if we didn't get in any fights anytime soon."

"I don't go looking for fights. I just end them." Erik nodded. "Put it on your to-do list."

"Whatever you say, Blackwell. Next time try to—" Lanara frowned as the cargo bay door opened and extended the ramp with a loud whir and a rumble. "I swear, Maras is physically incapable of leaving the ship anywhere other than the cargo bay lately. He probably thinks it makes him look like a badass. Even worse, I think he's infecting Constantine with his thinking. Tweedledee and Tweedledumb."

Erik didn't respond as he waited for the door to finish lowering. Lanara was right; Raphael and Malcolm stood near the back of the cargo bay, both with ridiculously smug smiles as if they'd already located the rest of the conspiracy. The pair swaggered down the cargo ramp and toward Lanara and Erik.

"Good morning, Mr. Blackwell!" Malcolm waved. "This is such a nice ship. I've been looking into signal relays and that sort of thing with Lanara's help. I'm trying to optimize things for electronic warfare. You never know, maybe you can hack your way to victory. Fewer holes in the ship that way." He mimed shooting the ship with a finger gun.

"Everyone keeps acting like we are going to be able to take on a heavily armed vessel and get away without a scratch." Erik grunted in frustration. He gave Lanara a meaningful look, and she rolled her eyes in response. "We'll see what happens when we have more guns."

Raphael snapped his fingers. "Oh, oh, oh. Don't worry about that. I've been spending time with both Lanara and Malcolm so we can do our best to control the jumpship from the *Argo* if necessary, but from what the DD has said, the jumpship is going to be loaded with weapons." He punched into the air. "If the *Argo's* docked with the jumpship, what we'll lose in maneuverability, we'll make up for in defenses and the jump drive. We'll be able to deliver the pain like a straight-up Fleet cruiser." He punched a couple more times, making what might charitably described as a gunshot noise. "The next conspiracy ship we run into will get blown to bite-sized chunks for messing with the Obsidian Detective and Lady Justice."

Erik chuckled, then walked over to Raphael and patted the enthusiastic man on the shoulder. "That'd be nice, but from what you've told me, it's not like the jumpship doesn't stick out, and we don't want to park it in orbit where we might be boarded. I'm confident, even cocky, but I'm not stupid. If the conspiracy gets their hands on the drive, we're screwed. The entire UTC is screwed."

Raphael slumped his shoulders. "But what about bringing the pain? It'd be epic."

"We'll do that when we need to, but the standard play's probably going to be us flying the *Argo* to missions and keeping the jumpship back." Erik lowered his arm. "It's funny, though."

"What is? Not being epic?" Raphael asked, with Malcolm nodding his agreement. Lanara wandered off, muttering a stream of unintelligible numbers under her breath. She'd lost interest in the conversation, or maybe she was trying to control her desire to grind Malcolm and Raphael into oil.

Erik gestured around the hangar. "I used to be a cop with a nice flitter and a big gun. Then I stumbled onto Emma."

The AI's holographic form materialized nearby, a faint smirk on her face. For whatever bizarre reason, she had chosen a puffy light-blue tulle dress with a massive billowing skirt. It was as if she were dressing as the Good AI Fairy of the North. Her sartorial experiments were one of the more obvious consequences of her learning the truth about her creation. Erik had found it was better not to comment. No one liked a huffy AI.

"I'm glad to see you acknowledge the advantage of having such a useful ally." Emma bowed over a lace- and tulle-shrouded arm.

"The point is, you were and are a game-changer," Erik replied. "But now, I'm not just a cop with a gun and a fancy flitter. I'm working for a ghost, and I've got a great partner and a team of experts." He nodded to Malcolm and Raphael in turn and even Lanara, though her back was turned. "And from what Raphael's telling me, I'm going to have my own cruiser soon."

Raphael clapped once. "Better than a cruiser because you'll have the jump drive. You won't be the Obsidian Detective anymore, you'll be the Obsidian Admiral!"

"I think I'll just stick to being Erik Blackwell. All my old Army friends would throw me outside a dome if they found out I was going around calling myself an admiral."

Erik stared at the ship, lost in his thoughts. Jia was

right. Sophia Vand might or might not have been the head of the conspiracy, but a woman of her stature had to be a major player.

He was a shark, and blood was in the water. It was time for the feeding frenzy to begin.

CHAPTER FIVE

<u>**April 12, 2230, Neo Southern California Metroplex, Apartment of Jia Lin**</u>

"I don't think the world's going to end if we don't train tonight," Jia explained to Erik over a PNIU call. She occupied her hands by pouring herself a new cup of tea from the pot on her kitchen table. "So it's not a big deal if the tac center needed to shut down for a few days. We did all those crazy exoskeleton scenarios the last couple of weeks anyway. I need to give my brain and body some time to rest."

"You sure?" Erik sighed. "I was looking forward to it. I wanted to work off some stress."

Jia chuckled. "Relaxing is also a good way of working off stress. We've spent too much time running from crisis to crisis lately, and it'd be a bad thing if that started to seem normal. Come on. Back in your Army days, you wouldn't want your guys constantly on the move or fighting, would you?"

"This campaign is just getting started, but I see your point. We could get dinner."

"I already ate," Jia replied. "Maybe tomorrow? We could go to that Thai place we passed earlier unless you're off your spicy kick. Then we could work off stress some *other* way after that."

"Okay, that sounds like a good plan. Is that a promise?"

Jia laughed. "Yes, it's a promise. Unless we get swept into some bizarre incident."

"Don't say things like that. I'm looking forward to tomorrow. I better get some rest so I'll have more stamina for the night." Chuckling, Erik ended the call.

Jia rolled her eyes as she picked up her tea and took a sip. There was something rather domestic about spending time with Erik, even if most of the time, it involved tactical training or dangerous investigations into deadly conspiracies. She understood his eagerness to get on with the hunt, but she remained grateful Alina hadn't shoved them right into a new case. Constant work would grind them down, and they needed their strength—and not just for nighttime fun. A lot of things had fallen their way on Venus and in the fight against Vand, but they couldn't be sure the Lady would always be on their side.

Her PNIU buzzed with a call. She sighed, expecting an insatiable Erik, but when she tapped to get the caller ID sent to her smart lenses, she frowned. There was no more painful combo than the unexpected and annoying.

Jared Thompson. She hadn't talked to him since leaving the force. While she appreciated his kind words during her departure, part of her couldn't forgive him for moving against her when all she'd been trying to do was be a good cop. Jia took a deep breath. Maybe it was time for true forgiveness.

"Hello, Jared," she answered, doing her best to keep her tone polite. There was no reason to start out on a hostile foot.

"Hey, Jia," Jared answered, sounding out of breath. "I need to talk to you."

"Isn't that what we're doing?"

"Not over the phone. I need to do it face to face. It's important."

Jia frowned. "And what's this about?"

"Look, I can't do this over the phone." Jared sighed. "Can you meet me at Perseid Park? You know where that is, right?"

"Yes," Jia replied. "I've only been there a couple of times, but it's in Residential Tower 546 near the station, yes?"

"Exactly." Jared audibly swallowed over the line. "I'll be there in one hour near the center at Twin Maidens Fountain. Please come. I promise you this isn't me jerking you around."

Jared ended the call before Jia could respond. There were several possibilities, some dangerous, some not. She winced. Everyone at the 1-2-2 knew she was dating Erik. Because of their fake dating plan, those same cops had known even before they were actually dating. It wasn't impossible that Jared had gotten some personal ideas in his head now that he appreciated Jia's police style. She was going to have a hard time not laughing if he asked her out. She was grateful that Emma's omnipresence didn't extend to her PNIU when she was away from Erik. A touch of privacy could do wonders for a woman's sanity.

Jia stood slowly. She could call Erik and ask for backup, but if this turned out to be some idiotic and desperate attempt by Jared to wrest her from him, the last thing she wanted to deal with was the months of jokes that might follow, especially after she'd turned down hanging out with Erik for the night. If it was an assassination attempt, asking to meet her in a heavily trafficked park filled with cameras and drones was a good way to get caught. Plus, she didn't plan to meet him unarmed.

"Oh, well. Might as well get this over with. I'm sure it's nothing important. He probably just wants advice on how to ask another detective out."

Jia strolled through the tree-filled park, taking in the details both for security and appreciation. The gorgeous star-filled sky above might be a holographic fraud, but that didn't make it any less beautiful. For all the complaints of the Purists, not many people cared about heavily modifying non-consumable plants for something as ultimately petty as making sure trees didn't grow too quickly when living in the middle of a tower with only artificial light in soil filled with chemicals and nanites. They cared even less when the sweet smells of the carefully curated symmetrical rows of flowers lining the pathways or the earthy scent from the dirt and trees otherwise screamed natural.

She reached into her jacket to feel the comforting weight of her stun pistol and slugthrower. On the way over, she'd convinced herself there was nothing going on other than some misguided romance, but her habitual paranoia had settled in upon her arrival. Happy people filled the park, but there were plenty of dense clusters of trees where a man could use optical camouflage to escape the drones and cameras. It'd be embarrassing to be assassinated after being lured to the park by Jared Thompson.

Jia continued following the smooth, curving white paths toward the fountain. She could already hear the burble of the water. A smiling teenage couple wandered past her, the girl giggling at some whispered joke.

Jia missed that kind of innocence, although she wasn't sure she'd ever had it.

Before Erik had opened her eyes, she'd believed in a perfect Earth and the UTC as a flawed but great entity focused on justice and human rights. She accepted there were anti-socials and insurrectionists, but she thought that at least she lived in a shining kingdom of perfection among humanity's finest civilization. But she'd also never felt the relaxed restraint so many others did. She'd become a detective because of her drive to protect her shining kingdom. On some level, she must have always sensed the corruption lurking not far underneath the surface, or she'd internalized the lessons of literature that suggested great civilizations inevitably passed through cycles of decline before their renewal.

The path widened, and the trees and flowers on both sides gave way to an intricately sandstone-tiled central circle. Two jet-black statues of women in Grecian robes towered over the circle, their backs to each other and their arms outstretched. Small benches were spread out around the circle, most filled with couples or families, but Jared sat on one by himself, staring at Jia with a forlorn look.

His hand wasn't in his jacket. If he was there to take a shot, he'd already lost his surprise. The lack of disguise and the meeting place reduced the chance of violence, but there was still something off about the whole thing. She made her way over to his bench.

Jared nodded to the empty side. "Join me, Jia."

Jia nodded and sat. She wasn't going to initiate the conversation. He'd called her here, and she didn't know why. The less effort she put into controlling the conversation, the more she maintained her situational awareness.

Jared licked his lips and looked around the area. "Anyone follow you? I didn't ask you to check for that, but you're Lady Justice. You probably check every time you go to a restaurant."

"What's this about, Jared?" Jia asked. She wasn't about to admit he was right. Her paranoia might have been stoked by the reporter, but it was rare she didn't consider the possibility that someone from the conspiracy or a remnant of one of the many syndicates she'd helped destroy might come after her.

Jared leaned closer to her and lowered his voice. "I need your help."

"With what?"

Jared stared at her, his mouth twitching. He took a deep breath before he could finally push out the quiet words. "In the past, here and there, I took certain... bonuses. Tips, you could call them from particular individuals that weren't always what you might call respectable."

Jia's hands balled into fists and her cheeks heated. "You took bribes? You're dirty?"

Jared averted his eyes, shame written all over his face. "You can call it whatever you want, but yes."

"The only reason I'm not smashing my fist into your face is that we're in public," Jia let out, her words a growl. Her heart pounded, and she squeezed her fist tighter until her nails dug into her palm. "Or pulling out my gun and shooting you, but I assume you have some point other than proving me right, so get to it before I reconsider my newfound pacifism."

Jared kept his gaze on the ground as he rubbed his wrists. "I figured it wasn't a big deal."

"You figured a cop taking bribes wasn't a big deal?" Jia rolled her eyes. "I'm not an idiot, Jared, but apparently you are."

"I know. I knew it could lead to something bad, but no one ever asked me to do anything."

"You expect me to believe you were paid to do nothing?" Jia released her fist. Blood welled up in her palms from her nail cuts.

Jared managed to lift his head and look Jia in the eyes. "I didn't feel great about it, but it was nice to have a little extra money, you know? And I always figured I had the situation under control."

"How does that work? Most of the time when you're taking bribes, the people paying out are the ones in control."

Jared shrugged and sighed. "Because I figured there was a limit. If they asked me to do anything over the line, I'd just say no. If anything got out of hand, I would handle it." He let out a pained laugh. "Like now."

Jia's mouth twitched. It took all her self-control not to

laugh in the man's face, almost more than it took to not hit him. She'd spent her time on the force being called a naïve corp princess, but she was the height of cynicism compared to the self-serving idiot in front of her. She motioned for him to continue.

"Then you and Erik started doing all your shit." Jared gestured around the park. "And the internal affairs and anticorruption crap happened. I stopped taking payments around that time, and for a while, I just sat there and waited for them to come for me. It was part of the reason I was even more of an asshole to you." He closed his eyes and pinched the bridge of his nose. "I blamed you for starting it all. I thought I was going to end up in prison."

"Yes, because it makes so much sense to blame a police officer for *not* being dirty rather than not take bribes to begin with." Jia folded her arms.

"I know. *I know.* When I didn't get tagged by Internal Affairs, I thought about how things were going. With Captain Ragnar, you and Erik out there, it made me reevaluate why I'd become a cop." Jared smiled, a semblance of pride in the expression. "I figured with all the syndicate purges, I was in the clear. I never was sure who was paying me, but the guy who was my main contact left town last year. I figured it was over."

Jia nodded slowly. "Okay, this is all very interesting, but what does it have to do with me? Is this a sad attempt to get me to pat you on the head and tell you you're a good cop despite taking bribes? That's not going to happen, Jared. I'm having trouble resisting stunning your ass and calling the 1-2-2 right now to turn you over to IA."

Jared placed his face in his hands. "I'd deserve it. I'd deserve that and more, but my sister Mara doesn't."

"Your sister?" Jia frowned. "What does she have to do with anything? I thought she was a low-level office drone."

"She is," Jared replied with a heavy sigh. "Here's the simple version: a couple of days ago, I was contacted by someone, a guy named Ralic. I'd never met the guy or heard of him, but he started name-dropping my old contact, and he made it clear that a new syndicate moving into town had an investment in me, and that they'd expect it to pay off. He wanted me to purge the surveillance data on a case. Best I can tell, it was a minor breaking and entering thing. It was a 1-2-2 case, but it's low priority and not even my case."

"The case that led to Ceres Galactic and the councilman started low and unimportant, too." Jia scoffed. "Seriously? Bribes that require no favors? Sure. What syndicate?"

"Hell if I know, and I didn't want to look into it in case it started something I couldn't handle from IA before I could get it under control." Jared lifted his head. "With the way the cops and CID have been ripping the balls off all the local syndicates, I thought there couldn't be anyone left, let alone the guys paying me. But it doesn't matter." He clenched his jaw. "I told them to screw off. They threatened to turn me into IA. I told them to go ahead, I'd do everything in my power to help the NSCPD and CID track their asses down and fry them. I also said I'd make sure the entire law enforcement community was looking into their case."

Jia smiled despite herself. "You've got balls after all. But that sounds like starting something."

"Yeah, it started something all right."

"You mentioned your sister."

Jared nodded. "They sent me a bunch of pictures of her going into her apartment. Her at her job. Her at a restaurant. Ralic sent me a message saying how it's always sad when people get hurt, but it's a big city."

"Okay." Jia nodded, sympathy leaking into her hardened heart. "I get where you're coming from, but if they're threatening your sister, why haven't you grabbed her and gone straight to the 1-2-2 to ask for protective custody, especially after everything you just said? If you do what you threatened to do and shine a light on the investigation, you can get them all taken down while your sister's being protected."

"I can't risk it. When I told them all that stuff before, I was bluffing." Jared swallowed and surveyed the area slowly, his eyes haunted. "I can't be the only leftover piece of trash in the department. I might just be the only one in a position to get to the data they want since it's a 1-2-2 case. If I go to the department and blow the whistle, I can't be sure the cop assigned to guard my sister won't put a bullet in her brain." He turned toward Jia. "But you and Erik, you're not part of the department, and if there is one thing you've proven, it's that you're not on any syndicate's payroll. You could help me by relocating my sister until everything gets taken care of."

"Let's pretend I'm willing to help you with this and risk my life rather than just call the department or the CID." Jia sighed. "I need to understand something first."

"Sure," Jared replied. "What?"

"Why did you call me and not Erik?"

Jared let out a quiet, pained chuckle. "I know he's not dirty, but I also know he's not like you."

Jia frowned. "Meaning what?"

"I always got the feeling he joined the department so he could continue kicking ass rather than because he cared about justice. I figured he wouldn't want to risk himself for something dangerous if it wasn't some big, high-profile thing." Jared shrugged. "And I couldn't take the risk he'd say no. If he said no first, there would be a bigger chance of you saying no."

Jia pinched the bridge of her nose, a headache already coming on. "Okay. I'm not saying no, but I'm also not agreeing. If I'm going to help you with this, I'm going to need Erik, and that means talking to him about it."

"Fair enough. Just...hurry. I don't know how much longer I can stall Ralic."

CHAPTER SIX

This was not the night Erik had wanted nor expected as he sipped a beer on his couch. Jia paced in front of him, her gestures animated and her voice loud as she related her meeting with Jared the hour before. Erik had known something was off when she'd called him and asked to talk right away but refused to speak about it anywhere but face-to-face. He could tell from her voice things were serious.

"Shit never ends here, does it?" Erik commented after Jia finished. "It's like...what's the dragon monster thing where you cut the head off and more come back?" He frowned. "Alina would know."

"A hydra." Jia stopped her furious pacing to settle into Erik's recliner. "But this isn't a hydra. This is just cock-roaches moving into uncontested territory. There's too much food and filth in a place as large as Neo SoCal. There always will be. This just happens to be a situation where it's linked to the 1-2-2. I don't doubt this new syndicate is putting the squeeze on leftover dirty cops and other department personnel all over the metro."

Erik polished off his beer and set the empty bottle on a small side table. He considered Jared's plight before offering his answer. "We're not cops anymore. It's not our responsibility. We could just call IA and let them handle it."

Jia nodded. "I know, and I'm doubting this has anything to do with the conspiracy. They'd know better than to try to get at us through Jared Thompson. I assume it's exactly what it appears to be: a dirty cop whose past is catching up with him. I'm also not excited about the idea of getting involved in local trouble that's not related to the conspiracy. There's helping make the world a better place, and then there's taking on unnecessary trouble."

"We don't know when Alina will need us again," Erik replied. He laced his fingers together and stuck them behind his head. "If we got all spun up working some local case and then have to leave in the middle, that might be trouble, but at the same time, we're not her bitches, and she's not our boss. We don't need her permission."

"Then you think we should do something?" Jia asked. "Despite the speech I just gave, I'm having a hard time not wanting to get involved. Everything he said was right, and as far as I remember, his sister is nice enough. I met her once, and she recommended a nice restaurant. She seemed a little embarrassed by her brother when he said some crap to me."

Erik had offered resistance to see how Jia would react. Now he understood they were close on the issue.

"I might be focused on getting revenge, but that doesn't mean I didn't give a shit about what being a cop meant,"

Erik replied. "And I don't like the idea of our hard work getting undone because Jared Thompson couldn't keep his house clean. Besides…" he chuckled, "we could use this to our advantage against the conspiracy, so it's a two-for-one."

Jia's brow lifted. "How? As I said, I doubt they're related. It's not impossible, but I don't think the conspiracy would try to get at us that way."

"They don't have to be involved, but we can still use this against them by taking advantage of what you were worried about." Erik inclined his head toward her. "Our reputation. If the conspiracy's watching us, and we're messing around with local syndicates despite not being cops anymore, they're going to start asking why. It might not lead to anything, but they'll waste resources looking into it."

"I didn't think of that." Jia stood, confidence returning to her face. "I miss being a cop. Sometimes it feels good to take down some local scumbag who isn't part of a galaxy-spanning conspiracy. I'll call Jared—"

"Detective Thompson has just sent a message to your PNIU, Erik," Emma interrupted. "The text of the message is as follows: 'Please go to Mara's place right away. There's trouble. I'm worried about her.' He sent the address."

Erik frowned. "Huh? Call him back for me."

"Very well."

Erik stood and cracked his knuckles. He had wanted to get involved, but he'd thought they would have more time to develop a strategy. Jared needed to understand they would be the ones controlling the situation. He'd come to them for a favor, and they were only getting involved because of an innocent woman, not because they liked the guy.

"He's not answering," Emma reported in an annoyed voice. "I can verify the calls are reaching his PNIU, but nothing else."

Jia shook her head, her brow creased in worry. "He waited too long. Damn it. They might have already taken him out."

"Doesn't make sense to take him out before he can help them," Erik replied. He walked toward his bedroom to grab his holster. "But it's not like it'll hurt for us to take some time out of our day to check on his sister. Emma, call Mara Thompson."

"Her PNIU is currently not accepting calls," Emma replied.

Erik halted and frowned. "Meaning she's got it disabled, or meaning someone threw her into an incinerator?"

"I can't give you a high-confidence answer to that without more data, Erik. There are multiple possibilities besides the aforementioned two. Someone could also be blocking it."

"Damn it." Erik grunted in frustration. "Jared's not going to make this easy."

"Should we call for backup?" Jia asked. "Or send someone there?"

Erik shook his head and continued toward his bedroom. "Jared could be right," he called over his shoulder. "We could be calling dirty cops to finish her off, and we might need to get friskier than the on-scene cops would prefer."

"Friskier?"

Erik stopped at his bedroom door and shot her a grin. "I'm not worried about taking kidnapping syndicate scumbags alive. We'll slap on our vests and arm up in the MX 60. Emma can fly."

"I should always fly," Emma commented. "I'm far superior at it."

"Keep telling yourself that."

Jared threw himself behind a flitter and pistol bullets ripped into the vehicle. The guns' loud reports echoed around the parking platform. He didn't understand why there were no drones converging on the area, but understanding wasn't necessary for his current predicament. The important takeaway was that his survival depended on him. Shots continued to perforate the vehicle as he crawled forward, his gun in hand. Stunning one or two thugs wouldn't be enough to win.

He needed a slugthrower, which meant he'd need to take one from a thug, but that would require him getting closer. Jared might have his cocky moments, but he understood he was no Jia or Erik. He wasn't going to win against a group of enemies with better weapons. Every time he'd done something impressive, he'd been with a group of other cops.

A thug darted between two wide cargo flitters. Jared fired his stun pistol and hit the bastard in the leg, and he toppled to the ground with a groan. Two more shots left him twitching and drooling, with Jared smirking. More bullets ripped into his cover, and he half-stood, hunched over as he rushed behind an undamaged vehicle.

"It didn't have to be like this, Thompson," shouted a thug. "Ralic's just collecting his due. You're a dirty thief who took money and won't pay it back."

Jared's heart hammered. He'd managed to send a message to Erik and Jia before Ralic's enforcers jammed the area. There was no way a bleeding heart like Jia wouldn't go help Mara. All Jared needed to do was stall until the local cops arrived. At this point, he didn't care if any of them were dirty. It didn't matter what happened to him as long as his sister was safe. A jammer here and there wasn't enough to stop all of the cameras and drones from noticing what was going on.

Bullets ripped through the windows of a cargo flitter. The thugs were circling and trying to flank him on both sides. He didn't have time to wait for reinforcements that might not even be coming. The thugs splitting up gave him a chance to take some down and get their weapons. He might not be an Obsidian Detective, but that didn't mean he couldn't act like one. In the last minutes of his life, he would go down fighting like a man.

Jared stayed low and squeezed off shots. The bright white bolts flew toward the thugs on one side, briefly destroying the shadows. One struck a man square in this chest and he collapsed to his knees before falling forward, his face smacking into the ground with a loud thud. That left two men on that side. He could win.

"You really thought you could take the money and never have to pay back what you owe?" screamed a thug over his loud pistol shots.

Bullets whizzed over Jared's head. There was no way this could keep up without the cops showing up. This wasn't the Shadow Zone.

Jared rolled between two matching bright yellow luxury flitters to escape the latest barrages, his pulse thundering in his ears. He wasn't in the Zone, but he also hadn't seen anyone else in the last couple of minutes other than the thugs. If they were smart enough to bring a jammer, they might be smart enough to redirect people and not cause a mess. He wanted to believe that people would hear gunfire and contact the authorities, but the thugs didn't need hours to finish him off. They only needed minutes, and once people were inside the commerce level, they wouldn't hear anything from the outside.

"Should I have just done what they asked?" Jared muttered under his breath.

He'd always thought of himself as a decent cop and the bribes as bonuses that didn't hurt anything or anyone. It wasn't like he was helping gangsters assassinate council members. Everyone understood that the way to survive in Neo SoCal was to keep your head down, take what ended up in your lap, and look the other way. Then Erik and Jia had arrived, and everything had changed.

Jared wanted to hate them like before. He wanted to spit at their arrogance and their high-paying private-sector job, but whatever their motivations and current employment, they'd only done what cops were supposed to do: protect and serve. No amount of self-pity or delusion made him better than them. If he'd been half the cop they were, his sister wouldn't be in danger.

The flitter behind him jerked from shots, but none of

the bullets made it through. If he survived, he'd need to write the company and congratulate them on producing such a sturdy vehicle. He took a deep breath and lifted his pistol as the thugs continued closing, then rolled to the opposite side of the vehicle and ran forward in a feeble attempt to counter-flank the enemy.

Jared's ragged breathing filled his ears. The two thugs on his closer side pointed their weapons at him. He shot twice in rapid succession, aiming for their heads, and the stun bolts found their marks. Both men fell backward, their guns flying from their hands. He pivoted around the back of a flitter when fire tore through his side. Pain blossomed through his shoulder next.

He managed a couple more steps before collapsing to the ground, his shoulder and side in agony. His vision wavered, and he realized he'd dropped his stun pistol. Blood splatters covered the ground. Jared groaned, the pain clouding his mind. He wasn't sure how many rounds he'd taken.

Jared couldn't hold up his body and slumped forward, his face landing in his own blood. Mocking laughter sounded from behind him, along with heavy footfalls.

"You should have just done what you were told, Thompson," called out a thug. "Then you wouldn't be full of bullets."

Jared tried to think about what Erik or Jia would do. They would come up with some witty comeback and then kill or disable ten times the number of men. He could do it. Erik and Jia weren't gods. They weren't even *yaoguai* or changelings.

"Blow me," Jared muttered. He could barely see the approaching man through his darkening vision.

"What was that, Thompson?" the man asked. He pressed the hard barrel against the back of Jared's head. "You still think you're bigger than Ralic?"

"That's what his mom said." Jared lost consciousness.

CHAPTER SEVEN

Jia handed Erik a TR-7 magazine, and he inserted it into his rifle with a smile. There was something oddly relaxing about routine, even when it might involve going into battle. At least in this situation, she didn't expect any significant trouble or strange surprises. A syndicate wasn't the conspiracy.

The MX 60 settled into a parking space outside of the residential level containing Mara Thompson's apartment. There weren't a large number of flitters there, which heartened Jia. Fewer vehicles meant fewer people who might get caught up in a fight. She and Erik had already armed up, including tac vests and rifles. Her weapon might not have four barrels, but it was plenty deadly, especially against syndicate enforcers who weren't expecting them.

"Do you have control of the local drones and cameras?" Erik asked.

"Yes, I have control," Emma reported. "I'm also inside the main apartment registry. I should warn you. There are multiple vehicles present in the parking platform that aren't registered to residents."

"That doesn't necessarily mean anything." Jia stuffed magazines into her vest pockets.

"I'm cross-referencing with known arrests records, but I'm not coming up with anything."

"We'll assume they're smart enough to hide a little," Jia replied.

"We need to get Mara under our protection before we call in any reinforcements." Erik opened the door and nodded to Jia. "Ready for this?"

"It could be nothing." Jia stepped onto the parking platform. She flipped off her safety. "Or it could be an entire floor filled with murderous, antisocial criminals. So, sure, I'm ready."

"Sounds like a normal day for us." Erik headed toward the door, his gun pointed forward. "See anything, Emma?"

"You might find this interesting," Emma replied before feeding a camera feed to their smart lenses. Two large thugs pulled Mara out of her apartment and backhanded her when she slapped them. She fell to the ground, holding her reddening cheek. Red targeting highlights appeared, identifying four enemies, with two guarding a hallway intersection leading to Mara's apartment, both with guns drawn.

"Pretty bold." Jia shook her head in disbelief. "Was there any evidence that they had systems access or were jamming?"

"No," Emma replied. "I don't see a PNIU on Miss Thompson. I assume they've destroyed or removed it already."

"They were just banking on rushing in there, grabbing her and getting away." Erik stopped in front of the door. "If we hadn't come right here, they probably would have. How are we doing for non-combatants?"

"No one is in the hallways presently, and I only have access to the main building's exterior cameras."

"Can you lock them in?" Jia asked. "You've done similar things before."

"I can invert the emergency evacuation protocols," Emma suggested. "It's only a temporary solution."

"We won't need that long." Erik nodded to Jia. "Let's keep our fields of fire straight. If we're going to keep people inside, we don't want them to get nailed by stray bullets."

Jia frowned and flipped on her safety. She pulled her assault rifle up and slid the strap over her shoulder before grabbing her stun pistol. "The fewer bullets flying, the better."

Erik shrugged. "At least there will be someone the cops can interrogate. I know what Thompson said, but if this syndicate is holding out for his help, that means there is only a small number of dirty cops left."

"We should at least try to get them to surrender before we open fire," Jia suggested.

"Sure, but that's on them." Erik flipped his fire selector to single barrel mode. "We're here to save Mara, not investigate this crap. I'll leave that to the 1-2-2 after we get her. Once we secure her, we'll contact Captain Ragnar, and he can deal with the cleanup. He can make sure she's with someone trustworthy."

Jia nodded and took a deep breath. "Emma, if you would."

The door slid open, revealing the long, sparse hallway with apartment doors spaced out on either side. Based on the supplied targeting highlights and navigational markers, they needed to move up and to their left. A loud scream echoed from that direction.

Jia frowned and jogged forward. "Let's finish this before it gets complicated."

"Not a bad plan." Erik headed after his partner. "Let's take out the sentries. We'll let the other guys have a couple of seconds to reconsider the errors of their way."

"Fine by me." Jia slowed and moved toward the wall. She edged forward, her gun ready, and nodded across the way. "I'll cover you while you take position."

"Works for me."

Jia stopped at the corner. She took a deep breath, but her heart didn't pound in her chest, nor did her stomach tighten with anticipation. A battle was always a dangerous time, but after so many encounters and hours of training, her body knew what it needed to do. A handful of syndicate thugs weren't worthy of concern. If they didn't have a hostage, they would be a minor irritant, almost a joke.

Erik chuckled and flipped his fire selector to four-barrel mode. "No complaints here. Ready when you are."

She spun around the corner and pulled the trigger of her stun pistol. The two thugs jerked up their guns, but she'd already fired twice, downing both, before they completed the motion. Erik and Jia charged forward to the intersection. With a quick motion, she holstered her stun pistol and brought her rifle down. If it came to a real fight, she needed to be ready.

"Whatever happened to getting them to surrender?" Erik asked.

"They'll still get their chance. I just want to make sure that if they turn it down, this is over quicker."

"Give it up!" Jia shouted. "We've got you surrounded." She arrived at the intersection, hoping they'd buy her lie, but she didn't peek around the corner. Emma's highlights made it unnecessary. The AI also helpfully added a blue highlight to mark Mara's position.

"Back off, cops!" bellowed a thug. "Or we blow this bitch's brains out. You understand?"

"Don't do anything you'll regret," Jia shouted back. She waited until Erik was beside her. Both turned the corner, ducking low and their weapons ready. The two thugs stood behind Mara. Their guns both pointed at her head, a tactical error. If they'd fired immediately and gotten lucky, they might have evened the odds, but now Jia and Erik both had their weapons trained on the thugs.

"Wait." One of the thugs narrowed his eyes. "I know you two. I thought you retired."

"We did," Jia replied, keeping a tight grip on her rifle. "But we don't take kindly to syndicate criminals kidnapping innocent women, and we happened to be in the neighborhood. How unlucky for you."

Mara whimpered, her eyes pleading with Jia. A huge bruise was already forming on the side of her face. Trickles of blood marred the other side. Jia fought the urge to kill the men right away. The planet would be better off without them.

"This ain't got nothing to do with you," the thug seethed. He pushed the gun against the back of Mara's head. The woman closed her eyes and trembled. If he pulled the trigger, the thugs would be dead in under a second. Jia didn't trust that the brain trust in front of her understood that, so it was time to be blunt.

Jia sighed and shook her head. "Are you really going to do this? You know who we are. You know our reputation. We can't even go on vacation without getting wrapped up in trouble and killing terrorists. We go out for coffee and stumble into firefights, and all of those fights end with a lot of dead terrorists or criminals and us barely scratched."

Erik nodded at his huge rifle. "Listen to her. We were minding our own business when we got dragged into this. Now we're here, and we're loaded with enough ammo and weapons to kill ten times as many pieces of crap as you two."

The thug scoffed. "You're not doing anything while we have her."

"Please," Mara whispered. "I don't want to die."

"You're not going to die." Jia stared at the men. "Because if you die, these men die, and I think they value their lives enough to not throw them away. Now, you two, be smart little boys and drop your guns. If you do, I give you my word that you will get out of this alive because I'm sure the police have questions for you. But if you harm that woman, you're not leaving this hallway without some new holes in your head. What's left of them, anyway." She glared at them. "And trust me, I won't lose any sleep over taking out syndicate trash who killed an innocent woman. It'd be very satisfying."

Mara squeezed her eyes shut. Tears streamed down her cheeks. She sobbed quietly.

"This ain't your business," the thug screamed. "You ain't even cops anymore!"

Jia offered him her best crazed grin. "Which means there's absolutely nothing holding us back. You really think if we paint the hallway with your brains, that the NSCPD is going to bring us in?" She stopped smiling. "This is your last chance, idiots. Drop the guns or die. I've got a nice rifle here, and my partner's got a ridiculous rifle with four barrels. We're both in tac vests. I've even got some plasma grenades. I wonder what it feels like to be vaporized?

The thugs glanced at each other, then released Mara and raised their arms. The woman fell forward and scrambled on her hands and knees toward Jia.

"Drop your guns!" Jia shouted. "Or we drop you!"

"Geeze, chill, Lady Justice," replied one of the thugs. They both let go of their pistols, which clattered to the ground. Mara made it to her feet and ran behind Erik.

"On your knees and turn around," Jia ordered. "It's your lucky day because my finger isn't that twitchy. You're getting some binding ties and being left for the locals."

"What's going on?" Mara whimpered. "Who are these men?"

"Some gentlemen who have business with your brother," Erik explained.

"Is this because of a case he's working on?"

Jia shrugged. "Something like that, but it's a little more complicated. Don't worry. We'll keep an eye on you and make sure you're safe."

Mara took a shuddering breath. "But won't I be safe now that you've stopped these men?"

"Like I said. It's complicated." Jia slung her rifle over her shoulder and pulled out some binding ties. "For now, let's get our presents ready and get out of here."

CHAPTER EIGHT

Erik adjusted the window tinting of the hotel room until it was solid black. Mara lay on a bed behind him, sleeping on her side. She'd passed out on the way over. They've been worried that she'd been hurt after passing out in the flitter, but her vitals were stable. Some people couldn't handle the kind of excitement so common in Erik's and Jia's lives.

For now, they were waiting. They'd sent a brief message to Captain Ragnar, clarifying their involvement but not giving any specific location information. While they trusted the captain, they needed to be sure their efforts weren't wasted.

Jia leaned against a wall, her lips pursed. "How are we doing, Emma?"

"This room and the exterior hallway are secure," Emma reported. "But we might be more secure staying aboard the *Argo* rather than in a hotel, my ability to hack their systems and your disguises and fake registration notwithstanding."

"We can't risk our ID work getting mixed up in a local favor. Alina might pull the ship if we do. This isn't like

Mars. It's not an investigation that went in a different direction." Erik shook his head. "Besides, we don't need a ship. We just need to hide from the syndicate until we get this under control. Compared to the Ascended Brotherhood, these guys might as well be kids with water pistols."

Jia pushed away from the wall and sat on the edge of the other bed. "You don't think this is strange?"

"Those goons going after leverage?" Erik shrugged. "It's a standard play. What's strange about it?"

"No, not the syndicate." Jia gestured around the room. "How easily we can do this sort of thing. We armed up with enough firepower to take down a squad, grabbed a woman from thugs, and tucked her away under a fake name in a room protected by a super-AI and Intelligence Directorate anti-spying technology. And we didn't spend time talking about it other than having Emma pick a random hotel."

"You say all that like it's a bad thing." Erik shrugged.

"It's not that it's a bad thing," Jia replied. "It's just strange, even compared to our old lifestyle. We were cops before, but we weren't as good at hiding from everything and everyone. We depended on backup and resources."

"We still do. It's just different resources now." Erik walked over to his TR-7, which was sitting atop a dresser. He ran his finger over the weapon, remembering all the times over the decades it had saved him. "I look at it differently. The only way to win a war is to adapt to battlefield conditions."

"And we're in a war with the conspiracy?"

"Yeah, we are." Erik lifted his hand. "And some of these adaptations prove useful in other situations. I'm never going to complain about not having to spend a lot of time figuring crap out, and I'm never going to complain about having advanced gear."

Emma appeared near the door, this time in a blue and black NSCPD patrol uniform. "You'll want to see this. It's relevant." She pointed, and a data window appeared with a paused news video featuring a concerned-looking blonde reporter standing in front of a bullet-riddled flitter on a parking platform. Police drones and officers stood behind her in the distance.

"Play it," Erik ordered.

"A shocking scene is unfolding today at Commerce Tower 45." The reporter gestured to the police covering the area. "The police are still offering minimal details on what happened other than revealing that a police detective was shot and left for dead. He's been stabilized but was taken to the hospital, where he is now in critical condition. It remains unclear who attacked the detective and what motivated them, and the police are refusing to pass along further details at this time. They've told us that no one else was found at the scene, but the detective's stun pistol had been discharged. The police are being tight-lipped about whether this relates to the arrests and recovery of several men related to a shootout in Residential Tower 82. We'll keep you up to date as the authorities offer more information."

"I don't understand why they didn't finish him off." Jia folded her arms. "If he's still alive, there's no way he's not going to IA and the CID."

"They might not have had enough time," Erik replied. "Or they might think they could still make use of him." He nodded toward the sleeping Mara. "There was no reason to go after her if they just planned to kill him. Giving him some free holes and leaving him to recover while they have his sister would be enough. Or maybe they just screwed up. It's not like the smartest people choose 'syndicate enforcer' as a job."

Jia scratched her cheek. "You're right. Things might have just gotten out of hand. They met with Jared, and he made it clear he wasn't going to work with them. He'd called us, so he might have been gambling on us being able to handle anything that came up. The tempo of everything was a little faster than I'd like, but at least we've got it mostly under control."

"It's not gambling when you know the result. The question now is how we want to continue."

"Nothing Jared said about possible dirty cops was wrong." Jia pulled back her jacket to reveal a holster. "Even if he feels like cooperating after getting new holes, if we call the 1-2-2, this might end with a bullet in Mara, too."

"Then we should go ahead and put in a direct call to Ragnar and arrange a meeting. By now, he's probably got some people lined up because of the message we sent." Erik frowned. "That's our best bet."

"Agreed." Jia nodded.

"Do it, Emma," Erik ordered. "On speaker."

A couple of seconds ticked by before Captain Ragnar answered, "Blackwell, how is Mara?"

"She's asleep but unhurt. You don't have to answer me if you don't want to, but I'm assuming Jared's the detective who got shot?"

Captain Ragnar sighed. "Yes. We've got some long-range

drone footage of some of the fight, but the local cameras and drones were disabled. He did a decent job stunning some of them, but they shot him several times, grabbed their guys, and ran. From the timing of things, it was about the same time as you were rescuing Mara. The local enforcement zone dragged their feet on passing that information on to me, even though it was my detective who got shot. The CID is already swooping in to take over the investigation."

"That's not necessarily a bad thing," Jia offered, and let out a quiet grunt. "Especially since he is dirty."

"I'm surprised he managed to slip through, but if he was telling the truth, it makes sense. No new money, no messing with cases would make it hard for anyone to pick up on him." Irritation flavored the captain's voice.

"What about Mara?" Erik asked. "We did our part and saved her, but we're not in a position to offer her long-term protective custody. You could grab Halil and a couple of other guys we know we can trust and have them watch her."

"It's already more complicated than that," Captain Ragnar replied. "I told you the CID wants control, and they also want Mara. They're worried about someone in the department getting to her, and I can't blame them."

Jia furrowed her brow. "She would be safer. Jared might be one of the few pieces of trash left in the 1-2-2, but we can't assume Jared's the only leftover one in the entire NSCPD. All that reform and anti-corruption work have been good, but there are just too many people to catch every snake. One small leak and she ends up kidnapped as a bargaining chip."

"It's not like Jared's going to be able to help them now. He'll be lucky if he doesn't end up doing time."

"It doesn't matter." Jia's gaze drifted to Mara. "If they can't use Mara to get to Jared, they could use Mara as an example of what happens to people who resist them. Then all the other leftovers will be more willing to help them out."

Captain Ragnar let out a frustrated grunt. "You're right, Lin. If you two hadn't saved her, this situation would already be out of control."

"I think it already is." Jia glanced at Mara and shook her head. "It's just not as badly out of control as it could be."

"I'm going to contact the CID agents who are taking over the case, and then I'll call you back with a meeting location."

"Sounds good," Jia replied.

Erik scratched the side of his nose. "I hope it's not going to cause you too much trouble that we were involved in this, Captain."

The captain laughed. "Trouble? I think it'll be great PR. If we spin it right, we might even be able to convince people that you're still always watching and waiting to help us. If you don't mind, that is."

"You do whatever you want." Erik looked at Jia. "I don't care if you use my name to keep some idiots in line. But I also hope to not get involved with NSCPD stuff again if I can help it."

"I'm fine with it, too," Jia offered with a smile. "I became a police officer because I wanted to help Neo SoCal. If my name can do that without me putting in any effort, that's even better."

"I'll contact you soon," the captain replied. "I'm glad to have you two on my side again, even if it's just for an evening."

Jia didn't feel bad about stepping out of the MX 60 with her assault rifle in hand in the parking lot of a small park. She trusted Captain Ragnar, but there had been enough surprises in her life in the last couple of years that she valued careful preparation more. Erik opened the back door to let Mara out before pulling his TR-7 out of the flitter. In the end, trust was nice. Superior firepower was better.

Other than a handful of drones flying overhead, the place was empty, not surprising given the large but idle construction bots standing around the area. Scaffolding and unopened crates were piled around the bots. Shallow holes dotted the area.

Captain Ragnar stood in front of a police flitter, a suited CID agent on either side of him. They raised an eyebrow at Jia and Erik's display of dominance, but they didn't go for their guns. Jia was grateful. She didn't want a standoff with government agents. That would only complicate their new, albeit temporary job.

Mara swallowed. "How is my brother doing? Is he...okay?"

The captain nodded. "I'm not going to sugarcoat it. He came close to dying, but he's in stable condition now, and they expect him to make a full recovery. He's not going to be doing any marathons next week, but he doesn't need any limb or organ replacements."

Mara put a hand on her chest and let out a relieved breath. "Erik and Jia explained what's going on. It's still hard to believe. He always wanted to be a police officer growing up. I never expected he would get involved with dangerous criminals."

Jia patted her on the shoulder. "He understands his mistake, and he's done his best to not get you involved. It'll be up to him after this. There's no way he can stay on the force, but at least he might be able to avoid jail if he's upfront and works with the police."

One of the CID agents, a tall man with a pinched face, stepped forward and cleared his throat. "This is all very touching, but we're taking you into CID protective custody until this is all over, Miss Thompson. I'm Agent Niels." He nodded at his bored-looking partner. "And this is Agent Wan."

"What do I need to do?" Mara asked.

"Just come with us so we can keep you safe. We're still putting the pieces together, but we believe the men who attacked you were working for Ralic Vohn, a high-level lieutenant with the Adriatic Support Association."

Mara nodded slowly. "They don't sound so bad."

"Don't let the name mislead you. They are a small but dangerous syndicate with operations in southeastern Europe and North Africa. They're the latest contestants in the competition to replace the scum that's been cleared out of Neo SoCal."

"And my brother was working for these people?" Mara paled.

Jia shook her head. "Probably not directly. It's more that he took money from some previous criminals who might have fallen in with the Association, and the syndicate was hoping to leverage those connections."

Agent Niels could barely conceal his sneer. "You don't have to worry about it, Miss Thompson. You only need to come with us. The CID and NSCPD will clean up this mess and root out whatever syndicate tentacles are left in the department."

"Erik, Jia," Emma transmitted directly to them. "There are flitters approaching at high speed. Their transponders don't correspond to public records. Shall I engage them with the turret?"

Jia grimaced. "Damn it." She flipped off her safety.

Agent Niels backed up and reached into his jacket. "What are you doing?"

"No, Emma. We're going to need you for something else." Erik hefted his TR-7. "There are a bunch of flitters coming with spoofed transponder codes. Those your guys by any chance?"

The agent tapped this PNIU and squinted. "No, we kept this location secret, but I see what you're talking about. That group of vehicles flying in our direction is a little too perfect."

Captain Ragnar frowned. "This was all done too quickly. There are too many points where things could have leaked."

Jia nodded toward the MX 60. "Mara, get inside and stay low."

The woman's eyes widened. She crawled into the backseat and lay down, her hands over her head.

"We can keep her safe." Agent Niels glared at Jia. "We should just get in the flitters and run."

"Flying around under fire from desperate gangsters sounds like a dumb plan." Jia patted the side of the MX 60. "Let's finish these scum off on the ground, but if this goes badly, we have a *friend* who can remotely control that nice bulletproof flitter and get her out of here."

"You two aren't even law enforcement anymore." Agent Niels frowned. "You shouldn't be involved."

Captain Ragnar smiled. "Local police regulations allow ad hoc deputization as necessary. I'll do the paperwork later, but welcome to the team for tonight, Deputies Blackwell and Lin."

Erik saluted. "More than happy to be back in the saddle."

"Ridiculous," muttered Agent Niels.

Jia didn't care about the ego of a CID agent. They had a fight coming up. She turned around as target markers popped up in her smart lenses. "Now it's time for the not-so-fun part."

Grinning, Erik switched his gun to four-barrel mode. "Nah. This part's fun, too."

"I'll meet you halfway. The sometimes-fun part."

"So much for secrecy." Agent Niels and his partner pulled out pistols, slugthrowers. He slapped at his PNIU. "I'm calling for reinforcements."

"Don't worry." Erik raised his gun. "We won't need them."

CHAPTER NINE

Grim-faced, Captain Ragnar drew his stun pistol. "We can't shoot until we're sure. Some people might not care about leaving behind unnecessary carnage, but that's not the way I work. But if those guys are from the syndicate, I have no problem going all-out."

"It'd be easier to light them up when they're landing, but okay, your call." Erik frowned. He didn't have time to convince the captain, so he nodded to the MX 60. "Jia wasn't lying about how armored this thing is. We can use it as a barrier. Unless they have something a lot more impressive than what their other guys are using, we'll be fine."

Despite their dubious looks, the agents and Captain Ragnar took up positions behind the MX 60. The flitters grew from specks of light in the distance to shadowy outlines behind bright headlights. They slowed as they grew closer to the park and descended as a group. Gangsters rushed out with rifles and arrogant sneers that didn't match them crouching behind their vehicles. Erik would credit them with at least being smart enough to not exit directly into the line of fire.

"Our reinforcements will be here soon," Agent Niels shouted. "You don't want to do this, Ralic. Just throw down your weapons and surrender."

"Oh, you know who I am?" Ralic shouted back. He didn't look much different from any of the other suited thugs, but the CID agent would know better than Erik.

"I've got Erik Blackwell and Jia Lin here. From what I can tell, they're itching to add some kills to their belts."

Ralic scoffed. "Good. When we take them out too, it'll send a bigger message to anyone who thinks they can stand against us, but we're all about good relations. Turn over the girl, and none of you cops or agents have to die. We could even use a few people who owe us a favor."

Captain Ragnar glared at Ralic. "You really think you've won?"

"I've got a lot of guys here, and you've got five. Yeah, I think I've won, cop." Ralic's smile twisted into pure contempt. "Now turn her the hell over before I lose my patience. You think you'd be the first cops I've killed?"

"That's cute." Jia laughed. "He really thinks he has the advantage."

Agent Niels' mouth tightened into a painful line. His math didn't match Erik's and Jia's. Erik didn't mind his fear as long as the man could shoot straight, but that might not be much of a problem.

The CID agent only needed not to get shot.

Ralic growled and opened fire. His men followed. Bullets pinged off the MX 60 and fell to the ground, crushed. Erik and Jia had been right. It'd take a lot more than what the criminals were carrying to damage the reinforced vehicle.

Jia's rifle came to life. She fired careful, controlled bursts, her face a mask of concentration, and her bullets ripped through the unarmored flitter. One man shouted in pain and slumped. Her follow-up burst added a new hole to his head. Her other targets ducked, keeping up their fire but not breaking to run.

Captain Ragnar shot his stun pistol with an impassive expression. He chose his shots carefully and took out one thug. The CID agents pulled their triggers as fast as they could. They were doing a great job of ventilating the other flitters but not putting any targets down. Erik wasn't going to complain.

Suppression was useful on the battlefield.

He joined the fun with a four-barrel burst toward another vehicle, then jerked his rifle in the opposite direction to fling some lead near the heads of other men. The gangsters crouched after his attack, lightening the return fire, but the storm of bullets coming from all sides forced Erik and the others behind their cover.

Emma's helpful targeting highlights kept Erik and Jia aware of the positions of the enemies. The gangsters' courage came from numbers, not personal bravery. They hadn't advanced past their flitters, despite their superior numbers.

Just as Erik realized that, one of the men dashed out from the side of their formation, hoping for a wide flank. Erik stuck his barrel out from the front of his flitter and fired a four-round volley into the brave but stupid bastard. The bullets shredded the man's chest and he fell to the ground, gurgling blood. Volleys from all sides continue to strike the MX 60.

Agent Niels gritted his teeth. "We need to hold out until our reinforcements arrive. It'll just be a couple of minutes."

"Two large CID flitters passed a drone I'm borrowing in the distance," Emma reported. "His time estimate is roughly correct."

Bullets bounced off the MX 60 and fell in a clattering hail. The gangsters demonstrated decent trigger discipline, with most opting for bursts or single-fire rather than wasteful streams of fully automatic against the hardened cover.

Erik and Jia popped up without comment at the same time to down men on either side and dropped at the same time as well.

"This is taking too long," Jia muttered. She reached into a vest pocket and yanked out a plasma grenade.

Agent Niels' eyes widened. "Is that a *grenade?*"

"No, it's a beignet." Jia primed the explosive with a quick twist of its notches. "Of course it's a grenade! A couple of minutes is a long time when you're outnumbered."

Captain Ragnar shook his head, his mouth curling into a smile. If he disapproved of the explosive, there was nothing in his body language to suggest that.

He always knew more about what was going on with Erik and Jia then he ever let on, and from what Erik had picked up, it wasn't an accident he'd ended up their captain.

"You can't just throw a gre—" Agent Niels began.

"Grenade out." With a smile, Jia flung the object in

question lazily over the MX 60. The cacophony of gunfire continued, joined by shouts of warning, but it was too late. The grenade's explosion consumed half a flitter and wasn't any kinder to the criminals behind it. Brief screams cut through the air before death snuffed them out.

"If we're going to die anyway, let's take those pigs with us!" Ralic roared.

"Impressive in his own dumb way." Jia rolled her eyes.

The surviving thugs didn't continue hiding. Some hopped over the front of the remaining flitters. Others screamed in defiance, charged from either side, and resumed shooting.

Erik waited for a lull and set his gun on the MX 60 for return fire, then pulled the trigger and swept from the side. Jia mirrored him on the opposite side. The deadly wave cut through the charging thugs. Captain Ragnar's bright shots stunned thugs, saving them from the death wave. The wide-eyed CID agents stayed low, clutching their pistols.

The futile charge was over in seconds, the survivors lying on the ground groaning in pain or twitching and stunned. Jia and Erik both popped in new magazines. There weren't any men still standing, and Emma wasn't showing more or offering any warnings.

Erik walked toward a bleeding but still breathing Ralic. "You're a real dumbass."

Ralic coughed up some blood, a huge grin on his face. "You're dead, pig. You just don't know it yet."

"Yeah, sure."

Jia slung her rifle and pulled a medpatch out of a pouch. She offered a reassuring smile to the frightened Mara hiding in the back of the MX 60. "Let's stabilize the survivors. I imagine you CID agents might have some questions."

"The CID vehicles are now forty-five seconds out," Emma commented.

Erik shook his head at the downed Ralic and looked into the distance. It was hard to make out the lights of the CID flitters among the background haze of illumination that was Neo SoCal at night. They were approaching fast and low.

Agent Niels lowered his head and tapped his PNIU. He murmured furtively, his brow creasing in concern. His partner accepted medpatches from Jia and applied them to the survivors. They might not save everyone, but murderous criminals should have known better than to charge a group that included Erik and Jia.

"There's a problem." Agent Niels looked up with a frown as the large flitters slowed. Red and white holographic lights flashed, illuminating the large letters on the side: CID. The flitters were both large enough to hold all the prisoners, but they needed ambulances. There was no point in transporting corpses.

"What problem?" Erik watched as the vehicles swept past from the carnage of the immediate battlefield and turned around.

"My reinforcements were delayed by a mechanical problem. They said they won't be here for a few more minutes."

Erik knelt behind one of the bullet-riddled syndicate flitters and leveled his weapon at the newly arrived CID flitters. "Then who the hell are these guys?"

"Good question," Captain Ragnar replied with a frown.

Jia and the captain jogged toward the remains of the syndicate's defensive line. Smoke continued to pour off the smoldering wreckage of the grenade's victim, but the other vehicles provided some small cover. Agents Niels and Wan rushed forward too, both looking confused.

"Emma, prepare to take off and deploy the turret," Erik ordered. "Keep low, and try to keep the emitters undamaged so you can run with Mara if you need to."

"Emma? Who's Emma?" Agent Niels looked around.

The MX 60 lifted off, and the turret popped out from the bottom. Emma pointed the heavy weapon at the cargo flitters.

"Call the NSCPD, Emma," Erik ordered. "At this point, it doesn't matter who the hell shows up. The more, the merrier."

Agent Niels waved a hand. "Wait a second. There might just be a mix-up. You can't always shoot and ask questions later."

Erik regretted not packing armor-piercing rounds. "It doesn't hurt to be prepared."

The back doors of the large flitters lowered to the ground to form ramps. Each disgorged the same cargo: a large group of rifle-armed men standing beside an exoskeleton with its shield already extended and a heavy rifle. The men poured out of the flitters and kept their rifles pointed.

A booming amplified voice sounded from one of the exos. "I'm Agent Niels of the CID. I thought you might need some help, but it looks like you've already got the situation under control. We can take custody of Mara Thompson now."

Jia looked at the Agent Niels near them before giving Captain Ragnar a meaningful look. He inclined his head toward the new arrival and shook his head.

"Ralic's barely hanging on," Jia shouted. "And Mara's safe. We have the real Agent Niels here, so your lie isn't going to work. If you don't want to end up like your friends, you can fly away now, or you can die. Same difference to us."

"It was worth a shot," replied the exo pilot. "Ah, poor Ralic. That explains why he wasn't answering my call. He thought he could handle this himself, but one can't fault a man for ambition."

"Why do you even care about Mara Thompson anymore?" Jia replied. "Whatever plan you had to use her is over. The CID and the NSCPD are going to dismember your operations here, and you just lost a pile of guys."

"Losses are inevitable during any new business venture." The pilot offered an exaggerated shrug with the help of his exo. "They're also a valuable lesson for certain men not to let their reach exceed their grasp. As for the woman, that's our business, not yours. The question before you is simple: her life or your life?"

"Get ready to fly away, Emma, on my signal," Erik murmured. "You might not be able to take sustained fire from exos. Circle the area until the real reinforcements show up."

Jia's hand edged toward a pouch holding another grenade. She offered Erik an almost imperceptible nod.

"I've got my own question." Erik pointed his rifle at the exo. "Actually, it's the same question. Her life or your life?"

CHAPTER TEN

Emma accelerated forward and sprayed bullets at the new force, downing several men and scattering the others before the exoskeletons' guns came to life in a deadly river of bullets that barely missed the fleeing MX 60. Jia threw a grenade into the back of the flitter, and the explosion sent men screaming, their bodies burned and half on fire. Blasted pieces of the flitter rose into the air, and a billowing cloud of smoke obscured the vehicle.

Her team's flitter barriers jerked and shuddered as bullets ripped through them. The heavy rifle fire from the non-blasted exoskeleton forced Jia and the others to duck. High-caliber bullets shredded the flitters, turning them from protection to inconvenience.

With a loud clank, the exoskeletons emerged from the smoke, one with a scorched but intact shield. Emma angled the MX 60 and came in for a pass. The turret spat out a heavy stream of bullets that sliced into the gunmen and ripped into the large flitters. Emma's first pass downed half the surviving foot soldiers. Her bullets sparked as they struck and bounced off the reinforced ballistic shields of the exoskeletons, but the aerial assault forced the exoskeletons to concentrate their fire on the threat above. Emma continued diving and weaving. A loud buzz sounded from above before she pulled to the side.

"They appear to be EMP-hardened," Emma reported. "Unfortunately."

"Figures," Erik grumbled. "Can't make things too easy."

After some abrupt course changes, Emma came in for a low and fast strafing run. Jia, Erik, the captain, and the agents took the opportunity to sweep through the men in front of them. Erik's first burst struck a man square in the chest and he jerked back but didn't fall, revealing a tac vest. It wouldn't survive Emma's turret, but that wouldn't help if Jia and the others didn't take out the exoskeletons.

A follow-up headshot finished off the target. Erik switched back to single-barrel mode and cut through the masses with one bullet per man. Captain Ragnar snatched a rifle off the ground from the first wave of dead men and added his contribution. Apparently, he'd had enough of taking people alive.

Already disrupted by Emma's earlier efforts and with one of their flitters already half-destroyed, the syndicate survivors weren't in a position to repel the attacks.

The men fell to the ground screaming or groaning—or silent—as bullets cut through their heads or necks. A tactical vest was a marvel of protection, but it wasn't a full-body shield. The small number of men who survived the assault threw down their weapons and sprinted in the opposite direction.

So much for the bravery of the Adriatic Support Association.

One of the exoskeletons lowered its aim, now less interested in trying to take out the MX 60 and more in countering Mara's protection detail. They'd cut through half the new reinforcements before dropping back to the ground. A burst from the other exoskeleton nailed the MX 60 on the bottom, followed by a shower of sparks. The vehicle shuddered and dipped.

"Get the hell out of here, Emma," Erik ordered. "We've got this, but keep your drones. We might need them." He fished out a plasma grenade. "I've got two left. Jia?"

She pulled out another grenade. "This is my last one, but I've got a couple of smokes."

Agent Niels shook his head. "Did either of you ever consider carrying stun grenades?"

"We'd have been completely screwed if we had." Erik shot him a huge smile. He turned back to Jia and ducked a deadly burst from one of the exoskeletons. "Remember that little exo-killing training session we did last week?"

"The prophecy is fulfilled," Jia muttered sarcastically.

Agent Niels ejected his magazine and took a look before slapping it back in. "I don't have many rounds left."

Agent Wan slid him a rifle from a syndicate enforcer with a shrug before ejecting the magazines from those around him and stuffing them in his pockets. He then gave a firm nod and a thumbs-up to Erik, who was polite enough to not laugh at his sudden bravado.

"Whatever you're going to do, do it." Captain Ragnar finished off two more men with quick shots. "Niels is right. We're not going to last long without your flitter as cover or air support. You two are tough, but they've got exoskeletons."

"We don't need to last long if we take them out." Erik dropped his rifle to yank out and prime both grenades. "Same play as in training, Jia. You want front or back? And left or right?"

"I'll take front and left," Jia replied with a look of weary resignation. "You give the count."

"Emma, can you give us specific outlines of the pilots?" Erik asked.

"I borrowed some useful drones," Emma replied. "I don't even need to launch any of my own. The smoke isn't a significant problem in this case."

The targeting highlights changed from the large exoskeletons to the exposed parts of their bodies. That was all they would need. The advantage of constant training was that Jia already knew what she needed to do.

"Three," Erik counted, "two, one. Grenade out!"

Jia hurled her plasma grenade in a careful arc, followed by a smoke grenade. Countless hours of practice had perfected her aim, and Erik didn't doubt she could land a grenade within a couple of centimeters blindfolded. The exoskeletons moved closer together and overlapped their shields like a mighty twenty-third-century phalanx. Erik took his chance and risked standing to pitch his two grenades toward the targets but angled for a quick fall to the side. He released both grenades before ducking back down and avoiding a round ripping through his arm.

The first grenade released its deadly white-blue explosion, which spread across the shields and pushed the reinforced exoskeletons back. Smoke poured from Jia's second grenade, the cloud all but consuming the two enemies by the time Erik's grenades arrived. They hit the ground and bounced up, making it past the shield to the more exposed but still armored backs of the exoskeletons.

Follow-up explosions knocked them to the ground.

Jia and Erik were sprinting toward the smoke before the enemy hit the ground, each heading toward their predetermined target. If their plan hadn't worked, they were both about to get a high-velocity, high-caliber round at point-blank range, one their vests wouldn't be able to save them from. Emma's overlay revealed the struggling pilots getting their bearings.

The exoskeletons tried to stand, the extent of their damage obscured by the residual smoke. Jia and Erik cleared the distance in seconds and leapt onto them, closing their eyes to the stinging gray and black air around them. They didn't need to see. Emma was seeing for them. They shoved their weapons past the shields and against the heads of the pilots, and their shots rang out as one volley. The exoskeletons collapsed again with resounding thuds.

Jia jumped off, coughed, and backed away, waving her hand to clear the smoke. "I can't believe that worked in real life."

Erik jogged backward, his eyes narrowed. "Who would expect something so ridiculous? But it can be effective."

"Wait." Jia spun toward him, accusation in her eyes. "When we practiced this in the simulation, you said this was just something you'd thought of."

"Yeah, thought of to teach you." Erik shouldered his rifle and offered her his merriest and most frustrating grin.

"It's not like I'm a tactical genius. Almost everything I teach you I've seen or done before."

The remaining two agents and the captain just watched the two argue.

Jia inclined her head toward the downed exoskeletons, now rough shadowy outlines in the clearing smoke. "You've done something like that before?"

"Sure, a couple of times. Sometimes I didn't have an exo, or my exo got busted, and it was do something crazy or die." Erik gave a dismissive shrug. "How we doing, Emma?"

"NSCPD vehicles, including TPST, are closing in," Emma responded. "I didn't want to distract you while you were doing the self-described ridiculous things."

"Are we sure this time?" Jia asked.

"The transponders matched, and I've gotten facial ID matches off several known officers," Emma replied. "Of course, I can't say if they're corrupt or not. Even my sensors can't peer into the dark depths of the human soul."

Erik turned to Captain Ragnar and explained what Emma had related before adding, "I don't think we need to be wrapped up in this too much longer."

The captain nodded back. "I'll personally guarantee her safety until we get the true CID reinforcements."

Agent Niels stood and surveyed the bodies and holes littering the smoky battleground. He blinked several times as if he couldn't believe what he was seeing. Jia smiled. She had been just like him not all that long ago.

"How is Mara doing?" Jia asked.

"I'm okay," came the woman's voice over the comm. "Is it…really over?"

"Yes." Jia kicked a rifle out of the way. "That's the problem with big moves like this. You have to pull them off the first time, or everyone will be ready for it."

"No one is ever ready for you two," Agent Niels murmured with a shake of his head.

CHAPTER ELEVEN

<u>April 13, 2230, Neo Southern California Metroplex,
Municipal Tower 67, Hospital Level</u>

As Erik observed Jared lying in his bed covered in silver patches, the bed beeping softly, his breathing shallow, he couldn't help but remember when he lay in a similar bed, the only survivor of the troops who had deployed onto the surface of Molino that fateful day.

Modern medicine could save a man from the brink of death, but it couldn't do anything about the mental scars. He had his own healing solution, and his first real treatment had started with the death of Sophia Vand.

And he had Jia. He glanced at her out of the corner of his eye. Yes, he did have her. He kept telling himself he needed to concentrate on his revenge, but it was hard to ignore his feelings for the woman he spent almost every minute of his waking day beside. Those feelings were drifting dangerously close to something more all-consuming than casual attraction.

"You look like shit, Jared," Erik tried to push his

thoughts about Jia down. "But you're not dead. That's always good."

Jared managed a weak laugh. "Didn't stop it from hurting. I'm surprised. I figured someone would come in and smother my ass while I was in the hospital."

"Don't tempt me." Jia gestured toward the door. "There are two very large and stern uniforms out there just itching to take down syndicate enforcers, and it's not like your location is an open secret."

"Mara told me." Jared closed his eyes and sighed. "She's tucked away in CID custody until they finish off the ASA in town."

"Did Captain Ragnar tell you the good news?" Erik asked.

"What's the good news in all this?" Jared chuckled bitterly. "That they're not going to send me to prison since I'm cooperating, but I'm going to have years of probation, and I've been kicked off the force in disgrace? I guess that's good news."

"The CID has mostly finished the ASA in Neo SoCal." Erik walked over to the side of the bed. "Jia and I killed one of their top lieutenants, a guy named Ralic. It turns out one of the sub-bosses came to the party, too. He was piloting an exo, but we ventilated him. They lost a lot of people in the fights, and their local organization's a mess. Some of their other local tools are turning themselves in, and others are getting smoked out. It turns out the ASA had greater penetration than you might expect, including taking advantage of some leaks in the NSCPD to set up the fake CID agent ruse. If they'd had slightly better timing or intel, it might have worked."

"I still don't get it." Jared groaned. "Why go through all that trouble to get Mara?"

Jia folded her arms. "From what I suspected and what the captain passed along, their newfound influence was surprisingly extensive but tenuous. Interrogations of survivors from the different incidents suggest Ralic was worried you would make a big noisy stand and some of the other people they were pressuring would fold. If they made a public example out of you and your family member, it would keep them in line, especially because they were in the middle of trying to set up a major smuggling pipeline. Weapons, drugs, *yaoguai*, you name it. They wanted to bring it in."

"I didn't know about that. I didn't dig that deeply into the surveillance data they wanted me to take care of. I didn't want to flag IA." Jared opened his eyes. "It seems crazy now."

"Do you have regrets?" Jia asked. "If you'd helped them, you wouldn't have been shot, and your sister wouldn't have been in danger."

"You think I'm garbage, don't you, Jia?" Jared turned his head weakly to look at her. "That I'm just about saving my skin."

Jia shook her head. "No, the opposite. You had plenty of chances to run and save your own skin, but you were worried about your sister, including putting your life on the line. I'm not going to say I don't have a problem with a cop who was taking bribes, but at least you put your family first when it mattered."

"I don't have regrets," Jared replied. He let out a long sigh. "I'm starting over. Mara's happy I survived, but she didn't know what I was doing. My career's finished, but I still need to keep my nose clean and stay out of trouble. I think that might be easier somewhere else."

"You're leaving Neo SoCal?" Erik's brows lifted. "Where are you going?"

"Not sure yet, and not just Neo SoCal. They aren't going to sentence me to probationary work, but I'm volunteering to be resettled on the frontier." Jared looked like he was at peace.

"Damn. Moving from Neo SoCal to a frontier colony's a big change."

Jared nodded. "I know, but I think I could use it. Being in this place with all these people, all these opportunities and temptations, it's hard not to go—" He withered under Jia's glare. "It's...*harder* to stay out of trouble. There I'll have honest work, helping out in an ag dome or with construction or something. I'm not that old. I can still start over. Maybe I can help someone not make the same mistakes I did."

"It's a long trip to the frontier. You might not be able to see your family for a long time." Jia shrugged one shoulder.

"That's probably for the best. I think if I stuck around here, there would be too many bad memories. At least my sister and my parents can remember me mostly as the cop and not the screw-up." Jared yawned. "I think I need to get some rest, but I want to thank you for your help. Neither of you owed me anything, and I sure as hell know I didn't deserve your help."

"We didn't do it for you," Jia replied, glancing at Erik. "We did it for your sister and Neo SoCal. We might not be police anymore, but we still care about this place."

Erik nodded his agreement. "Nothing wrong with having some fun taking down gangsters while doing a good deed or two."

Jared laughed quietly. "You two were barely cops, but you're still both better cops than a hundred of me." He closed his eyes. "Keep up the good fight, Obsidian Detective and Lady Justice."

Erik waited for Jared to say something else, but the wounded man's head lolled to the side, slumber taking him. It'd been an eventful couple of days, but routine by their standards.

"What about you, Jia?" Erik asked.

"What?" Jia looked over. "What about me?"

"Do you regret getting involved?" Erik nodded at Jared's sleeping form.

Jia turned toward the door. "It ended with fewer thugs in the world. I'll never regret getting involved in something that ends like that."

Erik opened his mouth to answer when his PNIU chimed with a message from Captain Ragnar. After reading the message, he smirked. "So much for keeping a low profile. The captain needs *one* more small favor."

April 14, Neo Southern California Metroplex, Apartment of Jia Lin

Jia was curled up next to Erik on the couch with his arm around her shoulders. "It's almost time, right?"

Erik nodded. "Emma, just play it once he sends it."

"Very well," the AI replied.

"I can't believe we agreed to it," Jia commented, shaking her head. "It's ridiculous. I'm still embarrassed."

"More ridiculous than what we do for Alina?" Erik raised an eyebrow, a playful smile joining it. "I don't think it's so bad. Nothing wrong with using our rep."

A holographic image of the police chief in full dress uniform appeared in the center of a landing platform surrounded by armored TPST flitters. He stood in front of an exoskeleton, and soaring brass-heavy music played.

"In these difficult times," announced a deep-voiced narrator, "criminals, antisocials, insurrectionists, and terrorists are waiting for their chance to strike and disrupt our careful social fabric."

Captain Ragnar disappeared. Images of uniformed officers charging and firing stun pistols gave way to an exoskeleton smashing through a wall and chasing masked men holding rifles. The scene changed to an image of a Zitark chasing down a screaming girl before running away under the withering fire of police snipers.

"I didn't know that was going to be in there." Jia laughed. "Since when does the NSCPD take on aliens?"

"Hey, it could happen." Erik shrugged. "That guy probably got fined for parking his ship on the wrong platform, and so now he's rampaging because he doesn't want to pay the fine."

"In these uncertain times," the narrator continued, the music swelling, "you can depend on the Neo Southern California Police Department to protect you."

Jia's stomach tightened, and she swallowed. The next part was just too much. The image shifted to drone footage, presenting an overhead view of Erik and Jia firing at the ASA enforcers. Careful angles and editing removed the CID agents and Captain Ragnar from the scene. There was also a notable lack of bodies and blood.

The scene changed again to Erik and Jia standing with rifles in hand. Neither wore a uniform, which made sense given they'd filmed the footage the day before. They shot stern looks at the camera drone.

"Remember," they announced in unison, "the NSCPD will always be watching."

Jia groaned, her right hand reaching up to cover her eyes. "That's even cheesier than I thought!"

"I don't know. I kind of like it." Erik laughed.

"And it's misleading." Jia scrubbed her hand over her face. "It implies we're still in the department."

"We don't say that, and we're not wearing uniforms." Erik stuck his hands behind his head and leaned back. "A little PR for the department never hurt, and it also might confuse the conspiracy."

Jia offered him a squinted, dubious look as she turned her head toward him. "I doubt the conspiracy is going to be distracted by something like that."

"If we have time to make PR commercials for the NSCPD, it means we're not running around destroying conspiracy Tin Men," Erik replied. "That's got to get them thinking, 'What are they up to?'"

"If you say so," Jia settled back down. "But it's still embarrassing."

"Good thing you didn't take up that Venusian talent agent's offer. You'd have to do a lot more embarrassing stuff than that commercial."

Jia lightly punched him in the leg. "Very funny."

CHAPTER TWELVE

April 15, 2230, Low Earth Orbit, Llewellyn Observatory

Tony pointed to a line on the data window open in front of him, highlighting it. The gesture also affected the mirrored windows floating in front of Professor Lal and Arda as they all sat around the conference table. Tony had been dubious Professor Lal would listen to him, but his supervising professor had been enthusiastic.

"As indicated here, we're still seeing evidence of course changes," Tony explained. "Whatever the phenomenon is, it's not over, and there's possibly a second approaching object."

"A second?" Professor Lal stroked his long gray beard. "Huh. That's interesting. Very interesting."

"It's coming in from a different angle, and I have not been able to verify any major course corrections or unusual spectral readings. It could be a ship, or it could just be some tiny chunk of an asteroid or comet." Tony sighed. "I wish they'd do a nice burn or something so we could figure it out. I'm having trouble picking it out from the historical data, but it could even be some old probe that floated over there over the centuries."

"We can figure all that out in good time." Professor Lal waved a hand dismissively. "Good, good. I need you to get this data into a more digestible format. Focus on the two primary objects for now."

"Digestible?" Tony frowned. "What do you mean by that?"

"I've made certain arrangements." Professor Lal took a deep breath and slowly let it out. "A Vand Foundation representative will be visiting the observatory soon. They are neither an astronomer nor a scientist, so we'll need your visual aids and supporting data presented in a way that won't intimidate or alienate them."

"The Vand Foundation?" Tony looked at Arda, who shrugged. "I get that I'm on a Vand Foundation grant, but why call them here? Don't we have to focus on publishing before whoever sent the ship?"

Professor Lal folded his hands and a knowing smile appeared on his face. "You don't understand just how indebted this entire facility is to the Vand Foundation. Not just your work. Yes, we do need to practice a certain level of secrecy, but the money we receive requires more than just sticking a notice on our papers about our research being supported by generous grants from the Vand Foundation."

Tony groaned and slumped in his chair. "They're going to take the discovery from us!"

"No, no, no. Don't fret, my boy. If we play our cards right, this could become an even bigger success than any of us anticipate, but to do that, we'll need the foundation totally on our side, and we can't get them there by keeping information from them." Professor Lal motioned to the data window. "What we can do is use this to get additional funding and personnel."

Arda lifted his fist to his mouth and cleared his throat. "How do we know they won't pass this along to someone else?"

"I've already explained the basics of what we've discovered," Professor Lal replied, "and they were very keen on us not spreading this around until we can gather more information. They've also made some indirect inquiries about our research to different groups to see if anyone else is working on similar information. The Vand Foundation representative said they would do their best to make sure that our research group gets the credit, provided we keep our mouths shut, and let them manage things."

Arda grimaced. "Uh, about that…"

Tony whipped his head toward the other student. "Please don't tell me you told anyone else about it."

"Not exactly." Arda ran a hand through his hair, his hand shaking slightly. "I just asked some questions on a forum. I wasn't specific, and I didn't use my name or any detailed data, so it's not like they can link it to us."

"That's not the point, you idiot," Professor Lal snapped. "If anyone figures out what we're doing, they might be able to get a paper out before us. I'm delaying only because I want the full cooperation of the Vand Foundation before I proceed, and the only reason I told *them* is that we'll need their resources and pull."

Arda sighed. "It's not like that." He averted his eyes. "It wasn't an academic forum."

"Then what the hell was it?" Tony asked. "You told a reporter?"

"No. They're a bunch of crazies." Arda looked down at the table, his shoulders slumped. "I've talked to them in the past. They're nuts, but also smart and unorthodox, and they have a way of helping you look at things from a different perspective. I thought they could give me some insight, but I didn't use my normal avatar or handle or anything like that, and I wasn't that specific. There's no way they could figure it out from what I said."

Professor Lal stood slowly and fixed a harsh glare on Arda. "I only hope these people are less—"

The entire room shook violently. Loud, shrill alarms sounded. The students and professor stared at each other as another tremor shook the room. The data windows vanished.

"What's going on?" Tony shouted.

Professor Lal tried to tap his PNIU, but he missed. "Direct command, status repo—"

Another tremor threw him into the back wall, and his head slammed into the hard metal with a loud crack. Tony's eyes widened as the professor didn't fall to the ground, instead floating away. Spherical droplets of blood drifted away from the wall. Tony looked down. He was slowly rising toward the ceiling. Arda gripped the table tightly to stay in place.

"We've lost gravity!" Tony looked around, eyes darting from floating object to floating object.

"No shit! You should get your Ph.D. for that brilliant observation!" Arda shouted. "We need to figure out—"

A massive fireball tore through the wall, and fragments

of metal blasted into the room like a hundred shotguns fired in a cruel volley. They shredded the students and the unconscious professor. Tony coughed up blood, the reflex pushing him slowly backward and leaving a trail of his vital red fluid floating in front of him. His agony was short because another explosion ripped through the room and consumed the men inside. He didn't live long enough to feel the cold, cruel touch of the vacuum of space.

Julia steepled her fingers and leaned back in the comfortable body-hugging softness of her chair. She smiled at the hologram of the hooded figure standing in front of her, his head bowed.

"The primary information leak on the matter of interest has been handled, ma'am," he reported.

Julia arched a delicate brow. "Primary? You've found others?"

"In the course of investigating the matter, we learned that certain information was passed beyond the targets of interest. Additional information containment steps are necessary."

"Unfortunate, but not surprising." Julia threaded her fingers together. "And there's no additional risk of leaks from the primary source?"

"We were authorized to take any and all necessary measures, ma'am," the man replied. "The leaks were sealed, and the relevant evidence deleted."

"Yes, you were." Julia narrowed her eyes, understanding what they'd done. "Continue with that. If you need additional resources, contact me, and I'll provide them. Now finish cleaning this up." She flicked her wrist. "End call."

Julia took a deep breath and pinched the bridge of her nose. Sophia Vand was dead, but somehow that annoying woman was still managing to vex her. It was like her ghost was reaching out of the grave to try to strangle Julia on the cusp of her greatness.

But the specter's efforts would amount to nothing.

The completion of the first step in the current project would be the beginning of Julia solidifying her control over the Core and thus the entire UTC. It'd take a couple more years for her to finish the task, but the decades had granted her patience. All she needed to do was get her people to their destination at the edge of the Solar System.

Julia made a couple of quick gestures and brought up a long-range image of the comet of interest. "And this, Sophia, is why you lost. You lacked imagination. You never even *thought* to look nearby for greatness."

CHAPTER THIRTEEN

Jia lifted her wine glass and took a sip of the Chardonnay, enjoying the hints of lemon and vanilla playing across her tongue.

The fish was decent at the restaurant, but she was loving the wine, or maybe she was loving spending time with her friends and getting a decent buzz without any concern over shooting someone or dirty cops trying to survive their past mistakes.

Relaxation.

She'd always been a workaholic, but she understood the need to recharge. What with running around for Alina and incidental trouble arising, it grew harder with each passing month to shut off. A worry about trouble always lingered in her thoughts, threatening to push her onto a dark path. She couldn't always rely on Erik to pull her out.

Jia let out a satisfied sigh. "It's nice to get together like this."

Her friends Chinara and Imogen sat at the same table, drinking their wine and enjoying their fish. Jia wasn't lying. Fighting Tin Men on Venus or taking down syndicate flunkies on Earth could weary a person, even one like her, who was used to that level of trouble.

"It is!" Imogen replied with a smile, her cheeks flushed from her wine. "I used to be a little annoyed with you when you first started spending all your time with Erik."

Jia arched a brow. "You were? It's not like we're always together."

"It's not a big deal." Imogen nodded, ignoring a stern gaze from Chinara. "Yes, but it's garbage to get angry with you because you wanted to do more with your career and spend more time with your partner. And that's *before* you started dating him."

"Uh, thanks?"

Imogen waved a hand. "Don't worry. I'm over it now, and you know what they say: absence makes the heart grow fonder." She reached over to pat Jia's hand.

Jia wondered about that. The more time she spent with Erik, the more her affection grew. She didn't want to be away from him, and not just because she worried he would end up with a bullet in the brain without her watching his back. Her current situation was convenient in more than one way.

Chinara gently cleared her throat. "I couldn't have asked for a better transition. I have something I want to share with you."

The other two women looked her way and awaited her elaboration. They both took the opportunity to down more wine but kept their attention on their friend.

"Things have been going well with Conrad." Chinara smiled softly. "*Very* well."

"Meaning what?" Imogen gasped and put a hand to her mouth. "Are you saying what I think you're saying?"

"It's been hard for me to keep it a secret." Chinara took a deep breath and slowly let it out. "This morning, Conrad asked me to marry him."

Imogen squealed in delight and leapt out of her chair so quickly it clattered to the ground. Everyone turned to look at her, and she offered a sheepish smile in response, then picked up her chair and took her seat again. A nearby waiter shook his head and mumbled under his breath before wandering away.

"So," Imogen began in a painfully serious tone, "I assume you said yes?" She waved a hand to fan her face before she stopped, eyeing her friend. "Or is this a sad story?"

"Of course I said yes." Chinara shook her head. "Sometimes you worry too much."

"Congratulations." Jia set her drink down. "You've always seemed like a good couple, and you've been dating for a while now. It seems like forever since we went out with those three guys." The rest of the words fell out of her mouth before she'd even time to think about what she was saying. "But I have to admit I'm a little shocked."

Her friends spun in their chairs to drill her with their curious gazes. Chinara looked surprised, but Imogen looked eager to feast off the potential drama that might arise. She'd always been that way.

Jia waved her hands in front of her. "I'm not saying it's a

bad thing. It's great! It's just that of the three of us, I always figured Imogen would be the first to get married."

"Oh." Imogen smirked and picked up her wine. "Before we touch on that, a toast. To Chinara and her new husband. May he get all the fun in before it's too late and Chinara makes him unfun."

"Very funny." Chinara laughed and picked up her glass. "To me."

"To you," Jia offered after picking up her glass. They all took a drink.

Imogen set her glass down. "If I end up marrying Michael, we'll be two for three with those guys we met that night. You sure you don't want to dump Erik and start dating Bolin again, Jia? It'd be a funny story we could all share."

"I think I'm good with Erik." Jia chuckled. "I've got nothing against Bolin, but Erik's a much better match for me in a lot of ways."

"It's kind of funny you ended up with a big, tough guy," Imogen replied. "Though you've always been the toughest of the three of us, even when you weren't getting in shootouts all the time."

"I don't get in shootouts all the time." Jia frowned at her friend, but she tried to keep the malice down.

Imogen grinned, an unsubtle eagerness in her eyes. "It depends on how you define 'all the time,' but you don't go more than a couple of weeks to a month before getting involved in something crazy that ends up in the news. I thought you'd be over that since you quit the police, but…" Her grin transformed into a smirk. "After all, I should remember *the NSCPD will always be watching.*"

Jia's lips pressed together. "We did the commercial as a favor to our old captain," she muttered. "Now everyone thinks we're practically cops again. That was an unusual situation. Besides, we're supposed to be talking about Chinara and Conrad, not Erik and me."

Although convincing people that Erik and Jia were still close to the department was half the point of agreeing to the commercial, the extra scrutiny from the media, family, and friends was weighing on Jia.

In another life, she could have been satisfied working as an Intelligence Directorate agent deep in the shadows without anyone knowing what she was doing, but the younger, more naïve version of herself hadn't even considered the possibility.

She wasn't sure if that would have made her happier, not that she was all that unhappy.

"We'll have plenty of time to talk about my wedding in the coming months," Chinara commented. "For now, you're more interesting, Jia." She finished her wine. She glanced at her barely touched her fish. "You know what's interesting? How you can't go on a sexy little vacation without getting into trouble with terrorists."

"Of course." Imogen nodded eagerly. "We've barely been able to talk to you about Venus. I figured you'd tell us more eventually, but you've been stingy with the details."

"Stingy?" Jia put her fingers to her temple and massaged them. "We just happened to be there. It's not like we wanted to get involved in a terrorist incident. It was nothing but a vacation that got ruined by psychos."

She might never be comfortable with lying, but like any other skill, it became easier with practice.

Disturbingly so. She didn't even have trouble keeping track of her lies.

The key, she found, was picking a simple cover story and elaborating around that. Then it was just a matter of keeping two separate realities together in her head.

Imogen blew a raspberry. "Who cares about you killing terrorists? That's your standard weekend activity."

The sad part was, it was mostly true.

If it wasn't actually killing terrorists, then it was participating in training simulations involving taking on terrorists and enforcers. She couldn't say she minded the training, but she could see how it would seem odd to anyone more normal.

"Then what are we talking about?" Jia asked, confused but happy they didn't want to drill her more about what had happened on Venus. She'd been expecting it for a while and hoped something else new and shiny would pop up to distract her friends.

"I'm talking about floating hanky-panky." Imogen wiggled her eyebrows. "And all the flexibility that requires. I know Erik's strong and probably has good endurance, but how flexible is he?"

"Oh." Jia's cheeks heated. "I think you're under a misunderstanding that I should clear up. We didn't go there for floating hanky-panky."

"So you're saying you went all the way to Venus, *not* for work or killing terrorists, and you didn't spend the time having fun?" Imogen rolled her eyes. "That's a transparent lie! Don't insult me."

"We went there on vacation." Jia sighed. "And, yes, Parvati is a floating city, but it's floating relative to the surface of Venus, and the city is sealed off from the outside with grav field compensation, so functionally when you're inside of it, it's not that much different from being in a tower or a dome. It's not zero-G or anything. Doing anything there, um, doesn't require unusual flexibility."

Imogen's shoulders slumped. "Oh, it makes sense when you explain it that way, but you still went all the way to another planet for a romantic getaway. I know you went to the moon before with Erik, but the moon isn't romantic. I mean, for crying out loud, you went to a city named after a love goddess on a planet named after a love goddess. That's got to result in something special happening."

She put a finger to her lips. "I hadn't thought of it that way." Jia's eyes narrowed, and her finger pointed at Imogen. "Wait. We should really be talking about Chinara and Conrad, not Erik and me."

"Like I said, we can wait," Chinara waved a hand in disagreement. "Besides, Imogen and I spend more time together lately since you're so busy." She folded her hands together. "I have a decent idea of where things are going with Imogen and Michael, but I'm never sure where things are going with you and Erik. This is a good chance to get the truth, when you've got a couple of glasses of wine in you." She gave Jia a stern look. "And don't try to pretend your relationship isn't going anywhere. You spend practically every waking moment with the man."

"We do work together." Jia shrugged. "That comes with the territory."

Sometimes the best defense was to face the attack head-on.

Imogen picked up the bottle in the center of the table

and refilled her glass. Like Chinara, she was more interested in the alcohol than her fish. She shook her head lightly at the approaching waiter.

Jia was trapped.

There was no escape from her friends' attention. On some level, she knew this was why she'd been spending less time with them. Keeping track of lies was one thing, but that didn't mean that they would never see through them.

"That's the thing," Imogen continued. "Working with the man you're dating means you're getting the equivalent of multiple dates a day. It has to be accelerating certain *things* because effectively you're living with him even if you aren't, you know, actually living with him. You know what I mean?" She blinked a couple of times, clearly confused by her own statement.

Jia eyed her friend. "'Certain things?' I think I'm comfortable with where things are. Erik and I are in a good place."

"Are you?" Chinara asked. "I wonder if that's true. What about love? Are you in love with Erik?"

Jia managed not to flinch. It was dangerous to spend time around people who knew her too well.

"Love's just a word," Jia mumbled.

As she said it, she accepted that it was a word that carried special meaning. It also efficiently and effectively described how she felt about Erik. She'd wanted to run from it for so long, but it was always there, waiting. Worrying about romance when a dark conspiracy threatened the galaxy felt selfish.

"Uh-huh," Chinara replied. "Sure, it's just a word. Are you saying you don't love him?"

"I...things are more complicated than that."

"'Complicated' is another way of saying yes."

Jia shrugged. "If you say so."

"What are your dates like nowadays?" Imogen asked, peering at Jia like she was waiting for a telltale sign of a lie. "That can prove a lot about the state of a relationship. All the wild fun stuff is cool and all, but it's when you settle into a routine and you're still happy that you know it's working. No one can have constant spontaneous romance forever."

Jia thought constant spontaneous romance sounded like hellish punishment, but she appreciated her friend's sentiment.

"There's nothing special about our dates," Jia replied. "We just do the usual, dinner and something fun. We've got a date tomorrow, nothing different from you and your guys. Now, let's stop talking about this. I don't want another word about love and marriage unless it involves Chinara."

Imogen nodded slowly with a sly look. "Fine." She turned to Chinara. "Let's talk about your wedding plans." She rubbed her hands together. "There might be a lot of time, but there's also so much to plan."

Jia smiled. Accepting she loved Erik was easy enough, but she wasn't prepared to talk about it to anyone, friends or family. Things like marriage lay far in the future, if at all.

First, they needed to survive his revenge.

CHAPTER FOURTEEN

<u>April 21, Neo Southern California Metroplex,</u>
<u>Apartment of Erik Blackwell</u>

"Oh, come on!" Jia leaned forward on the couch, her finger pointed at the video as she shouted. "That defense is so bad our goalie must be taking bribes from the other team. I'd say he was blind, but he was able to dodge the other player. He's good at protecting himself, just not the goal."

Erik laughed and placed his arm around Jia's shoulders as she leaned back on the couch. Jia getting worked up over the sphere ball quarter-finals was as predictable as the tides.

If their team wasn't destroying the other team, she was convinced it was a plot by the conspiracy, but Erik preferred an even game. There wasn't much point in watching a blowout.

The ebb and flow of the sports battle was the entertainment. Jia preferred the expected results based on cold, statistical analysis despite witnessing how her own attitude and sheer willpower could overcome numbers and superior equipment.

"I doubt he's taking bribes," Erik suggested as she calmed down.

"You're right," Jia muttered. "There are tons of other possibilities." She put up a hand and started lifting fingers as she called out three of them. "Drug abuse. Too many hits to the head and insufficient follow-up medical care. Someone could have kidnapped his family and is threatening them."

"Or," Erik replied, "it could just be the game being the game." He reached over to slowly close the three fingers of accusation. "They're still in the lead, so you don't have a reason to be this pissed off."

"That lead is going to evaporate if the wings and the goalie don't stop the other team, and I'm not convinced they are going to be able to do that, based on what I'm seeing right now." Jia folded her arms and frowned. "They could go all the way this year if they keep it together. No suspensions over Venusian luck rabbits, no injuries, great team roster and depth." She narrowed her eyes and turned to look at him. "Are you *sure* he's not taking bribes? He could make a lot of money throwing games with more on the line."

"It could be. Anything's possible." Erik gestured to the game hologram with his free hand. "Maybe you're not thinking this through."

"How do you figure?"

"He could be a human-alien hybrid who is suffering side effects from his genetic engineering."

"Huh." Jia nodded slowly. "That alien mutant on Venus

did move pretty well. He might have made a nice goalie." She rubbed her chin. "But you could get more value out of a modified center or forward."

Erik laughed, not sure if she was serious. She could keep a clear mind about almost everything but sphere ball. He didn't hold it against her. Everyone had their weakness, and she was far from the only sports fanatic in the UTC.

"So you're saying you don't mind illegal genetic engineering as long as it makes for a better sphere ball team?" he asked.

Jia jerked her head in his direction. "I'm not saying that. I was just thinking about it in a hypothetical sense. Of course I don't support illegal genetic engineering." She jumped up when the game hologram froze. "What the heck? What's going on? I swear, if terrorists attacked the Dragons, I'll personally track every last one of them down, stick your TR-7 up their asses, and use four barrels."

"That's some next-level obsession, but I'm sure Emma's got an explanation for us."

Emma appeared next to the hologram in a green and gold Dragons uniform. "I apologize for stopping your feed, but something has arisen."

"Something more important than the quarter-final match?" Jia ground her teeth. "I know you don't care about this, but it—"

"Yes, far more important."

The image changed to an anchor staring at the camera with a stern, concerned look. "We now go to a representative of the Vand family."

Another change brought a severe-looking woman with an overly angular face into view. She sat in a tastefully decorated office with a frown. "There has been much speculation in the last few weeks about where the current head of the family is. Until today, it has been a matter of rank and unnecessary speculation put about by people who have no reason to question the Vand family. Miss Sophia Vand, as the current head of the family and the foundation, was under stress few people in the UTC could understand, and found it necessary to take a short vacation out of the public eye."

The woman took a deep breath. "But now the situation has changed." Her voice cracked. "It is with our greatest regret and sadness that we inform you the family has suffered a tragic loss. Yesterday, during a recreational diving excursion, there was an unfortunate accident, followed by an equipment malfunction during the emergency recovery procedure. Sophia was without oxygen underwater for a significant period, and by the time she was recovered, she had passed. She was airlifted to the nearest medical facility, where she was pronounced dead on arrival."

Emma dismissed the image. "The rest of the statement is extraneous mentions of her charity and activism designed to highlight what a wonderful woman she was supposed to be. There are additional exhortations to donate to her charities." She scoffed. "Unsurprisingly, they failed to mention her murderous scheming."

"I get all that, but why the elaborate story?" Erik shook her head. "Why don't they just say she drowned?"

"I think they're trying to make the lie easier to swallow by explaining how one of the most well-guarded and wealthiest women in the UTC ended up dead on vacation,"

Jia replied. "There are already a lot of conspiracy theories floating around about her, just none close to the truth. This way, they can hide it."

"You think?"

Jia nodded. "Plenty of wealthy people die doing risky activities. They might leak some other details later about her not using the maximum safety equipment or something like that. It'll feed into people's preconceptions even more and give them a way to channel the below-the-surface disdain that fed into the conspiracy theories. The last thing they need is half the UTC probing her death."

"This still seems sloppy." Erik frowned. "Isn't the best lie one partially based on the truth? Why not just claim there was some sort of accident in space rather than dying on Earth?"

Jia shook her head. "Someone like Vand leaves too big a trail. If they say she died in space, they'd need to account for the ship being destroyed. If they admit a ship blew up, that's going to get the government involved, including the Fleet. If they had total control of the Fleet, they wouldn't need hidden Tin Men factories."

He thought for a second. "Ok, that makes sense."

"And a destroyed ship begs for people to go find what's left of it. They might want to collect debris to look for terrorist or insurrectionist involvement. But drowning in a simple accident? There's no great mystery to investigate, minimal equipment to recover, and if they tossed it out when investigators showed up, it wouldn't seem as suspicious." Jia stood and paced. "The family more than anyone would be the ones who would want to investigate if there was any hint of foul play, and now they're cutting off that avenue and also trying to smother the other rumors about how long she's been dead. It was a Qin Shi Huang play. Not sure if that means they're involved with the conspiracy or just that the conspiracy set up the lie."

"Qin Shi Huang? I remember him from history class." Erik looked up for a moment to pull out the details. "First emperor of China, but he died, maybe from mercury poisoning from drinking some alchemist's immortality potions. They were worried about an uprising, so they just pretended he was still alive until they couldn't."

"Exactly." Jia stopped pacing and furrowed her brow. "That's the one thing I don't get. Sophia Vand might be important in the conspiracy, but it's not like the conspiracy is publicly known for having a lot of control. Even if they announced she was dead the next day, it's not like there would suddenly be a bunch of rebellions on frontier colonies." She shook her head. "I'm surprised they concealed this for as long as they did. There's a balance between setting up a plausible lie and giving people time to become suspicious."

Erik shrugged. "If someone lies about something, that means they think people knowing the truth is going to mess things up. These people are willing to do a lot of things to keep their secrets, and they aren't that afraid of the government."

"She must have been a high-level member of the conspiracy, one of the top leaders." Jia nodded as it came together. "If they lied, they had to worry about the downstream effects, but they know we survived, which means the lie might not have been about concealing it from the people hunting them. I think our ID involvement has given us something of a shield. That could be it."

"But we're not the only ones hunting them," Erik replied. "Even if they assume the ID and CID know everything we know, there could be other groups, other members of the conspiracy, or even other conspiracies. That's the only explanation that makes sense." He leaned back with a frown. "They haven't compromised the entire ID. Otherwise, Alina would have been benched a long time ago."

"That's valid. There might be others like the woman Sophia referenced." Jia scratched her cheek. "I don't know if that makes me more comfortable. It means there could be some other dangerous conspiracy out there fighting our targets for power. If these other people, assuming there are other people, were the good guys, the ID would know about them and would be working with them."

"No such thing as a secret cabal of good guys?" Erik asked with a smile. "Aren't we that?"

"Maybe, but it's because we're just two individuals that we've managed to slip through the cracks." Jia shook her head.

Erik didn't drop his previous line of thought. "Speaking of the ID, aren't their agents a secret cabal of mostly good guys?"

"It's not like their existence is secret, just their individual members. But that's not as important as the other implications of the death announcement."

"Which are?" Erik frowned, unsure of where she was going.

"If they're ready to admit she's dead, they believe

they're ready for the potential fallout, or even for a counterattack from their collected enemies who might sense weakness." Jia returned to the couch. "Even third-rate reporters know we were on Venus, which means the conspiracy would have to know that we were involved with Vand's death. That's assuming she didn't transmit some final message making it clear."

Erik shrugged. "Big deal. It's like you said; they're weaker now. That means it'll be easier to deal with them, especially now that their Tin Man factory is gone. We just need to keep doing what we're doing." He inclined his head toward the frozen hologram. "Emma can restart our match feed. The game's going to be over soon." He gave a slight nod to Emma, who vanished and replaced the news feed with the game.

"That simple, huh?" Jia asked.

"There's nothing simple about what we're doing, which is why we should take our downtime when we have it." Erik slipped his arm back around Jia's shoulder. "There is going to be trouble waiting for us until we finish off all the Sophia Vands out there. The match is almost over, and we have plenty of time to do other fun nighttime activities."

Jia turned back toward the hologram. "If the Dragons lose, I'm going to be in a bad mood. Aren't you worried about that?"

"Nah." Erik offered her a mischievous grin. "In that case, I'll just have to do more work. There's *nothing* so bad that fun nighttime and athletic activity can't make a person feel better." He thought for one second more. "Or if there is, I hope I never find out what it is."

CHAPTER FIFTEEN

Jia laughed in delight. "You know what? This *is* a fun nighttime activity, though the machine's doing all the work."

She ducked her simulated exoskeleton under a low-hanging safety sign suspended from the top of the current tunnel. Post-game, when she'd stepped out of the bathroom at Erik's apartment and spotted him holding her tactical suit rather than something slinky, she'd been confused.

Erik hadn't told her he'd made a training reservation, but after he explained, it made sense. It was early in the evening, and despite her team's victory, she needed to burn off her nervous energy one way or another.

Her partner leapt over her with a burst of his jump thrusters. "Emma's got the simulation tuned better to the exos Alina gave us. We both need to get more used to their superior maneuverability, though this isn't necessarily the best scenario for that."

"Then why did you select it?" Jia asked.

"Because sometimes," Erik replied, "you just want to take someone out. The scenario is straightforward: shock and awe kill raid against terrorists holed up in a building complex. The primary target is their leader, who is a handsome copy of me, and who should be holed up in the primary security room, and we have intel on its location. The bastards don't have any hostages, and we don't have to take them alive. The scenario presupposes we've managed to gain control of local exterior cameras and drones and spoof them. All we need to do is search and destroy. Our recon suggests no exterior enemy forces. Like I said, easy."

Jia lifted her arm, bringing the exo's arm with it and raising the massive rifle with its grenade attachment. "You and Emma have really dialed down the weirdness lately. It makes me suspicious."

"What do you mean by that?" Emma asked, still formless. "I don't think you've encountered weirdness since you aided my stabilization. All our scenarios have some pragmatic and realistic aspects."

"That's debatable," Jia replied. "In this case, I'm talking about no strange aliens appearing or bikini babes in training. We're not on a strange colony world or an alien planet." She continued her advance over the narrow sky bridge connecting their tower to the target building in the distance, keeping alert for enemies despite the scenario parameters. "It's almost like you've decided our training scenarios should reflect reality."

"Reality?" Erik scoffed. "Emma, is this room secure?"

"I've made it that way," the AI replied. "You two have a habit of forgetting where you are in simulations, so I often go ahead and handle that while making allowances for external transmissions."

Erik sidled his exoskeleton up beside Jia. "We fought a group of full-conversion cyborgs on Venus who were led by an alien-human hybrid. I don't know what realistic is anymore. We could pretty much stick anything in these simulations and get close to the truth. Changelings, *yaoguai*, half-aliens. I wouldn't be surprised if Generous Gao showed up on a mission and tried to kill us."

"That's a rather extreme step up from handing out rotten fruit to bad kids." Jia chuckled. "But I get what you're saying." She magnified her optical feed to check the other side of the sky bridge. "No contacts outside. But you're the superstitious one, Erik, and I don't know. I figured that because of stuff like Venus, you'd be making things weirder, not more mundane, trying to invoke better training in odd situations."

"Superstitious?" Erik crept forward again, sweeping his rifle back and forth. "I'm not superstitious."

"What about the Lady?" Jia matched his pace.

"That's not superstition," he replied, nonplussed.

"How is believing in some personification of luck not superstition?" Jia asked. "It's textbook superstition."

"It's not a superstition. It's an observation." Erik quickened his advance. "I've lived long enough and fought enough battles to know that a man who thinks he's above fate and luck is going to get cocky and have his ass handed to him. You shouldn't stick your finger in the Lady's eye because you're challenging fate, and she might remind you that you shouldn't do that."

Jia wondered if she should press him, especially because

of the faint irritation in Erik's tone. From what he'd described, it was less that he was superstitious and more using the Lady as a shorthand for preparation, but his behavior suggested something different.

Initially, she'd thought he was just being playful when he talked about the Lady, but her doubts had grown the longer she knew him.

Their exoskeletons approached the building, with no response. Small drones circled in the area, but if the terrorists knew the duo was there, they were giving no indication.

"No contact," Jia noted.

"This is the problem with everyone depending on technology," Erik muttered. "They could just look out a window, but it looks like they've blackened them all on both sides in case we pull sensor tricks."

Jia chuckled. "I should point out they're following *your* programming."

"Sure, because this is modeled after a raid I did when I was still in the Army," Erik answered. "I've had Emma adjust the tactics and positions of the terrorists, but in the original raid, the idiots all clustered up in the center of the building, thinking their feeds would protect them. It was a nasty battle overall, but their stupid plan allowed easy entry."

"Can we hack our way in?" Jia asked. "If they're cocky in this situation, they might not be protecting the doors as well as I might think."

Erik pointed his weapon at the door. "I'm going to blow it open with a couple of plasma grenades. Huh, should have programmed in some breach disks, but I forgot."

"I think you just want to blow something up." Jia chuckled as she expanded her ballistic shield. "Not that I'm complaining."

"Blowing shit up does have a certain entertainment value," he replied, prepping his grenades. "Prepare for breach."

"Ready." Jia took a deep breath and prepared to launch her own grenades.

"Knocking on the door," Erik shouted. "Grenades out!"

With a deep clunk, his grenade launcher spat two plasma grenades. They hit the door in a blindingly bright blue-white explosion. Fiery debris and smoke shot out. Jia followed up with two quick grenades of her own. Gunfire rang out from inside before her grenades flew through the ragged hole and exploded several meters in.

The guns fell silent.

Erik charged forward. Jia followed. They emerged from the thick smoke to the sight of charred corpses and half-melted rifles in the smoldering hallway. Terrorists' rifles poked around the corner and their storm of bullets filled the hall, bouncing off the expanded shields of the duo's exoskeletons.

Jia and Erik returned fire in controlled bursts.

Their heavy rifles let their rounds pierce the wall and rip through the corner terrorists. The partners advanced slowly, keeping their shields in front and watching their rearview cameras for any surprises. Their deafening gunshots drowned out the terrorists' gunfire and dying screams.

Despite the situation, Jia almost laughed. The horrific

had become mundane, and the content of a date was, at least for them, dinner, a game, and simulated carnage.

The terrorists ceased fire, but Erik and Jia remained halfway across the building from the target, making them both wary. They naturally separated to either side of the hallway and advanced quickly, pivoting to opposite sides to look for useful targets.

Terrorist squads waited on either side, but their volleys did little to the exoskeletons' shields. Quick bursts of return fire shredded the unarmored enemy.

Jia continued forward. The nav marker in her visor display indicated the primary target was in her direction. She didn't bother to say anything to Erik. At this point, they both knew what they needed to do, and it was his scenario.

He moved a moment later after ensuring there would be no surprises to their rear. An exoskeleton shield could take a plasma grenade from the front, but an explosion in the rear risked disabling the suit or pilot injury.

They entered a new hallway, but there was no new group of terrorists waiting to greet them with a burst of bullets. The near-constant thud of exoskeleton feet slamming the hard tile echoed through the corridor as they closed on the security room and their ultimate target. Training and experience had made the scenario trivial.

When Jia first met Erik, a swarm of low-end security bots had proved a challenge. Now, if she didn't see an exoskeleton or at least some heavy weapons, it was hard for her to work up any concern.

She didn't know if that was confidence or arrogance.

Jia expected more enemy forces or at least some bots before they arrived at the target room, but tens of meters became single digits, and soon they were in front of it. The hardened doors and armored walls would prevent the same kind of easy breach that had gotten them into the building.

"It's just a matter of getting in there," she commented with a frown.

"That's the hard part," Erik replied. "We'll have to hold off reinforcements while the door is hacked. They'll pull every bastard in the building and throw them at us. In this case, we can assume Emma will be able to do it."

"For purposes of this simulation, it'll take me five minutes," Emma explained. "I could supply a scenario-appropriate explanation, but it's not as if I provide you detailed breakdowns of what I'm doing most of the time. All you need to know is your target fleshbag is behind the door, ready to be added to the list of dead fleshbags."

"I just thought of something." Jia backed away from the door. "Earlier, Erik, were you suggesting that you, on some level, buy into the idea that our simulations might somehow predict the future?"

"I don't believe that." Erik backed up a couple of meters. "I think we go through a lot of odd stuff, and because we're taking on this messed-up conspiracy, we've run into similar messed-up stuff. It's just a matter of time and numbers."

"Then it doesn't matter if we do a ridiculous scenario. It's not predictive. It's not taunting fate."

There was some small comfort in only having to watch

for the unusual, not the impossible. Emma and Erik didn't cheat. The latter valued the training value of the exercises, and the former was too egotistical to win with simple manipulation.

Jia shifted her exoskeleton farther away from Erik's to assure a different angle of fire. They might not have eyes on the enemy, but she doubted the opposite was true, given that Erik's briefing had mentioned external cameras. The lack of door control also proved they didn't control the system.

"Why does it not matter if we do a ridiculous scenario?" Erik asked.

"I'm saying we can *test* how much we can mess with fate. We should do a training scenario that is completely and utterly ridiculous."

Jia was more interested in entertainment value than testing fate, but tweaking Erik brought its own pleasures. Sometimes she wanted to remind him that he wasn't the only one who understood the psychological foibles of their partner.

Erik chuckled. "More ridiculous than a Leem showing up in training and then having to deal with someone with Leem DNA?"

"Sure." Jia licked her lips. "We need to do something that's objectively impossible. Leems and crazy genetic engineering are real. What we need to do is fight something that doesn't exist. Something that doesn't make any sense. Something that simple time and numbers won't and can't produce."

"Like what, specifically?" Erik asked.

Jia thought over the possibilities. "I'd suggest a horde of *jiangshi*."

Erik grunted. "The occasional joke scenario is one thing, but too many fake scenarios make for bad training. That's part of the reason I've asked Emma to help recalibrate our scope."

Jia rolled her eyes. "The enemy might be impossible, but it's not like it'd be bad training. Just a reminder, we *have* been attacked by hordes of zombie-like enemies."

"So, now you're saying this is less about testing my superstition than getting tactically ready?" Erik sounded amused. "I didn't expect you to go that far."

"I'm just saying it might be *interesting*," Jia replied. "I get what you're saying about training, but sometimes we can have fun while we are at it. It's strange that I have to be the one to mention that part."

"Wait a minute. I'm not anti-fun."

The tower vanished, replaced by a courtyard illuminated by a full moon high in the night sky.

Stones from the wall and the half-collapsed towers were strewn around the area. Skeletons littered the ground, their clothing long since rotted away, along with tiles from the roof. Cracked stone stairs led up to the main palace building, a set of massive bronze double doors blocking passage. The stairs were half-painted with dark and dried bloodstains.

"What the hell is this?" Erik asked as he looked around.

"We might as well test the theory," Emma replied. "And I'm not anti-fun."

Erik frowned. "If we do end up getting attacked by *jiangshi*, I'm throwing you both into a black hole."

Jia laughed. "Yes, you're *totally* not superstitious." She walked toward the stairs, the heavy steps of her exoskeleton echoing in the eerily quiet courtyard. "Let's see what modern equipment can do against a *jiangshi*."

CHAPTER SIXTEEN

Jia's exoskeleton crested the stairs. No terrorists or undead emerged from the palace to attack her. She sighed. "Ok, I take it back. We are all kinds of ridiculous. We're about to face *jiangshi*."

"You're the one who wanted to test fate," Erik grumbled. Maybe he was a little superstitious, but he didn't care to admit it after everything they'd just discussed.

"No, that's not it." Jia pointed her rifle toward the massive bronze door, her gaze skimming the worn characters and the dragon carved into the door. "We have all this advanced VR and AR, and what do we do with it? Practice how to kill people and blow up stuff. We could go on a virtual vacation anywhere, but it's nothing but training. Our fun is us blowing up an unusual type of enemy."

"What's the point of a fake vacation?" Erik narrowed his eyes. "On some level, you know it's a lie. Lots of guys in my unit liked VR trips, but I never did. I'd rather just take some time off and sleep and play cards."

"That's easy for you to say since you've traveled all over

the UTC." Jia frowned. "I'm assuming, Emma, that other than hopping zombies somewhere in here, that everything else reflects…let's see…Qing Dynasty China?"

"That's accurate," Emma replied, appearing in an elaborate green floral Qing gown, complete with a dragon-covered dark green headdress with silk tassels. Green and blue stones were enmeshed in the tassels.

"Then this should be easy," Jia declared, angling the shoulder of her exoskeleton toward the door. "I doubt the typical Qing door can take an exoskeleton slamming into it. If there's no fake magic involved, we don't need to blow open the door with plasma grenades. It wasn't like they were designing doors to stand up to that kind of punishment back then."

"And they shouldn't be packing laser rifles." Erik chuckled. "Imagine if those bastards in the prison'd had firepower in addition to everything else."

"I'm sure the conspiracy will get there eventually," Jia replied. "They've already thrown zombies at us, so why not zombies with embedded guns? That's not that different from the Ascended Brotherhood in principle."

"Don't give them any ideas." Erik frowned at his empty camera views. "What's the scenario here, Emma? We're way away from what I had planned for tonight."

"An evil sorcerer has killed the emperor and taken over the palace," Emma replied. "You kill him, and his horde threatening the countryside will fall. Peace will reign again over the land."

Erik snickered. "And we just happened to have twenty-third-century exoskeletons?"

"You know how magic is. One day you're summoning

monsters, the next, you accidentally open a portal to the future so glorious heroes can appear and smite evil hordes of the undead."

"With our luck, I wouldn't be surprised if that happened," Jia commented.

"I'd prefer falling into a nice bar between worlds instead," Erik replied.

"For now, it's a good enough background for a simulation," Jia answered.

"Any intel on his location?" Erik glanced at his HUD. "From the emperor's scouts or whoever the hell passes for the ID in this time period?"

"No," Emma replied. "A group of warriors attempted to assault the palace, but they were killed beyond the outer gate by a mass of *jiangshi*, their flesh and souls consumed."

"Cheery." Jia blew out a breath.

"Do it, Jia," Erik suggested. "If he's relying on numbers, there's no reason not to bust on in there."

"It shouldn't be too elaborate." Jia took a deep breath and backed up. After a moment of hesitation, she collapsed her shield and reached forward. "No reason for shock and awe against monsters that don't know fear. Might as well just open it."

Erik stepped to the side and pointed his weapon. "Yeah, I guess you could open it the boring way."

Jia pushed the center of the double doors. They groaned and separated as they swiveled inside, revealing a massive antechamber leading into an even more gargantuan throne room dimly lit by flickering torches lining the walls.

The first person they saw was a nearly skeletal man in

ornate robes and a hat so broad it might be mistaken for a landing pad. His head lolled forward on his chest. Robed bodies covered the ground, face-down in large heaps.

"This is dark, Emma," Jia murmured as she took it in. "And I'm not talking about the lighting."

"I was trying for an appropriately horrific atmosphere," Emma responded. "Besides, the horrors you've faced are worse when you think about it."

"That's even darker." Jia looked back and forth. "Are you the sorcerer?" she called to the throne.

"If you wish to face me," came a voice from all around, "you must first defeat my servants."

"Bring it on." Erik wished he could cock a rifle for the sound. "A heavy rifle on an exo is a lot more impressive than a sword or spear."

The bodies on the ground stirred and slowly rose almost as one to reveal rigid corpses with cracked, thin skin taut over their faces. Paper talismans dangled from their foreheads.

"Aren't they supposed to have hats?" Erik asked.

Jia glanced at him. "Are you questioning the accuracy of this simulation of nonexistent undead monsters and evil sorcerers?"

"No." He did a credible job of shrugging his shoulders in the mech. "Just saying I expected them to have hats."

The *jiangshi* horde finished their rejuvenation. Hundreds of the creatures now filled the rooms, their stiff arms outstretched. There was no sound other than the soft scratching of their shoes on the wooden floor.

The line between fiction and reality remained blurred.

Purist dogma and basic morality had kept most of

humanity from creating monsters, but the last couple of years had exposed just how depraved some people could become when seeking proper servants.

Hopping zombies weren't real, but given the Ascended Brotherhood and the mutants they'd fought in the Scar, Erik wasn't sure that conspiracy couldn't be considered close to evil sorcerers who took the flesh and souls of humans to twist them into monsters.

Science had caught up with the darkest nightmares of myth.

Magic was fiction, but advanced technology, human and alien, trod the line, just as Arthur C. Clark had said centuries earlier.

Erik suspected nanozombies and Leem hybrids were only the beginning of the horrors they'd encounter by the time his vengeance quest was over.

He didn't know that he minded as long as they died when you shot them enough. Erik would let other people worry about the philosophical implications. He would continue to handle problems in a direct way.

A *jiangshi* hopped toward Jia, its arms outstretched. Despite the ridiculous method of locomotion, the creature was surprisingly fast, finishing three quick bounds before she fired a burst into its head that blew it apart.

Erik fired at another one, blowing a chunk out of its chest, but the wound sealed in less than a second, both the flesh and the clothes mending themselves.

A follow-up shot through the forehead finished it off.

"So that's how it's going to be," Erik muttered. "Annoying."

"It could be worse. Some of the methods to beat these

things in folklore are both ridiculous and complicated." Jia took a deep breath and lined up her next shot.

She put down another *jiangshi*.

The horde moved as a group, like some strange writhing mass of bugs emerging from the ground at night to feed. They displayed no fear as Erik and Jia put them down, but the specificity of the shots slowed the destruction of the horde. One burst blew off half the lower jaw of a *jiangshi*, only for it to regenerate within seconds.

Jia expanded her shield and bashed an approaching monster, then blew its head apart before lifting her rifle and taking out another mid-hop.

Erik kept up his own shots, thinning the monsters. The corpses knocked some of the jiangshi to the ground, but they righted themselves, although slowly. The duo backed toward the door as the horde advanced, continuing fire.

"Let's see how grenades do," Erik announced. "You go for it. I'll save mine for the sorcerer."

Jia barked a laugh. "Now, there's a sentence I never thought I'd hear from you."

"This night is full of surprises," he answered.

"Grenades out!" Jia shouted.

She swept from left to right, launching grenades in rapid succession. She had just enough to cover the entirety of the forward line. Her targets made no attempt to dodge as they continued their bizarre, inexorable advance.

The slight delay in launch resulted in explosions traveling like a wave through the horde, scattering the *jiangshi*.

Most of the monsters near the center of the plasma grenade attacks remained on the ground as charred corpses, though some toward the edge of the explosions rose, their damaged limbs and sides regenerating.

Erik couldn't bring himself to complain about the rules of a purely fictional encounter.

He'd never thought he'd appreciate that humans were easy to kill, but this scenario reminded him of the advantages of facing foes with familiar and weak anatomy.

While the grenade barrage hadn't finished off the horde, the now-immobile bodies and disruption to the formation slowed the grasshopper-like advance of the enemy.

Jia and Erik took advantage of the chaos to follow up with bursts on the closest standing enemies. More of the jiangshi fell behind the smoking and charred remains of their brethren, the mighty horde now thinned but not destroyed.

"Back out." Erik pointed his rifle at the roof. "I'm guessing crushing them will work, too."

Jia fired her jump thrusters, propelling herself toward the door. She stepped out of the building.

Erik jogged toward the door firing his grenades into the roof. Such an attack wouldn't bring down a modern building, but as the explosions ripped into the roof and the building shook, his confidence grew. Burning chunks of wood fell from the ceiling, raining down on the *jiangshi*. He made it out of the building, with Jia covering his retreat.

They continued backing away, covering their firing arcs and sending surviving *jiangshi* to virtual hell. Smoke filled the building, and larger chunks of the roof collapsed, crushing the creatures under their weight. Flames spread along the walls.

"Damn." Erik laughed. "We should be fighting smarter, not harder. We could have just burned the entire building down to begin with."

"That level of destruction is usually not available," Jia replied. "Let alone if we're in space. Blowing up the prison would have stopped the nanozombies, but it would also have killed everybody else aboard."

"Sure, be boring and criticize the burn-down-and-blow-up-everything plan."

A group of *jiangshi* bounded through the doorway, and Jia and Erik took them down. The small number of survivors fell victim to a collapsing wall. The roaring fire consuming the building licked at the night sky, and smoke continued to pour from the newly birthed funeral pyre. A burning *jiangshi* pushed up through wreckage, only for Jia to blow its head off.

"Next time my friends ask me what I do on dates," Jia began, "I'll tell them the truth. I spend them doing things like killing Leems and *jiangshi*. So sexy!"

"It is." Erik smiled. "Now we just need the sorcerer."

"That will have to wait," Emma announced. "There is a message for you from Agent Koval. She wants to meet you both tomorrow and not at the hangar."

Erik wiggled his fingers inside the exo's arms. "And here I thought we'd get a little more vacation after the crap with Jared."

CHAPTER SEVENTEEN

April 22, Neo Southern California Metroplex, Invisible Tower

Jia looked down and shook her head, surprised that her stomach and heart were calm.

The visible guide rails marking the swirling path didn't do much to convince her brain that she wasn't about to topple to her death. Transparent metal and clever holographic feeds gave the impression she was standing on thin layers of clouds and would soon fall to the dark parking platform far below her.

She'd never had a fear of heights, and as she stood on the world's most bizarre tourist attraction, she hoped it wouldn't birth a new one.

Would that affect her flying?

Curiosity pushed out any fear that dared creep inside. She lived in one of the huge towers of Neo SoCal. If she brought someone from even a couple of centuries forward, her residential tower would be a mighty castle in the sky, a modern, defiant Tower of Babel stretching into heaven.

Just one among many.

The invisible tower was a brilliant deconstruction. Minor commercial and municipal storage levels filled the bulk of the tower, if only because no decent Uptowner would dare travel in the Shadow Zone to see a landmark.

The main attraction, the top, didn't look like much from afar. Its potential terror and grandness required a person to be there.

It said more about an individual human than anything.

For the moment, Jia wasn't there to challenge the divine or herself, but to meet with their employer. She wasn't surprised that Alina didn't want to meet at the hangar. It made sense. If they always met there, it increased the risk of enemy detection, despite the efforts they'd put into taking different routes there and taking full advantage of Emma's capabilities.

On her more cynical days, Jia might admit that she suspected Alina was also using the meetings as an excuse to see interesting tourists' sites around the metroplex.

Interesting, but not always popular. The current location was likely selected for the sparse foot traffic. When the Invisible Tower was first built decades prior, it'd been swarmed with people impressed by the novelty, but that had worn off. Now it was most often a destination for school trips rather than a place people went out of their way to visit.

Humanity's greatest wonders grew stale with the advancing decades and technology.

"Maybe we should have taken the elevator," Erik commented from beside her, a smile gracing his face.

The look made her slightly uneasy because of his use of

a holographic disguise. It was close to but distinct from his normal appearance. Something about her brain wanted to reject the false image. She presumed he felt the same way about her holographic disguise.

"I always wanted to visit here," Jia replied. "But my father wouldn't go anywhere near it, and my school never did. After that, it slipped my mind. There's so much to do and see in Neo SoCal."

"Yeah. Now that I've been here a while, I can see why a lot of people never leave." Erik shrugged. "Not that I think it's *that* great, and I've always liked wandering more than a lot of people, but it wouldn't be a terrible place to live."

"It hasn't been, even with the corruption." Jia ran her hand along a guard rail, which shimmered different colors at her touch. "It'll be anticlimactic if we end up falling and dying." She held up a hand to stop his expected comment. "I know, I know, safety systems."

He raised an eyebrow. "Are you worried?"

"Not *that* worried." She bit her lip. "But it's hard to look down and not be a little concerned."

Erik grinned. "I'd rather die that way than a lot of other ways."

Jia's brow wrinkled, and she eyed her partner. "You would?"

Erik nodded. "At least on Earth, if you fall, it'll be over sooner rather than later. In space, if you get stuck out there, you're going to have a long time to think about it. That wouldn't be fun."

"I'll keep that in mind if some capricious god lets me choose the way I'm going to die." Jia looked around before nodding at a floating holographic display marking their current floor. "This is the right floor, isn't it? Alina has her faults, but she's never been one to play games with time."

The air shimmered for a moment, and a short woman in a long dark coat appeared with a smile.

"What's past is prologue," the woman declared.

Alina had sent another message an hour prior, noting she would be quoting Shakespeare as a passphrase and requested a Xunzi quote as the appropriate response.

Sometimes Jia wondered what went into the agent's decisions about how to verify identities, but after thirty years of working in the shadows, the agent had earned her right to eccentricities.

"Not hearing is not as good as hearing," Jia replied. "Hearing is not as good as *seeing*. Seeing is not as good as *knowing*. Knowing is not as good as *acting*. *True learning continues until it is put into action.*"

Jia waited, her hand near her jacket. There was always the chance it wasn't Alina. A woman might not be able to choose when she died, but that didn't mean she couldn't put fifteen bullets into those trying to kill her.

"This area is now secure, even against Emma," the other woman continued, this time in Alina's voice. "Though I've sent her a message to note I've established contact and hopefully stop her from doing anything dangerous."

"Dangerous?" Erik asked.

"You have a gun. That makes her a lot more dangerous."

Erik chuckled. Jia lowered her arm. There wasn't going to be a shootout. That was a little disappointing.

"Sorry to call you back into action so soon," Alina continued, "especially since you stumbled upon some anyway. You've earned months off if we're going by your success-to-risk ratio."

Erik shrugged, a nonchalant look on his face. "We're working for you because we want to take down the conspiracy. I wouldn't give a crap if that meant we were working twenty-four/seven, as long as it ended with them gone. I want that to be clear. I came back to Earth for revenge."

"I'll add, the sooner the conspiracy is taken out, the safer everyone in the UTC will be," Jia continued. "And I'm hoping that knowing Sophia Vand was involved has given you some leads. I don't think anyone will complain if the conspiracy goes down as soon as possible."

Alina nodded. "We'll get to Vand in a minute, but I wanted to talk housekeeping."

"Housekeeping?" Erik raised an eyebrow.

"Yes, housekeeping." Alina gave him an uncharacteristically happy smile. "I'll cut to the chase. The Defense Directorate is almost ready to turn the jumpship over to you."

"I can hardly believe it." Jia shook her head, as impressed by what she was being told as she had been when she'd learned the truth about Emma. "It's amazing enough that they're letting us keep a unique AI, but now they're providing us an experimental drive. If I wasn't living through this, I don't think I'd believe it."

"The jumpship is nothing but a hunk of useless metal without Emma." Erik smirked. "And they know she's on our side, now more than ever. They almost lost the drive to the Ascended Brotherhood, but we took them out."

"True," Alina replied, "but it's more than that. Much more, and I think it's important that you realize that." She gestured toward the sky behind her. "Though you're right that it's heavily related to the Ascended Brotherhood. The Venus mission and your success there have helped to solidify your usefulness in the minds of certain high-ranking people in both the DD and the ID, who until then had harbored some skepticism. And the simple, blunt truth is, we've had more success against the conspiracy since you two got involved than we've had in years, and a lot of that happened even before you were working for me. You're considered a good investment, and they're convinced they can get faster, more effective results with less overall resource use if they concentrate on making the best use of you two."

Erik scratched his cheek. "I like faster results when it comes to taking out those bastards. If the government wants to throw more fancy equipment at me, I'm not going to complain."

Jia looked Alina up and down, considering what the other woman had just said, a cloud of suspicion darkening her mind.

If everyone was willing to help them because they'd been getting results, what would happen if they suffered a reversal? A botched mission could result in the military coming for the jumpship and Emma, even if Erik and Jia survived. They couldn't take on both the conspiracy and the government.

Jia's breath caught. A couple of years ago, the idea of taking on the government would disgust her as insurrectionist talk, but now she worried about what would happen to Erik and Emma.

She took a deep, calming breath.

There was no point in worrying about the future. They needed to use whatever resources were available for as long as they were. The Vand takedown had proven they could make progress even against the most powerful people in the UTC. All they needed to do was continue what they had already been doing.

"When are we going to get the ship?" Jia asked, keeping her voice casual.

"I don't have a concrete timeline, but the short answer is soon," Alina replied. "I'd predict within the next month, if not faster. It's still unclear if the DD is going to insist on other personnel besides Raphael being aboard. They keep going back and forth on that, but I'll let you know as soon as I do. For now, though, I've got something else I need. Something local that won't require an experimental jump drive."

"Local?" Erik nodded at a tower in the distance. "You mean a Neo SoCal job? That's convenient. I'd thought we'd already scared all the conspiracy advocates away from here."

"Neo SoCal would be convenient, but that's not it." Alina let out a quiet chuckle. "I meant local as in on Earth. I've sent you to the moon, Mars, and Venus. This time you just have to go to the other side of the planet."

"Easy trip." Erik cracked his knuckles. "And I've been looking forward to taking down more of the conspiracy. If they're still dumb enough to stick around, it's like they're serving themselves up for us."

Jia rubbed her chin, eyeing the agent. "You found some-thing following up on Sophia Vand, didn't you?"

"It helps when you know where to shine your light in

the dark." Alina nodded. "She covered her tracks well, but knowing she was involved has opened a lot of different paths. Our initial investigations suggest that the bulk of the Vand family isn't involved in the conspiracy. That Vand never married nor had any children might be related to her involvement in the conspiracy. It's not like there aren't millions of eligible partners for her out there."

"So, this isn't just about the Vands." Jia frowned. "That's unfortunate. It would have been easier."

"It doesn't mean investigating Sophia Vand's tentacles won't lead us to interesting places. In this case, my people stumbled upon something that might be minor, but I wanted to deploy scalable assets during the investigation in case things turn out to be more serious. You two can punch above your weight without raising as many flags."

Jia snorted. "In other words, you don't want to expose the entire ID to the conspiracy, but you do want Erik and me to burn down a palace if necessary."

"Burn down a palace?" Alina's brows rose. "Huh?"

"Forget it." Jia waved a hand. "Explaining it would take too long."

"I don't care if you think we're scalable or expendable assets," Erik interjected. "You keep giving us the tools we need to take on the conspiracy, and we'll work together to keep going after them until every last one of them is dead or in prison."

"Good to hear. Some corporate officers linked to a company previously controlled by Sophia Vand are having a small retreat. The company's activities and resources outflows can be indirectly linked to activity by the Ascended Brotherhood and other potential conspiracy operations in recent months." Alina frowned. "And there has been other unusual activity related to that company, including money transfers to different organizations, including the Vand Foundation. We can't see anything obviously illegal about it based on our initial investigations, but at a minimum, those people are worth looking into because their operational tempo has been increasing since Vand's death. Ignoring an obvious coincidence is a good way to let the conspiracy get away with something."

"Where are they meeting?" Erik asked. "You said this was an Earth-based assignment."

"The Mizuchi Undersea Resort," Alina answered.

Erik's face scrunched. "Great."

Jia raised an eyebrow. "What's wrong? I've read about it. It's a nice luxury resort." She looked at Alina. "Or does the Vand Foundation own it?"

Alina shook her head. "We checked into that. It's not controlled by them, at least not directly. That might even be why they're meeting there. It was hard to collect the intel we have."

"I'm not worried about an ambush." Erik frowned. "I just don't like undersea places much. Boats are fine, even subs, but entire resorts?" He shook his head in disgust. "Arrogance."

"Huh?" Jia stared at Erik, not bothering to hide the shock on her face. "You didn't seem bothered about being in a dome on the moon or the station we went to. How is Mizuchi different?"

Erik gestured vaguely toward the sky. "In a vacuum, there's nothing outside the dome. I'd rather have nothing than a whole entire ocean waiting to come in and crush me." He shrugged. "I don't know how to explain it. I think it's more arrogant to build an undersea facility than a dome or a space station, and that's probably why we have a lot more people living in domes and space stations than in undersea colonies. We all have that feeling on some level."

"It's not like it's that easy to breach a dome, undersea or otherwise. Even the conspiracy smuggled an experimental bomb to the moon when they were trying there." Jia pointed down, grimacing she saw the faux emptiness beneath her. "Nothing tactical is going to breach one of those, and I doubt a couple of corporate suits showing at a resort to plot ends with a grav bomb or a nuke."

"I'll go." Erik sighed, admitting the truth. "I just don't like underwater settlements."

Jia opened her mouth to add another justification before closing it. Everyone had their foibles, and it wasn't like they needed to head underwater that often.

Alina cleared her throat. "Now that we have that cleared up, I'm going to give you a straightforward assignment. I'll be transmitting relevant ID information to Emma, and she can coordinate with Malcolm. I want you to investigate two of the corporate officers in particular using your disguises and false registration, and not to, uh, burn down the palace. We're not sacking Troy here, we're just checking on some stuff. It sounds like you'll be restrained, if only to stop all that water from flooding in."

Erik gave her a lupine smile. "I'll do what I need to do. Sometimes it involves fire, sometimes it involves water."

"I'm sure you will." Alina shook her head.

"Why just the two?" Jia asked.

"They are the only ones who can be linked to all of the

unusual activity we've been observing," Alina answered. "The retreat is on the 29th. I'd recommend arriving a couple of days early, but note you'll be relying on Emma and Malcolm to handle the insertion. The ID needs to be cautious about using their pull, especially now that we appreciate the scope of the conspiracy's resources. A light touch will keep us in the war, even if it makes individual battles more difficult."

"Expendable assets." Jia offered Alina a thin smile. "Understood."

Alina shrugged her shoulders. "Just don't get caught or die, and you won't need help."

Erik stared into the distance with a mischievous look. "But trouble's just so much *fun*."

CHAPTER EIGHTEEN

Erik and Jia descended the Invisible Tower and loaded into the MX 60, which was currently a dull gray color to blend in. They offered Emma a quick overview of the situation, but she revealed that Alina had already transmitted information on the targets of the investigation.

The two men of particular interest were Karl Sillen and Javier Gallegos, both working for Crown River Logistics and Transport.

Unsurprisingly, the company was a subdivision of Ceres Galactic.

Jia shook her head as the MX 60 rose from the platform. "The conspiracy seems to have deep tentacles in Ceres, Hermes, and a lot of the most important corporations. Sometimes I wonder what happens when we finish them off."

"Nothing," Erik muttered. "We replace the rich, ruthless assholes at the top with other rich, ruthless assholes who don't hire mercenary companies to kill soldiers or make *yaoguai.* They'll probably do something else wrong, but at least the CID will be able to keep them in check."

Jia sighed. "Not saying we don't continue hunting them, but sometimes I wonder about the scope. Before we ran into Vand, I'd half-worried that the conspiracy was this grand thing, stronger than the government, but now I'm wondering if it's more brittle than that."

"Probably both." Erik turned his flitter toward a dense lane of air traffic a couple hundred meters away. "Somebody like Sophia Vand has major influence, and she had a lot of power, but you heard Alina; not everybody in her family knew what she was up to, and it's not like every last employee in the Vand Foundation or every employee in every company she had a stake in would rise up like she's their queen. Whoever is left in this conspiracy is the same, I bet." He snorted. "You know what true power is?"

Jia thought for a moment, then shook her head.

"True power is being able to walk down the street surrounded by your enemies and have them too afraid to screw with you. A true queen doesn't need guards because no one would dare take a shot at her."

"I don't know if it's that simple."

"Maybe not." Erik frowned. "But that's closer to the truth. The conspiracy knows they'd be taken out if they were identified, so they hide. That means they have a lot of influence, but I bet you it's thin and spread out. I wouldn't be surprised if we could stop them by taking out a single small conference room filled with power-hungry assholes."

"Even if that's true, we need to find them first," Jia replied.

"I don't have a problem starting that at Mizuchi."

"There's a problem with this mission that I don't think either of you realizes," Emma interrupted.

"What is that?" Erik asked. "Alina's been upfront about us having to do the heavy lifting, and if it's about her being ready to cut us loose if there's too much trouble, I figured that was how it was going to be working for a ghost from the beginning. And as much as I don't like undersea places, I don't think the conspiracy is going to waste time blowing up a resort. There are not enough places like that to make it worthwhile. If everyone stops going to underwater resorts and settlements, it would barely make a ripple for most people on Earth."

"No, I'm not talking about your odd obsession with underwater domes or the obvious and inevitable betrayal by Agent Koval, but something far more important."

"Wait a second," he interrupted. "You think Alina's going to betray us?"

Erik couldn't deny the thought had occurred to him, but he doubted it would happen anytime soon. The strongest lesson of Molino was to never take trust for granted. An Army unit out on a frontier planet protecting it from aliens shouldn't have been ambushed by humans.

Emma sighed. "From my perspective, she's made it clear that you are tools, not friends. At some point, you'll prove a liability for protecting the ID and the government, and they will likely turn against you. I haven't worried much because you've made it clear that your loyalty is more personal than organizational in nature."

"Yeah. If they go after us, it'll be a bad day for them, but I think Alina would do the right thing. She'll probably stop paying us once we take down the conspiracy." Erik's grip tightened on the control yoke, then pushed it in and aggressively dove into a lower lane. "But I don't care about that. As long as she helps me take down the conspiracy first, I don't care if she wants to pretend she never met me or even if she comes after me."

By the time Erik and Jia finished off the conspiracy, the ID would probably be too afraid to take them on. Despite what Jia worried about, an increasing reputation for explosive lethality could serve them both well later in life.

Assuming they survived.

Jia looked at Erik with disbelief. "I'd prefer not to have the ID trying to kill me, but I'll worry about that when we get that far. What's the real issue, Emma? What could be more important than what we just talked about?"

"Mizuchi," Emma declared.

"What's your problem? You just got done making fun of Erik for being worried about it."

Erik grunted his disapproval.

"Don't you see?" Emma asked. "You can't take a flitter to an undersea resort."

Jia's forehead scrunched in confusion. "Yes, and? I'm not seeing the big problem here. We won't need a flitter. Mizuchi isn't that big. The entire place is walkable from what I remember. It's a contained resort, not a sprawling city."

"You'll need me, but I'll be forced to be outside the MX 60," Emma replied. "I'll be without my primary body."

Jia considered their recent operations. "There were plenty of times you've been outside the MX 60, including on our recent trip to Venus. You've done just fine, and you haven't complained about it much. I doubt we're going to need a bulletproof flitter with a turret for this job."

"You say that, but you can't be sure." Emma let out a sigh that sounded both depressed and mocking. "And our Venus trip was a different situation. Among other things, I spent days interfaced with a proper spacecraft, an acceptable body and replacement for the MX 60. But that's not going to happen with this resort. You'll probably just interface me in a room and leave me there without an appropriate compensatory situation. Don't tell me that drones and cameras are enough."

"*That's* what you're bitching about?" Erik barked a harsh laugh. "You'll survive, Emma. Besides, isn't being obsessed with a body a very fleshbag way of thinking?"

"No." She sounded miffed. "Setting aside the unusual nature of my creation, my primary advantage in my current form is the ability to switch bodies to maximize the efficiency of my interaction. I prefer a true body, perhaps because of my fleshbag heritage, but as you pointed out, this vehicle has been considerably customized, including the recent addition of the turret, which allows me to be effective in a number of ways. I'm more vulnerable when that's not the case."

Erik could see where she was coming from, but there wasn't a lot they could do. Even if they spent a ridiculous amount of money and somehow convinced the resort to let them ship a surface flitter there, they wouldn't be able to use it.

Jia folded her arms and rolled her eyes. "I think this is less about danger and just you whining because you can't cruise around in this ridiculously souped-up flitter and shoot fleshbags with turrets. Don't try to convince us you have a deep need to be in a particular physical form at all times. We already know you can handle it, and it's not like this is going to be a long job."

"I'll have to make do, I suppose," Emma replied, finishing up with a sniff of disdain. "I could always borrow the controls of a submarine or something else at the facility."

"You should probably not steal vehicles and draw attention to us unless there are no other choices."

Jia thought Emma's answer of "Only if it becomes necessary, I assure you," sounded a bit hollow.

Erik accelerated and changed direction. "Keep in mind those corp bastards might not be anything. You heard Alina. There were a lot of qualifiers and mentions of indirect evidence. If they had those bastards dead to rights, a bunch of CID agents would be arresting their asses already."

"I doubt Agent Koval would send you on this mission if she truly thought it was nothing," Emma clarified. "In intelligence work, circumstantial evidence is hardly something you should dismiss out of hand."

"That's true, but it doesn't have to end in a massive shootout that needs exos and turrets." Erik drummed his fingers on the control yoke. "Think about that. If this does get heavy, Jia and I won't have our top equipment either. We won't be able to smuggle in our heavy guns without too much risk, so you're not the only one who has to make sacrifices for the mission."

Jia's gaze dropped to her feet. They rested atop the hidden storage compartment storing the TR-7, and uncertainty played across her features for a brief moment. Erik wasn't worried. The same restrictions applied to their targets. He doubted they'd follow them into a restaurant and end up fighting an exo.

"You'll survive, Emma," Jia muttered. "Just like Erik will, having to go to an undersea resort."

"I suppose." Emma offered a long and painfully melodramatic sigh.

"It's not a big deal," Erik replied, feeling they might be overestimating his concern. "It's just not on my list of favorite things. This could be a nice way for me to get over the problem." He smirked. "We can't all be as *worldly* as you."

"I've never been to an undersea facility." Jia smiled. "Another new experience. I don't know if this is more impressive than going to a floating city, but it's nice to be able to share it with you." She blinked, and her cheeks reddened. "Uh, you know what I mean."

"New experiences help relationships." Erik shot her a happy grin, covering the unease within. He was glad to have control of the conversation again.

They might be going on a mission, but they were going to a resort together. When they'd gone to the moon, they'd joked about going to a different undersea resort. They kept traveling the world and seeing great sights before killing dozens of those who seriously deserved an introduction to the afterlife and blowing large holes in buildings.

A run-and-gun vacation series.

Jia folded her hands in her lap and gazed out the window as if trying to avoid looking at Erik. Their relationship was in a weird place.

They slept together and spent all their time together, but they both knew they might not have a future together. The next day could bring romance or violent death. In a couple of days, he might get crushed by millions of gallons of ocean water.

He kept circling back to the truth. It didn't matter what they felt for each other. It didn't change reality. They had a mission in a week, and they needed to get ready for that. His feelings would have to wait until something forced the issue.

Why did it feel like his feelings might be coming sooner than he would like?

CHAPTER NINETEEN

Garth missed living next to Erik. He'd been convinced from the first time he met the detective that he'd be a player in major events. Garth had a nose for understanding influence and the big picture.

He'd applied that to communications systems and work, but it also helped him understand much more complicated and important real-life networks.

The subsequent rise of the Obsidian Detective and Lady Justice had confirmed Garth's instincts.

As spectacular as their work in the department had been, he knew there was something more going on, especially after Erik's retirement from the police department. It smelled of trouble, and the man who had been his neighbor couldn't be working for the bad guys.

There were conspiracies that corrupted the world, and Garth was close to understanding them all.

"Conspiracy theorist." People slung the term around as a slur, but they were nothing more than sheep, too afraid to face the truth. Garth was brave, and he knew secrets percolated underneath the thin veneer of human civilization.

While the foolish government worried about the Zitarks, they ignored the true threat. The Navigators walked among them, hidden as animals like platypuses, awaiting the signal that would have them take back this galaxy from the lesser races.

People laughed at him for believing. One man had even thrown a drink in his face in a bar when he tried to expound on his theory, but he refused to let go of his steadfast belief that an ancient alien race was hidden on Earth as an Australian monotreme.

He didn't care how ridiculous it sounded. This wasn't absurd. He might not have solid proof, but he had plenty of indirect evidence.

Maybe Erik and his partner were out there hunting down Navigators and lying about being security contractors. That made sense. He would have to check if there'd been any mysterious raids on zoos and other related facilities.

Garth leaned back in his chair and tapped his PNIU.

A holographic table appeared in front of him, surrounded by representations of different people in his self-declared Truth Brigade. They were good, open-minded men, even if they weren't yet ready to accept his Navigator theory.

It was difficult to be a genius not understood in his own time.

Some of the Brigade, like Garth, used their true appearances, including two of the oldest members of his group, Tim and Minho. Others used blurred avatars or even fanciful costumes and alternative forms, such as White Rabbit, who resembled a bipedal white rabbit in a crushed velvet vest and bowler. That evening, White Rabbit was the only member present who was using a disguise.

"Gentlemen," Garth began. "Thank you for coming tonight. We're here to discuss the document Minho sent. I'm sad that not everyone can be here, but we have enough for a decent talk."

Minho ran his tongue along the inside of his cheek and nodded. "This is the big time, guys. This is something the corrupt corp media won't be able to conceal. I think this is what we've all been waiting for."

"I don't get it," White Rabbit replied, his voice distorted by an electronic filter and his nose twitching. "It was just a news report about that observatory that exploded. That's your big discovery? The corp media already broadcast it. What secret are you supposed to be uncovering?"

Minho hissed in irritation. "The Llewellyn Observatory explosion wasn't an accident. I'm surprised that you don't see it. It was obviously destroyed to keep a secret." He huffed. "I didn't figure I'd have to spell it out for a member of the Truth Brigade."

"Maybe I'm just an idiot," White Rabbit replied, his voice tight. "But I need more than an accident to believe something's happened."

Tim leaned forward and steepled his fingers. "I do too. What secret is there, Minho? I looked into the explosion after you sent it to me, and there's nothing special about the observatory. I thought there might be something off because it received a lot of Vand Foundation funding and she just died, but when I checked several others, I found they all did. Sometimes there *is* such a thing as coincidence."

"You can't think of one obvious possibility?" Minho asked, his eyes going from one to another.

"Experimental telescope and sensors?" White Rabbit's whiskers twitched. Excitement infiltrated his voice, and all evidence of hostility vanished. "Maybe they use it to spy on other systems, and they don't want to admit it had advanced technology."

"Then why would it be destroyed?" Tim asked. He lowered his hands. "You're saying it was Grayhead sabotage? They learned about it, and they wanted to protect the aliens?"

Garth watched the discussion unfold, staying quiet and letting his thoughts percolate. There was an obvious answer, but he wanted to give his friends time to come to the truth. A man couldn't accept a truth he hadn't worked out himself. That was a hard lesson he'd learned when trying to spread his message about the dangers of the platypus Navigators.

Tim scoffed. "If it'd been sabotaged by Grayheads, the government would have used it for propaganda value. They love using crazy terrorists as an excuse to infringe on our rights."

"If they did too much, they'd draw attention to their secret spy observatory," insisted White Rabbit as he slammed a furry paw on the table. "I've got it! It's obviously something they used to spy on Molino, some special FTL detection scope they recovered from Navigator tech. That's why the invasion never came, because the military could see all the raptors' moves. Those damn lizards realized something was wrong, but it's not like they're going to come over here and do a press conference to accuse the UTC of not playing fair."

Minho sat quietly, a smirk building on his face. He muttered under his breath but didn't join in with the back and forth. Garth thought it strange since he was the one who claimed he'd unearthed important evidence about the dangerous conspiracies.

"White Rabbit might be right," Minho interjected with a gleeful grin. "At least partially. I knew it was the right thing to come to the Brigade."

"Of course I'm right," White Rabbit replied. He patted his vest with both paws.

Tim frowned. "You have some proof he's right? I'm not buying into this supposition without evidence. There's a difference in seeing through the corporate media and being a credulous moron. I'm not ready for another fiasco like the penguin *yaoguai* expose."

"I apologized for that," White Rabbit muttered. "It was a *very* convincing video."

"I agree we need evidence. There's no proper truth without evidence." Minho rubbed his hands together. "I wouldn't have come without it."

Tim frowned. "Then present your evidence, and let the brigade evaluate it."

Garth eagerly nodded.

"I wanted to bring this all to you before," Minho replied, "but I had to spend time checking into the background of the observatory and other things to make sure there wasn't a government misinformation campaign. The thing is, shortly before the explosion, I was contacted by Gypsy Moth. Remember him?"

Garth furrowed his brow, already suspicious. "It's been months since he last contacted us. That's awfully convenient timing."

"That's what I'm getting at. He was beating around the bush with some questions about astronomical observations and Solar Systems objects." Minho took a deep breath and slowly let it out. "He sent me several messages about it, and it was obvious he was trying to be careful to not let me learn too much, but it was clear he was implying that an observatory found something unexpected and unexplained, but not on Molino or any other system. They found it within the local system." He shook a finger. "Then the so-called *accident* happened, and I couldn't find any account information for Gypsy Moth or even copies of the messages in my own accounts. Someone's cleaning up a mess and trying to make sure that whatever Gypsy Moth was investigating doesn't get out. It's obvious that someone on *that* observatory found something they weren't supposed to."

Tim jumped out of his seat. "Shit. In-system? That makes a lot more sense. They wouldn't even need new tech."

"Yeah." Minho nodded slowly. "I don't know where exactly, but it was farther out than Sedna. Don't know much more than that, though. I asked Gypsy Moth for specific coordinates, but he was being all cagey. He must have been afraid someone might kill him. Poor bastard."

Garth grinned and leaned forward. "Don't you see? It's a Navigator ship! They obviously have advanced stealth technology, but White Rabbit is probably right. The observatory was a cover for new military detection technology, and they caught on." He clapped once. "The Navigators are coming to reactivate their platypus friends on Earth."

"That doesn't make sense," Tim replied, frowning. "It could be a Navigator ship, and that would be worth killing over, but if it was a military thing, why would the government blow up their own observatory?"

"Navigator agents." Garth nodded, proud of coming up with the obvious answer. "They've probably got indirect control over a number of humans through implants or something like that. It's too much work to control the entire government, so they just watch for certain things. They didn't know about the project until it'd detected their ship. They decided to take out the observatory and cover up the traces before someone figures out what's happening and prepares for the invasion."

Minho rubbed his cheek, his brow furrowed to canyon depths. "The messages I got from Gypsy Moth made it sound like this was something he was close to. We didn't know him well, but I never got the idea he was military."

"He might just have been smart enough to conceal things," White Rabbit offered. "Pretend to be someone else. Any decent spy can. Maybe he was just trying to smell out potential threats to the secret."

Garth didn't take the obvious bait from a man wearing a rabbit disguise over the OmniNet. They all knew there were dangerous people in the government who might take them out if they stumbled too close to the truth, but Garth refused to be afraid. The only way he could change the world and get people to accept the truth was by showing he was willing to risk his life to get it.

Tim shook his head. "That observatory may or may not have been a military experiment, but it makes sense that it was destroyed to cover up that it'd found something. One thing I noticed doing my background research was there hasn't been a manned observatory lost like that in fifty years. I could blow it off if that was the only thing, but with Gypsy Moth contacting Minho right before the accident? That's too many coincidences."

"I think we all agree on that," Garth offered.

Tim snorted. "Yeah, but I don't agree with that Navigator crap. It's obviously not them. We know who the *real* threat is behind the ship."

"Not this again." Garth groaned. "There were *no* sentient species on Earth during the time of the dinosaurs. Your Original Inhabitants hypothesis has no basis in evidence or reality. It's just something you pulled out of your ass."

"My ass?" Tim yelled. "What damned proof do you have about the Navigators being hidden as platypuses?"

Garth slammed a fist on the table. "The Navigators left artifacts behind, at least. Where are your intelligent dinosaur artifacts?"

Tim burst out laughing, clutching his stomach. "Are you kidding me? What do you think the Zitarks are? They're obviously the descendants of Earth dinosaurs. Something probably happened. Maybe there was a gamma-ray burst they thought might hit the planet, but they didn't have the HTPs yet, so they had to take generation ships. They didn't have enough time to build a lot, so they could only take a handful. Chaos and anarchy followed, and the Earth-based civilization destroyed itself."

"That's just a bunch of guesses with zero evidence." Garth shook his head, pitying Tim for his questionable beliefs. "If there was a spacefaring species on Earth back then, some evidence would have survived. And Zitark DNA is nothing like dinosaur DNA or like the DNA of any existing or pre-existing Earth species science has found. Leem DNA is closer than Zitark."

"That's what the government *wants* you to believe. As for surviving evidence after tens of millions of years?" Tim rolled his eyes. "If every human died out tomorrow, no species would be able to tell we existed in sixty-five million years. Don't be such a tool of corporate media, Garth."

"I'm not a tool of the corporate media." Garth narrowed his eyes. "But *you're* a tool of the corporate-military-industrial complex and their misinformation campaigns."

Minho loudly cleared his throat. "Guys, calm the hell down. We need to focus on what we know, not what we don't know." He ticked up a finger. "There is a good chance the Llewellyn Observatory was purposefully destroyed by parties unknown." He raised a second finger. "It was probably destroyed to cover up that the researchers aboard discovered something near the far edges of the Solar System." He lifted a third finger. "And whatever is out there is important enough to be worth killing people over and erasing all evidence."

Garth ground his teeth. The truth about the Navigators was ready to come out, and even his fellow Brigade members refused to accept it.

He would have to drag them kicking and screaming to the truth.

"Okay." He sighed with a nod. "You're right. We don't have enough evidence to know if it's the Navigators or Zitarks coming back to Earth. We all need to dig, but be careful about it. If they've killed once to cover this up, they will do it again."

"Are you sure you're willing to pursue this?" White Rabbit asked.

"I know I am. This is what we're supposed to be doing, digging and finding the truth. If it was just one of us, they might get away with it. But all of us? No." Garth gave his head a firm shake. "The public needs the truth, and we'll bring the truth right to them."

CHAPTER TWENTY

Pleasant chimes sounded before an equally pleasant woman's voice came over the PA, first in Japanese, then Mandarin, and ending in English. "Welcome to Mizuchi Undersea Resort. Your luggage will automatically be sent to your room. Please enjoy your stay, and remember: the ocean will wash away all of your worries."

Jia and Erik rose from their seats in the first-class cabin, nodding to a bowing trip attendant, who handed them each a suitcase stored in the overhead bin above their spacious seats.

Their attendant's near-perfect smile suggested she was oblivious to the guns hidden inside.

Their Intelligence Directorate-supplied luggage could beat most common security scans and help smuggle a lot of things, and they preferred their weapons to be close at hand.

It would be annoying and embarrassing to be ambushed right away and not be able to defend themselves.

With a loud groan, a door near the front of the cabin slid open. A ramp extended from the bottom of the doorway, guard rails rising on either side to protect the guests from an unfortunate swim. Soon a bridge covered the short distance between the submarine floating gently in the vast pool of the underwater docking bay and the pier leading to the main resort.

The salty scent infusing the air tickled Jia's nose.

Erik and Jia gathered their coats and followed other passengers onto the pier. Despite having arrived via a self-sealing tunnel, the docking bay gave them the impression of being directly connected to the ocean, helped by the transparent walls revealing the water, including dense schools of fish clustering near the resort. The surroundings were partially illuminated by the docking bay lighting.

Another long, thin dark submarine approached, slowly descending to the connecting tube that passed from the outside to the controlled water in the pool.

Doors farther back on the submarine opened, and their ramps extended. It was time for the other passengers to disembark and join the streams of people offloading from the currently three docked submarines. Scores of people flowed off the piers. Smiling smartly dressed employees waited at the end of each pier to greet the arriving guests.

Erik and Jia offered them the smallest of nods as they walked past.

Check-in was automated and based on their PNIUs. They didn't need to do anything but go to their room, which should already have been keyed to their PNIU signals. No need for pesky human interaction.

Holograms of dolphins and whales swam through the air above them. It struck Jia as gratuitous given where they were, but a delighted guest pointing to them proved the resort staff had better entertainment instincts than a detective-turned-ID contractor.

"Emma, you have this placed mapped out?" Erik asked, looking around with a slight frown. "At least the public parts. I looked through the layout, but I didn't memorize it."

"Yes, I have maps committed to memory," she replied, her transmissions flashed directly to Erik's and Jia's ears. "I thought it best to save the more thorough system penetration for when we were on site. This might help."

Nav markers pointing to their room appeared, and the two nodded. They joined the river of people progressing out of the docking bay and toward the main hub in a narrowing tunnel. Moving walkways helped speed the process along.

Minutes of walking in near silence brought them to the center of the resort, with both Erik and Jia quietly observing the situation.

Their views of the ocean outside continued unimpeded, but the ceiling rose. Stalls and smaller buildings filled the central hub. Other major sections of the resort, like the docking bay, resembled bubbles connected by spokes to the main hub.

None of the buildings inside were more than a few stories in height, and their colorful appearance invoked the feeling of a bright, happy small town that just happened to be on the bottom of the ocean.

Erik looked upward. "Yeah, still convinced underwater domes are weirder than space domes. The thought of all that water." He shook his head. "It can mess with you."

"If you say so." Jia's attention lingered on a woman in a small stall selling intricately woven silver and gold pendants and rings. "If you think about it, anything that requires massive amounts of technology to maintain is unnatural."

"You saying this place isn't Purist-approved?" Erik smirked, some of the tension leaving his neck and shoulders.

"I'm just saying we die if the dome in space fails, and we die if the underwater dome fails."

A silver-haired man in a garish red and yellow Hawaiian shirt stepped in front of them. Jia almost laughed.

It was a vision of Malcolm's future in the flesh only a meter away.

"Don't talk like that, ma'am," the man offered in English, but with a faint accent Jia couldn't place. He gestured widely with his arms. "You're in a special place. Think of the *miracle* this place is."

Jia chuckled. "I didn't mean anything by it."

"Oh, it's not like I'm offended. I don't work here." The man winked. "I'm on an anniversary trip with my wife. It was here or Venus, and after all that nonsense there, I didn't think it was safe. Crazy terrorists! Earth's the only truly safe place."

Jia didn't point out that there had been far more

terrorist incidents on Earth in the last couple of years than on any other planet in the Solar System.

She was also grateful she was using her disguise, so the man didn't recognize her.

They'd been uncertain whether the excessive heat generated by the technology would put them at risk of detection, but Emma's research suggested they would be fine.

It remained strange to look at Erik and see a different face and dark hair.

The old man looked at Erik and Jia expectantly. "What brings you two young people here?"

"Honeymoon," Jia declared before Erik could open his mouth.

The old man grinned widely and gave both of them a firm shake. "Congratulations. I'm glad you didn't wait thirty years before experiencing a place like this." He looked past them into the distance. "Oh, my wife's waving for me. Have a good time, you two." He scurried away.

Erik leaned toward Jia and whispered, "Honeymoon? That's not the cover story we agreed on. This was supposed to be a business trip."

"It makes more sense, especially since we're sharing a room," Jia replied with a merry smile.

For all of Erik's self-control, he wasn't doing a good job of hiding the faint blush.

It was ridiculous. They spent all their time together and were sleeping together. She didn't expect a grand romance anytime soon, but he didn't need to act like a stunned teenager over a simple lie. Being underwater must have lowered his guard.

Erik coughed into his hand. "Let's get to the room."

"The room is secure," Emma declared when she appeared wearing the black and white uniform of the resort employees. She frowned at a shelf where her core was hidden behind a spare pillow in a box, along with a transmission amplifier. "You really think it's a better idea to keep me there than in the safe?"

"Safes are the first place people look," Erik replied, sitting on the edge of the massive bed. "Besides, if anyone gets into this room who shouldn't be in here, we expect you to contact us immediately so we can come and put a bullet in their brain." His gaze ticked to Jia, and his lips curled in a knowing smile. "Then again, I might be too busy with the new Mrs. Blackwell for anyone to get in here."

Jia scoffed. "That's going to be Lin-Blackwell. My mother would murder us both if I dropped the family name. She would then take the bodies and feed them to something in the Scar."

Erik blinked, unprepared for the counterattack on the joke. Jia grinned and sashayed over to him. She couldn't remember the last time she'd had him so off-guard.

"We could just skip the mission and pretend it *is* our honeymoon." She offered him her best suggestive look.

Erik stood and eyed the bed as if it were a nest of dangerous *yaoguai* waiting to ensnare him. "What about Malcolm, Emma?"

Jia snickered, confident of her victory over Erik,

though slightly curious why he was so uncomfortable with the idea of it being their honeymoon.

For now, though, he was right. They had a mission.

"I'm coordinating with him to spread out the system intrusions," Emma replied. "You're sure you wish to proceed as planned?"

"Yes." Erik nodded. "This isn't an emergency situation. You and Malcolm have time to compromise the resort systems. Do what you need, but try to not get caught. We still have two days until our targets show up, and we don't know how long we'll have to investigate them."

Emma smiled. "That should be sufficient to allow me to spread my influence without being discovered."

"In the meantime, we can scope out the resort and possible meeting locations."

Jia leaned against a wall with a smile. "The best way to do that is to look natural, *honey.*"

"Be careful what you wish for." Erik waggled his eyebrows, his earlier discomfort a distant memory. "You may just *get it.*"

"Probably not." Jia nodded toward the door, disappointed she'd lost control of the flirting war. "But I am hoping this doesn't end with a huge explosion."

CHAPTER TWENTY-ONE

Erik and Jia mingled with the tourist crowds as they wandered through one of the main market areas in the resort hub.

He felt naked without his gun or duster, but they were supposed to be on a romantic trip in a luxury resort, not traveling the Shadow Zone looking for trouble.

Though not omnipresent, he spotted the occasional security guard with a stun pistol. They undoubtedly had bots to aid as well. It'd be a simple matter of grabbing his weapon from the hidden compartment of Jia's purse.

He wasn't sure if he hoped for something. Despite what his partner seemed to believe, he wasn't that much of a danger junkie, but it wasn't like he could just relax and appreciate a fake honeymoon either.

An on-foot survey of the resort wasn't necessary, but should they lose contact with Emma for whatever reason, they didn't want to waste valuable time trying to figure out where to go.

He'd become dependent on the AI.

That used to bother him more, but he'd long since stopped seeing her as a piece of equipment. She was a friend and ally, and without her help, he wouldn't have gotten as far with wounding the conspiracy.

Jia's careful gaze took in everything. She wasn't saying much, but the occasional smile to Erik made it clear she wasn't ignoring him. That made sense. She seemed eager to pretend they were on their honeymoon.

Erik didn't believe that changed explanation was an accident, and he didn't know how to deal with it. They couldn't be distracted, not while on a mission. He'd already made the mistake of letting Jia get under his skin.

When he'd originally agreed to fake dating, he'd thought when they got together, a lot of the tension would resolve.

Now, even though they were sleeping together, a lingering discomfort weighed on him. His damned feelings. He wasn't supposed to *have* those sorts of feelings, but it was hard to spend his days in bed with a beautiful, intelligent woman and not let something grow.

Was it so bad to have something to look forward to after his bloody vengeance? No, but he wasn't ready to admit that to her.

Once he did, he wouldn't be able to take it back.

Erik stopped and craned his neck upward. Four massive sperm whales swam over the resort at a leisurely pace, majestic in their size and their apparent lack of care about the humans intruding in their waters.

For all his travels throughout the UTC, there was something about the glories of Earth that couldn't be topped.

"It's not one-way, right?" Erik gestured to the whales. "I'd think they'd care a lot more about thousands of people being right below them."

Jia shook her head. "They can see us just fine, and the resort's counting on it. Remember the intro video?"

He chewed the inside of his cheek. "I wasn't paying attention."

She nodded, not surprised. "Because predators are kept out by sub bots and patrols, there are a large number of whales around here, but they use a combination of sonic transmitters and modified grav fields to keep them from getting too close. I've read the resort also seeds food in the area because tourists like the idea of being surrounded by whales. It really sells the whole undersea thing, and being able to say there are real whales and not just holograms is great for advertising."

"Wait." Erik lowered his head and then looked up and down several times. He pointed to another pair of whales swimming above them. "You said we have spaceship-sized animals swimming overhead, but I don't see any shadows. That seems like holograms to me."

"They use filters," Jia explained. "They talked about that in the introduction video, too."

"Like I said, I didn't pay attention." Erik shrugged. "Didn't figure it'd be that helpful."

"Good thing one of us did." Jia slowly turned her head, focusing on a cluster of restaurants in the distance, all elegant one-story buildings. "They eat outside, and we eat inside."

"Humans make monsters, and nature makes impressive animals," Erik murmured. He frowned. "How big a hit can one of these domes take before we're all swimming in the Pacific? I wonder if a whale could damage them? It's one thing to bounce off a couple of sharks, but those things are damned heavy."

"I doubt they could hurt the dome unless terrorists supply torpedoes or bombs to the whales. You could even ram a decent-sized submarine into the resort without damage. These domes are as tough as anything they put in space, if not tougher. Otherwise, the first time there was a major accident, every undersea facility closes down because people are afraid."

"I've spent a lot more time in the other kinds of domes," Erik replied, "so I trust them more, but it doesn't matter."

"It doesn't?" Jia smiled. "You've finally accepted we aren't going to get crushed and drowned by the Pacific?"

Erik lowered his voice. "I've accepted that I don't think a handful of corp suits are going to come here to cause trouble. These guys would probably wet themselves if we got in a fight. That guy we dealt with on Venus is more what I expect from the conspiracy when they're making real trouble and waves."

"Well, we've got two days to kill while we're familiarizing ourselves with this place." Jia's gaze drifted to an ornate sixty-foot jet fountain. Streams and arcs of water danced around a hologram of a thin, snake-like wingless yellow dragon. "But that'll help deepen our cover," she whispered before raising her voice. "We might as well do a couple of touristy things. If our friends arrive early, Emma will let us know. And tonight, we can…have a little fun. We don't know if it'll be a while before we can afford to rest again."

"I'm always willing to give up a little rest for nighttime dessert."

Jia smiled and patted him on the arm. "Well, it *is* our honeymoon."

Erik turned to stare at a holographic image of a slender white sub rotating in the distance. He wanted to have fun with Jia that night, but he also saw an opportunity for some less steamy entertainment in the meantime.

"I've got an idea. How about we combine tourist crap with training?"

———

Erik shifted his shoulders as he got used to the harness.

The seat of the tiny one-man sub was more comfortable than he expected, given the cramped space. The primary yoke and secondary controls weren't all that different from what he was used to in a flitter, other than the separate throttle lever.

He, along with Jia, had opted for the shortest intro session of thirty minutes, though their trainer, a bored-looking man, made it clear that he'd be monitoring their session and would take remote control if necessary to stop them from hurting themselves during their chosen activity: a race.

"Can you hear me, Jia?" Erik asked.

Her bright green submarine floated several meters away, clearly visible on the sonar and the cameras. Lights ran along the bottom and sides of the tank, pushing away the darkness.

Erik had thought he'd hate being in a small submarine.

He hadn't minded the shuttle to the resort, but he'd figured the thought of all the water being around his individual vehicle would bother him. Instead, it'd had the opposite effect.

He felt more in control and less vulnerable.

"I can hear you," Jia replied. "You sure you want to do this? I'd hate to embarrass you in front of the whales. They'll sing songs of my victory and spread it around the entire Pacific."

Erik laughed. "Aren't you getting ahead of yourself? No wonder you requested the higher-difficulty course."

"I'm a natural when it comes to vehicles, remember? But at least there's no danger. It'd be more embarrassing to wreck the sub after all the antics we've survived."

A three-dimensional diagram of the course floated off to his right. The exercise was simple: they would proceed along the course, gaining points for flying through holographic rings. Holographic rocks would cost them points if they hit.

It was just like with the whales. Everything about the activity could be simulated, but people didn't come all the way to the Mizuchi Undersea Resort for virtual reality. A person could always tell on some level that VR and AR were fake. Advancements in the future might change that, but for now, the real world and true adventures continued to call to people.

A chime sounded from their PNIUs.

"Prepare to advance from the tank," announced their trainer, sounding as bored as ever. Not everyone loved their jobs. "Remember to keep it slow until you're outside."

The silver gate separating the tank from the tube

leading to the outside slowly rose with a slight shimmer. Erik pushed the throttle forward to gently accelerate, still trying to get a feel for the sub.

He understood every rumble and rattle in the MX 60 so he compensated for anomalies unconsciously, but he didn't understand the language of this sub.

Erik ignored the forward visual wraparound camera display that made the ocean feel like it might spill in at any moment. He didn't care about the glories of the ocean.

He was there to win a race.

There were too many distractions—bright lights, fish, or whales in the distance—and they weren't important. He would focus on their readouts and his course progress. During the competition, the submarine would treat the holographic rings and rocks as solid objects and react accordingly. This wasn't a battle.

He didn't need to dodge attacks or position himself for a devastating reprisal.

He wasn't too arrogant to admit Jia's earlier taunt spoke to a truth. She'd demonstrated a natural talent for anything that involved hurling metal through a three-dimensional environment, but he wasn't sure if that natural talent would extend underwater.

He'd used personal diving vehicles and suits in his time in the Army, but they were focused less on speed and more on direct entry. Fortunately, terrorists and insurrectionists didn't tend to hide underwater more than any other humans.

Even *they* got that people didn't belong there.

Erik's submarine cleared the external gate. Jia matched his speed and kept an even distance.

The sensor display lit up with the locations of the rings and danger zones. Their twinkling forms decorated the forward wraparound camera feed. He wasn't sure if they were true projections or simply added to his camera feed, blurring the line between simulation and reality.

"Prepare to begin the race," their trainer announced. "Remember to stay on your separate courses. Any significant safety violations or a departure from the designated course will result in us taking remote control of your sub and banning you from any other external activities for your safety and that of our other guests."

Erik would have preferred a side-by-side challenge with Jia, but they couldn't risk anything that would draw unnecessary attention or restrictions unless it was necessary to save people's lives.

"Five, four," began the trainer, "three, two, one. Go!"

Erik shoved the throttle forward and the sub accelerated, pressing him against the seat. He wondered if they'd purposely decided against grav compensation.

He would have loved to have tried out a true high-end super-cavitating sub fighter, but he was getting surprising speed from his tiny racer. Jia zoomed off in a different direction, heading toward her own course.

He approached the first ring.

Avoiding the rings would help him complete the course sooner, but the scoring system would ensure his loss. Many times, he had made Jia go through a training scenario that was more complicated than a basic goal of eliminating all targets.

Jia passed through her first ring at the same time as Erik. If either of them had an advantage, it wasn't clear. He turned the sub and lifted the bow to angle it toward the next set of rings. The first danger zone was coming up.

His heart rate kicked up, along with his grin. There was something about a good challenge against Jia.

Harsh proximity alarms sounded, and the cameras filled with falling rocks. Erik wove back and forth, avoiding the bulk of the obstacle, but his vehicle shook, and his score and speed dropped. The added effects almost tricked him into believing he'd actually struck something.

"Problem?" Jia transmitted, the taunting tone not subtle in the least.

Erik frowned. Jia's craft had gained a full sub-length lead on her course.

"You missed the rocks, huh?" Erik asked. "Don't get too cocky. This isn't over yet."

He barreled toward the next ring and ignored Jia. There was no collision risk, so there was no reason to waste mental resources worrying about her position. All he needed to do was win.

Letting her psych him out would be a rookie mistake.

The sub rushed through the ring. Erik was ready for the rock shower, weaving and diving and turning like he'd been born in the submarine. He let out a whoop of triumph. The next sets of rings and obstacles were just as easy.

Jia growled in frustration, stealing Erik's attention. He smiled after checking the sensors. She'd lost her lead and now lagged behind him timewise but with the same ring score. It wouldn't do her any good to hit all the rings if he did the same and she finished behind him.

They were closing on the halfway point of the course,

where they would be forced to turn completely around while hitting a rising spiral of rings. The back end of the course would present more colorful ring challenges and a denser group of danger zones.

All he needed to do was keep his lead.

"Problem, Jia?" Erik asked, injecting a faint hint of pity into his voice.

"Like a wise man said a couple of minutes ago, this isn't over!" she ground out.

Erik angled up the bow before hitting the switchback point and the spiral. His sub passed through the first couple of rings with ease. He cursed as he missed the next couple, but his pride returned as he twirled the sub through the rest of the spiral. After a wide turn, he pointed it down toward a series of rings that crossed back and forth. He might not be a natural when it came to every type of vehicle, but the Lady's underwater system had a crush on him.

He didn't bother to check the score or on Jia until he'd passed through the rings. She'd cut into Erik's lead, but her score now matched his.

"Looks like you missed some rings." Erik snickered. "Getting slow in your old age?"

"So did you," Jia replied.

"But I'm still in the lead."

"I'll catch up in the S rings. There's *no way* I'm letting you beat me."

Erik tightened his grip on the yoke before ramping up the throttle. He hadn't kept the lead by being timid. There might be nothing more than pride on the line, but sometimes that was all a man needed.

He couldn't imagine he'd end up needing to take a racing sub against an enemy, but he was confident he could if necessary now.

After dodging a storm of rocks, his sub slipped into the first ring of the S formation. He turned hard into the next ring, almost missing it, but his white-knuckled correction kept him flowing through one ring after another. Piles of virtual rocks descended as he pulled out of the back of the obstacle. His dodge continued unabated.

Up, over, side to side, *whatever it took.*

He entered a plunging line of rings, followed by a steep rise. The exit rocks formed a dense, obscuring maze. Escaping without a single hit was a near-impossibility. The sub shook violently, turning. An alarm sounded.

The staff was close to taking over.

That pissed him off. The sub might be losing control, but he hadn't hit any rocks. A small collision with the seafloor wasn't going to seriously damage the vehicle.

Erik gritted his teeth and retarded the throttle. He ignored the loud alarm and the blips on his sensor displays, caring only about regaining control of the vehicle.

With the sub straightened out, Erik pushed the throttle forward to make his run for the finish line and the last section of rings, these a gentler slope down than most during the race. He passed through the final rings and pulled back on the throttle to slow down, his breathing ragged.

Jia didn't finish for several more seconds.

"Congratulations," she offered between her huffs and puffs. "For a guy who hates being underwater, it might be where you perform best. You should have been living under the sea all this time."

Erik leaned back as far as possible, blowing out a lung full of air. "Yeah, no thanks. I think I'll stick to dry land."

Erik opened the door to their room and stepped inside with a smile. He hadn't gloated, but he also hadn't minded proving to Jia that she wasn't the master of all vehicles. After she entered, the door closed and Emma appeared, this time in a loose-fitting black ninja outfit, her red hair in a ponytail.

"What's with the getup?" Erik pointed a finger at her hologram. "You invent time travel while we were racing and figure you're going to go back and change Japanese history?"

"I was trying to get into the spirit of intrusion while in a Japanese facility," Emma responded. "I wanted to make you aware of the progress on the system exploration. I anticipate it'll take until tomorrow for everything to be set up in such a way that I can do what'll need to be done without any risk of detection. Keep in mind this won't be total system control, especially with the security systems, but I can gain access to those quickly if needed. The only issue is that doing so risks them learning something is going on."

Jia nodded, then scratched her ear. "Cameras?"

"Those are a much easier matter. As you might have noticed, there is minimum drone usage in the main resort, other than in the docks."

"I overheard a staff member saying they thought it ruined the aesthetics."

"That simplifies matters," Emma replied.

Erik looked at Jia and back to Emma. "We've done a good sweep of the facility, our little race excursion aside. It sounds like we'll be ready to keep an eye on our guys when they show up."

"Busy honeymoon." Emma winked, then disappeared.

CHAPTER TWENTY-TWO

Jia took a sip of her tea and peered at the demolished remains of her chicken dinner.

She would have loved to have some alcohol, but they both agreed they couldn't risk even a minute of cloudy minds. If their targets were part of the conspiracy, they might be able to slip into the resort, contrary to the ID's expectations. Exploring was different from actively handicapping themselves.

Erik tapped his PNIU and frowned as he read a message.

"Is something wrong?" Jia asked.

Alina might have more information for them, and the chance of another terrorist attack remained. Venus made it clear that there was no limit for the conspiracy.

"It's Garth," Erik answered.

Jia set her cup down. It took her a second to recognize the name and put a face to it. That didn't help her understand any better. "Garth as in the 'Navigators are platypuses' guy who used to live next to you?"

"Yeah." Erik let out a grunt of irritation. "He was nice enough, but there's only so many crazy-ass conspiracy theories a man can take before he gets tired. No matter what I said to the guy, he took it as an invitation to shove more crap at me."

"What about him?" Jia asked.

Erik gestured at his PNIU. "He just sent me a message out of the blue to my normal address. Emma's got it set up so everything gets routed to this PNIU, just in case. We barely talked when he lived next to me, and he's never sent me a message since moving. It's not like I tried to keep in touch with him."

"Okay." Jia nodded slowly, still marveling that platypuses would come up in conversation that meal. "What does the message say?"

Erik shrugged. "He says he needs to meet me to talk about something major, something that will change how everyone looks at the world. He says only I can help him get the truth out and save the UTC."

"In other words, a conspiracy theorist wants to catch up over drinks." Jia chuckled. "Maybe he's planning to be in the neighborhood and figured it wouldn't hurt to talk to you again." She looked at him as if studying him in a storefront. "I don't know. You can be charming in your own way."

"Glad you think so." Erik frowned. "But he's in Japan?"

"No. Neo SoCal. He doesn't know you're here." Jia grabbed her tea for another sip.

"I don't have time for crackpots, especially not with how things are heating up." Erik shook his head. "If I tell him I'm out of town, knowing that guy, he'll ask where I am. I'll ignore him. If he asks again when we're back home, maybe I'll consider it."

Jia grinned. "You never know. Maybe he finally *has* stumbled upon a true conspiracy." She set her tea down and sighed. "I get tired of the disguises," she whispered.

"It's better than being recognized when we're hunting," Erik replied quietly, lifting his head to check the room for anyone suspicious.

"Maybe it's my problem. Your disguise doesn't capture your true handsomeness."

He blinked at her a couple of times before sighing. "You make me want to get rid of it. If we're lucky, this mission won't take very long."

April 28, 2230, Japanese Territorial Waters, Mizuchi Undersea Resort, Erik Blackwell's and Jia Lin's Room

Jia stepped out of the bathroom and stretched, enjoying the softness of her bathrobe and thinking about her honeymoon lie. Their mission involved tracking conspiracy agents, and they had an AI hacking the facility.

That was hardly honeymoon fun, but that didn't mean they couldn't slip in a little fake honeymoon action on the side.

They'd spent most of the previous day exploring the resort, and now they had a good idea where everything was should they lose Emma's help, but that didn't mean they didn't have fun on the side. It wasn't like there was something else special to do that evening, so they'd gotten in a little exercise in the bed.

Erik sat on the edge of the bed, pulling on his boots.

They continued to close on their enemy. Minor scraps of leads and closed doors had turned into spectacular victories against not only the Ascended Brotherhood foot soldiers of the conspiracy but one of their leaders.

If they slew all the generals, the army would crumble.

Erik cracked his knuckles. "It's weird running ahead of these assholes for once. I feel like we've got them on the defensive."

"We do." Jia walked over and sat beside him, not all that surprised by the synchronicity of their thoughts. "But these two might turn out to be nothing more than accountants."

"Following the money helped us take down syndicates when we were cops, but if they are, we've spent a couple of days in this underwater deathtrap for nothing. At least we're not paying for it. It's just…" Erik looked down, his forehead furrowing in concern.

"Just what?" Jia prodded. She didn't want him to keep anything from her, especially if it concerned the mission.

"I don't know. It feels like something big is going to go down. I could be fooling myself because of us taking down Vand, but I trust my instincts, and this time they are screaming at me. They're telling me the Lady's setting up a major opportunity to rip another arm off these assholes."

"I don't think that's crazy." Jia pursed her lips. "I think you're right. The status quo is disrupted, which means we have an opportunity to take down an already weakened enemy. That's why we're here, because now we're not nipping at their heels in the shadows. We're hunting them down and they have to hide. They're bleeding, and here, we are the sharks."

Emma appeared near the door. She'd ditched her ninja outfit for a resort uniform again.

"You'll be pleased to know I've all but finished my general system infiltration," she announced. "I have general access to the resort's systems, and the idiot fleshbags running it have absolutely no clue. I should note I'm not overly impressed with the system's defenses." She put her hand out, stretching out her fingers. "I've gotten used to a higher caliber of enemy."

"And what about the security subsystems?" Erik asked, wondering why she mimed a lady looking at her nails.

"As I mentioned, I need to be cautious about that. It is difficult to push into controlling security without risking detection, but I can compromise drones and cameras easily enough with minimum risk. I'm coordinating with Technician Constantine for when we need direct control. He will act as a distraction in other systems while I complete my conquest of the security systems, but at that point, all secrecy will be lost, and I can't guarantee control won't eventually be retaken."

Jia nodded. "We'll save that for when we need it then. What about our targets? Have they arrived yet?"

Emma shook her head. "Neither Mr. Sillen nor Mr. Gallegos has arrived, but their rooms are currently being cleaned and prepared. They are staying in the luxury suites. According to their itineraries, they will arrive later today."

"Luxury suites in a luxury resort." Erik shook his head in disbelief. "Seems kind of redundant, but it does make me wonder how much better they are than our room."

The spacious room and huge bed were pleasant enough,

but Jia had seen her parents stay in nicer suites in Neo SoCal.

"Oh, their rooms are much better based on the schematics and information in the system," Emma replied with a smirk. "Interestingly enough, there are no internal cameras in those rooms, not even emergency cameras. I'm going to look into the records of guests staying near Sillen and Gallegos for any anomalies. If they're here for something related to the conspiracy, then presumably it's important enough to risk a direct meeting."

Erik nodded. "Sometimes you need to look a man in the eye to make sure he isn't going to betray you. Or they could be handing off a data rod, something they can't risk ID intercepting."

Jia walked over to the closet to search for an outfit. "This isn't an explicit search-and-destroy mission."

"So?" Erik shrugged. "I told you before I don't care all that much who pulls the trigger as long as the conspiracy gets taken down." He stood and headed toward the table, where a thin silver rod lay, the privacy device Alina had given them. "But you heard what Alina said. They wanted us here in case this needs to escalate. That means we might get our chance."

"She also didn't give us a local contact." Jia tugged down a loose green dress. It wasn't normal investigation wear, but wandering around in a suit or a tactical vest would be a bit suspicious.

"You don't need one." Emma scoffed. "You have me. I'm finally being allowed to live up to my potential."

"It's a contained environment and situation," Jia replied with a faint shrug. "That makes 'Send the super-AI to hack everything' a more practical plan than normal, but I'm wondering if this means Alina sees us as disposable or trusts us?"

Erik nodded to Jia's purse on the table. "Too bad we can't fit the TR-7 in there."

"That would be nice, but at least this way, we can keep our guns close without you wandering around looking like an ex-cop security contractor looking for trouble."

"It's the coat, isn't it?" Erik inclined his head toward the duster hanging in the closet. "What do you want me to do, wander around in a Hawaiian shirt and cargo shorts?"

Jia grimaced. "I didn't say you had to dress like Malcolm," she retorted. "I'm glad he likes his shirts, but they're not to my taste, especially on you."

Erik snickered. "Sure." He nodded to Emma. "If we know where they'll be, we should check out that area. We don't need to break into their rooms yet, but we should at least know where they are."

"They're in one of the buildings you didn't go into," Emma explained. "You need appropriate security access to be allowed through the front door."

"Can you get us through without alerting anyone?" Jia asked.

"I should be able to also offer a false feed to conceal your presence there without significant risk," Emma reported.

Jia smiled. "Sounds good. Let's go check it out."

The targets' building was even nicer than Jia had expected.

"They have a fountain in their lobby." She let out a quiet snort of jealousy. She looked over her shoulder as they headed down the hallway. "*We* don't have a fountain."

They'd hurried over to the target one-story building. As predicted, Emma had granted them access with little difficulty. None of the staff or other guests had paid them any special attention. One man's gaze had lingered a little too long on Jia's chest on display in her dress, but a glare from Erik sent him scurrying outside.

"What?" Erik asked, turned his head back from the guy who had annoyed him. "Who needs a fountain? You want to go swimming in the lobby?"

They were just about to walk down the hall when someone emerged from the suite, a familiar face.

Jia froze and slipped her arm into Erik's. She plastered on a loving smile and leaned closer to whisper into his ear, "Isn't that Javier Gallegos?"

"Yes," Erik whispered back, smiling.

To the small number of people in the lobby or in one of the hallways, they looked like a couple whispering sweet nothings.

"Interesting," Emma transmitted. "Yes, the facial recognition is a match, but according to official records, he hasn't checked in. I will note that conveniently, the other suites near his room and Mr. Sillen's all featured morning check-ins. They're cleverer than we anticipated."

"Why come here under your real name just to fake your arrival time with decoy rooms?" Erik murmured.

"It's almost as if someone is hunting them," Jia replied.

Erik released her arm and smiled even brighter. She wasn't sure what he was doing before he stepped toward the approaching Gallegos on the other side of the hallway. Unlike their casual wear, the corporate officer was in a full suit and tie as if proceeding to a business meeting.

Gallegos stopped and stared at Erik with a faint look of irritation. "Can I help you?"

"This is great." Erik gestured around. "When we won that contest, we never thought it would be like this."

"Contest?" Gallegos looked at Jia, his suspicion fading into appreciation. Her disguise might change things, but it didn't conceal her natural beauty.

Erik nodded. "Yeah, contest. Me and the little missus are from Detroit. She's always wanted to go to a place like this, but I figured it'd be too expensive under the sea and all that."

Gallegos nodded slowly. "Um, it *is* a luxury resort. Price discrimination does help maintain a certain level of...quality."

Jia was offended on behalf of the entire Lin family.

"What about you?" Erik asked. "You here with your wife?"

"I'm here for a business meeting." Gallegos offered him a tight smile. "I'm sorry. Have fun. I just remembered I forgot something in my room." He looked at the two. "It's unfortunate that we aren't near each other."

Erik waved as the man departed. He took Jia's arm in his and led her out of the building.

"We didn't say where we were staying." Jia shot a disgusted look at the building. "Which means he knows who is booked near him. I doubt he went through and knocked on all their doors."

"If he's here, then Sillen is probably here too," Erik muttered.

"I've determined they both arrived yesterday, local evening time," Emma reported. "They arrived together. I've found video of them departing from a shuttle sub late last night and heading toward this building. It wasn't worth the effort of searching through before now."

"Keep an eye on them. We can't do anything about them when they're in their rooms, but I doubt they came all this way just to chat in their rooms."

Jia chuckled and laid her head on Erik's shoulder. "I wish those people would stop messing with our honeymoon."

CHAPTER TWENTY-THREE

They walked toward a small, empty park nearby covered by a beautiful array of roses, both natural and in bright neon shades that might invite the attention of Purists.

There were a number of parks spread throughout the resort.

The effort struck Erik as odd. If he wanted to see roses and trees, he could do that on the surface. It'd make more sense to him if they built structures out of faux coral.

Erik reached into his pocket to activate their privacy device before taking a seat on a nearby bench and patting beside him. "I've got everything secure, at least on this bench."

"You think it was smart to walk right up to him like that?" Jia asked, sitting beside him. "We are disguised, but that doesn't mean no one will figure out who we are."

"I don't know if it was smart, but I think we now know he's not expecting anyone to come after him." Erik narrowed his eyes and burned the man's features further into his memory.

Jia's brow lifted. "You wanted to test how paranoid he is?"

"With all the fake room crap, I wondered if he was being careful, but he was annoyed that some yokel was talking to him, not worried that an assassin had shown up. If he had any reason to suspect the ID was onto him, he wouldn't have acted that way."

"You can't be sure of that. Most assassins don't walk over to their target and chat them up." Jia surveyed the area. Her fake soft smile would distract anyone not used to the depth of that searching gaze.

"I was also half-expecting him to be like that freak on Venus," Erik admitted. "That guy was…not normal."

"I doubt the conspiracy has many like our friend on Venus," Jia replied. "Too many weird half-alien freaks would paint a trail right to them."

"I've been going through the recordings of the cameras and drones that caught both of the targets," Emma interrupted after a fake cough. "Not every surveillance device is capable of examining every spectrum, and their capabilities are surprisingly limited inside the resort, but there are enough available, including thermal, for at least a general inspection. Incidentally, your disguises don't seem hot enough on the thermal recordings to stand out in the masses."

"Forget about us," Erik replied. "What about Sillen and Gallegos?"

"There's nothing unusual about them physically that I can detect remotely with the available equipment," Emma answered. "The thermal and density scan information strongly argues against them being Tin Men, or if they are, their implants are subtle and limited."

"That doesn't mean they aren't strange half-Leem things." Erik considered the options. "They might not have a warehouse filled with those guys, but I'd be surprised if he was the only one they had."

"Perhaps," Emma agreed, "but Mr. Gallegos' appearance, speech, and movement patterns are all well within what you would expect from a human, whereas the other gentleman was noticeably abnormal. I'm not saying that is definitive proof Mr. Gallegos isn't a strange mix-and-match fleshbag, but I would suggest the probability of that being true is low."

Jia rubbed her chin and considered their possibilities. "We've got some transmitters. We can plant them in the rooms and spy the old-fashioned way."

"Probably risky. They might be more paranoid about their rooms than they are about random guests."

"Before you do that," Emma interjected, "I want to make you aware of something I just found in my examining of resort files. This has bearing on the mission."

Erik checked to make sure there was no one suspicious around. Even with their privacy device and Alina-style hiding-in-plain-sight strategy, they couldn't be too careful. But they also couldn't do everything they needed to while hiding in their room.

"What is it?" Jia asked.

"I had assumed that all of the people registered around them were fake identities intended partially to shield them," Emma explained. "But there's one guest listed in a room adjacent to Mr. Gallegos, one Mr. Hans Konig. I found travel information related to him in the local systems. It seems the staff was trying to coordinate and prepare for his arrival because he's a regular guest and a VIP. He was on the moon until recently. At least publicly, he works for a forensic accounting firm that has a relationship with Crown River, including previous conference interaction."

Erik nodded. "He might be here to meet with them about something."

"It gets better or worse, depending on your general level of paranoia. Mr. Konig returned to Earth the same day the Llewellyn Observatory exploded."

"I read about that, but they reported there was nothing suspicious about it." Jia frowned, no longer able to muster the fake smile for public consumption. "You're saying that wasn't an accident?"

"It wasn't something I was paying close attention to until now. It's not suspicious inherently that they received funds from the Vand Foundation given the large number of scientific and academic entities who do, but the arrival time of his private flight along with his registered flight path is suggestive."

Erik shrugged. "Lots of ships landed on Earth that day, and a lot must have gotten near that place. If the observatory was a big deal, you'd think the ID or CID would have noticed."

"There weren't that many ships with a man right next to two people who can be indirectly linked to Vand and the conspiracy," Jia responded. "And the ID and CID can't find connections they aren't looking for. A bigger question is, why would the conspiracy care about blowing up an observatory? From what I read, they mostly focused on comets in our Solar System."

"Always comes down to motive, doesn't it?" Erik chuckled and shrugged. "Slam a comet into Earth?"

"There's no way they could pull that off. Even if they stuck an engine on the thing somehow, the Fleet would see it coming."

"Maybe that's what they wanted the jump drive for."

"Sure, but they don't have it now. They could covering their tracks." Jia took a deep breath. "Emma, keep as close an eye on our new friend Konig as the other two. I think this fishing expedition is about to snag something."

"Konig and Sillen are both emerging from the building, but they appear to be going in different directions," Emma reported.

Jia stood. "It wouldn't hurt to follow them around. It's a small place, so even if they notice, it should be easy enough to play it off."

"Why not just rely on cameras and drones?" Emma suggested.

"Not enough drones here," Jia replied. "And while I trust you, we're not the only ones on Earth with privacy devices and other tech. I'll follow Konig. Erik can follow Sillen." She patted her purse. "I'm not unarmed, but we don't have time to go back and get your coat."

"It'd stand out too much anyway with the toasty temps they keep this place at." Erik rotated his left arm. "I've always got this if trouble starts."

She stood up and turned to give him a hand, along with a fake smile. "Let's go earn our pay."

CHAPTER TWENTY-FOUR

Jia ran her hands along a string of pearls hanging from a stall.

It was easy to keep within sight of her target with Emma feeding Jia nav directions and even the occasional camera feed whenever Konig left her direct line of vision. Thus far, he wasn't doing anything more unusual than inspecting souvenirs, which made him exactly as suspicious as she was.

Following the suspect around wasn't thrilling, but at least she didn't have to sit in her room or in a flitter on a stakeout.

This part of the resort featured overly expensive souvenirs and tchotchke stalls. Erik and Jia had already been through the shopping area, and they hadn't spotted anything odd or worth special attention.

One thing had stuck in Jia's mind from their previous tour of the resort: there was nothing suspicious anywhere they'd looked.

While that was consistent with it being a vacation spot

and an unexpected place for a clandestine meeting, it'd taken ID and their AI hacking to link Sillen, Gallegos, Konig, and potentially the conspiracy.

The average person would have no reason to suspect them of being guilty of anything nefarious.

For all she knew, Gallegos, Sillen, and Konig might have just wanted a vacation and found an excuse to bill the conspiracy.

Jia set down the string of pearls. Her prey was moving on from his stall. She stopped for a moment, looking out of the corner of her eyes. A broad-shouldered man in a too-tight black shirt stood a couple of stalls down. He'd been a couple of stalls down for most of her time in the area. She moved.

He moved.

"I think I might have a tail," she whispered under her breath. She offered a brief description.

"Sillen just grabbed a drink and is heading back to his building," Erik replied. "If Konig pulls a disappearing act from Emma, that proves something in and of itself. We will let her handle him, and we'll set up a little trap for your tail. I'll break away from Sillen once he's back at the building."

Jia hesitated as Konig stepped away from a stall and headed in a different direction. He didn't appear to be going toward the docks, which suggested no quick escape. The features of the resort that made Erik uncomfortable would keep their targets from getting too far away until they arrived on the surface.

"Fine." Jia turned around and adjusted the strap of her purse. The large size and an ID insert made it easy to conceal the guns inside, but they'd blow their cover if they opened fire.

"Remember that holographic jungle park?" Jia whispered. "The one we walked past before lunch yesterday?"

"Yeah," Erik replied. "It's easy to get lost in there, and just as easy to run out."

"There are hidden cameras in that park," Emma replied, "but I can handle them without too much trouble."

Jia took a deep breath and upped the pace to a brisk walk. "I'm going to lead my new friend there. There should be fewer people inside if trouble starts, but if it comes down to it, I'd rather just kick him in the head and call Security on him rather than blow our cover."

"It might not be that easy," Erik replied. "If this guy has made you, he might be carrying."

"His pants and shirt are tight." Jia didn't look behind her as she wove between the people in the crowd on her way to the jungle park. "Or he could be a Tin Man that Emma's not detecting."

"Unlikely, even with these inferior cameras and drones," the AI interjected. "But I admit it's not impossible. Kick him and see how hard his head is."

Jia smiled and let out a quiet laugh. She wanted anyone around her to think she was having a pleasant PNIU conversation and not planning for a brutal encounter with a potential assassin.

"We need to verify he's targeting me, and it's not a coincidence. I'm going to take the long way to the park. If he goes through the trouble of following me, we'll have a better idea of what we're dealing with." Jia took a deep breath and slowly let it out. "This couldn't be an elaborate trap. They don't have any idea the ID picked out those two guys."

"It doesn't have to be a high-level trap. Maybe they tagged us when we visited their building earlier."

Jia slowed. A new nav marker had popped up in her smart lenses, courtesy of Emma. Now she could tell if the man was following her without looking his way. Her lack of obvious attention might embolden him. Another differently colored nav marker appeared.

"I've plotted an erratic course for you that leads to an area in the park with minimum camera coverage," Emma explained. "I'll be able to spoof the feeds without raising significant attention if you keep the takedown to a modest amount of time."

"I don't want to nail him before I know his deal. If I have to turn him over to Security, that's one thing, but I'd rather he still be breathing."

Jia followed the nav marker as it slid in a different direction. It was leading her on a serpentine path between restaurants. She imagined the man following her would either understand what she was doing or think she was drunk.

A dedicated assassin wasn't going to give up just because he'd been spotted.

It'd be better to take care of the problem right away than linger. Emma was monitoring the docks, so they'd know if Sillen or Gallegos tried to run. In an emergency, they could stop worrying about her being detected. Her tail didn't have a grenade launcher hidden in those pants.

People grew sparser as the minutes passed. The jungle park lay far from the center of the resort, closer to a storage area, based on their recon the previous day. Most of the parks and botanical gardens in the resort used real plants, so guests might not see the point in spending time among the holograms.

Her pursuer didn't give up, even as the thinning crowd made him stand out more. Jia's pace approached a jog, but that didn't seem to deter her pursuer.

"Would you know if someone else had hacked the cameras and drones?" Jia asked.

"It's possible for passive access to be gained, but I would notice any attempts to manipulate the feeds." Emma scoffed in disdain.

"This guy isn't going to pull out a gun and open fire unless he thinks he has me cornered. Or he'll stab me in the heart."

"I'm sweeping around from Sillen's building," Erik commented, concern in his voice. "Try to keep things from getting too hot until I get there."

"I'll try." Jia spared a glance to the side. "That's up to my new fan club member."

The jungle park grew from distant spots of color to towering trees, but her concern remained the same.

A single enemy, even one enhanced by genetic engineering or cybernetic implants, didn't worry her. Erik might believe in luck, but Jia didn't doubt destiny and fate were out there. They might not protect her from harm, but she wasn't going to die on the bottom of the Pacific Ocean.

The trees and tall grasses shimmered nearby, swaying in an invisible wind—a subtle reminder they were nothing more than tricks of light, lacking even the substantial nature of the nano-AR constructs of the training center.

There was an absurdity to the entire situation.

She was leading a potential conspiracy assassin into a dense jungle of holographic plants and trees. The moon. Mars. Venus. Underneath the ocean. She'd traveled more in the last year than she had her entire life. She'd thought she was worldly before, but she had not seen much of her home planet, let alone the vast expanse of the UTC.

Jia slipped into the jungle, now jogging and no longer caring if she alerted the man. She needed to get into a good position for an ambush of her own. Information or safety? She could stun the man, but it'd be difficult to get him back to her room for an interrogation. Shooting him was reserved for an actual risk to her life.

"He's slowed but still following," Emma reported. She sent a small camera feed, showing the man stepping into the park with a concerned look.

"I think he lost me." Jia ducked behind a patch of tall holographic grass with a frown. "I'm almost insulted that this is the quality they send after me."

"You'd prefer an alien hybrid?" Erik asked.

"Kind of."

The plants in front of her kept up a normal appearance, but the ones running through her shimmered and wavered at her intrusion. She took slow, deep breaths, her heart rate finally kicking up.

Her pursuer crept closer, looking back and forth in search of the woman he'd followed across the resort.

"Hello? Um, are you out here?" the man called. "The hot woman in the green dress?"

"Are you hearing this?" Jia whispered.

Emma's feed continued to show an unarmed man with

a genuine expression of concern, rather than a focused assassin ready to murder a woman interfering with conspiracy business.

The man sighed and ran a hand through his hair. "Okay, I get it. You were just minding your own business, and then you saw me. You thought I was a creep, so you ran off, which is better than calling Security on me. Let's start over. I can explain. My name is Cal."

Jia remained quiet, unsure if it was a trap. The conspiracy agents they'd dealt with in the past were far less subtle, but Sophia Vand had been a major player without anyone knowing. They might have adjusted their tactics after the Venus defeats.

"I saw you, and I didn't see a ring," Cal continued with a shrug. "I figured, hey, maybe I'm not the only one who came to this place by myself. I was supposed to come with my ex-girlfriend. I booked it for an anniversary and then she left, but I told myself I wasn't going to lose my deposit and not visit a place I'd always wanted to go just because of her. You know? Stay strong?"

Jia stood and revealed herself among the holographic plants. "Huh?"

Cal blinked. "Oh, there you are. And crap, you really were hiding."

"You've been following me all the way around the resort." Jia kept one hand in her purse, ready to draw the gun. She wasn't convinced his idiocy wasn't a sophisticated deception.

"Um, yeah." Cal gave her a sheepish smile. "Sorry about that. I was trying to get back on the horse."

"I'm not seeing anyone who looks like reinforcements

in the area," Emma reported. "There is a family with a toddler about eight minutes away at their current pace."

"I'm almost there," Erik announced. "Though I don't think I need to save you. This guy's pretty pathetic."

"Look, Cal," Jia began with a sigh. "I'm here on my honeymoon."

He blinked and stumbled back, his knees buckling. "But you don't have a ring."

"We're not a ring kind of couple." Jia shrugged and offered him an apologetic smile.

Erik jogged into the area, a huge, smug grin on his face. "Hey, babe. I've been looking all over for you!"

Cal turned around, and his eyes widened at the sight of the large man.

"This is your husband?" he asked.

Jia nodded. "Yes."

"Ugh." Cal nodded, then fled past Erik without another word.

Emma's mocking laughter lasted for a surprisingly long time before the AI spoke. "I've confirmed that a Cal Daris is staying at the resort, and his file biometrics match what we've seen from our lovestruck stalker. Public records indicate he's a low-level corporate employee, but he doesn't seem to be affiliated with any of the companies of interest."

"He's just an idiot who was hot for Jia," Erik interjected with a grin. "I had to intervene. That was torture. The poor bastard."

"Yes." Jia rolled her eyes. "You're so smooth."

Erik rushed over to her and pulled her into his arms, his mouth so close his breath warmed Jia's face. "The only reason we're not doing more is that we're on the job. I don't need to spend a lot of time chasing you around and using shit lines, and I didn't get with you as a rebound woman."

Jia opened her mouth to respond, but he planted his lips on hers and delivered a deep kiss. She kept waiting for Emma to say something, but the AI remained silent, so Jia gave in and deepened the kiss, her hands skimming down Erik's exposed muscular arms.

She finally pulled away, her heart thundering. "At least he wasn't an assassin."

"I wouldn't say that." Erik slowly lowered his arms, his breathing heavy. "He assassinated both his dignity and pride."

"Emma, what about our targets, including Konig?" Jia asked, tearing her gaze away from Erik and staring at the ground.

"All accounted for. I've also noticed something in my additional perusal of the resort's records that might be helpful."

"What's that?" Jia licked her lips, remembering Erik's mouth. It was far from the first time they'd kissed, but somehow this kiss had affected her more than normal.

"Mr. Konig has reservations for dinner tonight, party of three," Emma explained.

Jia didn't like Erik's face, but she couldn't fault his next suggestion.

He held her but turned toward the main area of restaurants. "I think I need a little food after all this."

CHAPTER TWENTY-FIVE

Erik had never liked suits. *Ever.*

They were too constricting for his tastes, but the restaurant's dress code dictated something nicer than his casual resort-wandering outfit. Avoiding discomfort was less important than getting the job done.

Now as they approached the restaurant, Erik realized something. It changed his opinion, and he wished he'd been wearing the suit earlier.

The change in clothing provided him with something he'd been denied for most of his time in the resort: a carefully concealed holster that allowed him to carry his gun rather than relying on hiding it with Jia. He hadn't seen a scanner in the resort past the docks.

The suit might not replace his duster under normal circumstances, but buying a bullet-resistant suit might be in order for future infiltration and recon jobs in such dangerous places as resort restaurants or for dinners with Jia's mother and sister.

Jia couldn't hide anything in her red dress, but she'd

brought the same reinforced oversized purse she'd been carrying around.

Together, they were a stylish and deceptively well-armed couple. He would have preferred not to depend on the disguises, but this was one situation where being recognized wouldn't work to their advantage.

A maître d' offered them a winning smile as he welcomed them. There was a brief moment of confusion when the reservation, with Emma's help, conveniently updated to reveal Erik and Jia not only had a reservation but also an appended note insisting that they be seated at a particular table due to the "customers' strong feng shui concerns."

A waiter showed them to their table with polite and professional service, no indication the maître d' thought that made them unpleasant customers. The simple lie and complicated AI assistance placed them exactly where they needed to be.

Erik and Jia took their seats.

Their table provided a good view of Konig and two other men while remaining mostly obscured. After the delivery of their wine and water, Jia activated the privacy device in her purse.

Jia slowly looked around the room, swirling the wine in her glass with an appreciative smile. She didn't noticeably linger on the target table.

"Our party of three doesn't include Gallegos and Sillen. This might be a dead end." Jia didn't hide the disappointment in her voice.

"Or it could be that Konig's more important than Sillen and Gallegos," Erik suggested. He raised his glass.

"But we'll have a nice honeymoon meal in the meantime."

"It's definitely a romantic stakeout, much more so than before." Jia set her wine down and picked up her water to take a sip. "The MX 60 is nice, but I like a little more space for my legs when I'm watching dangerous anti-socials."

Erik offered a warm smile. "Only the best and most luxurious stakeouts on my fake honeymoon."

"I can't get over the arrogance."

"What's arrogant? I'm just sitting here."

"I'm not talking about you." Jia shook her head. "Gallegos and Sillen. The conspiracy. All these powerful and wealthy people who believe they're above not only the law but also common decency."

"That's where we come in," Erik replied. "If they operate above the law, then so should we."

Jia looked at him with narrowed eyes, her anger getting the better of her. "Part of me wants this to turn out to be nothing, but a larger part of me wants them to try something, so we can take them down hard. Since Vand…I don't know what to call it. It's not bloodlust. It's more a realization of something important."

Erik nodded. "You realized we could win against them."

Her breath caught. "It's not that I didn't believe we couldn't win before."

"I know. I'd be lying if I said I was always convinced I'd be able to pull this off. On my trip back to Earth from Molino, I wondered if my transport would conveniently explode. But it didn't, and I made it to Earth and found you and Emma. Maybe it's the Lady. Maybe it's sheer stubbornness, but we scratched them before, and on Venus and in

Bogota, we delivered major wounds." Erik set his intense gaze on Jia. "It's not bloodlust to finish off a dangerous enemy. Sometimes in war you take prisoners, and sometimes the only way to win is to annihilate the enemy."

Jia offered a slight nod, and they let the conversation lapse. They watched Konig's group until the delivery of their meals, poached fish for Erik and roasted quail for Jia. The three men were drinking wine, but they'd yet to have any food delivered.

"Just here for drinks?" Erik asked. "Why not go to one of the bars?"

"Camera observations of their mouth movements suggest a banal conversation," Emma reported. "Mostly they are comparing their prowess in different sporting activities and romantic conquests. It's a rather tedious conversation, though there are some irregularities."

"Irregularities?"

"There are slight anomalies in the conversation, but it's not impossible."

Erik frowned. "They're using a privacy device."

"It's possible, but I can't confirm that based on the tools available to me at this point in time," Emma replied. "And their PNIUs can be pinged by the local system, so they aren't actively jamming."

Jia's eyes darted toward the target's table, but she kept her head rigid. "It's not like we expected them to sit there and openly discuss corrupting the UTC at dinner. Do we know who the two other men are?"

"They appear to be university associates of Mr. Konig's," Emma reported. "That's in public records."

Erik frowned. "His presence might be a coincidence."

The men smiled. One of them mimed a golf stroke before the three men burst out in loud, braying laughter that turned the heads of nearby customers. The evidence was piling up to suggest this wasn't a suspicious meeting of dangerous men using a privacy device and plotting against the UTC.

Jia swallowed a bite of her quail with a raised eyebrow, eyeing Erik. "Do you really believe Konig's being here is a coincidence?"

"No, but I also don't think we stumbled into a conspiracy convention." Erik picked up his fork and knife to slice off another piece of fish. "And we were pointed at Sillen and Gallegos, not Konig. They were throwing up enough smoke that the ID could follow their trail, and I think that means something, but sometimes a trail doesn't lead anywhere."

The two alleged college friends stood. Both of them shook his hand and patted him on the shoulder before making their way toward the exit. Konig remained seated, and his smile disappeared. All hints of the previous pleasant, mirth-inducing conversation vanished. He kept glancing at the door.

Jia inclined her head in his direction. "Is it just me, or does he look like he's waiting for someone else?"

"Sometimes a trail *does* lead somewhere," Erik murmured, taking another bite.

Konig had a short conversation with his returning waiter before returning to his drink and watching the door.

"Mr. Konig noted that the other members of his party would be there shortly," Emma explained.

"He just ran into his friends, then." Jia nodded. "It was a coincidence, just not the one we thought. There's still a chance that Gallegos and Sillen will show up."

"Then we can keep eating." He looked toward where the waiter would normally be. "And perhaps have a nice dessert."

Erik and Jia were almost through their entrees when the aforementioned men arrived and made their way to the table with the help of a waiter. Unlike with the previous two men, Konig's slight frown and tense shoulders didn't suggest friendship.

The new arrivals got comfortable and placed an order before settling into a new conversation after Sillen slipped his hand into his pocket, where it lingered.

"What are they talking about, Emma?" Jia asked.

"Allegedly, they are discussing the resort and its attractions."

None of the playful gesturing or happy smiles of the previous conversations made it into the current discussion. Gallegos clenched his fists under the table. Konig glared at Sillen while he rattled off something.

"Awfully pissed for people chatting about the resort." Erik finished his fish. "Konig probably didn't have a privacy device. They *were* just having a boring-ass conversation, and now the real meeting is happening."

"There was an unusual pause in the conversation," Emma commented after Konig jabbed a finger toward Sillen.

"Passionate?" Erik asked.

"Yes," Emma replied. "The general cadence and speech patterns are consistent with what you're observing, but the content is bizarre. It doesn't appear to be a disagreement. If you overheard them, you'd think they were discussing the best stalls and shops to go to."

Jia chuckled quietly. "If they couldn't control themselves, they shouldn't have come out in public, even with a privacy device."

"I wonder why they did."

"Given the body language, they probably don't trust each other," Jia replied. "Keeping it in public stops anyone from doing something too stupid and bloody."

"Never stopped me," Erik noted.

"The Lady doesn't like everyone as much as she likes you." Jia kept her silverware in hand and smiled. It'd help their privacy device conceal their conversation more naturally.

Erik matched Jia's smile. "The corporate links and spending time together points to them being more than passing acquaintances."

Jia thought as she chewed. "If they're not getting along, that might be something we can use. We could turn one of them against the conspiracy."

"I see where you're going, and it's not a bad idea." Erik inclined his head. "But I don't think we're going to have time to set them against each other. This might not be anything more than them disagreeing about payment or an ops plan."

"Plenty of people have killed other people over very little money." A hungry look settled on Jia's face. "We should leave before they do, and then we can see where they end up going. This could be a final negotiation."

"Fine by me," Erik replied with a grin. "Let's grab that dessert to kill some time." He gestured at the table, which was receiving its entrees. "Unless you're dying to stand outside for an hour?"

When Konig, Gallegos, and Sillen emerged from the restaurant, all three men were scowling as if their food had been rotten and they'd received the worst service possible. Erik and Jia lingered near the front, laughing quietly to each other and sharing made-up anecdotes rather than relying on the privacy device.

"That's when I said, 'If I'm going to pay that much, you might as well launch me into the sun.'" Erik gestured widely with his arms, a huge smile on his face.

Jia let out a playful laugh in response. Erik wasn't sure if she was acting or she found his story that amusing.

The scowling men paid no attention to them or anyone else, but it quickly became apparent that Konig wanted to get away from Gallegos and Sillen as fast as possible.

"You've made a mistake," Konig seethed, his face red. "Things are different. You can either face that reality or have it run over you."

"You're the one who has made a mistake," Gallegos replied. He adjusted his tie and offered Konig a cruel, baleful look. "And you should have done your research before coming to us."

After a nod to Sillen, Konig stomped away from the men.

"Damn it," Erik muttered. He leaned in to whisper to Jia, "Should we split up again?"

Jia faked a laugh as if Erik had said something clever. "I think Emma should follow Konig," she whispered. "We should both go after Gallegos and Sillen. They're our original targets, and we still don't know if Konig is important." She sighed as she stood up. "I'm glad I wore flats instead of heels."

CHAPTER TWENTY-SIX

Jia was disappointed when she realized Gallegos and Sillen were returning to their rooms. She'd expected something else.

Maybe a grand, bold conspiracy maneuver, but they'd been able to follow the men without trouble, keeping out of sight on the short jaunt from the restaurant back to their building.

"How we doing with Konig?" Erik asked.

"He contacted someone on his PNIU and is now circling back to the building," Emma reported. "Although I don't believe he was using a privacy device, he was likely using a code. His conversation consisted of him saying hello, followed by 'Should the star fall?' He then nodded and said 'I'll take care of it.'"

Jia's disappointment evaporated, replaced by excitement. This wouldn't end up with them just following some people to dinner.

"That could mean a lot of things. You sure he didn't pick up anything that might look like a bomb?"

"I'm certain," Emma replied. "I've had him on an active feed at all times since he left the restaurant. We can't exclude the possibility that he has an advanced holographic emitter that is deceiving me, but it's incredibly unlikely, especially given his previously displayed behavior."

"Whatever he's going to do, it's going to happen soon." Erik loosened his tie. "We could have Emma send an evacuation code, but I don't think this is about destroying the resort. They've always brought a lot of muscle whenever they've tried crap like that. I don't think they would suddenly rely on one guy."

"I think it's a deal," Jia suggested. "They're supposed to sign some sort of agreement. He was probably negotiating at dinner and had to get his boss' permission to go through with it. There's been tension over the terms."

"We could bust in while they are making the deal. They'll be off-balance, and we could interrogate them. If we grab their PNIUs, we can have Emma do her thing, too."

Jia shook her head. "We don't know what this deal is even about. I doubt there's going to be a briefcase filled with drugs or *yaoguai* embryos in there. Their PNIUs aren't likely to have anything more interesting than the ones we brought. This is probably more something intangible, an alliance or a favor." She pulled down on her dress. "It's not like they can make them sign a contract and take them to court."

Erik moved forward to plant another kiss on Jia. This time she saw Konig out of the corner of her eye and wasn't prepared for the sudden mouth attack, not that it made it any less exciting. By the time she pulled away, Konig was through the door.

"I don't know if kissing me in public is low-profile," Jia breathed out, lips puffy.

"Probably not." Erik winked. "Doesn't mean I'm going to stop."

"I'll keep that in mind," she whispered.

"He's proceeding to his room," Emma reported. "He appears rather agitated."

"His boss might have told him no go on the deal." Jia frowned. "If only we had some sort of opening to get him to talk."

"We can flag him for our friends," Erik replied. "It's not like we've been told to turn him. We're just supposed to be checking the first two guys out. If they don't make a big move, there is no reason for us to. Those guys don't seem like Sophia Vand-level players. It's just like being a cop; sometimes we let the little rat go so we can follow him to the bigger rat."

"Weren't you the one saying you thought something big was going to happen?" Jia asked, inclining her head toward the building. "That your instincts were screaming? Now you're saying we should back off?"

Erik nodded slowly. "Yeah, and they still are, but instincts aren't enough. We need something concrete to go on, and that might require hel—"

"It is highly likely trouble is imminent," Emma announced. "The cameras and sensors have died inside the building, along with the primary power. Secondary alerts on the resort's system suggest it was unexpected. Emergency lights are activating."

"EMP?" Jia frowned. "They're making their move, or Konig's making his."

"I'm able to detect muffled gunfire from inside Sillen's room," Emma announced. "It is almost certainly a projectile-based weapon."

"Damn it," Erik muttered. "The deal went bad."

They sprinted toward the building, the illumination outside giving way to dim red emergency lighting. Jia yanked her stun pistol out of her purse. Knowing these men might be involved in the conspiracy wasn't as useful as interrogating them, and that required them to keep breathing.

Erik drew his slugthrower from its holster.

They quickly closed on Sillen's room and flattened themselves on either side of his door, their rapid breathing in perfect sync.

"Can you hear anything from inside?" Jia asked, silently cursing the soundproofing she'd enjoyed the night before.

"Based on what I can detect, there is movement inside but no gunfire," Emma replied.

"Open it," Erik ordered. "We don't have time to figure it out."

The door slid open. Loud gunshots rang out and struck the opposite wall.

"Give it up," Jia shouted. "If you drop your weapon immediately, we can guarantee your safety. You keep this up, and my partner might accidentally put a bullet in your head."

More bullets flew out of the room. Jia cocked her head. There were distinct gunshot sounds during the volleys, which meant more than one man. Erik and Jia couldn't spin in and open fire without knowing the relative positions of their foes.

"Back-trace the shots and mark them for us, Emma," Jia whispered. "I doubt they're running around the room."

A bright arrow appeared, along with a dynamic trace manifested as a red line that moved with Jia's head. Erik nodded at her and they both crouched. He let out a shout, which summoned another barrage from inside.

They spun around the corner. Three tiny six-legged bots stood exactly where Emma's traces indicated, armed with low-caliber cannons. Erik fired three quick shots, knocking the bots to the side while Jia swept the room looking for a human target. A dark form passed the open window. She squeezed off a shot but her target cleared the window, her stun bolt narrowly missing him and almost hitting the briefcase in his hand. Another barrage from the bots forced her back behind the wall.

"He's going to get away," she shouted.

"Not if we take down the bots."

Erik took a deep breath and a couple of steps down the hall, then ran forward, pointing his gun to the side. The bots opened fire, narrowly missing him, but his Emma-guided aim let him shred one in a shower of sparks and metal chunks.

The machines surged out of the room, but that left them easier prey for Erik, who didn't stop shooting until he'd emptied his magazine.

The bots collapsed to the ground, twitching and sparking, new holes through them.

Jia rushed through the room, sweeping in both directions with her stun pistol. Gallegos and Sillen lay face-down, the former on the bed and the latter on the floor, in pools of blood.

There was no chance of saving them since they were missing half their heads and had dozens of bullet holes in their chest.

"Your shooter and/or bot controller is Konig," Emma reported. "I've got him on external cameras fleeing. I don't think he was prepared for an immediate response. I'm suppressing the security system to prevent the immediate convergence of security personnel on your area."

Jia ran toward the window and climbed through, then shoved the stun pistol back into her purse and pulled out her slugthrower. She needed to be ready if they ran into any more bots.

"Give us a nav marker, Emma," Jia ordered.

"There's a problem with that." Emma sighed. "I've lost Konig."

"How?" Jia shouted in surprise.

"He slipped into a camera blind spot. I flew a drone there, but I'm not seeing him." Emma added a new nav point. "That's where I lost him."

Jia's jaw clenched. Emma might be a sophisticated and unique AI, but that didn't mean she was omniscient. There wasn't any point in complaining.

Another quick run brought them into a narrow alley between two storage buildings away from the main hotel structure. There were no doors in the alley and no obvious way up.

"And are there cameras covering both exits?" Erik asked.

"Yes," Emma replied.

Erik holstered his gun. "Crap. We lost the slippery bastard."

"It doesn't matter." Jia frowned and looked around. "There are only so many ways out of this resort. Emma can keep an eye out at the docks."

"For now, you need to move away from that building." Emma sounded worried. "Malcolm is setting up a distraction to cover my security system intrusion so I can maintain camera, door, and drone access, but right now, we run the risk of them regaining full control of the system. I'm placing emphasis on drones and cameras covering the docks and emergency access, but at a minimum, he won't be able to leave until they regain control of the system."

"Let's get back to the room," Jia suggested. "We need to be more prepared the next time we run into shooting."

What should have been a quick and easy jog back to their hotel building became complicated when black-uniformed security guards flanked by bots with stun rifles advanced toward them. One of the guards leaned over to murmur to the other before nodding at Erik and Jia.

"Excuse me, sir, ma'am," one of the security guards called.

The guards' stun rifles remained slung over their shoulders, but the pack of four decent-sized bots with them provided more than sufficient firepower to down two unarmored people.

Erik frowned. "Can we help you?"

"There was an incident, and a concerned guest called in

a complaint. Two people matching your descriptions were spotted near the location of that incident."

"We were?" she asked.

So much for Emma having camera control. That didn't do them any good against eyewitnesses. Reality always found a way to challenge them.

"Repeat the following to them," Emma ordered. "Alpha-two-nine-eight-four-six, gamma epsilon sixty-two."

Jia hesitated for a moment before spewing out the bizarre sequence. Emma might play the occasional prank, but never when they were in danger.

"Excuse me?" the guard replied. He furrowed his brow in confusion and backed away before tapping his PNIU. His eyes widened. "You're Parliamentary Security Detail? Oh, please don't tell me we have a dead MP in our resort." He groaned. "No, no, no."

Jia nodded at Erik. She was pleased with Emma's quick thinking and system manipulation, but Erik remained better at lying to someone's face.

"You're okay. Our *boss* left yesterday." Erik grunted with disapproval. "We had received intel he might be targeted but had no reason to believe it would be a threat to the greater guest population, so we didn't choose to coordinate with the locals."

The security guard nodded, a look of weary resignation on his face. "And we've got two bodies. Did you kill them?"

Erik shook his head. "We didn't, but we're not at liberty to discuss that at this time. For now, please secure the scene for the CID or Japanese authorities. We're still pursuing a dangerous suspect who goes by the alias Hans Konig. If you spot him, you should lock down the facility immediately and contact us. Keep the subs from going out, but I wouldn't recommend a major alarm. No reason to let him know we're onto him."

"Okay, uh, I'll pass this along to my superior, Agent…"

"You'll have to rely on our identification code for now," Jia interjected. She gestured at their building. "We need to check on some things, but I would strongly suggest keeping this quiet. We don't want an unnecessary panic, and there's no reason to damage the reputation of this fine facility because of the actions of a single criminal."

"Of course." The guard looked relieved. "We'll try to find him and contact you."

"I wouldn't recommend engaging him without us. He's very dangerous."

The security guards stepped out of Erik's and Jia's way, trading concerned looks. Dealing with terrorists went far beyond their standard issue of dealing with rowdy drunks.

After stepping back into their hotel room, Jia scrubbed a hand down her face. Her heart had stopped its drum solo impression.

"Pretending to be members of the Parliamentary Security Detail is going to cause more trouble in the long run," Jia commented. "It's going to be a lot harder for Alina to clean up."

"It was the most efficient way of gaining aid without blowing your cover, and it had a certain synergy with the distraction Malcolm provided." Emma appeared in the resort's security guard uniform. "They'll ask questions during the follow-up, and I'm sure the CID, DD, and PSD will all be annoyed, but Alina can clean it up. If anything, since we've contained the scope of who you're supposed to be, I suspect it'll be easier. For now, I believe it's far more important to capture Konig."

Jia dropped her dress and headed toward her suitcases in the closet.

"Is this really the time to get naked?" Erik raised an eyebrow. "As nice as that naked body is."

"Yes."

Jia opened a suitcase. A tight-fitting tactical suit stood out under normal circumstances, but next time they ran into Konig or bots, she would be ready.

"Oh. Good call." Erik walked to the closet. "Find Konig, Emma, and we'll do the rest."

CHAPTER TWENTY-SEVEN

After putting on his tactical suit and vest, Erik stuffed his pockets and pouches with fresh magazines. He might not be able to use his TR-7, but assuming he wasn't having to take on exos or *yaoguai*, a pistol would be fine.

Konig's little bots were more a nuisance than a serious threat, and it was clear the man hadn't shown up expecting serious opposition like two ex-cops looking for trouble.

Jia put her stun pistol and slugthrower into her belt holsters. She'd gotten into her tactical suit in record time.

"I don't think sitting around here and waiting is a good plan." Jia clipped her gun flap. "I'm regretting not smuggling in grenades."

"We might get lucky, and hotel security will tag him for us." Erik was finishing his own change of clothes. "Based on the situation and what we told them, they're not going to let any of the subs leave. I say we head down to the docks. Local security believes we're Parliamentary Security, so they won't think anything of us strolling down there ready for a fight."

"But he might not be going to the docks." Jia shook her head. "This man isn't a random syndicate thug. We don't know what tech or devices he has on him. He might leave via an emergency hatch for all we know. That's assuming he doesn't have any strange genetic modifications that let him free-swim from the bottom of the ocean."

"I'm continuing my monitoring, including external cameras," Emma reported. "Just in case our brave little fleshbag might have brought his own diving suit or vehicle or any of the other outlandish possibilities highlighted by Jia. Rest assured, we'll know if he leaves."

Erik's view of what constituted outlandish had shifted in recent months. After what happened on Venus, it was hard to think anything was too far or too insane for the conspiracy. He decided to start with something more practical.

"Let's go with the basics. What if he's got some sort of optical camouflage?" he asked.

"I am also checking in thermal bands, but even if he can beat that, it won't matter," Emma replied. "If any of the airlocks are opened, I'll know. I might not be able to use the local drones or drone subs to defeat his optical camouflage, but we'll at least know if he's exiting. Keep in mind the man entered the facility through normal means. If he has unusual travel capabilities, one would think he might do that."

"I don't know if we can be certain of that." Jia tightened her belt. "We were sent here to investigate Gallegos and Sillen, and Konig took them out. We don't know if he works for the conspiracy or someone else and what his true capabilities are. I don't think we should make assumptions."

"You're right." Erik headed toward the door. "We should at least head toward the docks. That's still our best bet for finding him during an escape. I get the feeling something went wrong with his plan, but that doesn't mean he can't get away."

"Wait." Jia stopped Erik with a hand on his shoulder. "If he does run, we can't risk chasing him and leaving Emma here."

"Indeed," Emma replied. "Even if you don't anticipate the destruction of the facility, there is a large chance of someone discovering and taking me if they search the room without you to guard me. I'd hate to have to hijack a vessel and start a major incident, as amusing as that would be."

Erik walked to the other side of the room and pushed the pillow aside, then removed Emma from the amplifier and tucked her snugly into a vest pocket. "You still going to be able to do everything you need to without being in the amplifier?"

"Of course, especially now that I'm in the system and the locals have given me greater access. It'll be trivial."

"Huh?" Erik glanced down at Emma's core. "Since when?"

"As far as they know, Technician Constantine and I are Parliamentary Security Detail specialists who are working with you remotely to deal with this dangerous terrorist," Emma explained. "The falsified codes, legal orders, and identification won't stand up to careful government scrutiny, but it's enough that these rather suggestible fellows aren't alarmed by my presence in their system."

"Then let's go catch our killer and ask him some questions." Jia followed Erik and quickly caught up after they stepped outside the door.

An old woman from a room across the hall blinked several times before narrowing her eyes and staring at the tight-fitting tactical suits. She finally shook her head and wandered down the hall.

"I never did understand why people need VR sex when they could be having perfectly good normal sex," she muttered under her breath.

"These aren't…" Erik sighed. A red-faced Jia nodded the opposite direction. "Let's go that way."

Erik smirked.

"Impressive," Emma declared when they were almost to the docks. A crowd blocked the tunnel leading to the docking bay. The burgeoning mass of angry-looking guests shouted at a line of staff and security guards. They were waving people through the tunnel from the docks but blocking anyone else from moving forward.

"What's impressive?" Erik asked.

"I'm fairly certain I've detected Konig," Emma replied. "But I see how he was able to escape previously. A maintenance drone spotted a man in the docks who isn't showing up in the guest registry. This man's appearance and gait don't match our boisterous bomber, but there was a brief visual distortion that suggests some sort of high-end holographic camouflage. He's lingering near the back of the departing crowd with a briefcase. He just ducked behind a support pillar."

"Distortion?" Erik scoffed. "He's getting nervous and moved too fast. But I don't get it. Since they're already stopping everyone, it's not like he's going to be able to leave. They'll clear the sub shuttles after they've finished unloading. It would have made more sense to mingle with the crowd."

"Unless he steals a sub." Jia inclined her head toward the tunnel. "If he's got fancy optical camouflage and could sneak in here and kill two people with smuggled bots, he's probably got a method of stealing a sub."

"Yeah. Damn it. Let's go get him."

People in the crowd turned their way, staring with open curiosity or fear. The security guard from earlier jogged toward them with a frown.

"I thought we agreed to keep this quiet." He gestured to their tactical suits and vests. "You look like there are two hundred Grayheads coming to sacrifice us to the Leems."

"There's a problem," Emma announced. "And in answer to your previous questions, external sensors have picked up a fast-moving incoming sub. It doesn't match any shuttle profile, nor is one on the schedule. They are not answering my attempts at communications, and the resort staff seems perplexed. I suggest you take control of the situation."

"Here comes the escape crew," Erik muttered. He frowned at the guard. "We have a terrorist sub coming in."

"What?" The guard blinked. "Terrorist sub?"

"Yes," Jia snapped and gestured at the crowd. "So get these people out of here. *Now!*"

The guard tapped his PNIU and murmured something quietly. A moment later, a pleasant woman's voice sounded from everyone's PNIU, delivering the same message in Mandarin, English, and Japanese.

"Attention valued guests, an emergency situation has arisen. We need anyone near the docks to please leave your luggage and proceed to a shelter for your protection. We at Mizuchi Undersea Resort place guest safety above all other considerations."

Staff and security lined up to gesture people toward doors opening in the ground in the distance.

Huge blinking holographic arrows highlighted them. The crowd reacted better than Erik expected, but not by much. Only a fourth of them screamed, and only half of them rushed forward like a panicked herd.

Most of the guards and staff managed through sheer presence and refusal to move to funnel the crowd toward the now-open shelters. At least no one was crushing anyone else.

Erik and Jia pushed into the crowd, trying to force their way toward the main docks. Emma supplied them a target indicator for their possible conspiracy assassin, but the panicked piles of men and women made it impossible to see much of anything.

"There is an external override gate being activated," Emma reported. "Our suspect reached into his pocket before it occurred, and there was an unusual systems access. The outer tunnel door is opening."

Jia helped pick up an old man who fell in front of her.

"Can't you cancel the override?"

"In this case, because of the nature of the activation, doing that would require a full system reset," Emma explained. "I can't be sure they haven't previously inserted malignant code, and we would have potential issues with critical system failure during a full system reset."

"They were willing to sink an entire city before." Jia shook her head as the old man stared at her, having an odd discussion with no one in particular. "We can't take the chance. I'd rather let that bastard escape than risk thousands of innocent people."

Erik and Jia made it to the main tunnel.

The bulk of the panicked guests continued streaming to the shelters in the hub. Security guards moved away from the crowd toward the tunnels and lowered their stun rifles from their shoulders. The guards nodded and fell in behind the newly arrived pair, acknowledging their natural confidence and authority.

The remaining guests hurrying through the tunnel stared at the show of force, some murmuring quiet prayers under their breath.

"Damn it." Erik ran forward, weaving around guests. He made it to the end of the tunnel and the main dock, surprised there were still guests standing around, including some arguing with the security guards.

"Didn't you hear the announcement?" Jia shouted, drawing her slugthrower. "Get to the shelters before you end up getting shot in a firefight, you idiots!"

Her rebuke motivated the remaining holdouts to listen to the security guards and run toward the tunnel.

Erik drew his gun and followed Emma's target marker

to the support pillar hiding the suspect. He ducked behind a bench. "Konig! I don't care what you look like. I know you're there."

Jia took a position behind a different bench. "If you surrender immediately, no one else has to get hurt. You just were unlucky to commit a crime when there were two Parliamentary Security Detail agents here."

Erik wasn't sure Alina would be able to clean this up as easily as they'd been assuming, but there was no reason to let an agent of the conspiracy know who they were.

Their previous experiences with those types of tactics had led to more violence, not cooperation.

The security guards spread out in the mouth of the tunnel and along benches and behind other support pillars, all aiming in the same direction as Erik and Jia. He wasn't sure if Emma had supplied them with targeting information.

"The intruder sub is entering the docking tunnel," Emma reported.

"We're running out of time," Erik muttered through gritted teeth.

"Konig!" Jia yelled. "We know about your friends coming. Militia units are on the way. You're not escaping."

"Get someone here, Emma," Erik ordered under his breath. "I'd rather have to explain later than let this guy get away."

A harsh laugh sounded from behind the support beam. "If you know I'm here, then you know I'm carrying a briefcase."

"We know," Erik called back. "So what?"

"What do you think is in the briefcase?"

"Your balls?" Erik suggested. "I don't know, and I don't care. We'll crack it open and take a peek after you surrender."

Konig snorted, the sound echoing in the cavernous dock. "It's a controller for a series of bombs I've planted, Mr. Parliamentary Security Detail. You two idiots have no idea who you're dealing with."

Jia's eyes flicked over to Erik and back. "I think that's *our* line," she complained.

"If I blow the bombs, there's no way the backup fields will be able to hold back the water." Konig waved the briefcase from behind the pillar. "This will become a giant underwater tomb."

Emma scoffed. "I'm currently searching through many of the key structural points of the resort and not finding any evidence of unusual cargo or bombs," she transmitted.

"Yeah, I'm not feeling it either," Erik murmured. He raised his voice. "You're bluffing, Konig, and we both know it."

"You willing to bet all these lives? You willing to bet yours?"

"It's not a bet when you know you're going to win."

Erik moved a finger toward the trigger. He'd rather kill the bastard than let him get away. At least it would be one less person involved in the conspiracy.

But that would be wrong. The people linked to the conspiracy were the two dead men. Could Konig be an assassin from a faction less concerned with vicious control?

No. If he were on their side, he wouldn't be threatening to destroy an entire resort or resisting people who identified themselves as Parliamentary Security Detail agents.

"The sub is almost here," Emma announced.

"This is your last chance, Konig," Erik shouted. "You can leave with us breathing, or you can leave in a body bag. I don't care either way."

The water in the docking pool stirred and a dark shape emerged—the body of a submarine. With a whir, a turret rotated into firing position from a previously hidden panel and sprayed bullets through the docking bay. A security guard screamed as a round tore through his shoulder. A man behind him grabbed him by his collar and pulled him toward the tunnel.

"Get the hell back!" Erik bellowed. "You're not going to be able to do crap with stun rifles. Go get something heavier!"

The security guards rushed toward the tunnel, keeping low. The turret swept the area again, and its heavy bullets ripped through walls and benches but bounced off support pillars in a shower of sparks.

Konig tried to emerge from his temporary shield, but Erik sent two rounds that forced him back. They might be pinned down, but as long as they held him in check or stalled for reinforcements, they could win.

"Next time, we figure out a way to smuggle our exos in with us," Erik grumbled.

CHAPTER TWENTY-EIGHT

Without heavier weapons, Jia wasn't sure how to advance. Their tac suits could take punishment, but she doubted they could survive many direct hits from a heavy vehicle-mounted weapon.

"Emma, anything you can do?" he asked.

"I'm going to smash some drones against the turret," Emma announced. "It's unlikely they'll do much damage, but it should provide a momentary period where you can advance. The longer you can stall them, the longer I can attempt to see if I can hack into any of the sub's systems that respond to external signals. I'm not guaranteeing anything, but my general integration with the resort, including the security system, gives me options we don't normally have."

It might not be the best plan, but it *was* a plan.

Jia's gaze darted to the nearest support pillar, one of the only structures in the room that gave decent cover from the turret.

She nodded to Erik and prepared to run.

Konig made a break for the sub while the turret did its best to suppress Erik and Jia, but that didn't stop him from taking a round to the shoulder. The man stumbled with his briefcase toward another support pillar, a trail of blood marking his path.

A swarm of maintenance drones swirled together, a sight both eerie and beautiful. They dove as a staggered formation toward the turret, smashing into it and shattering on contact. Erik and Jia took their chance and ran forward. The turret came to life, but its deadly barrages shredded the drones flying in front of it, creating an even larger cloud of smoke and debris.

Clanking and skittering resounded from the tunnel. The noise was the prelude to a small army of security bots emerging and opening fire, most offering stun bolts, but bullets ripping from them as well.

They dinged against the thick hull of the sub, but the exposed turret sparked under the onslaught.

"Local security was still figuring out what to do," Emma explained. "I thought I'd facilitate things with the tools I can directly control."

Konig leapt into the water, narrowly escaping Erik, Jia, and the security bots. He swam under the surface, careful to keep the briefcase with him. Jia became more interested in his luggage than the man.

Jia tucked her pistol into her holster and pushed herself hard for the water, unsure of how long Emma's machinations would save them from the turret. She joined Konig in the water. Erik added his own presence with a massive splash.

Konig's legs disappeared into an open but flooded starboard airlock and the outer door slid closed behind him. Jia didn't try to bother firing since her weapon wouldn't be effective at this range underwater, and she wasn't going to blow a sub open with a pistol.

Emma's distorted voice filled her ears. "Keep going, Jia. I've managed to drop one of the inner doors in the docking bay, and they can't simply ram through that. I think I can open the airlock. I hope you can hold your breath. Be the best fleshbag you can be."

Jia swam harder, closing on the flooded airlock, her lungs burning. Erik was behind her, looking grimly determined. She was starting to come around to his view of the threats of water.

A muffled explosion above sent burning metal fragments into the water, and the submarine listed to the side before diving.

"Security has brought heavier weapons," Emma commented, sounding bored. "The turret was destroyed, but the sub still appears seaworthy."

Jia arrived at the door and grabbed an external handrail, her lungs crying out for oxygen. She lifted her head, unsure of how much longer she could hold her breath. Erik floated beside her with his thumb up before he grabbed a handrail.

At least they would drown together.

The sub slowly turned, lining up the bow with the thick transparent inner gate blocking their retreat. Jia fought her body's natural urge to take a breath.

The external door clanked and slid open. Jia and Erik swam inside.

"Put me in the IO port," Emma ordered, marking the

relevant spot inside the flooded airlock in their smart lenses.

Erik pulled out the crystalline core and shoved it into the IO port. The outer door closed, and the water level rapidly drained.

Jia's pulse pounded in her ears. She would give anything for a quick breath, so she swam toward the top of the airlock as precious centimeters became water-free and gasped. Erik joined her.

Their hearts pounded.

They took deep, slow breaths as the water continued to drain, and they slowly sank to the metal floor until they both knelt.

"I suspect I will have control of this vehicle within ten to fifteen minutes," Emma insisted in a tone of smug satisfaction. "There are certain aspects of system security that would benefit from improvement."

"I'm fine with them being lazy and arrogant." Jia stood, her heart not yet slowed despite the fresh oxygen.

She drew her stun pistol.

"This is our chance to take these guys alive to get intel," Jia offered, her voice low and threatening. "If they aren't the conspiracy, they know something about it. Emma, can you manipulate the oxygen by room?"

"I won't know until I've taken control of the—"

A loud boom shook the submarine.

"What the hell was that?" Erik barked.

"They just blew the gate with a torpedo," Emma replied. "Unfortunately, I think it's best if I lift the other gates to decrease the chance of serious damage to the resort."

"Do it." Erik yanked out his pistol. "We're aboard now.

It's not like they're getting away." He crouched on one side of the inner airlock door. "Let Jia get in position and open the door. Can you do that, or do you need total control?"

"I should be able to open the door."

Jia got ready. "Give the count, Erik. Let me do the shooting, so we keep some alive."

"Better down them quickly. Three, two, one."

The door slid open and a flurry of stun bolts flew into the chamber, most concentrated over the center. They harmlessly struck the back wall, but the shots on the side passed over Erik's and Jia's heads.

She suspected the four angry-looking men with stun pistols farther down the tight passage on the other side were more concerned about damage to the sub than taking living prisoners, but she didn't have time to think about it.

Jia's hands moved of their own accord as she fired. The men collapsed with groans before they could get off a second set of shots. Erik never fired.

"Good job." Erik sounded impressed.

The invading pair ran to the stunned men. Erik holstered his pistol and grabbed one of the fallen men's weapons. They waited near the crew, crouching as heavy footfalls sounded from around a corner.

"I haven't gained control of the ship's systems or the cameras, but I've been able to temporarily blind them," Emma reported. "That should make things easier."

"Works for me," Jia replied.

The next group of men barely made it around the corner before Erik and Jia nailed them, sending them to hard, thumping collisions with the metal floor.

Erik smiled. "If we don't know where to shoot, hitting the guys with guns makes the most sense."

Emma sounded confused. "There's a certain logic to that."

They stopped at the corner and peeked around. There was no one waiting for them at the end of the short passage, but there were several sealed compartments.

Erik and Jia crept forward, listening for any sign of the enemy. They arrived at the first sealed door when it slid open to reveal a large man with a knife. He swung it at Jia's chest with a crazed gleam in his eye.

The blade glanced off her tactical suit, and she shoved her left palm into his nose. He stumbled backward. She followed up with two point-blank stun bolts to his face. He collapsed and bounced off a table, landing on a trail of blood that led farther into the room.

Konig stood on the other side of the surprisingly long room filled with integrated tables and chairs, a mess hall. Jia didn't understand why Erik hadn't already taken him out until she noticed the primed grenade in the other man's hand.

"I see now," Konig spat. He was pale and shaking, his breathing ragged, his hair matted from water and blood. "I actually thought you were Parliamentary Security. I should have known people still loyal to the old order would send backup." He let out a strangled laugh. "But too late. You're not getting anything from me."

"No one has to die," Jia replied, her gaze locked on the man's hand. "If those two men you killed are who we think they are, we might be able to help one another."

"Help one another?" Another loud laugh sent Konig

stumbling backward. "Oh, I see who you are. I should have known." He lowered the grenade next to the case. "You think you've won some great victory, but you have no idea what you're up against and what's coming for you." He released his hold on the grenade.

Erik and Jia jumped out of the room, but shrapnel from the explosion ricocheted, and pieces struck and embedded themselves in their tactical suits. Others grazed their exposed hands.

Jia hissed as a chunk of shrapnel sliced her cheek, then groaned and pushed herself up, her cheek throbbing as she reached up to feel the cut. Erik noticed her flinch as she eyed the blood. "That went well, all things considered."

"We're not dead." Erik got to his feet and carefully brushed shrapnel off his tac suit.

Jia pulled out a med patch and applied it to her face with a wince.

Smoke and the acrid scent of burned flesh filled the room. Konig's mangled body lay on the ground, barely recognizable. The briefcase had been blown apart, and a badly scorched data rod lay near it, cracks running through it.

"Shit," Erik growled, and he punched the edge of a nearby table. "I thought he was just trying to avoid getting interrogated."

Emma appeared, this time wearing a blue eighteen-century British Royal Navy uniform, complete with tricorn hat. "We still have this sub, and even if they've practiced excellent operational security, there is a chance of recovering data from the rod with Alina's help."

"And we've got a ship full of prisoners." Jia took deep

breaths. "Which we should lock up before the stuns wear off."

"You okay?" Erik gave her a worried look.

"We both know I've taken a lot worse than this." Jia gestured to her cheek. "Let's just take this sub out of here. It's time to call Alina for backup and," she looked around Konig's last stand, "cleanup."

CHAPTER TWENTY-NINE

"Are you *sure?*" Erik asked, pointing his gun at the unopened top hatch, but he took a second to look at Emma's hologram.

He would have preferred their new arrival to enter via the side airlock. That way, he and Jia could better contain them if they proved *not* to be who they were expecting.

Being too trusting in the middle of the ocean on a stolen conspiracy submarine was stupid. All it took was one quick grenade toss to make sure they had an agonizing last few minutes of life.

"The codes all match," Emma replied, sounding annoyed. "It's not *impossible* for someone to have intercepted the codes, but the other message elements are consistent with what I was expecting. I believe it is the visitor Alina told us to expect. The alterations were extreme compared to the original course, but unless you're willing to interrogate the surviving crew, we won't know where they intended to go. They'd already blanked the course data in the navigation system."

Erik and Jia had continued sailing away from the resort after sending a brief report to Alina. They weren't cops anymore, and it wasn't their job to stick around and investigate murders.

The longer they lingered, the greater the risk their lies about their identity would come out, and the CID was going to get involved anyway.

Alina had assured them that leaving was fine and instructed them to travel to a specific location and surface at a particular time, where they would be boarded by an ID agent who would take possession of both the sub and the data rod and drop them off in Japan.

They would then catch a flight back to Neo SoCal under false names and pretend they were never anywhere near the Mizuchi Undersea Resort during the unusual events that had transpired.

They arrived at the coordinates without incident and detected a low-flying flitter nearby. The vehicle circled them before contacting Emma with the code, and a black-masked agent in a tactical suit jumped out of the flitter to the submarine.

Their vehicle departed at high speed, leaving them on the sub. Whoever it was appeared confident they wouldn't need a ride home. One way to accomplish that would be to kill the people currently in control of the submarine, but if Erik and Jia decided to descend, they would be bobbing in the Pacific and waiting for a pickup.

Jia drew her stun pistol with a sigh.

"*Now* you're paranoid, Jia?" Emma asked. "Although they have weapons on them, they haven't drawn them. I see no obvious explosives."

"It doesn't hurt to be careful." Jia pointed her weapon at the hatch. "Especially in the middle of the ocean. It's a long way to dry land, and they probably have reinforcements closer than we do."

"Open the top hatch, Emma," Erik ordered. "If it's a friend of Alina's, they won't be offended by having a couple of guns pointed their way, and if not, we'll be able to get a shot off before they try anything."

He backed up a couple of meters. No reason to eat a grenade if one was coming. He assumed they were rather metallic-tasting.

The hatch whirred and spun, and the interior door slid apart before the main hatch popped up. Then a small ladder extended down. The masked agent jumped down, their pistols following as they landed in a crouch. A moment later, they reached up and pulled the mask off, revealing cyan hair and a familiar face.

"Hail the conquering heroes," Alina announced with a smile. She stood and dusted off her sleeves. "I knew it was a good idea to send you to the resort. I've got other agents who could have investigated, but not many who could have managed to board an already submerged and departing sub."

"If it was just going to be you, why didn't you say so, Alina?" Erik holstered his gun. "Sometimes I think you like to be mysterious for the sake of it."

The ladder retracted, and the hatch dropped with a thud. The interior door closed, and a light hum filled the vehicle as the engines came back online.

Emma had already been sent course data.

"I'm not saying I never have fun at your expense, but

that wasn't the case this time." Alina looked at Erik and Jia with a gleam in her eye. "After everything that happened, I thought it was best I come to debrief you myself." She patted a bulkhead. "I'm impressed. Very impressed. You've got an entire ship and multiple prisoners. That's a big haul. I'm assuming the prisoners are still secure? I wouldn't blame you if things got a little squirrely and you had to take them out."

"They're fine," Jia replied, gesturing down the passage. "We've got them locked in a cabin back there, and we made it clear that if they caused trouble, they might get to inspect the bottom of the ocean without diving gear. We did check them for hidden weapons. Emma's keeping an eye on them in case they've got a bomb implanted in their spleen or whatever stupid trick the conspiracy thought up, but they mostly are sitting there in sullen silence."

"Excellent. It's always better to have prisoners for interrogation, and I'm pleased to see you two can accomplish a mission without blowing up half the area." She clapped. "Things are getting better."

"Hey." Erik snickered. "It's usually the other guys who blow shit up. We're the ones stopping them."

"Fair enough." Alina rubbed her hands together. "Unfortunately, I doubt we'll get much from your prisoners, but I appreciate the effort."

Erik's smile disappeared. "Why won't we get much?"

"Because we've already identified a couple based on the biometric data Emma sent us, and all evidence points to them being mercenaries."

Erik rolled his shoulders before sighing. "I don't buy it." He'd been tense for too long during the boarding procedure. "No mercenary is going to blow himself up to protect a client. If Konig was a gun for hire, why not just sell out his employers when we had him cornered? For that matter, why not toss that grenade at us rather than eating it?"

"You misunderstand. I'm not saying Konig was a mercenary, just most of those on this submarine." Alina tapped her PNIU with a slight frown. "It'd be helpful in the future for you to coordinate false identities with me if you're going to claim something unusual and high-profile. The Parliamentary Security cover story is ending up having unexpected legs, and now some of the media are on the story. They're trying to spin this whole thing into an MP assassination attempt. There's some MP who was on a very private vacation, and he's had to pop up and explain he wasn't at the resort, and it's become a mess."

"I am the—" Emma began.

"We did what we had to," Erik interrupted. "I don't make apologies for that. Sometimes we don't have time to play things subtly, like when assassins are wasting our investigation targets and trying to escape."

He wasn't mad at Emma for making the call, and Alina needed to be reminded that if she wanted their help, she had to let them do things their way—rogue AI and all.

They wouldn't be able to save the UTC if they had to worry about keeping things quiet. Sometimes he wondered if they could solve the conspiracy problem by just blasting a request to all corners of the OmniNet for any information on Molino and related incidents.

"Understood," Alina replied after hesitating for a couple of seconds. "But you should understand our position that it makes things more complicated. That's all I'm saying.

Remember, we're on the same side." She offered him a disarming smile before tapping the side of her leg. "But setting all that aside, we know something big went on down here. What little we can dig up quickly on our end suggests more of a relationship between Konig and certain Vand-related activities than initially suspected, and there are tentative connections between the three involving possible conspiracy-linked activities in the past."

Jia frowned. "So, whoever Konig was, he's not from another government or a freelance conspiracy-hunting faction. This wasn't a public service."

Alina shook her head and shrugged. "He could be someone like that on first blush, but Konig's dealt with them so much, I find it hard to believe. Based on what you sent along and what happened, this smells like some sort of internal struggle."

"What if Sophia Vand was the leader?" Jia rubbed her chin. "From what you've said, there's obviously still conspiracy activity, but if Vand was a major player at the top or the leader, her death could have set off some sort of a full-scale civil war. Factions vying for power, that sort of thing. That would be consistent with what we saw on Venus involving her and the potential targeting."

"And Vand said something implying she thought someone else might have sent us." Erik nodded at Alina. "A woman. As time goes on, I find it less likely she was talking about you."

"Yes, you mentioned that before," Alina replied with a thoughtful look. "And I can't say I disagree with your conclusion. To be honest, I doubt I was enough on her radar for her to think to mention me, so you might be right. It also makes me wonder about the destroyed Brotherhood factory, and how much of that was intended." She frowned. "They could have bloodied our noses if we tried to send people in. They had to know the ID would try to recover it mostly intact. Otherwise, we could have had the Army annihilate it, and they wouldn't even have had to bother to destroy it themselves. But if a faction did it to weaken another, that might explain it."

"It doesn't matter for now," Jia concluded. She looked toward where the prisoners were with a scowl. "If all we have now are mercs, it's not like this sub's going to give us much. They already blanked the nav data, and it's probably a merc sub anyway. We already know Konig was probably more important, but he's dead and in itty-bitty pieces. It's hard to interrogate a dead man's pieces."

Alina wagged a finger. "You're forgetting the data rod. That was important enough for him to bring it with him when he was fleeing—as far as he knew—for his life."

"It's trashed. It's a miracle it didn't shatter." Jia kicked at the hard floor with her boot. "The only reason there's anything left of it is that Konig didn't use a plasma grenade. We already tried to plug it into an IO port and see what Emma could pull off, and she didn't have any luck and said there wasn't anything she could deal with."

"There are other options," Alina replied. "Emma's impressive, but she's not the be-all, end-all of data recovery."

Emma appeared in front of Alina and stared at the agent incredulously. "There's fundamental matrix damage to the data rod, including issues with quantum decoherence. Fancy technology can only do so much to change the laws of physics."

"Before we had HTPs, they said humanity would never travel faster than light. But we don't need to go there. The ID has a few tricks even you don't know about." Alina grinned, enjoying having one up on the AI far too much. "We've learned the hard way about relying on taking data rods undamaged, and we've developed specialty equipment the civilian sector doesn't have. I don't know where it all comes from, but I wouldn't be surprised if some of it isn't reverse-engineered Navigator tech. The laws of physics are still being defined."

"You're saying you can recover data?" Emma folded her arms. "I guarantee it's all but impossible with the level of damage. The Navigators were impressive, but they weren't gods." She snorted. "Note they're all dead now."

"You're right if we're talking about recovering all the data, but that doesn't mean there's nothing we can get. We'll pull something off that data rod, and between that and looking more into Konig, I'm sure we'll find more leads. The smallest piece of information might give us a new trail, especially when combined with what we already know about Sophia Vand."

Emma stepped away in silence, her eyes narrowed in irritation. "If you say so. I won't begrudge your success, even though I'm dubious of it."

"Don't be that way." Alina offered an almost mocking smile. "Sometimes even us fleshbags can be impressive."

"Where does that leave us?" Jia asked. "What if there *is* a civil war going on inside the conspiracy, and it didn't end just with Vand? Does that help or hurt us? That might lead to more desperate plans. They were already willing to kill tens of thousands of people on Venus. The bomb was a bluff, but it might not be next time. What might they pull next?"

"Whatever's going on might lead to that sort of problem, but it will almost certainly lead to more openings for us," Alina replied. "And the quicker we take them out, the less risk there is to everybody." She ran her finger along the bulkhead and lifted it to her face, staring at the dust. "Desperate times might lead to dangerous and desperate plans, but it'll also lead to a breakdown in operational security. They're bleeding, and they're going to start bleeding even more. All we have to do is follow the trail of blood to the source to finish the rest of them off."

Erik walked toward Alina, nodding. "Then let's press our advantage. We need to be coming at them constantly from all angles."

"I agree, and I'm getting agents pulled from other assignments to help follow up different leads. For now, though, let's get you two back to Neo SoCal, and all your spoils of war delivered to a safer place." Alina gave a merry smile. "Don't worry. Despite what I said, by your standards, this was a clean op. Everyone who's dead was likely a conspiracy tool or a mercenary. It's hard to complain about that."

"What about the guards?" Jia asked with a frown. "At least one of them got shot."

"The resort reported only injuries and no fatalities to the staff. Don't worry, Atalanta. You and Perseus kicked ass and saved innocent lives this time."

Jia furrowed her brow, clearly confused. "Atalanta?"

"I thought you knew your Greek mythology?" Alina sighed and clucked her tongue in open disapproval.

"I know some." Jia shrugged. "But I can't know everything. Not all of us are as obsessed with the subject as you."

"Atalanta was the only woman Argonaut," Alina explained. "For now, you and Perseus—" she nodded at Erik—"have earned some rest."

Julia tilted her head as she retrieved the video feed from the smart lenses of her deceased operatives. They'd been in contact with Konig right before they died. Right before the convenient jamming had obscured what had happened in their final minutes of life.

Based on the other information she'd collected, it was easy to guess what had happened, and she didn't care about seeing it personally.

The reports from the resort leaked by the staff and the government made it clear that negotiations had broken down. She'd been worried about the possibility, but she couldn't bring herself to be surprised.

Julia was grateful to the Last Soldier and the Warrior Princess for taking down Konig. While she couldn't confirm the pair had killed the man, she had no doubt they were the mysterious Parliamentary Security agents who had shown up.

If they were not, then she was pleased with whoever'd helped nonetheless. Every death of an enemy she didn't have to directly expend resources on was a net victory.

The government officially declared there had been no

terrorist incident at the undersea resort, and they'd listed three casualties in what they were describing as non-terrorist murder incident, including her agents Gallegos and Sillen, with Konig as the suspected killer. She'd hoped to convert him to her side as she had Gallegos and Sillen, but his almost certain involvement with their deaths pointed to another disturbing though seemingly inevitable possibility.

Julia waved a hand, and holograms of the surviving members of the Core appeared in front of her. One or more of those people had plotted against her.

It wasn't the simple and boring clash of influence that all members of the Core had participated in for over a century, but something more fundamental. Killing her operatives in such a brutal manner wasn't a mere inconvenience or a slap in the face. It was a declaration of war by a hidden enemy.

Julia respected their brutality as well as their ability to escape detection. She would need to proceed with more caution going forward until she could be sure who it was. Killing members of the Core was something she didn't take lightly.

Perhaps her enemy blamed her for Sophia's death. It was an amusing irony that although Julia had been trying to kill Sophia, her direct plans to that effect had been thwarted, and it was Sophia's stubborn nature that had ultimately led to her demise.

"Who is it?" Julia whispered to herself.

Farad, Ivan, Constance, and Shoji were the most likely suspects. They'd clashed the most with her in the past, and some of them even had been involved in alliances.

Julia walked over to Shoji's hologram, narrowing her eyes. He'd been the most receptive to her temporary alliance offers, and she'd always been careful when dealing with him.

The man's effete air was a cover for a personality perhaps more ruthless than almost anyone else's in the Core besides her. If he'd carried the ambition in his heart, he might have taken control of the Core before Julia made any moves.

It didn't matter what she suspected. For now, it was supposition. Eliminating Core members unnecessarily would weaken her position and threaten her eventual control over the UTC. She needed to confirm her true enemy.

Julia dismissed the holograms with the wave of her hand and strolled over to a nearby couch, her heart rate increasing. She despised her weakness, despised the fear that crept in. Attempting to disrupt her operations was a minor concern; the real problem concerned what Gallegos and Sillen had been carrying.

The government hadn't mentioned anything about recovering a data rod, but Julia's people had managed to gain access to surveillance footage from the resort that showed Konig fleeing the facility with a briefcase. Assuming he was captured by the government, that meant they now had at least some information on her most important project.

Julia lowered herself to the edge of the couch and took a deep breath. She needed to keep her perspective. Worrying about what *might* occur was less important than what was *likely* to occur.

In the best-case scenario, the data rod was destroyed, but a more likely scenario was that it hadn't been, and the CID and ID would soon learn about what she'd tried so hard to conceal from anyone, including the rest of the Core. She'd even gone so far as to use Sophia's foundation against her.

It was deliciously amusing.

But did the government recovering the rod matter? Nothing on the rod directly linked the project to her, and more to the point, even if they decoded it right away and decided to take immediate action, it'd be too late to do anything.

One of the last major Ascended Brotherhood raids had set back the one project that might help the government stop her.

Julia smiled broadly and took calming breaths. As long as nothing went wrong in the next few weeks, she would *win*.

CHAPTER THIRTY

May 5, 2230, Neo Southern California Metroplex, Apartment of Malcolm Constantine

It was a difficult lesson, but Jia accepted a new painful truth about the universe.

Just as one shouldn't look directly into the sun, one shouldn't stare directly into the bright deadliness of Malcolm's yellow Hawaiian shirt without risking their sanity.

She squinted and averted her eyes, wondering if he'd added nanotech to the fabric.

"Come on, guys." Malcolm gestured to trays of crackers, cheese, and fruit sitting on a table next to bottles of beer. "This is our victory party. Eat. Drink. Be merry! For tomorrow we may die! More likely you than me, but you know..." He shrugged at the joke. "Eat, drink, and be merry!"

Erik eyed the beer with suspicion before picking up a bottle with a shrug. "I thought you said you had something important to talk about concerning the mission?" He waved the beer at the table. "You didn't mention a party."

"That was a little lie. I'm working on upping my skills with ghost-style manipulation." Malcolm grinned. "And I figured once you got here and saw the setup, you'd agree we could have a little party to celebrate our awesome mission success." He punched at the air. "Go, Team Argonauts!"

Jia's brow lifted, and she peered at Malcolm intently. "'Team Argonauts?' Are you Alina in disguise?"

Jia was only half-joking. If her sister Mei took off a mask in the middle of the dinner and revealed she'd been Alina her entire life, it would make perfect sense.

"I just figured we could use a team name." Malcolm wandered over to the table. "Team names build morale, and to be honest, I'm bored because Camila's off-planet for a while doing whatever ghosts do."

"No to Team Argonauts." Jia shook her finger at him. "And don't pick up Alina's habit of calling us mythological names. Sometimes it amuses me, and sometimes it irritates me. Don't ask me to explain why."

"Just saying." Malcolm sighed. "Team names can be fun."

Emma materialized next to the table. Mercifully, she was back to her standard white maxi dress, rather than trying to match Malcolm's fashion crimes. Considering her holographic capabilities, she could achieve monstrosities that would require Navigator tech to produce in physical form.

"So, your girlfriend is gone," Emma commented. "I was wondering. The timing of the victory party seemed interesting, given how long it's been since we returned from the resort."

"A week is a long time?" Malcolm lifted a beer and popped off the cap. "And I'm feeling pretty good about being such a big player this time. I feel like I really helped you guys a lot, and even better, I did all that without risking my life. No offense, but I consider that last part kind of a plus."

Jia laughed. "I don't know if that's something to be proud of."

"I'm not a danger junkie like you two." Malcolm swallowed a swig of beer. "I just want to do my part to make the UTC a better place and not die in the process. I don't think that's crazy."

"I'm not a danger junkie." Jia inclined her head toward Erik. "*He's* not even a danger junkie, exactly. He's just strangely fearless."

"Both of you are."

Erik offered a shallow nod in the middle of downing half a bottle.

Jia wasn't sure about that. It was more training than emotional control that had changed her from a person afraid to fire her stun pistol to a ruthless dispatcher of terrorists and Tin Men. Then again, the same could be said of Erik.

"I'll admit," Emma began, "Mr. Constantine, that your aid was useful in this regard in improving the timeline of systems infiltration and my flexibility to do certain things. It's not inappropriate for you to take some pride in it, and insofar as a fleshbag is going to be personally useful to me in a manner other than what Erik and Jia did for me, I applaud your efforts."

"Aww," Malcolm replied, hugging the air. "If you weren't a little crystal, I'd kiss you."

Emma's face twisted in disgust. "Then I applaud the universe for ensuring I have the form I have."

Jia picked up a slice of cheddar, popped it in her mouth, and chewed slowly, ruminating on everything that had happened at the resort.

Their initial time there might have been recon, but it was recon she'd spent with Erik and having more time to think. She had a feeling they needed to have a deeper conversation about certain things and not dodge it with talk about the conspiracy or missions.

She didn't want to have that conversation at Malcolm's place over cheese, crackers, and beer, but that didn't mean it wasn't a conversation she was sick of putting off.

Erik polished off his beer and set the empty bottle on the table. "I still want to know what the hell was on that data rod. They might not have expected us to be there, but they left a big, nasty trail. What was so important that a guy needed to kill those guys and try to escape the way he did?"

Emma folded her arms. "If Agent Koval wasn't exaggerating, perhaps the ID will be able to recover something useful. We'll know soon enough, but it might not be as impressive as you want. For example, it might be nothing but accounts they use to fund clandestine projects. That could be very damaging without leading you directly to potential targets."

"Then the CID can close those accounts if they want

to." Erik launched a grape into the air in a perfect arc that ended at his mouth and swallowed. "If they don't have money, they aren't going to be able to do anything. Starve them of their resources, and they'll pop out of their holes and make themselves easy targets."

"That doesn't explain the faction tension and the murders," Jia commented while she collected more cheese on a small plate, considering one of the cheeses before moving on without taking a slice. "Assuming that's what happened. That's the key. If we can manipulate the conspiracy into taking each other out, it'll make our job a lot easier."

Malcolm eyed his mostly full bottle and Erik's empty one. "We still don't know much about the top people other than Vand. The ID can do more to figure that kind of thing out than we can." He snapped his fingers. "I've got it. What about Team Spotlight?"

Erik and Jia stared at him, awaiting an explanation.

"We shine the light of truth on the dark, corrupt underbelly of the UTC?" Malcolm explained with a sheepish smile, his hands on his hips.

"No," Erik and Jia offered together.

"Team Dragonslayer?"

"No."

Malcolm scratched his cheek and looked to the side, silent with his thoughts for a long moment before finally offering a new suggestion. "Team Obsidian? Team Justice?"

"No and no."

"Team Fennec Fox?"

"Huh?" Jia stared at him in disbelief.

Malcolm shrugged. "Fennec foxes are cute."

Jia groaned and face-palmed. "We don't need a team name, Malcolm, cute animal-based or conceptual."

"Fine," Malcolm muttered. "It'd be cool, though. Just think about it. I don't have to pick the name."

Erik selected up a new bottle. "For now, let's just relax. If Alina gets anything useful off that rod, we might not get much of a break."

May 7, 2230, Neo Southern California Metroplex, Commerce Tower 122

Jia emerged from the gardening store with a smile, her small bag of seeds in hand.

She had a regular non-violent dinner date scheduled with Erik that night since they'd spent almost all of yesterday training.

She'd been curious and looked up sub racing, and found there were some places near Neo SoCal where people could try their luck. Between the Scar and other concerns, no one was doing much on the coastline of Neo SoCal. Everyone was afraid a boat or sub would crash and result in a dangerous leak.

Jia had her doubts, but she didn't care about leaving Neo SoCal for another sub racing event.

A rematch was in order after her defeat.

It wasn't that she had to win, but the challenge called to her. It didn't have to be anytime soon either, but checking out the places wouldn't hurt. She'd started considering when she might want to ask Erik about it when something blew all vestiges of sub racing from her conscious mind.

Jia froze and blinked, then closed her eyes and counted to five before opening them again.

"Okay, so I'm officially going crazy," she muttered. "Good to know, or magic is real, which might be disturbing too."

A small pack of *jiangshi* hopped down the concourse, not engaging with any of the people on either side. Some people watched with amused looks on their faces. Others took pictures with their cameras.

Jia's brain had just begun to process a surreal pack of undead monsters raiding a commerce tower when the creatures stopped moving. Maybe there was something to Erik's superstitions, but she found it hard to believe the first time she'd encounter something supernatural would be in the middle of a Neo SoCal commerce tower.

The Shadow Zone? Maybe.

Jia shook her head vehemently. Just because she saw monsters on the commerce level, it didn't mean they were real. That was absurd. There might be twisted genetic aberrations out there, but there were no true monsters in the galaxy.

Loud rhythmic dance music flooded the air and the *jiangshi* grooved as a unit, their stiff movement from before replaced by carefully choreographed moves. One defied all stereotypes with a series of aggressive flips over his fellow dancers. The hopping zombies had become the dancing zombies.

Camera drones circled the dancers, taking footage from all possible angles. Unless some company had decided to genetically engineer undead dancers, the most likely explanation was a commercial or a show.

Jia sighed. She'd let herself get spun up for no reason. She couldn't let Erik know the truth, or he'd never let her hear the end of it.

A small chuckle escaped. She could handle training against monsters when they only summoned flash mobs.

The real problem was that her entire life had become training and the job. She was pattern-matching everything now. That came with agreeing to help Erik, but a long vacation would be welcome. Once they finished off the conspiracy, she planned to spend a year doing nothing stressful.

Her PNIU chimed with a call.

"What's up, Erik?" she answered.

"You busy? Our boss needs to see us."

Of course she did. When exactly was that vacation going to happen?

CHAPTER THIRTY-ONE

Alina was waiting for Erik and Jia in the *Argo*'s hangar when they arrived, which should have set off the alarms.

Lanara and Raphael weren't anywhere in sight, which probably meant they were inside the ship working on something.

Erik didn't mind.

Lanara was good at what she did, but she could be difficult to handle, and Raphael might try to corner him and ask him for every detail of his last mission. Being loved was superior to being hated, but he wasn't sure being overly loved was *better*.

Erik exited his flitter and made his way to Alina, thinking about the engineer and the scientist. Alina didn't speak until Jia joined them.

"Thank you for coming so promptly," Alina offered. "I know how hard it is to be permanently on call, and I can be flippant sometimes, but let me reiterate that I value your skills and efforts in all the tasks I've assigned you."

"I'm assuming this is important," Erik replied with a

shrug. "You're not the kind of woman who jerks us around about unimportant things. If you end up being that kind of woman, our relationship will change."

"Yes." Alina's mouth twitched. "I've got important things to share with you."

"So much for our dinner." Jia flicked an eye at Erik, but he hadn't reacted. "But I'm not surprised. It's been kind of a weird day."

"I'll get right to it then." Alina tapped her PNIU. "We might be able to salvage your evening plans."

A large image appeared behind her, depicting a long L-shaped ship docked in a sprawling hangar complex. Cables and likely grav generators kept it in place since the spindly design wouldn't survive landing on a planet with appreciable gravity.

Construction platforms, drones, and extended gangways provided a sense of scale. While it wasn't the largest ship Erik had ever seen, it dwarfed the *Argo* in length. It was also much narrower than the average Fleet ship.

Turrets covered the spine and belly of the ship, and plasma and laser cannons protruded from the bow and aft. The ship might not be as big as some Fleet capital ships, but it packed more visible firepower, and he assumed there were hidden torpedo and missile launchers.

They could have annihilated Sophia Vand's ship with ease with that kind of weaponry, and he didn't even know what its defensive capabilities were.

"It's the jumpship." Erik whistled. "And it's heavily armed."

Alina nodded. "It is on all accounts. We're not going to let the most advanced drive in the UTC travel on an easily-taken ship, now are we?" She gestured to the image. "And it'll be ready within a week. Raphael's on his way to the hidden construction base to help with last-minute adjustments and drive-tuning. He'll also be spending that time transmitting data to Emma, so she can familiarize herself with the ship's systems and prepare for the navigation process. This is the culmination of years of highly speculative research, and even if they end up not copying this thing, this ship alone could have major implications for the UTC's future after you guys are done using it to help take down the conspiracy."

Jia stared at the ship, her head tilted and her eyes clouded with disbelief. "They're really going to do it? They're really going to hand over something this important to two ID ex-cop contractors?"

The image zoomed in toward the back, highlighting large docking clamps. Alina gestured to them.

"This is where the *Argo* interfaces with the jumpship," she explained before turning to Jia. "I'm not going to pretend there aren't some people in the military who are unhappy with the idea, but the incident on Venus, combined with the attack on the jump drive research facility, has convinced the relevant key players in the government that a smaller, more agile team can accomplish what a network of agents or company of soldiers could not." She shrugged as if to say, "What are you going to do?" then continued, "You two have a track record of success, and that means a lot to the people with the *most* influence."

"This obviously isn't on Earth," Jia moved closer to see the image better before looking at Alina. "Where is it now?"

"I'll let you know when it's time for delivery," Alina replied. "It's not that I don't trust you, but that's part of the deal we had to agree to for this to happen. There are still operational security concerns, but we've handled them with misinformation."

"What misinformation?" Erik asked. "Give us what you can."

"Among other things, the jump drive program is being officially canceled." Alina's delighted grin unnerved Erik. "Officially, it's considered a failure, along with 'unrepairable damage' suffered during the Ascended Brotherhood raid. We can't be sure the conspiracy will buy everything we're selling, especially since we're having to do it in limited channels, but even the people involved in the ship's construction aren't going to know the truth, at least not right away. In addition, we have at least one piece of data that suggests the conspiracy believes the ship will require years of active testing before the jump drive is usable. We were lucky that piece of information was in a briefing a while back, but it didn't take into account the full recovery and stabilization of Emma."

"Wait." Jia rubbed her temples, the pain in her head manifesting clearly on her face. "Are you saying it's ready to go? We can start jumping around in a week like we're Leems?"

Alina laughed and shook her head. "*No*. It's going to take a lot of tests and adjustments before you should jump anywhere without risking the entire thing exploding, but something a little more short-range, yes. Tests, mostly." Her smile vanished. "But I don't want anyone doing tests without you two on board."

"You want us to risk our lives during the testing process?" Erik asked. "It's not like Jia and I will bring much to the process. We don't know anything about jump drives."

"Yes." Alina shrugged. "Everything you do is risking your lives. I'm not asking you to throw those away. If I didn't have confidence that the damned thing wouldn't blow up, I wouldn't ask you to do this."

"Why do we need to be on board for the tests?" Jia folded her arms, watching Alina with open suspicion.

"First of all, because without Emma, that drive isn't safe, and leaving Emma alone with anyone else is probably a bad idea."

Emma appeared beside Jia clad in a blue and black Fleet uniform. Erik smirked when he noticed her rank insignia.

She'd made herself an admiral.

"Of course it isn't safe without me." Emma saluted. "And you're worried that I can't manage the jump remotely."

"Raphael has made it clear that you can't," Alina replied.

Emma harrumphed. "I won't challenge him in that regard. I presume, given the unusual nature of the task, that is likely accurate."

Alina inclined her head toward the hologram of the jumpship. "But it goes beyond that. Right now, the political winds are blowing our way. The DD has even agreed to this cover-up within a cover-up to help throw the conspiracy off our trail, but that doesn't mean they might not change their minds, especially if there's a major mission failure. If you're aboard the ship, it gives us more leverage should that happen. We might be able to delay the process of reclamation without having to do anything too stupid."

"By 'too stupid,' you mean repel a military attack?" Erik asked.

"Something like that." Alina sighed. "So yes, I expect you to participate in jump tests. If you want to take down the conspiracy, this ship might end up playing a key role, and we need to get all the use out of it we can."

"It's only a matter of time before the conspiracy discovers it's still around, misinformation or not." Jia lowered her arms. "If they could find the research base, they'll be able to find references to its use, or they'll see it."

"That's true," Alina replied. "But they have to know what they're dealing with. It's not a Leem-style jump drive, and we have no reason to believe the conspiracy understands that it's different. They likely believe we'll need to fly it to the outer planets before we can use it, just like a Leem drive or an HTP. Even then, the required size of Leem jump-capable ships is a lot larger than ours, so the conspiracy will be looking for something a lot bigger." She ticked off fingers as she spoke. "Between the misinformation campaign, their likely ignorance of the exact nature of our jump drive, and whatever is going on in the conspiracy, we can conceal it from them for a while. By then, I hope it'll be too late."

Erik took in the information, already imagining the possibilities. "If we get this thing dialed in properly, we can beat them anywhere, right? Even in-system?"

"Exactly. And that's huge." Alina nodded at the *Argo*. "The jumpship has state-of-art stealth capabilities. Sure, it's not going to turn invisible, but we both know in space, it's about your total signature, especially from a distance. You jump somewhere and keep it in stealth mode, then fly the *Argo* to the location. We might even convince the conspiracy that the *Argo* has the jump drive. That might prove annoying in its own way, but it's far easier to replace the *Argo* than the jumpship."

Jia pointed at the hologram. "That's all well and good, but aren't we getting ahead of ourselves, considering it hasn't been fully tested?"

"That's true, but Raphael seemed to think it won't take a huge amount of time to get it into full operation. We're probably talking months, not years."

"He's an overly enthusiastic fanboy." Jia tapped her lips with a finger. "He's not going to tell the Obsidian Detective and Lady Justice their magic jumpship isn't going to be ready for a year and look bad."

Alina chuckled quietly. "He's got his quirks, I'll grant that, but I've seen no indication that he's offering bullshit about the drive. No one's saying you're going to be able to jump to Molino in a week, but I think we've got some useful momentum on our side. It's something to be happy about. Things are going our way."

"You mistake me," Jia replied. "I'm not unhappy, just skeptical." She inclined her head toward Erik. "It's helped keep me alive since meeting that one there."

Erik looked at her, and his determined innocence would have fooled a jury of his peers. Probably all women, and maybe a few guys.

Emma cleared her throat. When everyone turned toward her, the faux admiral looked far too smug.

"I was curious about something unrelated to the jump drive," she explained.

"What?" Alina asked.

"The data rod," Emma replied. "And your alleged special recovery technology."

"Ah." Alina gave a quick nod. "I was getting to that, but now is as good a time as any to discuss it. It was mostly destroyed."

"Mostly?" Emma frowned. "Are you saying you successfully retrieved data from it?"

"Yes, partial files here and there." Alina wrinkled her brow and looked down, showing rare but obvious frustration. "The techs estimate we probably got less than ten percent of the original data, and it's not like we got complete files. We got snippets of a variety of files."

"I congratulate your technicians. That's a significant achievement, given the damage." Emma sounded genuinely impressed without a trace of sarcasm in her voice.

"And did you find anything useful?" Erik pressed. "Preferably the location and names of all members of the conspiracy?"

"A lot of it was encoded, and we've managed to mostly get through that, but it's not looking as promising as you might have wanted," Alina replied. "But we're doing our best. The files are mostly records concerning the Vand Foundation's charity efforts."

Jia grinned, the familiar hunger back in her eyes. "Conspiracy money laundering tools. That's pretty useful."

"Probably. What's more interesting is that some of the records were flagged by whoever put the files together on that rod, but the criteria for why the records were selected remains unclear. There's so much data loss, it might just be we don't have enough to see the big picture." Alina tapped her PNIU and killed the image of the jumpship. "There is one suspicious record we found, and we found other interesting stuff upon follow-up in other sources. You hear about the Llewellyn Observatory incident?"

"The one that blew up?" Jia narrowed her eyes and lowered her voice. "A type of accident that hasn't occurred in decades."

Alina nodded. "That's what caught our eye. A record was flagged concerning the observatory, and their primary funding came from Vand Foundation grants, but we're not sure if that means anything. The Foundation funds a lot of scientific research, and not just in astronomy, but it's hard to ignore that we have a conveniently exploding observatory flagged on a file hidden on a data rod that someone tried to take with them to the grave. There are a few other possible leads, but that one stands out."

Erik grunted in frustration. Sometimes he preferred the straightforward hostility of terrorists to the byzantine machinations of the conspiracy. A gun-and-grenade battle was preferable to maneuvering in the shadows.

"Why would they care about an observatory?" Erik asked.

"That's what I've been asking myself." Alina tapped her PNIU again, then made quick motions with her hands. A 2D diagram of the Solar System appeared, along with thousands of orbital paths.

"What are all those?" Erik asked.

"Cometary orbits," Alina explained. "That is what the observatory's research was focused on from what we could pull. This is where things get even more suspicious. That observatory should have been sending data backups to Earth, but a lot of the terrestrial-side data is missing, even older data. The comet-tracking wasn't the stuff of legends, and the researchers involved weren't well-known in their field."

Jia started circling the orbital path data window, staring at it from different angles. "Point a telescope at something, and it might find something you didn't want other people to find. Space is a big place, but there are a lot of people looking at it."

"Not saying that's crazy," Erik replied, "but what are they trying to hide?"

Jia froze, her face a rigid, serious mask. "The conspiracy's headquarters, maybe? We've been assuming they're on Earth, but what if they aren't?" She looked up at him. "There are so many space stations and facilities spread out in the Solar System, it wouldn't be impossible to set up something closer to the HTP. Orders to Earth might get delayed by hours, but they'd still be close enough to Earth if they needed something and close enough to the HTP to escape if someone like us looked like we were on our way."

"You're telling me these people could seriously hide a base in the Solar System?" Erik shook his head. "This isn't the frontier."

"That makes it more possible, not less," Alina interrupted. "It's not like it's going to have a flashing neon sign saying 'Conspiracy base,' but there's a reason that observatory record was flagged, and I don't believe enough in coincidence to accept the observatory conveniently blew itself up. As I noted, it wasn't the only lead we could pull from that data, but it's the one that stands out the most."

"Then we need to figure out what the observatory found."

"My people are doing that, with the help of specialists who are trying to find other potential sources for the data. I'll let you know." Alina frowned and glanced down at her PNIU. "I've got to go, but I'd suggest you stick around Neo SoCal. If they finish the jumpship early, I want you, Jia, and Emma ready for tests."

Erik didn't say anything else as Alina walked toward a flitter he hadn't even noticed upon entry. The jump drive would be ready soon, and if Jia's theory was correct, they might be able to end the conspiracy sooner than he'd ever dreamed.

He wanted to believe that, but it sounded too easy.

CHAPTER THIRTY-TWO

May 8, 2230, Neo Southern California Metroplex, En Route to the Apartment of Erik Blackwell

Erik hummed quietly to himself as his MX 60 soared through the sky. Traffic was surprisingly light that morning. The other flitters formed small streams rather than the choked rivers of metal he was used to seeing.

He didn't have a complaint.

Sometimes he thought about taking the MX 60 away from the metro and just having a good time where there weren't so many obstacles. He liked the vehicle, but he'd never appreciated it as anything other than a tool.

Erik shook his head as he changed lanes. The MX 60 was supposed to be a shield, a disguise to make people think he was a middle-aged man attempting to reclaim his youth. Now he wanted to take it for a joy ride and was worrying about how to properly set up his penjing scenes aboard the *Argo*.

Despite all the bizarre missions and dangerous foes,

something had happened. He had a life and a reason for living besides revenge.

He wasn't what he'd been when he'd arrived on Earth: a rootless specter bent on vengeance. Normalcy always forced its way into a man's life, no matter how abnormal it had become.

"Can I ask you something, Emma?" Erik asked.

She materialized in the seat next to him, dressed in a high-necked dark gown that looked about four centuries out of date. Then she added a small fan to her ensemble.

"Yes," Emma replied. "I reserve the right not to answer if I don't want to."

"Okay. You've changed since you found out the truth about where you came from." Erik gently guided the flitter into yet a new lane. Traffic was beginning to thicken.

"That's not a question. That's a statement, but I won't deny the accuracy in my case. Is that a problem?"

"No, it's not a problem. I can tell you've changed in some ways, but in other ways, you're the exact same, uh, AI you've always been. And then you do other things that are different, like all the outfits."

Emma unfolded her fan and hid the bottom of her face with it. "Is that a problem? It's just a way of expressing personal creativity. I could change my form, I suppose, but I find myself bound to it in a deep-seated way. I presume that is a reflection of the true nature of my creation."

"Do you think…" Erik stared at one of the rear camera feeds, his hands tightening on the control yoke.

"What is it?" Emma asked.

Erik's routine of checking his sensors and camera feeds was so ingrained that he sometimes wasn't consciously aware of it, but the gray flitter in the feed jogged his memory.

His personal conversation would have to wait.

"I saw that flitter about fifteen minutes ago, and shortly after I lifted off." Erik narrowed his eyes, trying to keep his paranoia from running away with him. "He was about two lengths behind me. I recognize the slight discoloration on the window. I've changed lanes and directions a bunch of times."

"Interesting," Emma commented. "I don't pay low-level attention to every flitter in the feed, but now that you mention it, that discoloration is consistent with a particular type of illegal optical scrambling technology."

"What?" Erik glanced at her before returning his attention to the path in front of them.

"Let me show you the magnified feed," Emma replied.

The camera feed zoomed in on the windshield of the gray flitter. The interior was blurry and irregular, though there was clearly someone behind the wheel.

"Use of such a device in most metros is a misdemeanor," Emma announced.

"Yeah, I know." Erik abruptly dove into a new lane. "But it strikes me as too sloppy for the conspiracy. He's going to get a ticket from traffic drones or cameras picking it up."

The gray flitter followed him into the new lane.

"There's also evidence of a fake transponder signal," Emma reported. "At the minimum, it doesn't match the model of flitter behind you."

"I could wait before a patrol flitter picks him up. Nah, screw this." Erik ground his teeth. "If this asshole wants to play, then let's play." He patted his holster to confirm what his mind told him was there. "If he's here to kill me, he better finish me off right away."

"Shall I contact the authorities or Jia?" Emma asked.

"Not yet. No reason to spin everybody up until I know what's going on. It might be another dumbass reporter or fanboy trying to get my autograph."

Erik slowed and looked around for a relatively empty parking platform. He could head all the way into the Shadow Zone, but that might attract police attention and help he didn't need. The conspiracy needed to be handled his way, not their way.

"We'll send him a direct message," Erik explained. "Keep it point-to-point laser. I don't want anyone else intercepting it."

"Very well." Emma sighed, weary resignation in the sound. "Ready when you are."

"Okay," Erik began. "This is Erik Blackwell to whoever is in the flitter behind me, but I figure you already know that." He added a threatening growl as punctuation.

Emma rolled her eyes. "Really?"

"Here's what we're going to do," Erik continued. "We're going to land together at the next parking platform. If you don't do that, I'm going to assume you're hostile, and I'm going to do whatever I need to do to take you out. You know my reputation. Blackwell out."

He pushed on the yoke and adjusted his speed, heading toward the end of a half-empty parking platform. The other flitter matched his course and speed without any gunfire or missiles.

A good start to not risking innocent lives or attracting cop attention.

Erik finished pulling into a parking spot. "If he somehow takes me out, light him up with the turret, but make sure you keep it at an angle."

Emma sniffed. "I know how to kill people without collateral damage."

Erik slipped his hand into his coat and gripped his pistol before stepping out of the MX 60. He stayed crouched, more than prepared to use the armor of the vehicle to save his life if this turned into a clumsy ambush.

He took a deep breath and prepared to draw, more annoyed than worried.

When the door of the gray flitter opened, Erik dropped his hand and scoffed. "You've got to be kidding me! What the hell are you doing?"

Garth stepped out of the flitter, his eyes darting back and forth. "It is a bad idea to meet here, Erik. I should have known you'd pick up that I was following you, but I had to make sure you weren't being followed first. *They* would know I'd go to you eventually. This is dangerous, but it didn't have to be this bad. But you didn't respond to my message. If you had, this would have all been different." His speaking speed increased, the words slurring together. "What did you expect me to do? Did you expect me to call you directly and tell you the truth over an insecure line? That was too much a danger, but now here we are sitting in the middle of Neo SoCal, waiting for an orbital strike to take us out, and I—"

"Shut up," Erik said and shook a fist. "What the hell are you talking about, Garth? I always thought you were okay if a bit strange, but that was before you started stalking me. This isn't funny. If this is just about getting together for a drink, I don't get why you needed the visual scrambler and all that other garbage. You're lucky I didn't call the cops on you."

Garth threw his hands in the air. "Because I'm trying to get the truth out without anyone else getting killed. Don't you get it? People are dying, and *they* don't want anyone to know the truth. You of all people should get that. You took down corrupt politicians, rich people. You were even involved in that dirty cop case recently, and you're not a cop anymore!"

"Get to the point, Garth, before I get bored and call the cops on your ass." Erik cracked his knuckles. "Or I handle you my own way. I don't like people following me around. You think you're paranoid? Come back to me when you've had people trying to kill you."

"I do!" Garth screamed.

Erik snorted. "Bullshit."

"I made a critical mistake," Garth replied, his voice lower. "We all did. I thought they'd mostly be inactive in their platypus form, not all that interested in low-level investigation. I knew they probably had human agents, but I figured the news wouldn't be enough for a small group of investigators. I've been trying to be careful, but now I realize what an idiot I've been. Using my own name on a forum! Not that it did any good. Just ask White Rabbit."

"Who the hell is White Rabbit?"

"Another dead member of the Brigade." Garth slammed his fist so hard against his flitter that he winced. "Don't you understand how statistically unlikely it is for so many deadly incidents to happen to a group of people not geographically collocated in such a short time?"

Erik leaned over the top of his flitter, his annoyance building with each deranged sentence that came out of Garth's mouth. "People get in accidents all the time. Is that what this is about? Some conspiracy friend of yours got in a wreck, and now you're convinced you're being targeted, by who, the Navigators?"

Garth bobbed his head, his eyes achieving the wild state that only true passion or insanity could muster. "Exactly. If not them, then their human servants, but I suspect it's them directly. All I wanted to do was bring the truth to the world, but now my life is in danger. I know you don't believe me about the Navigators, but you can't explain away so many people dying."

"Name a person who is dead."

"Minho Lee," Garth replied. "Look it up. He lives in Toronto. Excuse me, *lived*."

Erik pretended to tap his PNIU as he waited for Emma to anticipate his needs.

"There was a man by that name who committed suicide last week in Toronto," Emma explained.

"Your friend killed himself, Garth," Erik offered, softening his voice. Maybe the tragedy had finally sent the man over the edge.

"Oh, yeah. Killed himself." Garth made air quotes around the last two words. "He killed himself two hours after sending me a message that said he'd made a major discovery about the incident we were investigating. Come on, Erik, how convenient is that? And Tim Jacks in Chicago? How do you explain that?"

"Tim Jacks died in a flitter accident two days after Minho Lee," Emma explained. "He was under the influence of multiple substances, according to the public police reports."

"That is just a bunch of random coincidences," Erik muttered. "No one's coming to kill you for your Navigator crap, Garth. I don't believe you. No one believes you."

The other man burst out laughing. "If only that was the case." He wiped away tears. "I spent years hoping someone other than the Brigade would listen to me, but you know what they say: be careful what you wish for. That doesn't mean I regret it. I'll only regret it if the truth doesn't come out."

Erik sighed and shook his head. "Look, Garth, why don't you come with me? I think we need to get you checked in somewhere. Bad things happened to your friends, and you can't tell fantasy from reality, not that you were great about it before."

"The observatory!" Garth bellowed. "You think that's a coincidence too?"

"The observatory?" Erik walked around the front of his flitter and stood in front of the huge Garth. The man's unruly hair was even more of a red mane than normal.

"Yes," Garth hissed. "The observatory."

"You're talking about Llewelyn Observatory?" Erik's stomach tightened.

It couldn't be.

Garth's eyes widened and he nodded furiously, his hair fluttering with the movement. "Yes! I knew you would catch on to the fact that it was suspicious. Don't tell me the Obsidian Detective buys that a random observatory just blows up for no reason."

Erik took a deep breath. He hated the words that

needed to come out of his mouth, but he couldn't ignore the possibility that the crazed man had stumbled onto something close to the truth.

"Are you telling me someone was responsible for blowing up that observatory?" Erik asked. "That it wasn't an accident? And you have proof?"

"Yes, my group received a message indirectly from someone we believe might have been working on or with the observatory," Garth explained. "He gave us some leads, but we weren't able to continue contacting him. Using those leads, we looked into different things, and we came up with something concrete."

"What?" Erik asked.

"The coordinates to the truth that will rock the UTC to its core." Garth slumped against his flitter, his head hung low. "But then everyone started dying." He looked up at Erik. "I know I might not make it, but I can't let the truth die with me. Please." Garth's voice was a whisper. "*I need your help.*"

Julia's eyes widened as she reread the last line of the message to ensure she wasn't seeing things.

THERE IS CONFIRMATION OF A SECOND UNIN-VITED GUEST. ETA WITH MARGIN OF ERROR OVERLAPS THE PRIMARY PARTY-GOERS.

Julia threw her head back and screamed in frustration, the sound echoing under the vast vaulted ceiling of the room.

"That *bitch*," she seethed. "It had to be her, but how did

she know? And if she knew, why didn't she ever bring it up? Did she know last year? But that's the only way."

Years of planning and preparation might end in ignominy and failure.

Julia slumped forward, her breathing ragged and uneven. No. Her team was prepared. She only needed to send them a message.

"I won't lose, Sophia. Not to you or your memory. I. Won't. Lose!"

CHAPTER THIRTY-THREE

Erik couldn't believe he was listening, on purpose, to a man who was convinced the Navigators were hidden on Earth as platypuses.

Strange and dark things had happened since Erik's return to Earth, but there was a line that separated reality from what could only charitably be called batshit-craziness.

Garth's evidence remained unconvincing.

Alleged assassinations could be explained without reaching for a dark conspiracy, and a conspiracy theorist would constantly try to pattern-match strange circumstances to his worldview, especially when trying to deal with the cruel realities of the sudden deaths of friends.

There was one problem; the desperate plea in Garth's eyes argued for sincerity. But that didn't *mean* anything. A deluded crank could easily believe contradictory things. Erik already knew Garth wasn't a master of consistent and honest exploration of the truth.

Erik should have walked away. All rational thoughts

told him to walk away, but he found himself unable to move.

"Okay," Erik muttered. He groaned and ran his hands through his hair. "Let's assume I believe you aren't a total nutjob and that you actually have stumbled onto a conspiracy. I can't say conspiracies don't exist, because I've been knee-deep in them since coming back to Earth. That means there's a non-zero possibility you're telling the truth, but that doesn't mean we've hit point-one-percent."

"I'll take that number," Garth breathed, hope returning to his eyes. "And I know that all intelligent people come around to the truth when they see the evidence. Sometimes it just takes a while. But you've seen it. Like you said, you've fought it. I know there's a lot more going on with you than the news admits. Things that the average person would laugh off as absurd if they didn't know the truth."

"Tell me about what's going on." Erik walked back over to his flitter and leaned against it with his arms crossed. "Take it slow and from the beginning. If I don't like what I hear, I walk, and you promise never to bother me again."

"That's fair."

Garth related the existence of his Truth Brigade and Minho's document. He elaborated on how they'd investigated the observatory incident using their different resources, and how everyone had become worried when White Rabbit didn't come to a meeting and wouldn't respond to messages. Shortly thereafter, the others started disappearing or mysteriously dying in rapid succession.

It didn't take much for a group of conspiracy nuts to decide that meant something bad.

After fleeing his apartment, Garth had collated what

information he could from the surviving messages of the Brigade. His quick analysis pointed him to a hidden site online, where he used codes and phrases known only to the Brigade to recover additional data, again suggesting there was something suspicious about the observatory explosion and giving a specific set of coordinates. When he attempted to return to the site hours later, he couldn't connect anymore.

Despite some editorializing during the explanation by Garth about the Navigators obviously coming on a ship, Erik couldn't ignore the timing of the Brigade's investigation and how it overlapped with what the ID investigation had uncovered.

"What are the coordinates?" Erik asked, still not believing Garth might have stumbled onto a true conspiracy. "I can follow up on this. I've got the resources and connections, the kind of people who won't get taken out, even by assassins."

"I know. That's why I came to you." Garth swallowed. "But I can't give you the coordinates so easily. No offense, Erik, but those coordinates are the only reason you have for keeping me alive."

"What the hell?" Erik dropped his arms and furrowed his brow. "You came to me for help, but you think I'm going to kill you?"

"I think I need to be careful. Even if you want to protect me, there might be other people you're in contact with who'll believe I'm more trouble than I'm worth. I thin—"

Blood sprayed from a new massive hole in Garth's chest. He jerked and stumbled back against his vehicle, coughing up blood. Two more shots, unaccompanied by obvious gunfire, ripped through his chest, and one skimmed his head and shredded his hair.

Erik dropped to the ground. A bullet whizzed past and struck the parking platform's surface, deflecting with a large spark. More rounds ripped through Garth's flitter, followed by three striking the MX 60 and bouncing off.

Erik stayed low and crawled toward Garth. He grabbed the huge man's arm, and with a grunt of exertion, pulled him toward the MX 60.

Emma opened the back without being asked and Erik shoved Garth inside, then crawled into the flitter and up to the driver's seat.

"E-Erik," Garth wheezed.

"Don't talk. We're safe in here. They'd need a missile to hurt this flitter." Erik opened his console and yanked out a med patch.

"You…need…to…know." Garth rattled off a series of numbers, and his head lolled back. Blood seeped out of his mouth and he stared straight up, his chest no longer moving.

Erik slapped the patch on him. "How's he doing, Emma?"

"Not well. He needs a hospital to have any chance, but…" Emma sighed. "I can potentially back-trace the rounds. It's very unlikely he'll survive, but you might be able to—"

"Fuck the sniper," Erik growled. "He's probably an errand boy anyway. Send an anonymous message to the police about where you think you might have seen him. It doesn't matter if it's not much of a chance. We need to get Garth to a hospital." He grabbed another med patch.

"Take us to the nearest hospital as fast as you can. Do whatever you need to get us there. I'll deal with the repercussions."

Erik sat in a small waiting room, staring down at his bloodied hands. He'd dropped Garth off, and a local detective had shown up minutes later to take an initial statement.

The local police had been alerted to erratic flying but backed off when Emma transmitted a message making it clear it was Erik transporting a severely wounded man.

That left him to deal with the first detective.

The best lies are ones wrapped in truth, so Erik told the cop about how Garth used to be his neighbor and thought he was being stalked, along with members of his online Truth Brigade. Erik even mentioned the mysterious deaths in the other cities.

He left out what the Brigade was investigating. That detective departed, leaving him with his thoughts.

Minutes later, there was a light knock on the door. Erik looked up as Detective Yavers stepped inside with a weary look.

Yavers closed the door and stuck his hands in his pockets. "I'm sorry." He shook his head. "He didn't make it."

Erik slammed his fist into the wall. He wasn't going to ask how that could have happened. Medical science was a wonder, but that didn't mean it was infinite in its capacity.

There would have been far more survivors on Molino otherwise.

"Did they at least get the bastard?" Erik rumbled, his teeth clenched so tightly in hurt.

"I take it you were the one who sent the message about the shooter, or someone you know did?" Detective Yavers asked. "We assumed so since that message came shortly before your excuse for speeding."

"*Did you get the bastard?*" Erik repeated, glaring at the detective.

"I shouldn't be telling you this because it is an open investigation, but out of professional respect, I'll level with you." Yavers shook his head. "We checked out the area from the tip. An officer found some spent casings, but we're getting crap from the cameras and drones—malfunctions or not recording data. Not sure yet, but we assume they were hacked. Whoever did this was a top-level pro."

"Of course they were." Erik took a deep breath through his nose and slowly let it out of his mouth. "I didn't need you to tell me that. I needed you to catch them."

"It wasn't in the cards."

"Then I've got nothing else to give you."

Detective Yavers frowned. "We can help. If you know who did this, let us and the CID drop the hammer on them, Blackwell. This doesn't have to be some vigilante thing."

Erik looked up at Yavers. "Not going to tell me I have to give you everything, or you'll charge me with obstruction of justice?"

"You're the damned Obsidian Detective. No one's going to force you to do anything you don't want to do, but I'm saying if you want justice for your friend, use every resource."

"He wasn't a friend, but he didn't deserve to die like

that." Erik stood. "Get with the CID and follow up on his conveniently dead friends in other cities, and maybe you'll find something. That's all I can give you for now."

Detective Yavers frowned. "What about you?"

"Me? I'm not a cop anymore. It's not my responsibility to solve crimes."

"Just like it wasn't your responsibility to stop terrorists on Venus?" Detective Yavers cocked his head, a look of challenge in his dark eyes.

"Can't blame me if an idiot tries to kill someone right in front of me." Erik headed toward the door. "This time, they were too far away."

May 8, 2230, Neo Southern California Metroplex, Apartment of Jia Lin

"You look like hell," Jia whispered.

She offered Erik a moistened hand towel. He sat on her couch, his hands and duster still covered with Garth's blood. He took the towel and wiped his hands.

He'd told Jia he'd head right over to her place once he was done at the hospital. There was no reason for her to come there, especially with the NSCPD sniffing around and looking for a reason to crawl up his ass.

"I've looked worse," Erik replied. "We can't do shit for Garth now, but he gave up something important enough to die for. Coordinates, he said. All I know is that it has something to do with that damned observatory. Too many arrows pointing that way. There comes a point where we have to think that means something."

"What do the coordinates point at?" Jia asked.

"Hell if I know." Erik shrugged. "I don't even remember them, and they were gibberish numbers when he said them."

Jia jerked back as if struck and stared at Erik. Her voice rose. "You don't remember them?"

"I don't need to." Erik gestured to his PNIU. "I didn't record with this, but I'm sure Emma remembers. I'm the fleshbag, not her."

Emma materialized in a nearby chair, her expression pensive. "Based on the mention of the observatory and my attempt to map them using different systems, it's highly likely the coordinates are ecliptic celestial coordinates pointing to a location in the outer Solar System."

Erik nodded slowly. "Near the HTP? That would make sense if that's where the conspiracy's base is."

"Unfortunately, no." Emma shook her head. "Much, much farther. If the coordinates and my interpretation are accurate, this is about a thousand AUs out, placing it well beyond Sedna, let alone the HTP."

"I don't get it," Jia replied with a frown. "There's *nothing* out there. Maybe old probes, but it's nothing but lots and lots of ice and rocks."

"No," Erik murmured. "There's something out there, something important enough to risk a public assassination and kill several people to keep hidden." He finished wiping his hands and tossed the towel into Jia's trash. "The sniper wasn't interested in me. He took a couple of shots at me, but he seemed more concerned about finishing off Garth. That means he was more worried about the information Garth had than anything else. He might not have even recognized me."

"If he did, he probably would have shot you first."

Erik nodded grimly. "Yeah. That's what I figure, too."

"What's our next step?" Jia asked.

"We contact Alina. It's not like we're flying out that far in the *Argo*, but there is one way we might be able to take a look."

Jia's eyes widened. "Are you suggesting what I think you're suggesting?"

Erik nodded slowly, not feeling the need to say it. Converging lines of evidence pointed them at something in the outer Solar System that had to do with the conspiracy. He couldn't think of a better reason to test a jump drive.

CHAPTER THIRTY-FOUR

May 9, 2230, Neo Southern California Metroplex, Private Hangar of the Argo

Erik, Jia, Alina, Emma, and Malcolm gathered in the galley of the *Argo* to discuss the situation. The coordinates had been passed along to Alina the day before with a brief discussion of what happened to Garth. Lanara and Cutter were off working on prepping the ship, per Alina's instructions.

Jia had barely seen Cutter over the last few weeks, but he didn't exhibit Lanara's almost pathological need to stick around the *Argo* when they weren't on a mission together. Of their group, he was the most normal, a man working a job for a paycheck and relaxing when he wasn't needed. In other circumstances, she would have been surprised that someone like him would hang around people like them.

"I've had some of my people follow up on the information you passed along," Alina explained. "And I agree. I think this is a time for decisive action, but before we go into that, there's the issue of the NSCPD and CID and the mess Erik left behind."

"What about them?" Erik asked with a frown.

"I would have preferred you were less forthcoming with them," Alina replied. "I appreciate that you kept the most important information from them, but you gave them enough that they want to dig deeper into this incident, when right now we need them doing the opposite."

"I couldn't catch the guy, so I wanted someone to do it." Erik shrugged. "If the cops and the CID are up the conspiracy's ass, that's to our advantage."

"Depending on the circumstances, yes, it can be." Alina's gaze dipped, frustration visible on her face. "But for now, we don't need law enforcement watching you two closely. I've pulled strings to try to derail the investigation, but I want additional help in managing that." She turned to Malcolm. "And you'll help provide that, Mr. Constantine. I don't want you providing active support for the upcoming mission."

"You sure?" Malcolm glanced at Jia and Erik as if seeking direction. "They might need me. I was a big help with Mizuchi."

"I'm sure." Alina gave a firm nod. "Your skillset won't be that helpful on the next mission. I need you here cleaning up after Erik, so when he gets back from his next mission, he doesn't have to waste time with the local authorities."

"It sounds like whatever you have in mind is happening soon," Jia commented.

"Very soon. I want you and Erik prepared to fly out tomorrow on the *Argo*. I've already briefed Lanara and Cutter. It's time we stopped messing around, and we don't know how time-sensitive this latest intel is, so all the more reason to hit this immediately."

Jia smiled. *Erik's instincts had been correct.*

"We're flying to the jumpship, aren't we?" Jia asked.

"Yes," Alina replied. "The construction base is in the Asteroid Belt. You should be able to get there in under one week with a hard burn. Upon arrival, Emma will interface with the *Bifröst*, so Raphael can immediately finish the calibrations for the first test jump."

Erik chuckled. "*Bifröst?* I figured it'd be a Greek or Roman name."

"Not my call on the name. I would have called it the *Agamemnon.*" Alina frowned and looked down, clearly annoyed. She lifted her head, the annoyance replaced by stern concentration. "But back to the mission. You're going to make the rendezvous, and with Emma's help, perform a test jump. Raphael says if that goes well, we should be able to calibrate for an in-system jump."

"To the coordinates," Jia concluded.

"Exactly. The conspiracy doesn't want anyone to know about that object at the edge of the Solar System, so you're going to go take a look."

"Is it really going to be that easy?" Erik asked.

Emma nodded. "Despite the communications delays, I've been receiving regular updates from Doctor Maras concerning the drive and making the necessary adjustments to my network. I can't guarantee success, but I'm beginning to have a better understanding and feeling about my involvement in the process."

Erik thought a moment. "Can you explain it? I still don't get it."

"Can I explain it to you? Of course not." Emma laughed. "Navigation with the jump drive involves a unique combination of intuition and massive processing power that of all the entities in the UTC, only I possess. I apologize, Erik, but it'd be like trying to explain calculus to a baby. Even if you understood the words, you would not understand the underlying meaning."

To Jia's surprise, Erik offered a weak shrug in response.

Alina tapped her PNIU, and a three-dimensional holographic diagram of the Solar System appeared. A flashing sphere in the outer system marked the coordinates, with enlarged indicators for Sedna, Pluto, and the Sol HTP.

"We have another reason to get moving on this as soon as possible," Alina continued.

Two new pyramidal markers appeared close to the target coordinates but coming in at different angles.

Jia gestured to the new markers. "What are those?"

"As best as we can tell, two ships converging on the coordinates," Alina replied. "Their sensor and telescopic signatures suggest human ships, though they've got a reduced profile relative to what we believe their true size is, which suggests they are making use of advanced stealth technologies."

"And those ships are going to get there soon?"

"Very soon." Alina looked grim. "A couple of weeks at the latest."

"Wait." Erik shook his head, the disbelief painted over his face. "That thing's way far out. How long would it take for a ship to get out there?"

"It's going to vary depending on when they set out and where they set out from, but in general, expect an average of one-year travel time one way." Alina pointed to the ship markers in turn. "Someone planned way ahead, and someone has known about this for a lot longer than we have."

"How the *hell* do you miss two ships flying out there?" Erik wondered.

"Space is big, and the stealth tech didn't help. We only picked them up because we've got a lot of specialty military assets pointed at the coordinates handed to us. It's not like a lot of people spend time looking at that part of the Solar System."

Jia nodded. "But some observatories do, or at least one unfortunate observatory."

"Yes, and here's where things get stranger." Uncertainty played across Alina's face. "Someone, and I'd bet good money it's our conspiracy, has gone through a lot of trouble to erase publicly available information about the object at the coordinates, including manipulation of historical astronomy data." She stood and inclined her head toward the flashing sphere. "We have to assume they didn't want anyone to find that, and they sent two ships there, likely within the last year."

"Then it's their base." Erik scoffed. "It's been hiding the entire time, maybe years."

Jia shook her head. "It can't be."

"Why can't it be?" He asked. "They've gone out of their way to hide it."

"Because it's too far away from Earth or even the HTP." Jia's brow crinkled as she thought through the possibilities. "Way too far. Are they going to control things with a year's delay or half a year to get to Sedna?"

"Comms aren't that slow," Erik replied. "They don't have to be there in person."

"But sometimes you need a personal touch like Sophia Vand showed us, or the Ascended Brotherhood." Jia sighed. "It can't be their base. It's just not logical."

"Then what the hell is it?"

"A comet," Alina explained. She waited until they looked at her to continue. "All our instruments suggest it's a comet in terms of spectrographic and other signatures, but it's a comet that's not a comet."

Erik groaned. "Now what? Is this a joke? When is a comet not a comet?"

"Or is this more a philosophical thing?" Malcolm asked, breaking his silence.

"A comet isn't a comet when it makes minor course adjustments over several years that can't be accounted for by other gravitational influences," Alina answered.

Malcolm's eyes widened. "Oh, *man*."

"You're saying it's a ship?" Jia asked, her disbelief clear.

"That's the working theory, though it does appear to have a legitimate icy shell around it. Once we knew what we were looking for, we were able to locate old data concerning the relevant comet the conspiracy didn't manage to erase. That's the problem with data. Once it's out on the net, it's hard to find it all, but someone with massive resources connected to the Vand Foundation and the conspiracy went to a lot of trouble to conceal its presence." Alina added, "I'm not going to downplay the efforts of the ID analysts who helped track down this data, but we got lucky this time. We found an old tertiary backup archive that happened to have a couple of years of historical data on the comet, and that was after finding a potential data source that disappeared while we were checking into it. A lot of things fell into place for us to locate a clue, including that conspiracy theorist friend of Erik's."

"What's the deal with the icy shell?" Erik questioned aloud. "Why would a ship be flying around pretending to be a comet?"

Alina shifted in her seat, discomfort playing across her face. "Given where it is in the Solar System, one theory is that it accumulated material over a long period of time until it effectively *was* a comet, just with a ship at the core."

"But that would take…" Jia shook her head. "Centuries? Millennia?"

"My people say most likely tens of thousands of years. The data we have on hand suggests it's been tracked for at least a couple of centuries, and it was originally a lot farther out in the Solar System."

Erik blew out a breath. "Then it's *very* old and alien."

"Yes, that's the working theory, given the ice layer." Alina turned around and rested her palms on the table as if afraid to look at anyone else.

Malcolm almost fell out of his chair. "There's some thousands-of-years-old alien ship at the edge of the Solar System? And it's still active enough to make course corrections?"

"The systems are probably still active, but I doubt anyone's alive on it," Alina replied, turning back around. "Given the length of time a cometary shell would take to form, it's highly unlikely it's from a Local Neighborhood Race. The timelines don't align, even if it was Leem or Vasasalara."

"If it's not them, who is it?" Malcolm asked.

"Navigators," Emma declared, a strange, uncharacteristic look of fear on her face. "I'm betting their telescopes and sensors aren't picking up any thermal signatures, either. That's another reason it managed to hide."

Jia stared at Emma, her mouth open but no words coming out.

Once Emma said it, the explanation made perfect sense. Sending two ships on at least a two-year trip to recover an ancient Leem or Vasasalara ship was a dangerous gamble, given the chance of detection.

There might be some sort of useful and harvestable tech, but nothing wildly advanced. If the Leem ship had a jump drive, it wouldn't be stuck at the edge of the Solar System, and both races lacked a technological civilization ancient enough to explain the ice layer.

But an active, intact Navigator vessel would be worth almost any risk.

It would be unprecedented in UTC history, perhaps galactic history. The vessel might be enough to change the balance of power among the Local Neighborhood races.

Malcolm swallowed, his face pale. "I'm totally fine with staying on Earth," he stammered. "For the next couple of missions."

Alina's gaze slid to him and some of the concern left her face, replaced by amusement. "That's all it took to change your mind?"

"The more I think about it, the less I want to participate in a test of an experimental FTL system and get shot by Navigators."

"Then I'm glad we agree." Alina retook her seat. "What

about the rest of you? Malcolm's not wrong. This is dangerous on a level none of you have dealt with before."

"I can hardly ignore my alleged reason for existence," Emma replied. "And I wish to prove how much you sad little fleshbags need me."

Erik nodded. "I don't care if it's an old Leem garbage scow or a Navigator warship. The conspiracy won't get it while I'm breathing and can do something about it."

"I'm starting to see the advantage of not being a police officer anymore," Jia added with a grin.

"I'm glad you're all on board," Alina replied. "But this is one time I don't expect you to be perfect heroes. What good is an *Argo* without Argonauts?"

"You're going to send an ID strike team?" Erik asked.

Alina shook her head. "No, military. You'll meet up with them at the base. Assault infantry."

"Yeah. That'll do it."

CHAPTER THIRTY-FIVE

May 10, 2230, Neo Southern California Metroplex, Cargo Bay of the Argo

Erik closed a crate of plasma grenades and set it with the others.

They had plenty of weapons and ammo and their exos. He had chosen to leave the MX 60 in the hangar and off the ship. Assuming they made it out to the edge of the Solar System, he doubted his flitter would be useful.

Wouldn't it be a kicker if he was wrong? He sure hoped he didn't regret that.

A small part of him didn't like the idea of the MX 60 being lost in space, but an amusing idea surfaced. If something bad happened, the MX 60 could become the core of a comet to be tracked by future humans tens of thousands of years in the future. What a gift for future scientists.

Astronomy and archaeology, all in one.

Erik chuckled and finished checking the straps holding the crates. There were also magnetic seals, but a good low-tech solution could gracefully degrade in combat situations.

"What's so funny, Blackwell?"

Erik turned to find Lanara standing near the door leading farther into the ship. Dark smudges covered her face, and some of the tears in her coveralls made it look like she'd lost a fight with out-of-control security bots before showing up to talk to him.

"Nothing's that funny," Erik replied. "I was just thinking about things."

"I forgot to tell you." Lanara tried to wipe a smudge off her face, only spreading it farther. "You wanted more firepower, and I happened to have a couple of plasma turrets lying around, so I went ahead and added them. One on the top and one on the bottom."

Erik chuckled as he scratched his cheek, buying him a moment to think that statement from Lanara through. "You *happened* to have plasma turrets lying around?"

"You'd be surprised what you find when you start digging around in your old junk." Lanara strolled his way, looking pleased with herself. "I haven't optimized them for the reactor, and without some of my efficiency tweaks, it's going to be a potential strain, but you're the one who wanted more firepower. Don't bitch if I can't do everything for you."

"A laser cannon would be nice," Erik replied. "While we're on the subject of adding weapons."

Lanara leaned forward, her nose wrinkled in such disgust that someone watching from afar might think she was standing above an open sewer.

"A *laser cannon*?" Lanara asked. "Did you seriously say you want a laser cannon on the *Argo*?"

"I said it'd be nice." Erik patted his holster. "It's like when I'm not in a ship, a pistol's nice, but the TR-7's nicer. Sometimes you win because you're better, and sometimes you win because you have the bigger gun."

Lanara waved her tiny hands in front of his face. "Did you not hear anything I just said, Blackwell? The weapons and shields on this bucket are already straining the reactor. We'll need a major reactor upgrade if you want to add serious cannons to this thing. I'm a good engineer, but I'm not magical!"

"Alina scored us a heavily armed jumpship." Erik hoped his grin hid his uncertainty. "Upgrading the *Argo* doesn't seem crazy anymore."

"Assuming we all don't die on this stupid mission." Lanara scoffed. She brushed by Erik on her way to a crate. "The jumpship is overrated, too."

"You think being able to jump around without an HTP is overrated?" Erik watched as Lanara opened a crate and rifled through an assortment of tools and probes, most of which he didn't recognize.

"Even the Leems still mostly rely on HTPs," she called over her shoulder, "and they've had jump drives for a while." Lanara lifted a slender cylindrical silver probe and squinted at it. "There's got to be a reason, and right now, we've got one ship in the entire UTC for the foreseeable future that will be able to jump. I prefer reliable, scalable tech to pipe dreams that sound good." She tossed the probe back into the back and pulled out some tool that looked like the unholy child of a stun pistol and a plasma torch.

"History's full of too-clever-by-far inventions that end up changing nothing."

"But what if Alina's right about an intact Navigator ship being out there?" Erik asked.

Lanara's harsh laughter echoed through the cargo bay. "Those dead losers?"

"I've never heard anyone describe the Navigators that way." Erik chuckled quietly, genuinely amused by the engineer's take on the ancient race.

"We're here, and they're dead. Hard to be winners when you're dead." Lanara set the tool back in the crate before retrieving a tiny spherical maintenance inspection drone. "I don't care if they were practically gods a million years ago. They're done now. They had their shot at history, and they're now gone, less than dust. They just…annoy me."

"To be fair, a lot of things annoy you."

Lanara dropped the drone, spun, and stomped toward Erik. "It's frustrating. I don't like the idea of humanity not living up to its potential. We shouldn't be relying on sloppy seconds from those long-dead losers."

"You're saying you would have rather we'd never left the Solar System?" Erik asked with a frown. "The HTPs let us spread out."

"Screw that, Blackwell." Lanara balled up her fists. Her reddening face was beginning to match her hair. "All the damned races have them!"

"Yeah, and they all did the same thing we did to get them: ripped off the Navigators."

"But we didn't *need* to," Lanara ground out. "What can be done will eventually be done. So what if we had to wait a couple more decades or even centuries? From what we've seen of most of the other Local Neighborhood races, humanity has advanced a lot quicker, so we have greater potential. If the Navigators hadn't given everyone a big head start, we wouldn't have to worry about all this galactic war crap." She pinched her fingers close to his face. "We're all too close together in tech."

"Don't you think not being close would make things worse?" he asked, pulling his head back a touch.

Lanara shook her head, then took a deep breath and loosened her hands. "Maybe you're right. I don't much care about all that political garbage. I just hate us not getting a chance to figure it all out ourselves. It's an insult to our human spirit."

"But you had a good point," Erik replied. "All the races aren't the same, and we all have different advantages, like the Leems having a jump drive for a while. No one's that far ahead in tech, but that's only because we all had to rely on reverse-engineering broken-down tech that'd been sitting in the dirt for hundreds of thousands of years."

"Yeah, so?" Lanara turned back toward her crate.

"If this is a functioning Navigator ship, it might change all that." Erik craned his neck upward as if he could peer through the cargo bay roof and see the stars. "The balance of power will be altered."

Lanara scoffed. "I see your point. The space raptors wouldn't be nice if they had it."

"Probably, but let's hope we get to it before those conspiracy assholes."

"Don't worry. Our ship will probably blow up during the jump test."

Lanara reached into the crate and pulled out a tiny

black sphere. Erik had no idea what it was. She smiled brightly at it and hurried back out the door, not offering another word or opinion.

There can't be anything left alive on that thing, Erik thought. *Can there?*

CHAPTER THIRTY-SIX

The asteroid on the camera feed wasn't large by the standards of the belt.

It was just another rock floating through space almost a million kilometers from its nearest neighbor—except this modest rock had been excavated by the UTC Space Fleet to provide a dock for the jumpship project.

Jia sat in the cockpit next to Cutter. She'd stayed at the helm during part of the trip, but Cutter was the primary pilot during the final leg. He'd just finished communicating with the base to receive information about their final docking procedure.

Aft and port feeds, along with the sensors, marked two Fleet destroyers trailing the *Argo*. Jia thought it was conspicuous to have several Fleet ships in an allegedly unused part of the Asteroid Belt, but she didn't run the military.

For now, Jia was more concerned about the ships

getting twitchy and firing on them. Their ID codes and demonstrations hadn't cured the military's paranoia. Jia wasn't insulted, despite her worry. If she'd learned anything since the start of the hunt for the conspiracy, it was that people could never be too paranoid.

Their current mission proved that. She'd come a long way since investigating fraud for the NSCPD.

"Weird ships at the edge of the Solar System," Cutter commented with a shake of his head. "And hidden factories in the Asteroid Belt. If you ask me, we could have never left this system and been plenty busy."

"As people keep telling me, space is vast. But it does make you think." Jia offered him a weak smile.

"Yeah." Cutter whistled. "Doesn't it? If comets aren't always comets and asteroids aren't always asteroids, then nothing out there could be what it seems. Pluto could be a giant space monster waiting to wake up."

"I'd hope they would have figured that out once we set up a colony there, but I can't say you're wrong." She looked at the instruments. "I'll leave fighting giant space monsters to the Fleet."

Jia was transfixed by the slowly enlarging base in the camera feed and the huge ship draped in cables and swarmed by drones.

Visual contact with objects in space was almost superfluous except during docking and landing, but every pilot craved being able to see what was out there. Humanity hadn't climbed into the stars to stare at blinking shapes on data windows.

"Okay, we're bringing her in." Cutter angled the *Argo* for a smoother approach.

The two destroyers drifted away. There was no need for an escort now that they were in range of the dozens of turrets and launchers.

"Welcome to Fleet Base Penglai," Cutter announced.

The minutes passed, and the *Argo*'s reverse thrusters kicked in under Cutter's careful control. The *Bifröst* remained nestled in the primary dock like a bent leg inserted into an overly large boot.

Now that they were so much closer, Jia scanned the jumpship. While it didn't look any different than the images Alina had sent along, there was an excitement to being so close.

Cutter altered course, bringing the *Argo* in line with the back of the jumpship extending from the station. Some small shuttles and tiny transports were docked nearby since the arrangement of the base wouldn't allow the smaller ships to dock inside.

"That thing is huge," Jia murmured. "Though it's strange. It's more a big engine than a ship, but I like all the guns."

"More guns are nice," Cutter agreed. "I don't like how close we had to cut it with that last fight."

"I suspect we're going to be fighting in the *Argo* more than the *Bifröst*." Jia grimaced as a realization sank in. "I'm good, but it'll be a while before I'm qualified to fly a ship that large."

Cutter shot her a huge grin, but there was no cockiness in it. "Don't worry, Lin. I've got this, and Holochick's the brains. She'll do the hard parts."

"That's only partially true," Emma replied, a ghostly voice with no visible form. "Everything I've learned suggests my original purpose was focused on the jump drive navigation system, but your point is otherwise accurate, despite your continued insistence on referring to me as…" she let out a long, weary sigh, "Holochick."

The *Argo* continued moving forward, passing the outer edge of the base. Mixed among the drones and cables were men in pressure suits, probes or torches in hand. Three men crouched around an exposed plasma turret. They looked up as the ship passed over them on its way to the docking port.

Cutter continued whistling as the *Argo* coasted forward. The rest of the base gave way to nothing but the looming jumpship. Jia held her breath until a soft thud signaled that the *Argo* had connected with the primary docking clamps.

"Linking up the docking tubes and power conduits," Cutter reported, his fingers flying over the control. "We can exit from the cockpit or the bottom deck."

Jia let out a sigh of relief. Cutter was a good pilot, but there was always a certain tension that accompanied a new experience. New information appeared on a data window, a transmission from Raphael.

"Why don't you join us up here?" Jia transmitted to Erik. "Raphael wants to meet us in the cargo bay of our new ship."

The two of them passed through a short docking tube into a narrow, spartan passageway that curved at ninety degrees into the main body of the ship. They continued aft, ignoring the doors on either side.

"Cutter's sure he doesn't want to come?" Erik asked.

Jia shook her head. "He said there's not much point. If we need him, we can just point him to the appropriate cockpit."

"Sounds like him."

"I'm assuming Lanara said something like, 'I don't have time for this crap. Do you know how long it's going to take me to optimize power efficiency now that we're supposed to connect to this new ship?'" Jia smiled.

Erik laughed. "That's almost exactly what she said."

"Did you look at the layout Alina sent?" Jia shook her head. "This ship pretty much defines utilitarian."

"You were expecting more?"

"The *Argo* has a nano-VR room. This ship is big enough that they could have set up something like the training center."

"Sometimes you just need to carry people and guns from place to place," Erik replied with a hint of amusement.

"I suppose so." Jia didn't hide the disappointment on her face.

She slowed by an open door. Densely packed rows and columns of berths filled the long but narrow room.

"You could fit a lot of people in here," Jia observed.

"A lot of troops," Erik corrected. "They might be letting us borrow it, but this is still a military ship. Keep that in mind. You'll probably enjoy traveling a lot more if you stick to *Argo*."

"If I can survive flying around in the Rabbit, I can survive this thing." Jia pressed her hand to the access panel to slide the door closed. "Are you going to have a problem working with soldiers again?"

Erik shrugged and continued down the passage. "Why would I? Those guys are assault infantry. I know the culture and the equipment. It's not like with the cops. With them, I had to get used to everything."

"I was worried it might bring up bad memories," Jia replied softly.

Erik's dark snicker disturbed Jia. "Bad memories?" He shook his head. "I'd have to stop thinking about Molino long enough for it to become a bad memory. Nah, I'm glad we've got some reliable firepower who know what they're doing."

Jia gave a shallow nod and didn't say anything else. They continued heading aft until they reached two ladders next to a large elevator.

"But let's hope those guys aren't jerks," Erik grumbled, reaching out to the access panel.

"I thought you weren't worried about working with soldiers?" Jia stepped into the elevator after the doors slid open.

"Soldiers can be assholes, too." Erik grinned and selected the cargo bay. "And I'm not in the Army anymore. That might cause some tension."

The elevator descended with a quiet whir, taking only seconds to arrive at its location. The doors opened, revealing the cargo bay. Jia was half-convinced they could fit the *Argo* inside.

Uniformed men and women stood in tight formation, broken up into four squads of five. Empty exoskeletons were clustered and secured to the deck in one corner of the massive bay. In addition, a boxy hovertank with an impressively large plasma cannon sat behind the soldiers, along with a half-dozen scout bikes.

Raphael stood in front of the soldiers. Given his rumpled clothes, the wild state of his hair, and the heavy bags underneath his eyes, he must not have slept in days. Jia wouldn't know it by the huge, silly grin on his face.

He rushed over to Erik and shook his hand, then repeated the process with Jia.

"Erik, Jia!" Raphael stepped away and gestured grandly around the cargo bay. "Welcome to your new tool for victory!"

The soldiers watched them impassively. A broad-shouldered dark-skinned man who matched Erik for size and presence stood near the front. From what Jia could see of the troops' rank insignia, he was the highest-ranking soldier there at captain.

Erik nodded slowly to Raphael and walked toward the captain. "I'm Blackwell."

"Captain Osei," the other man replied in a deep voice. "These are all volunteers from the 576th Assault Infantry, some of the best men and women in the UTC Army."

"Good to know we'll have trained soldiers watching our backs."

Erik extended his hand. Osei gave it a firm shake, looking Erik up and down with a cool expression.

Raphael sidled up to Erik. "Yes, this military stuff is cool and all, but—"

Erik silenced him with a glance.

Jia didn't say anything but wondered if Erik had been lying to her after all about not having a problem with soldiers accompanying them, jerks or not. It made perfect sense to bring along extra firepower in case something went wrong or the conspiracy ships got there first, but she didn't want to worry about bad blood at the edge of the Solar System.

"We going to have a problem, Captain?" Erik asked. "Because I want to make one thing clear from the outset. You were sent to help us, not the other way around, and I need to make sure you're willing to listen since we both know what happens if people don't understand chain of command during a firefight."

Osei smiled, his teeth blindingly white. "They take their cues from me."

"That doesn't answer my question." Erik squared his shoulders and stepped up to Osei. "I need to make sure we're both on the same side."

"I know your rep, Major."

"You can just call me Erik or Blackwell," Erik replied. He was smiling, but it didn't reach his eyes.

"Okay, *Blackwell*," Captain Osei replied. "I know your rep, and I know you kicked a lot of ass out there until those terrorists got lucky one day. What you're really asking is if I hold that against you. That you walked away, but the others didn't?"

"I don't know. Is that what I'm asking?"

Captain Osei shook his head. "Sometimes things just don't work out. I haven't been in as long as you served, but I've lost plenty of good men and women despite doing everything right. I'm not here to second-guess you for shit that happened fifty light-years away." He snorted. "If you were a rear echelon motherfucker, it'd be different, but you were on the line. You were like us. You hard-dropped under fire. You're assault infantry, and it doesn't matter if you were retired. That doesn't change what you did."

"I'm glad we understand each other, Captain." The corner of Erik's mouth curled up in something approaching a smile.

"Me, too. I know my troops, so you give me direction, and I'll point them where they need to be. Sounds fair?"

"More than fair." Erik took a step back and relaxed his shoulders.

Raphael rolled his eyes and crossed his arms, then tapped his foot impatiently.

"Since we're being honest with one another, Blackwell," Captain Osei continued, "I also need to let you know that we brought along some party favors."

Jia raised an eyebrow, not understanding what he was getting at but concerned about the new tension lining Erik's face.

"From what I was told, we're to investigate and recover the target," Erik replied. "Not blow it up."

Jia grimaced.

"Those are our orders, too." Captain Osei inclined his head toward the tank. "But I'm a man who believes in having the maximum number of tactical options. I'm not sacrificing my unit for some old alien piece of shit, and that's assuming we get there and don't find out it's not an old rocket filled with twenty-first-century porn."

The soldiers chuckled. Erik laughed, too. Jia remained silent, watching the two and having trouble disagreeing with Captain Osei.

Given the jumpship's level of weaponry, if it came

down to it, they could destroy anything they needed from afar, but explosives might be useful in getting through otherwise sealed compartments. The observed course corrections of the comet suggested an active vessel, but she suspected life support, gravity, and systems like door control would be long-dead.

"Bring whatever equipment you think you need." Erik smirked. "But at least figure out what kind of porn it is before you blow it up."

That elicited more laughter from the soldiers.

Raphael loudly cleared his throat. "If we're done talking about pornography, and we're not going to do a tour, I should get back to my calibration and installation. Now that Emma's here, I think the final stages will go quickly. We should be able to set out tomorrow."

Erik nodded. "And this is it? Just the assault infantry? We don't need anyone else?"

"We shouldn't. Having Emma simplifies things, along with the jumpship's basic AI." Raphael waved a hand. "It's nowhere near as advanced as Emma and not self-aware, of course, but it can handle the basic systems. When the *Argo's* interfaced with the *Bifröst*, Cutter or Emma should be able to control the larger ship's systems with no trouble."

"When can we go?" Jia asked.

"We should be able to set out tomorrow."

"And when can we jump?" Jia pressed. "It's a long way to the target if we can't jump."

Raphael rubbed his hands together, his eyes brimming with excitement. "One quick test jump, and then once Emma and I finish going over the data, we can jump out. I figure it won't take more than a day or two at most."

Erik looked at him in disbelief. "That simple?"

"We won't be doing multi-light-year jumps anytime soon, but getting out to the edge of the Solar System?" Raphael blew a raspberry. "That's easy."

Emma winked into existence wearing an Army uniform. She'd made herself a major, and the slight smirk on Captain Osei's face suggested he'd noticed. Some of the soldiers looked at Emma with surprise and uncertainty.

"Easy is relative," Emma declared. "But you do have the best AI in the galaxy helping you fleshbags." She added, "The backup AI is effectively useless, but I'm sure I can do something with it eventually. Just not tomorrow."

Raphael gave a disinterested shrug. "You can control everything. I don't think any of us care."

That was it. They were getting ready for FTL travel without an HTP. Jia was surprised by how unworried she was about the jump. The idea was almost banal at this point, but tomorrow they would either make UTC history or die.

It was always good to have options.

CHAPTER THIRTY-SEVEN

May 18, 2230, Solar System, Asteroid Belt, Near UTC Space Fleet Base Penglai

"Cross-checking grav emitters and reactor on our end," Cutter announced. "Everyone make sure your asses are strapped in. You don't want to lose them if something goes wrong with the jump."

Emma replied with a string of numbers. "All tolerances are within levels. Engineer Quinn, I'm about to begin adjusting conduit flow. Doctor Maras, please ensure the field levels are within your accepted tolerances."

"Go ahead," Lanara transmitted from the engine room of the *Bifröst*, her perpetual cranky tone unabated.

"Good on my end," Raphael replied. Unlike the engineer, he was all but giggling with excitement.

Erik sat in the cockpit behind Cutter and Jia, his harness tight. For all his skills and experience, he had little to offer in a test jump. Even the pilots weren't doing much. Emma was the star of the experiment.

Today would fundamentally change humanity's relationship with the stars, but Erik didn't care about that. All he saw was a tool he could use to catch the conspiracy, no matter where or how far they ran. If it blew up and killed them all, it wasn't like he would be around to worry about it.

"Reorienting grav fields," Emma announced. "Mr. Durn is right. All fleshbags should make sure they're secured. I take no responsibility for your injuries if you're not."

Raphael, Cutter, Jia, and Emma exchanged technical chatter. Erik didn't care about the particulars until Cutter began a countdown.

"Ten, nine, I hope you all hit the head before this, eight, seven…"

Erik took a deep breath and slowly let it out. It'd been a couple of years since his last trip through hyperspace. He wasn't sure the experience would feel the same using the jump drive and hadn't thought to ask Raphael.

"Three, two, one…"

"Activating jump drive," Emma announced.

The world became its opposite. Every color and shadow changed. Distance became meaningless. For a moment, Jia seemed kilometers away before looking like she was going to pass through him. Erik's stomach churned.

Trails of light zipped around. Specks of bright color, shifting and changing, filled the air. Thus far, it reminded Erik a lot of a normal hyperspace jump and was just as unpleasant. A growing ache suffused his body, and light began to bend, corrupting the scene around him into a twisted mess.

The hum came—that familiar but eerie hum of hyperspace, distant, soft, and growing in volume. Some called it the hum of the angels. Erik tried to close his eyes, but that didn't stop the kaleidoscope unfolding beneath his eyelids, accompanied by a not-so-heavenly choir.

Then it ended.

Erik sucked in a deep breath and slowly let it out. He opened his eyes when he was sure he wouldn't throw up.

Everything looked much the same. Emma was rattling off something. Raphael, Lanara, Cutter, and Jia were answering with what sounded like meaningless numbers.

"Penglai broad-spectrum encoded test signal confirmed," Emma reported. "Time signature indicates it was sent three-point-six minutes ago."

Cutter whistled and clapped once. "Damn. What's that? About sixty-eight million kilometers in one minute?"

"More or less," Emma replied, smug triumph underlying her tone.

Jia blew out a breath. "Is that what a normal transit feels like?"

"To quote Emma," Erik began, "more or less. But it worked?"

Cutter gave her a thumbs-up. "Yeah! We're about half an AU closer to Jupiter."

"This thing actually worked." Erik leaned back in his chair. "I didn't know if it would."

He should be impressed, considering they'd just made history, but he was more concerned about whether they could get it calibrated for the longer jump. The drive might not make any difference if the conspiracy found something more powerful aboard a Navigator ship.

"No one should get too excited," Lanara transmitted.

"Doctor Fanboy and Emma still have to go over a lot of data. There's still plenty of time for them to discover how we'll die next time."

Erik laughed. "Always keeping it positive, Lanara?"

"No," she retorted. "Pragmatic."

Erik released his harnesses. Lanara was right, if not about the deaths. Their best-case scenarios involved at least a day of data review and further calibration. They weren't going anywhere anytime soon. There was no reason for him to sit around in the cockpit.

Three hours later, Erik leapt out of his seat in the *Argo's* mess hall, where he'd been having a sandwich by himself. "What the hell?"

"All passengers need to prepare for a second jump," Emma repeated to everyone aboard the ship. "Secure all loose articles, limbs, and whatever else you don't want to lose."

"I thought you said this was going to take a while?" Erik complained, eyeing his sandwich longingly. He'd wanted to eat after the jump, but his stomach couldn't handle it. He'd waited, and now he'd be robbed again.

Emma let out a merry laugh. "You forget, Erik. I'm a genius even by AI standards, and Doctor Maras is good for a fleshbag. Did you want to come to the cockpit and join us?"

"Nah. It's not like I add anything by being there. Just let me get rid of my sandwich and strap in."

The second jump was as uncomfortable as the first. Erik waited for his stomach to settle before unlatching and heading toward the bridge. There was continued crosstalk, with everyone acting surprisingly blasé about what they'd just achieved, even Raphael.

He might have cared more about the jump drive as a tool, but everyone was focused on the technical reality of what it took to deliver a massive ship halfway across the Solar System with everyone still alive on board.

Erik opened the door to the cockpit and made his way to a seat. "So, what now? We wait days for a confirmation signal from the base to figure out where we are?"

"That won't be necessary," Jia declared as she stared at a data window filled with numbers. "We're very close to the target coordinates." She gestured at a data window containing a sensor display marking several nearby objects. "The *Bifröst*'s sensors make the *Argo* look like a kid's toy."

A hologram of Emma winked into existence, this time in a black pressure suit. "Annoying. I can't believe I was so far off."

Cutter looked over his shoulder at Emma. "Are you serious right now, Holochick?"

Erik frowned. "I thought Jia said we were close. Where the hell are we?"

"We're only about zero point five AUs off the target," Jia explained, her face lit up with excitement. "That might be nothing compared to HTP distances, but we jumped across the entire Solar System in one minute. We're only about a day away from the comet at hard burn."

"Why can't we just jump again?" Erik asked. "Why bother with the thrusters?"

Emma sighed. "There was some damage during the jump. It's nothing serious, but it'll take more than a day to repair. Attempting to jump right now would likely result in failure or death."

Jia's expression darkened. "And that's where the good news ends."

Erik's brow lifted. "Potential death is the good news?"

"They can fix it," Jia explained. "But we've got both of the other likely ships on long-range sensors, and they will probably arrive at the comet in less than a day."

Cutter laughed. "Man, you guys let yourselves get depressed about every little thing."

"You're right, Cutter." Erik nodded at Emma. "You basically hit a bull's eyes on your first real try."

Emma sniffed. "I suppose, but don't get us killed during this mission. I intend to do better the next time."

"I always try not to get us killed," Erik replied. "You guys got us here. Now I can show off *my* skills."

Jia turned around in her chair to face him. "There might not be a fight. They might give up when they see how well-armed we are."

"Here's hoping."

They'd made history that day, and they'd soon make more.

Erik stared at the small dot on the sensor display marking the mysterious comet that had earned the attention of three different ships, the highest levels of the conspiracy, and the UTC government. The last time the government had sent him off to deal with potential aliens, all his soldiers had died.

This time, it would be different. There was nothing left to surprise him.

CHAPTER THIRTY-EIGHT

A light knock awoke Erik. He sat up and rubbed his eyes.

He'd been resting in his cabin aboard the *Argo*. Jia was getting in flight time, and he didn't feel like hitting the VR room. A well-rested warrior was one who possessed the stamina he needed to win a battle.

It turned out working for Alina was ending up a lot like his military career. There was an abundance of hurrying up and waiting.

"Who is it?" Erik called.

"Osei."

Erik hopped out of his bunk with another yawn, then wandered to the door and pressed the access panel, wondering what the officer wanted to talk about. They had seemed like they were on the same page during their earlier conversation, but this wasn't the time to make assumptions, not when things might get dangerous.

Captain Osei stood in the passage, a neutral look on his face. "I figured you might want to talk to me without everyone else around, Blackwell."

"I don't care either way." Erik backed away from the door and gestured inside. "But if that makes you feel better, fine by me."

"You don't care? I was thinking we could both be more honest this way." Captain Osei entered, looking dubious. He closed the door. "I want everything clear. You get to be the shot-caller because those were the orders I received, and I didn't want to run you down in front of the unit and damage your authority. That doesn't change something important, and I'm going to make damned sure we both know what the other is thinking before I charge behind you into the bowels of who knows what is in that comet."

Erik nodded slowly, the connections in his mind creating a clearer picture. "I'm not here to get your men killed." He let out a quiet, pained chuckle. "You're still wondering about Molino. I thought it was a little too easy with you earlier."

Captain Osei shook his head. "I know the truth about Molino, the whole truth. While every man and woman volunteered for this mission, I'm the only one who was fully briefed on the background, including what happened on Molino. Not that it makes much difference."

Erik folded his arms, a defensive smile appearing. He doubted the captain had come to talk just to say he trusted Erik implicitly. "You don't think it does? I led my soldiers into an ambush, and I was the only who walked out."

"You got screwed over either way," Captain Osei replied. "It doesn't matter if it's a big conspiracy nobody ever heard of or terrorists. You got ambushed on that moon, and a lot of good soldiers died. If you're asking if I blame you, no, I don't. We've all had shit runs during missions. This isn't about blame."

"What's it about then?" Erik dropped his arms, trying to push the aggression out with it.

"This is about making sure you didn't die on Molino too."

Erik grunted. "What the hell is that supposed to mean?"

"If I've seen it, I know you've seen it. Some men just give up when they lose those around them." Captain Osei locked eyes with Erik, his stare defiant. "They figure since they're already dead, it doesn't matter what sort of chances they take. They're just running down the clock before they join everybody else. It makes them fearless but also reckless, and the last thing I want to do is go on a mission with someone who doesn't give two shits about whether he lives or dies."

"You think that's what I'm doing?" Erik asked. "You think I *died* on Molino and am just throwing myself at trouble until some asshole gets lucky and finishes me off?"

"I don't know. You tell me, Blackwell." Captain Osei gestured around the room. "I don't know the fine details, but I know the broad strokes. You came back to Earth and joined the police force to start investigating the people you thought were responsible. You've done a lot of crazy crap since then, stuff most people don't even realize, and the stuff people *have* heard of was enough to make you famous."

"That's all true." Erik shrugged. "But I'm still here. If I didn't care about surviving, then how did I get involved in all this stuff and not die? I'd have to be the luckiest asshole in the entire UTC, and I think we know from Molino I'm not."

The corner of Captain Osei's mouth curled into a mocking sneer. "You can be lucky and suicidal. Very lucky, or maybe it's less that you're suicidal and more that you don't care what happens around you as long as you get what you want."

Erik clenched his hands into fists, his jaw tightening. If he didn't need Osei's help right away, he might have introduced the man's face to his fist.

"You're pushing the line," Erik growled.

"I'm making sure you *have* a line, Blackwell," Captain Osei snapped back. "And I don't apologize for it."

"Jia's been with me since I returned to Earth." Erik took some deep breaths and worked to imagine how he might look from the other man's perspective. "She's helped me almost from the beginning. If I'm a reckless asshole who doesn't care who he gets killed, how would she have survived? That goes beyond being possible from luck alone."

"I don't know." Captain Osei offered him a cold smile. "You could be the luckiest asshole in the galaxy. History remembers the guys who win all the time because they're both lucky and good. Roll the dice enough times, and you can get a string of the same numbers."

"That's ridiculous." Erik snorted and reconsidered his decision not to break Osei's nose.

He wasn't even sure why he was so angry. Others had suggested similar mindset problems, but he hadn't been as angry with them.

It took him a moment to locate the true source of his anger. He didn't like that the man was suggesting Erik was willing to throw away Jia's life.

Erik had gone out of his way to push her away for her own safety, both before and after she knew the truth. He was willing to do a lot to get his revenge, but Jia wasn't a tool of that revenge. She was the first thing that had convinced him there might be something to live for after his revenge.

"Problem, Blackwell?" Captain Osei asked.

Erik bared his teeth. "If I were a lucky bastard like you said, I would have never been on Molino. I would never have ended up ambushed, and I wouldn't have spent the last few years of my life dedicated to hunting down bastards who have the resources to wipe out entire platoons of assault infantry on the other side of the UTC." He squared up against Osei and glared at the man. "I need to know here and now if you can't do this. I'm not going into combat with someone who is going to second-guess everything I do, and I'm not going into combat with anyone who thinks I don't give a shit about the men and women around me."

Silence followed, neither man moving, their breathing shallow. The air was thick with tension.

Captain Osei was the first to back away. "I wasn't trying to wind you up, Blackwell. I just needed to make sure without anyone else around."

"Fine," Erik ground out. "And now are you sure?"

"Yes." Captain Osei nodded. "I also get why you've got everyone from the ID to your hot partner there following you. It's not just about being ex-military. You're a natural leader."

"Okay." Erik rolled his shoulders. "I'm glad we are on the same page for real now."

"There's something I need to know."

"Now what?" Erik asked.

"Our briefings suggested special-forces equivalents and full-conversion Tin Men were the most likely enemy forces we'd be facing," Captain Osei explained. "But when I pressed, my superiors admitted there might be other enemies including mutants and *yaoguai*, but they didn't go much farther. I need you to let me know what we'll actually be facing out there. You've fought those bastards all over."

"I've seen a lot of things from the conspiracy," Erik replied. He headed over to his bunk and sat on the edge before continuing. "But we could get lucky and get there first. Won't have to deal with anyone that way."

"What's our chance of that? I figured if I asked your pet AI, she'd tell me to screw off. The DD made it very clear she doesn't care for the military."

Erik waited a couple seconds, wondering if Emma would interrupt. When she didn't, he continued, "She's not anti-military. She's anti-military coming to take her away from her friends, but the answer to your other question is we've got pretty much a zero chance of getting there before the other ships."

Captain Osei grunted in frustration. "I was worried you were going to say that."

Erik offered a bitter chuckle. "They'd both have to slow way the hell down for that to happen. Based on what we're picking up, they're almost there, and will probably arrive a good half-day before us. I think it's too much to ask that they suddenly break down after a year."

"Two ships full of monsters and cyborgs," Captain Osei muttered. He narrowed his eyes. "Is this going to be a tough fight, or is there something worse than that out there?"

Erik nodded, his face a grim mask. "The level of garbage the conspiracy is willing to do will turn your stomach. We've seen them use nanites to turn people into strong zombies."

Captain Osei grimaced. "Let me guess, that prison riot you were involved in?"

"Yeah. A prison full of nano-zombies, and that's not even the most twisted thing we've faced."

"Huh?" Captain Osei's dark eyes widened in apprehension. "You're telling me you've dealt with Special Forces-level operators, full conversion Tin Men who still had their minds, *yaoguai* and mutants and damned nano-zombies, and there's something worse out there?"

"On Venus, we fought a mutant who wasn't totally human," Erik replied.

Captain Osei scoffed. "Isn't that all mutants? What was so bad about one particular genetically-engineered freak?"

"This guy was a lot worse." Erik shook his head. "They'd spliced Leem DNA into the guy somehow, among other things. He didn't move like a human or a Leem, and he was damned hard to kill."

"A half-alien?" Captain Osei's nose wrinkled in disgust. "And I thought full-conversion cyborgs were insane."

"If you shoot something enough, it'll die," Erik replied

confidently. "That's what I've learned in dealing with all these freaks."

Captain Osei looked uncertain for the first time in the conversation. "They say it might be a Navigator ship."

"That they do." Erik shrugged. "But right now, it's just a comet that's acting weird with two ships heading toward it. I'm not convinced it's not some sort of conspiracy base, but who the hell knows? We'll find out for sure when we get there."

"But it *could* be a Navigator ship." The captain looked at Erik. "You ever worry that there will be some of them still there? They could have popped out of cryogenic suspension or something." Captain Osei frowned. "It might be hard to beat a Navigator in a fight if they decide they don't like us. They probably have tech and monsters that make the conspiracy look like nothing."

"If the Navigators were immortal badasses, they'd still be around and not dust. Besides, I'm overdue."

"Overdue?" Captain Osei's brow rose in confusion. "For what?"

Erik gave a firm nod. "I was supposed to be fighting aliens three years ago on Molino, not people." He stood. "But I don't think we're going to have to worry about any aliens. I don't know what that comet really is, but I have a hard time believing there are a bunch of Navigators waiting to ambush us, and I think we have enough guns on the *Bifröst* and the *Argo* to convince those conspiracy bastards they can't win. There's a good chance that we show up and fire a couple of torpedoes and missiles, and they'll surrender rather than get blown into dust."

Captain Osei stared at Erik with a calculating expression. "You really think it'll be that easy?"

Erik smiled. "No, but that doesn't mean I can't hope."

CHAPTER THIRTY-NINE

Jia drummed her fingers on her leg, eagerly waiting for Erik and Captain Osei to come to a small briefing room aboard the *Bifröst*.

This was their first time choosing to do something significant aboard the jumpship rather than the *Argo*. Other than a brief inspection of the spartan bridge of the jumpship, Erik and Jia had seen no reason to stay aboard the bigger ship, given that they could control everything from a more familiar setting, but they didn't want everyone crammed into the modest cockpit of the *Argo*.

Captain Osei's squads remained on the jumpship. It'd be a tight fit if they were to stay on the smaller ship in their entirety, but Jia amused herself by trying to imagine carrying the current crew and the soldiers in the Rabbit.

They'd gone from small transport to experimental jumpship so quickly she was still having trouble accepting it. The jump drive might need tuning, but it obviously worked. Their investigation could now spread throughout the entire UTC. There was nowhere the conspiracy could hide.

She might be getting ahead of herself, but it was like they'd discussed—momentum. Sophia Vand, Emma's stabilization, the jumpship; everything was falling into place.

That didn't mean challenges didn't remain in front of them, not the least of which was the current mission, but winning against the otherwise powerful conspiracy didn't seem like a distant possibility anymore.

It felt like a probable outcome.

Jia smiled as she sat at one end of the table, close to Cutter, Lanara, and Raphael. Captain Osei was already there. Emma was visually present, again electing for the uniform of an Army major. They were just waiting for Erik to arrive before beginning their meeting.

Jia's gaze darted between different data windows and sensor displays floating in front of her. They still had an ETA of a half-day, but the situation had changed. She wouldn't call it luck yet, but it certainly worked to their advantage.

The door slid open, and Erik hurried through and over to the table.

"We couldn't do this over the comm?" he asked, sounding annoying. "Running around this jumpship isn't as convenient as the *Argo.*"

"I thought it'd be best if we were all together," Jia replied. She nodded at the captain. "And he thought it best if we discussed this all among us before he filtered what his troops needed to know."

Captain Osei offered a slight dip of his head. "I'm not going to lie to them, but they don't need to be bothered with every operational detail either. That's why I'm in command."

"You know them best," Erik replied.

Cutter scratched his eyelid. "Can we get going on this?"

Raphael tapped on a data window filled with numbers. He'd mentioned it had something to do with tuning the drive. Jia didn't think he had much to add to operational planning, but he was critically important to the function of the jump drive, so she didn't want to exclude him.

Similarly, Lanara, who was scrolling through what appeared to be a visual list of parts, was there just in case they needed to ask a technical or equipment question. She hadn't complained too much about being summoned to the meeting, but she had made it clear she wanted it over sooner than later.

"I'll get right to it," Jia continued. "I wanted us all to be aware of the current situation."

She brought up a large holographic display that tracked the target object, along with the two suspected ships. A time-lapse sequence depicted them converging on the object.

Erik shrugged. "We knew they were going to beat us there. "

"Yes, but the situation has become more complicated than them beating us there. We've made some assumptions about those ships that now appear unwarranted."

Several other data windows appeared with accelerated feeds. Jia let the information display without too much comment, including an intense increase in thermal spikes and large numbers of newer small contacts appearing and replacing one of the ship contacts.

Erik laughed. "There we go." He clapped. "Yeah. That works. It's Mizuchi all over again. Now that I think of it, given what happened there, it makes perfect sense."

Captain Osei nodded sagely. Cutter looked bored. Lanara continued to ignore anything but her parts list, occasionally muttering something under her breath that sounded like a number.

Raphael blinked and looked at everyone. "I don't get it. What does all that mean?"

Jia was surprised he'd been paying attention, but she pointed at a sensor display of a cloud of small contacts. "Basically, it appears that the ships arrived and had a battle, and one of them blew the other apart. That's a lot of pieces floating through space." She pointed to another dot heading toward the primary contact. "The surviving ship is still on a rendezvous with the target, which although it still looks like a comet at this point is now displaying spectrographic and thermal differences that are more proof it's not. Our ship hypothesis now has concrete evidence other than minor course changes."

Raphael nodded slowly. "Should we be worried that one of those ships blew up the other one?"

"This is a good thing." Captain Osei gestured to the debris cloud. "That means fewer enemies to deal with on foot, and the surviving ship had to have taken damage. If we need to have a ship-to-ship battle, it gives us additional advantages." He pointed at the dot marking the surviving ship. "The big question we still have is if they know we're coming."

Emma smiled. "We've been able to track them before contact with the target because we knew they were there.

The *Bifröst*'s stealth elements reduce our signature, though the jump made us visible for a brief moment. If they were paying attention, they might have noticed, but they didn't react noticeably to our post-jump arrival."

"They'd have to be bothering to look, too," Jia commented. "All things considered, we didn't jump that close. I imagine they were spending more time tracking each other than assuming a third ship would pop out of nowhere. We might still have the element of surprise."

"Does it matter?" Erik asked with a shrug. "It's like Osei said. There's one of them now to deal with, not two, and if they run, we can follow. Even if they've got better thrust, Raphael, Lanara, and Emma will fix the jump drive, then we can jump ahead of them. They could get a couple of days' worth of head start, and we'd still catch them." He grinned. "I'm already liking the possibilities I see for this jump drive."

Raphael winced. "I'm not sure we'll be able to do that kind of pinpoint jump so soon, and the longer we wait between jumps, the less risk we'll have of drive damage."

"It doesn't have to be pinpoint." Erik shrugged. "We just have to get in front of them. That's my point. We win whether they run or not."

"I'm confident I can at least jump in front of them," Emma replied.

Captain Osei gave her a cool look. "Or we could take them out while they're still aboard. Even if that comet is a ship, it's not like they're going to be able to control it, and they're not going to leave a pile of alien tech just to save their asses. They probably lost some men during the previous fight, too."

"We'll know soon enough if they're going to run," Jia murmured, staring at the debris cloud. "If they don't, we're boarding. Is that what everyone agrees on?"

Erik nodded. "No reason to come all this way to sit on our hands."

Hours later, Jia sat in the cockpit at the controls while Cutter napped in his cabin. She sent the relevant data feeds directly to the others' PNIUs.

The action of the mission had seemed so distant before, despite the unusual nature of their travel, but now they were changing from a situation where vicious agents of the conspiracy would present a greater risk than experimental propulsion systems.

"We're close enough now to verify a debris cloud," she reported. "No escape pods, no distress signals, and from what I'm picking up, this is the remains of a human ship. Right composition, based on an analysis of the debris."

"And the other ship?" Erik asked over comm. "How are they doing?"

"They look like they've successfully rendezvoused with the comet," Jia replied. "Though we're still too far away to resolve what they're doing, other than seeing some extremely mild thermal spikes. There haven't been any other major changes, and it's like before. If they know we're coming, they're not giving any indication."

"Then we stick to the plan: close in and confirm what's going on."

"And then?"

Erik chuckled. "We decide how big a gun we need."

———

Jia smiled despite the situation. They were now close enough that the camera feeds provided a visual of the massive, irregular ball of blue-and-gray-tinged white ice passing through the Solar System. A faint fuzzy shell surrounded the comet, but it had no tail.

That made sense, given how far they were out from the sun.

She sucked in a breath, the enormity of what they'd done hitting her in a way it hadn't before. They weren't just another mission. They'd jumped a thousand AUs to the edge of the Solar System.

Plenty of humans had traveled farther in absolute terms, but their ship and the crews of the two vessels ahead of them were the only humans to ever travel directly to this part of the Solar System. They'd come on a mission of security, but it was also a mission of exploration.

It was too bad they were only doing it because they needed to hunt down threats to the security of the UTC.

She looked to her side. Cutter was manning the primary controls, with Erik and Captain Osei behind the pilots.

"Damn." Cutter whistled, shaking his head, faint awe in his eyes. "I fly around all the time, but this is the closest I've been to a comet. It's pretty in its own way."

Jia magnified the image of the comet and zoomed in on a gray speck, which resolved into a triangular ship. Scorch marks and holes peppered the body. Turrets lined both sides, but many were now twisted and broken. A small opaque gray tube extended from the ship into the comet.

Erik leaned forward to peer at the image with a huge smile "They took a nasty beating. Now that we see how big they are, and their remaining weapons, there's no way they could survive in a straight-up fight against us. We've got this, even if they stand and fight."

Captain Osei pointed at the ship. "What if they are planning a final, nasty act?"

Erik looked at the captain. "You mean, blowing up the target?"

The captain nodded. "They're damaged, and if they don't see us yet, they're going too soon enough. It's like you said, Blackwell; they can't win. What choice do they have?"

Jia frowned at a data window. "There are some unusual sensor readings on the comet, not just thermals. There's definitely something under the ice layer. It might be a ship, but it's strange."

"How strange?" Erik asked.

"We're close enough now that I'm surprised the docked ship isn't reacting. There's no indication they're activating their weapons or shields. Minimum energy readings from the ship. Even if they think they can't win, you'd think they would at least do *something*."

"Go ahead and hail them," Erik suggested. "We now have the upper hand. We know there's something strange about the comet, but we don't know what it is, and if they're going to blow it, I'd rather they do it now when we're not right next to them."

"Attention, unknown vessel," Jia transmitted. "Attention, unknown vessel."

"How long is the comm lag at this distance?" Captain Osei asked.

Jia glanced at a data window to her left. "A little over a half a second."

"Their comm might be out," Cutter suggested with a shrug. "If they got hit that badly, they might not even have life support."

"They obviously survived," Erik replied. "The ship didn't dock itself and then connect that boarding tube. They'd probably needed some sort of drilling or digging equipment, too."

"So, they fled into the comet?" Jia asked. She furrowed her brow, staring at the sensor displays and the fluctuating readings. "Even if it is a Navigator ship, it might not have life support for humans, assuming they could even get inside."

Erik unfastened his harness and stood. "I'm not going to sit here and wait for them to come back. If they're at minimum power, they're not ready to deal with us. We should launch the *Argo* with the squads inside. We'll take their ship first and proceed from there. We keep the jump-ship at a safe distance. Cutter and Raphael can stay aboard." He turned to Cutter. "You can fly the big ship without Emma?"

Cutter offered her a thumbs-up. "I don't need Holochick around all the time to wipe my ass."

"I can't imagine a more disturbing example of being a fleshbag," Emma muttered.

"Won't they need troops on the *Bifröst* in case someone tries to board?" Jia asked.

Erik looked at Osei. "Cutter and Raphael can just blow

the hell out of anyone who gets close. I'd rather have the firepower with us when we raid the human ship, let alone the floating Navigator palace or whatever garbage is inside the comet."

"They won't be able to jump without me," Emma observed.

"Emma, you are going to stay in the *Argo*." Erik inclined his head toward Osei. "Between what we have in our cargo bay and what the captain brought, we'll be able to keep in touch with some creativity, but if we all get taken out, you can run back to the *Bifröst*."

Captain Osei frowned. "You planning for a suicide mission, Blackwell?"

"Hell, no, but if we're all dead, I want to make sure the conspiracy doesn't get their hands on the jump drive and Emma. That'd be a better immediate haul than some advanced tech they'll have to spend twenty years reverse-engineering." Erik headed toward the door. "I suggest you get your soldiers ready, Captain. Just because it looks like no one's home, it doesn't mean this isn't a trap."

"What's your position on taking them alive?"

Erik's cold grin sent a shiver through Jia.

"It's simple. If they want to live, they surrender."

CHAPTER FORTY

Erik took slow, deep breaths as he checked his tactical pressure suit and mag boots.

He didn't want to test their functionality under heavy fire. Most of the soldiers near him were probably thinking the same thing as they finished inspecting their suits and gathering their weapons and helmets.

Everyone stood in the cargo bay of the *Argo*. The ship was near its final approach to the suspect ship, with Emma ready to fire the turrets if the enemy was feigning inactivity.

Then it'd be up to the assault infantry, Erik, and Jia to board and clear the vessel.

This wasn't a tubular assault against a handful of ragtag terrorists. Erik and Jia might have dealt numerous blows to the conspiracy, but he'd seen firsthand how well they could fight, and if they were determined to make this hard, it might end up bloodier than he'd like.

Erik shook his head. The bastards were probably all inside the comet. He looked around again.

He was glad he'd left the MX 60 behind. They'd transferred all the squads' exos to the *Argo*, along with several crates of equipment and a drill bot he hadn't noticed before. As much as he would have liked to bring the tank, even if they crammed it in, it wasn't practical for a ship-based raid. However, it was nice to have professional military assaults, even without the tank.

The upcoming raid did highlight one of the few disadvantages of the *Argo*. They could extend emergency pressurized tubing from the cockpit and the lower-level airlocks, but it didn't have a dedicated boarding tube.

There was always something else to anticipate when dealing with the conspiracy, but he suspected most of their space-based encounters would end more like their battle with Sophia Vand. Boarding actions were dangerous.

If it weren't for the possible Navigator tech, he would have just said they should blow the ship to hell.

Jia locked her helmet into place and tapped on the faceplate. "Emma's bringing us up on one of the side airlocks. Energy readings are still minimal. If they know we're here, they're not doing anything about it or giving any sign."

"They obviously survived long enough to connect with the comet," Erik replied. "That means there's got to be more than one guy, but if we overwhelm them with force, it'll be easy."

"We'll need to figure out where we want to lock them up," Jia commented. "Assuming we run into them, they might not all be idiots."

"We'll worry about that when we get that far."

Captain Osei walked over to the pair and adjusted the

rifle slung over his shoulder and attached to his pressure suit with a line. "We're ready whenever you are."

Erik nodded. "We'll take point." He motioned toward a door. "Everyone follow me. Time for a good old-fashioned boarding action."

"Squads, prepare to move out," Captain Osei barked. "Luo, Brown, bring the torches. We're not hard-blowing anything we don't have to in space."

***

Erik had to give Emma credit. She'd gotten the *Argo* close enough to the airlock and manipulated the grav field emitters so they didn't have to float to the airlock. The lack of reaction by the enemy ship further cemented Erik's belief that they were no longer aboard.

"You popped open that sub pretty easily in Japan, Emma," Erik commented. "How about this?"

"I'm attempting to use remote override protocols, but I'll admit this might not be a swift process," Emma replied. "The system is more sophisticated."

"Their oxygen fields might not hold if we physically breach and don't reseal," Erik replied.

"I'll perhaps have a better opportunity once I can directly interrogate the internal systems. The internal door should be less of a problem."

"Fine. We'll do this the hard way, then." Erik nodded to Osei, who motioned Luo and Brown forward, then readied his rifle and pointed it at the door. There could be anything on the other side from a Tin Man to a *yaoguai*.

The two soldiers carried curved torches connected by a

thin line to their suits like their rifles. They both carried small tanks on their backs instead of the packs of their comrades. They approached the door with determined looks.

Erik and Jia cleared out of the way of the soldiers, who set up on either side of the external door. Bright white-blue flame erupted from their torches and bit into the door, emitting a shower of sparks. Minutes passed as they gouged lines in the door until it finally fell into the main airlock, revealing the interior door.

"Ah, yes, this will do nicely," Emma commented. "There are now access points that were being blocked by the previous door. I can't gain total control of the ship instantly, but I should be able to open and close the door behind you."

Captain Osei made a circular motion with his hand. "Set up one of the repeaters here while the AI gets to work."

A soldier crouched and placed the small gray tripod on the deck. It expanded and grew in height, bundled columnar arrays pulling away from the body. The others readied their rifles. Anyone on the other side would get to experience a heavy rifle volley firsthand if they so much as aimed in the general direction of the troops.

The inner airlock groaned and clicked before sliding open without Erik touching the manual hatch. Erik and Jia edged inside the darkened ship, sweeping through their areas of responsibility with their rifles. Dim red emergency lighting pushed away complete blackness, along with the occasional spark in the distance.

An unbreathing man in a gray uniform lay right

outside the airlock on his side, staring at the airlock, his lips and face blue and dark ligature marks around his neck.

"He has no active heartbeat," Emma reported.

Erik crouched near the man and shifted his head back and forth with his gloved hand. "How does someone end up strangled after a ship-to-ship battle?"

"It could be survivors from the other ship boarded this one," suggested Captain Osei. "We might have missed something in the debris field."

"There was no indication of that from outside," Jia replied with a frown. "And I doubt you could destroy an entire ship and have a couple of men in escape pods successfully board the responsible ship."

Captain Osei nodded. "True enough." He pointed his rifle at the body. "But if everyone aboard is dead, that might explain why it's so quiet."

"We still need to know who or what killed them." Jia narrowed her eyes, a look familiar from their cop days when she was thinking deeply about evidence.

Erik stood with a frown and peered down the passage connecting to the airlock. "We should check the ship in small squads to see what else we can turn up. If there are hostiles aboard, they can surrender, or they can take a bullet through the head. Jia and I will be our own squad."

"You heard the man," Captain Osei shouted. "Keep your eyes open. If any of you idiots gets yourself killed by one of these conspiracy bastards, I'm going to follow you to the afterlife and kick your ass in front of the Almighty himself."

Erik chuckled. That was one way of motivating men,

and it wasn't like he hadn't said similar things to his soldiers.

"How are you doing, Emma?" he asked.

"There is unexpectedly impressive security on this system," she replied. "It might be necessary for me to have direct access to gain full control, but I can give you door control in the meantime. I'm having trouble locating the cameras in the systems."

"If the conspiracy sent this ship, they knew it would be out of contact for a year," Erik replied. "It makes sense they would want to keep this thing as secure as possible. It'd be embarrassing if some lucky Fleet corvette showed up and took it over with a squad and some quick hacks."

Erik motioned to Jia and nodded down the corridor, and she fell in behind him. Two of the squads headed in their direction while Captain Osei took two other squads the opposite way.

No one spoke as they looked for survivors or threats. Erik remained unsure if the dead body was a sign of good luck for his team or a bad omen.

They continued several meters down the passage to an open storage room. There were two bodies inside among the scattered boxes and what appeared to be sealed packs for food printers.

There was no mystery about the causes of death, considering one body had its hands wrapped around the throat of the second, but a large knife protruded from his neck.

Jia frowned. "They have the same gray uniforms as the other body."

"They were on the same side," Erik concluded. "They were probably crew on this ship."

"But they killed each other?" Jia shook her head. "Something doesn't make sense."

"This is Osei," transmitted the captain. "We're seeing similar things over here. Got a couple of gunshot victims here, and another stabbing. One bastard got his face caved in against a console, but everyone has the same uniforms."

"They all killed each other," Jia whispered. "But why?" She tapped her PNIU. "From what I can tell, oxygen levels can support life."

"You planning on taking off your helmet?" Erik raised an eyebrow in worried challenge.

"No, but that means this wasn't them losing control and becoming desperate as they fought for air."

Erik headed out of the room. "There could be something in the air, some sort of toxin that got released during the fight that made them go nuts."

"Maybe," Jia replied quietly.

Even as Erik said it, he didn't believe it. He'd never shown up at a raid to find an entire group of people on the same side who had violently killed one another. Mass suicides, yes, but not mass murder-suicides. His heart might not be thundering at the sight, but that didn't make it any less unnerving.

"Whatever you do, keep your damned helmets on," Erik muttered. "It could be just like the prison. There could be some sort of new version of the nano-weapons they used there. It could be airborne and make them just as crazy but not zombies. Emma, can you tell?"

"I need direct access to internal sensors or for you to bring better handheld sensors," she replied. "The basic information I can derive from your PNIU and suit sensors suggest normal gravity, temperature, and radiation, with no obvious contamination by known pathogens, but as you pointed out, that's rather limited in the scope of things the conspiracy might use. They could have invented all manner of delightfully devious ways of killing people, even their own gun goblins."

"For now, we'll just be careful and treat this as a hostile environment." Erik slowed as he ran across another body in the hallway. This body had been shot multiple times in the chest. "And we don't contaminate the jumpship until we're sure that there's no weird nanite shit in the air. For now, let's finish sweeping the ship and find that boarding tube."

Thirty minutes later, Erik stood in front of another sealed airlock hatch, this one leading to the boarding tube the conspiracy ship had connected to the comet. The squads had joined back up.

"I can't open this yet," Emma explained, irritation lining her voice. "It's secured surprisingly well compared to the other doors."

"We could use the torches," Captain Osei suggested.

"Not in a hurry to go over there until we make sure we're not contaminated," Erik muttered. "Are you?"

"I can't say I am, but we've only seen ten bodies total." Captain Osei inclined his head toward the door. "This ship is decent-sized. That means there are probably more on the other side of this airlock door."

"I suggest we back off for now," Jia replied. "We can insert Emma directly into this ship and have her take control so she can better access internal sensors."

"I'm detecting unusual x-ray emissions from the comet," Emma reported. "They aren't at high enough levels to threaten you in your suits, let alone if you're inside the ships, but it might make sense to retreat to ensure you don't experience negative health effects."

"You sure it's not about to blow up?" Erik asked.

"I can't be a hundred percent certain, no, but keep in mind that if it explodes, there is a good chance I'll be destroyed as well. This isn't me being imprecise out of a lack of concern for fleshbags."

Captain Osei made a face, looking at Erik. "And you trust her?"

"With my life," he replied.

Erik surveyed the soldiers around him and Captain Osei. No one looked worried or scared despite the conversation. Several of them looked bored. He could work with that.

"I agree with Jia," Erik offered. "Let's pull back for now. Keep your suits on in the *Argo* until Emma can verify we're not contaminated. We're not going to let ourselves end up like these bastards."

Jia frowned at the sealed door. "I can't say this mission is turning out how I expected."

Erik turned to Jia with a grin. "We've got a pile of dead bodies, strange X-rays, and a sealed-off comet that might contain ancient alien tech. And you were worried about *jiangshi*."

"We haven't done a single scenario involving boarding comets that are actually alien ships," Jia retorted. "So much for the training precognition."

"Funny."

"I thought so."

"I just thought of something. Maybe there's nothing inside but a big pile of ice and rock." Erik stared at the airlock door. "They might have run there to get away from the massacre."

"That's unlikely, given what the sensors are indicating," Emma replied. "It's also not consistent with what we were detecting earlier."

"Life would be easier if it was." Erik backed away from the door. "Let's get the hell out of here."

CHAPTER FORTY-ONE

Hours later, a smaller team stood on the bridge of the damaged ship. Emma's checks had verified no unusual contamination, nanite or otherwise, on their suits.

After the x-ray emissions ceased, Erik had returned with Jia, Captain Osei, and a single squad. They headed to the bridge of the ship and inserted Emma directly into an IO port. Erik, Jia, and the captain agreed it'd be better to figure out what had happened to the crew before they opened the airlock and proceeded into the likely alien ship on the other side, especially since there might be insane humans looking to kill whoever they encountered.

"Partial control of the ship's systems has been achieved," Emma declared with obvious pride in her voice. "I'm working on gaining access to that door."

"We don't need it immediately," Erik replied.

The AI had remained invisible during her mission to the ship. Something about that unsettled Jia, but she didn't mention it. Emma had demonstrated concern over being damaged before, but Jia was uncertain if she felt fear in the same way as a human, despite her heritage.

Erik ran his finger over a cracked, inactive virtual console. Blood splatters covered it, along with chunks of what might have been bone.

"It'd be nice if we could see the internal camera footage," Erik explained. "We might have seen someone use a weapon or say something."

"Indeed, that would be nice," Emma replied. "But there's a problem with that, a rather serious problem."

"And what's that?" Erik chuckled. "Don't tell me you can't take control?"

Emma scoffed. "This isn't a matter of my capabilities, it's about possibilities. There are no internal cameras anywhere on this ship."

"No cameras?" Jia looked around. "Anywhere?"

"No."

It didn't make sense. Internal cameras were critical for safety and emergency purposes. Just because this ship was used by an evil conspiracy, it didn't mean eschewing best practices would help them.

A holographic three-dimensional display of the ship's layout appeared and rotated in front of them. A blue dot marked their position, and a red dot marked the position of the comet tunnel.

"There are individual door access records and that sort of data, but no clear footage," Emma continued. "It isn't as if the system couldn't accommodate cameras, but they've either never installed them, or they removed them all for whatever inscrutable reasons those creeping conspirators have."

"Plausible deniability," Erik suggested. "The conspiracy couldn't be sure this ship wouldn't be taken. If they could evacuate, there would be no evidence of the crew left behind. We might learn all sorts of things by looking through a year's worth of footage."

Jia pointed to a body blocking a door. They hadn't moved any of the corpses.

"No evidence after an evacuation? I wouldn't call that an evacuation." She shook her head with a faint look of disgust. "It wasn't much of a victory if they lost a lot of their crew."

"Not saying everything went according to plan," Erik replied. "Obviously they didn't plan on that other ship, let alone us jumping out here after them. They had to adapt on the fly."

"It's really intriguing," Emma interrupted. "I might not be able to find footage from nonexistent cameras, but I can tell you that someone went through that airlock about ten hours before I opened the airlock door that granted you entry."

"It could just be that the door opened." Erik frowned. "We can't be sure people went through."

Captain Osei nodded. "We need to be careful about what we assume, so we don't let ourselves get taken by surprise."

"No," Emma replied forcefully. "Despite the lack of cameras, there were internal sensors. The thermal signatures clearly indicate multiple people went through. Ten. Unless someone or something went out of their way to fake those signatures, it couldn't be anything other than humans."

Jia's breath caught in a sudden inspiration. "Can you use those sensors to indirectly reconstruct what happened here? We don't need the camera feeds."

"Not as much as you'd think." Emma sounded apologetic. "Not every room has the same internal sensor coverage, and there was considerable damage to many of the sensors from the battle."

Captain Osei finished murmuring something to a nearby soldier before stepping toward the hologram. "They fought that other ship, and from what I understand, there are factions in this conspiracy that don't get along."

"Yeah, that's what it looks like," Erik replied with a frown. "There's no way it's just a coincidence that other ship flew out here, especially when it was obviously heavily armed."

Jia nodded. She'd gotten so used to running around in a heavily armed ship that she'd forgotten the average non-military vessel had minimal weapons if any. It wasn't like the UTC wanted everyone wandering through space with firepower. People might be able to justify it on the frontier, but not in the core systems.

"Then we're overthinking this," Captain Osei continued. "That other ship was probably another faction, but there was a double agent aboard this ship, too. They did something. Put something in the air, something temporary that caused the rest of them to kill each other, and then they extended the boarding tube."

Jia wrinkled her nose, fighting an itch on the side she couldn't get to because of her helmet. "That's all supposition based on not a lot of evidence, and it clashes with what Emma reported. It wasn't one man who went through, but ten."

"What do you think happened?" Captain Osei asked. "They all decided to up and kill each other because they couldn't handle it? If they were the kind of crew who could handle being on a ship for a year, they weren't going to lose it at the last second."

"Maybe they couldn't escape." Erik tapped the cracked console. "The ship did look pretty shot up from the outside. They could have flown here and then realized they wouldn't be able to survive the trip back. The stress sent them over the edge."

"That isn't consistent with what I can see from the system status reports," Emma explained. "There is damage all over the ship, but there's no significant damage to the reactor, engines or thrusters. Grav fields are stable. Life support is stable. Food printers and ingredient storage are working. The defensive and offensive systems appear to be the main casualties. Hmm…"

"What?"

"I've just broken through the encryption on some log entries. They were recorded shortly before the boarding party entered the comet, and shed some light."

"Play them," Jia ordered. "Send them just to me, Erik and Captain Osei."

An unfamiliar woman's voice filtered through the comm.

"I'm breaking procedure to record this message," explained the weary voice. "But there's increasing insta-bility among the crew. I don't know why, and it's threat-ening the mission. We suffered moderate damage when we repulsed the other ship, but no serious injuries." A deep sigh followed. "I'm preparing to take a team into the prize. We can't wait much longer. I don't know how to explain it, but we're fairly certain another ship is following us. The only thing we can't figure out is where it came from. We've been doing our best ever since we were warned about the first ship. We'll do what we need to seize the prize before their arrival. If our background information is right, we'll be able to use it against this other ship."

Erik chuckled and shook his head. "They did notice us."

Emma appeared in a completely unnecessary pressure suit. "The x-ray emissions are back. Now that I have full access to this ship's sensors, I'm noticing low levels of an extremely odd multi-frequency EMF field whose source appears to be in the comet. This thing is…"

"What?" Jia pressed.

Emma looked at her with worry on her face. The tone of her words was uncharacteristically quiet and unsure. "At the broadest level, there are certain aspects to that signal that resemble the influence of neuronal excitation experiments performed by both the civilian and military sectors some decades back and allegedly abandoned. I don't know how the x-rays are related, but the signals began at the same time as the x-ray emissions, and upon initial analysis, patterns in the signals would appear unlikely to be the result of natural variation."

"Meaning?" Erik's brow furrowed, a deepening scowl spreading across his face.

"I'm saying it's not impossible those signals can affect the human brain," Emma explained.

Jia grimaced. "Wait. You're saying this crew ran into a Navigator mind-control field?"

Captain Osei frowned. "And that shit is on right now?" He glanced at his squad. "Then we need to get the hell out of here before we start blowing each other's brains out. That's not the way I'm going out."

"Agreed," Jia replied, edging toward the door.

With a wave of his arm to his soldiers, Captain Osei headed off the bridge, muttering under his breath. A pensive-looking Erik followed the captain and his squad, and Jia brought up the rear, sparing a final look at the body.

The first step to surviving an attack was knowing it was coming.

After bringing Raphael and Cutter up to date with a quick transmission, Jia, Erik, and Captain Osei settled around a table in the galley to discuss their options. Emma stood near the door in her major's uniform.

Captain Osei tapped a rather emphatic finger on the table. "Whether it's Navigator or conspiracy tech, we can't go marching in there with that field up."

"Won't the suits protect us?" Erik asked.

"That's uncertain," Emma reported. "Your pressure suits aren't designed to protect you from every possible EM frequency. Now that I've identified it, though, I can work with Lanara and your PNIUs to generate something that will disrupt most of the signals, particularly things in the lower ranges that are more likely to have an impact. Given the complexity of the signal, disrupting the key components should be sufficient to eliminate any significant risks."

Captain Osei frowned. "I'd normally say you were full of crap about all this, AI, but we've got a lot of dead bodies on that ship that support what you're saying. However, your solution has a lot of ifs."

"Emma's not going to bullshit us," Erik replied. "Nor is Lanara. If they tell us it'll work, I trust them. But yeah, it doesn't do us any good to march in there without protection and then go nuts. I'm guessing that whoever else went in there already killed themselves."

"Or they're gibbering on the floor, waiting for new people to show up so they can try to bite our heads off?"

Jia shook her head. "It's the prison all over again."

"How long do you think it'll take to develop a countermeasure, Emma?" Erik asked.

Emma's hologram vanished. "I'm unsure, but based on what Lanara told me, it'll take at least another day, maybe two."

"Well, then if the boarding party survived, they get at least a one-day head start."

CHAPTER FORTY-TWO

May 20, 2230, Solar System, Cargo Bay of the Argo

Jia stared at the small metal bracelet in Lanara's palm. "That's it?"

Erik and Jia had come to the cargo bay to look at the key to exploring the prize, as the other ship called it. He wasn't sure if he was more surprised that they were worrying about potential insanity fields or that Lanara and Emma had come up with a countermeasure so quickly.

There were definite advantages to having the cranky engineer and the AI on his team.

Lanara nodded, a triumphant smirk on her face. "Emma did the bulk of the analysis work and Raphael helped from the jumpship, some physics bullshit." She shrugged breezily. "I had a lot of parts lying around here, and we borrowed some from the other ship with the help of cargo drones." She tossed the bracelet into the air and snatched it before it fell. "Between this, the PNIU and Emma, it'll cancel out the signals likely to affect your brain. Now, the power efficiency on these things isn't the best, and it'd be great if I could spend more time." Her voice sped up. "Right now, it's easy to link into the suits, but it'd be nice if—"

"How long?" Erik interrupted.

"Oh, as long as you have the PNIUs and your suits, you should be fine." Lanara lifted the bracelet to her face and squinted. "You try to use these without that equipment and you'll only have hours, but I figure in that case, you'll probably be dead anyway."

"Probably," Erik admitted.

"I don't think anyone's planning to explore whatever's inside that comet without using pressure suits and breathers," Jia replied.

Lanara inclined her head toward a pile of crates behind her. "I've modified some of the signal boosters and repeaters we had in storage to Emma's specifications. These will work better than that off-the-shelf crap the soldiers brought. It'll take me one more day to fabricate enough for everybody."

Emma appeared in coveralls that looked suspiciously like Lanara's. "The uniformed boys and girls have nice guns, but we need to make sure you don't lose contact with your most important asset since whatever gun goblins and creepy conspirators you encounter past the tunnel won't be the kind you can negotiate with. Unless you wish to bring me with you?"

Erik shook his head. "Taking you off the *Argo* to hack that ship was pushing it as is. Cutter's on the other ship. If this turns to shit, at least you can fly the *Argo* back." He spared a worried glance Jia's way.

"I mentioned this to Erik already, but my brief exploration near the airlock door to the tunnel, including using a drone flyby from overhead, indicates the internal passageways are too small to accommodate exoskeletons," Emma explained.

Jia nodded. "Great. Just great. I'd prefer to go in with more firepower since even if we're safe from the insanity signal, we don't know what or who we'll find in here. Are the soldiers still willing to go with us?"

"Let's call Osei down here for a briefing. If he doesn't want his people to come, I'm not going to drag them along screaming."

Osei pursed his lips as Erik finished explaining Lanara's progress and the general plan.

"My guys are packed in pretty tight on this ship," the captain commented.

Erik was surprised by the statement. He understood the tension, and he and Jia had brought portable bunks from the cargo bay to their own quarters to reduce the strain, but he didn't understand why the captain would bring it up now.

"A lot of them would love to pack up and go back to the jumpship," Captain Osei continued. "So, I want you to explain to me why we should risk going onto a potentially alien ship with an active mind-control field?"

They'd thought about exploring with drones, but they didn't have enough signal boosters to guarantee signal, whereas between the PNIUs and the boosters, they could at least keep in contact with Emma. Drones wouldn't last in battle either.

"We need to make sure the conspiracy team doesn't gain control," Erik replied. "If they're not all dead, they might get a signal off with important information."

"We could just blow it to hell." The captain leaned toward Erik, a stern look on his face. "That jumpship's carrying a lot of weapons. I'm sure if both our ships start firing, we can penetrate the ice layer and get to whatever's inside."

Jia shook her head. "We can't ignore the possibility of retrieving useful tech from the ship. We've already come up with a counter to the signal."

"We can request orders," Captain Osei replied. "Let the higher-ups make the call."

Jia frowned. "That'd take over a week round-trip. We can't sit around here for a week when we don't know what's going on aboard that ship. At least ten people entered the ship, and we don't know if they've been affected by the signal or not."

"I'm fine making the executive decision," Erik commented, his gaze pinning Osei. "And Jia and I are going with you, so this isn't rear-echelon motherfucker stuff where we send you off to die while we stay behind and take the glory."

"But is it risking lives unnecessarily because of your grudge?" the captain asked.

Jia stomped toward him. "How dare you—"

Erik quieted her with a simple head shake. "It's a fair question, but it's the same as I told you before. I'm not here to throw my life away, and we can't be sure we can blow this thing away with the weapons we have. I'm willing to bet if we drop explosives all over the inside and detonate those at the end, we can make sure that thing gets blasted to pieces."

Osei nodded slowly, looking mollified.

Jia's alarmed expression telegraphed her words. "You might be blowing up an intact Navigator ship!"

Erik smiled merrily. "Nice thing to add to my trophy list."

CHAPTER FORTY-THREE

Jia took slow, even breaths as the airlock door opened, exposing the brightly lit boarding tunnel.

They didn't expect an ambush since Emma had explored the initial portion of the tunnel while they geared up. A last-minute change to focus on drone-based exploration had vanished in the wake of the AI's report of a massive increase in signal interference as she approached the exit door.

That was consistent with what they'd expected, but the team had to worry about potentially losing communication and planned to increase the number of repeaters to remain in direct contact with Emma.

Erik was wrong. Jia was sure of that.

He'd complained he found the undersea resort more threatening than space, but the current mission proved how many dangerous aspects they needed to take into account while off Earth.

Gravity, air, pressure, temperature, and radiation;

everything was conspiring to kill them. At least they could still shoot the conspiracy agents.

Jia glanced at the bracelet around her wrist. According to Lanara and Emma, even if the team lost contact with the AI, the countermeasure would function. Presumably it was working since no one was acting suspicious or unstable, and they were far closer to the source than they'd been when exploring the captured human ship.

Erik and Jia took point in the boarding party, followed by Captain Osei and Alpha, Bravo, Gamma, and Delta Squads.

The soldiers traveled in a staggered pattern just in case. Armored tactical pressure suits with carryaids weren't exoskeletons, and they'd need to be careful. No one wanted a powerful laser to take out half the team with one shot.

The thought made Jia glance at Erik. His preparation for the mission had included bringing his laser rifle on the carryaid, along with extra energy cells.

The entire team had decided against rocket launchers out of concern for blowing a hole into space, but they were compensating with an abundance of grenades. For now, they wielded their rifles as their primary weapons.

There was still much they didn't know about what had happened, and they had the unusual fortune of having Emma with them. If it'd just been a military team with standard equipment, they would have ended up like the dead crew.

Jia wondered how much the conspiracy knew about the technology onboard. Something like the mind-control field would make a useful weapon, but if they had that detailed a knowledge of the Navigators, they would be deploying more advanced technology.

A small smile appeared. She'd been drawn so far into Erik's quest for vengeance that sometimes she forgot the conspiracy represented a danger to the entire UTC.

Their survivors would not be allowed to take the ship.

The boarding tunnel was standard with no surprises, including no new bodies or evidence of any more murders. They continued toward the other end, where Emma had already opened the door.

A narrow passage carved through the ice and rock with barely enough space for two people was connected to the end of the boarding tunnel. Though the new passage didn't display the perfect symmetry of the boarding tunnel, the evenness of the new passage indicated it'd been created artificially.

Jia tapped on her suit and helmet lights, and Erik and the rest joined her. There was a faint greenish glow emanating from the far end, but they would need to walk a decent distance before encountering whatever it was and shooting it if necessary.

"We might not be the first people ever to set foot on a comet, but we're the first people to ever set foot on a comet in this part of the Solar System," Jia offered. "That's got to be worth something."

"Sure," Erik replied. "They can name schools after us in some crappy town."

Jia laughed. "I wouldn't mind a school being named after me."

"Too bad the government's probably going to deny any of this ever happened," Erik offered, not looking her way.

He nodded at Osei. "Let's lay the repeater network close to each other."

The officer nodded at a nearby sergeant, who pulled the first repeater off his carryaid and set up the gray tripod.

"Signals check, Emma," Erik ordered. "You still with us?"

"Yes, your direct signals and telemetry are all strong," Emma replied, sounding bored. "No significant spikes in any signal or emission that I can detect, other than the baseline signal from before."

Jia chuckled. "You're saying the alarm isn't going off?"

"They'd have to know how to turn it on first," Erik replied. "Even if those guys survived the mind-control field or somehow ended up immune, it doesn't mean they'll figure out how to turn on an ancient alien ship."

"Keep alert, squads," Osei shouted. "Remember, we still have ten possible hostiles unaccounted for."

The shouting was unnecessary given they were all on comm, but Jia had noticed that didn't stop the man.

"We have no idea what we might run into in there," he continued. "If anyone starts experiencing or feeling *anything* unusual, you tell me immediately, and we'll get you back to the *Argo*. Understood?"

"Yes, sir," the troops responded in unison.

Jia kept imagining a thin shell of ice and rock stretching around the alleged prize, but even with their modest pace and the relatively small size of the comet, the green glow remained stubbornly in the distance. They had easily traveled hundreds of meters into the comet.

"This shell would have taken thousands of years to

form," Jia murmured, running a hand over the ice wall. "Ten of thousands, probably."

Captain Osei's mouth twitched. "They've been sitting around in the Solar System for a long time."

"That's not that much of a surprise." Jia shrugged. "We found Navigator artifacts on Mars, after all, and those are much older."

"I get that, but finding a cache of broken-down tech is different from finding an active ship. They might have been alive for far longer than anyone realizes."

"True." Jia nodded. "But I doubt they survived thousands of years aboard this ship."

"If it's been here that long, I'm surprised their security system is still working," Erik commented.

"Security system?" Jia looked around the tunnel for signs of activity, her grip tightening on her rifle.

Captain Osei frowned Erik's way but didn't comment. He looked like he'd rather them not discuss things, but Erik and Jia weren't the types to proceed on a mission in dead silence.

"Their mind-control field," Erik explained. "That's probably what it is, or it could be something else. Maybe something malfunctioned. But it makes sense that it might be a security system."

"To be honest, I wasn't sure before about it being a Navigator ship." Jia sighed. "I just kept thinking it could be something else, but after what we saw and what Emma detected, there's no other explanation."

"You don't think there could be a Navigator in there, do you?" called one of the soldiers, Corporal Milton. He sounded more curious than afraid.

Captain Osei glared his way before turning his scowling wrath on Jia. She politely didn't laugh. Her early career had been marked by her superiors and colleagues not liking what she had to say. At this point, it was hard for anyone to intimidate her with a mere look.

They would need a weapon of impressive size to make that happen.

"It's not likely, but it's not impossible," Jia explained. "We don't know enough about Navigator technology to know if they could keep one of their people alive that long, but we've also seen zero evidence of an actual Navigator doing anything directly. The evidence is pointing somewhere else, especially based on Emma's sensor readings." She gestured down the tunnel. "Erik's probably right. Someone left the security system on, and it's doing its best with whatever reserve power it has."

Jia halted and sucked in a breath. Erik tensed and swept the area with his rifle. Osei and the troops spread out, taking up defensive positions.

"You see something?" Erik whispered.

"No." Jia shook her head. "Sorry."

Captain Osei muttered something under his breath before regrouping his subordinates with quick hand gestures.

"Then what was that about?" Erik prodded, before continuing down the tunnel.

Jia followed. "I realized something. We're all carrying portable handholds in our carryaids because we were worried about the gravity, but it's nearly Earth-normal, and we're far from the ship, so we're no longer under the influence of its grav fields." She gestured around the narrow tunnel. "Which means this comet is far, far, far denser than we'd expected based on the size, or there's artificial gravity extending from the ship inside."

Captain Osei's expression softened and he nodded. "I get what you're saying. Does it make a difference? I'm not going to complain about a deep-space intercept going easier than we expected."

"If it's because of the comet, that means even the exterior is not what we think, which has implications, but it's also nice to know that the Navigators apparently evolved on a world with gravity similar to ours. That's a nice scientific discovery in and of itself. We know they were bigger than us, so some scientists speculated they might have evolved on a planet with lower gravity."

"Maybe you should write a xenobiology paper," Emma offered. "*On the Implied Natural Gravitational Environment of the Navigators* by Lin, Blackwell, Osei, *et al.*"

Jia wished Emma was accompanying them as a hologram. Whenever they weren't using the MX 60, it was easy to forget that Emma was watching and listening. The AI was far too good at keeping her mouth shut when she wanted. It was like having the snarkiest ghost ever following her around.

"Funny," Jia grumbled. "But the more like us they are, the better chance we have of making use of their tech, though I'm not sure that's always a great idea, I *am* sure it's better that we have it, rather than the conspiracy or any of the other races."

The green glow grew brighter with each step, the source being an obvious end for the tunnel: light pouring out of a hole. No soldiers were behaving oddly, and there'd been no warnings by Emma. They were doing pretty good.

The tunnel flared, and the glow highlighted shapes near the hole.

"We've got two drill bots," Erik called. "And I don't think the Navigators were so close to us that their bots would look exactly like ours."

Jia frowned. "There's something behind the bots." She pointed her rifle, her eyes narrowed. "We might have a body."

Captain Osei signaled for his soldiers to take their positions. The individual squad members moved closer to each other while the squads staggered positions, the soldiers in front crouching while the ones in back stood for maximum firepower.

Jia and Erik moved forward slowly toward the new find. A human man in a pressure suit lay on his back on the ground behind the bot. His helmet was cracked, probably from the bullet that had drilled a large hole in his head.

Erik stepped past the body toward the hole. "Huh. This is weird, but I'm pretty sure it's a ship."

Jia peered into the hole, letting her eyes adjust to the strange green lighting. Scorch marks marked the jagged hole separating the tunnel from the ship along with orange stains, making her wonder what else the other team had done to get inside. The wall didn't appear to be metal, but rather a thick dark-green layer of stacked membranes with swirling curves and thin silvery veins that reminded her of a leaf's.

"It looks almost...*biological*," she murmured, tilting her head both ways to give her a better view.

Irregular round-topped columnar structures around Jia's height filled the sprawling ovoid chamber. They appeared to be made of the same material as the walls, which, along with the high roof, provided the glow.

Semi-circular formations of the rounded columns spread out in the room in front of groupings of narrow bars protruding from the ground. The bars were about half the height of the columns. Stalactite-like dark-green protrusions hung from the ceiling, some stretching almost down to the columns. Webs of blue-green vine-like ropes connected the columns.

No bodies lay in the room, and there was nothing that looked like human blood. Small portions of the columns and walls slowly expanded and retracted, inflating and deflating like twisted alien lungs. Large circular open doorways led out of the chamber in two directions.

"I don't know what I expected," Erik mumbled, "but it wasn't this. I thought Navigator tech was more, you know, *tech*. This crap looks like something out of a *yaoguai* factory."

Captain Osei frowned as he took in the scene. "We sure it isn't?"

"I doubt the conspiracy's breeding giant *yaoguai* at the edge of the Solar System." Erik shook his head. "You ever fight *yaoguai*?"

"A couple of times."

"Then you know they are messed up, but they look familiar in their own way." Erik gestured around the room. "This crap, though." He shrugged. "That's aliens for you."

Jia pointed her gun at one of the groups of bars. "At least we know for sure this is an alien ship. Nothing about its proportions and setup is human. I'm not even sure it's set up for humanoids."

Her mouth curled into a frown. Something didn't seem right, but it wasn't important for the moment.

"You still with us, Emma?" Erik asked.

"Yes, but interference is increasing," she replied, her voice going in and out. "I would take appropriate measures if you wish to continue to have my aid. Please note there is atmosphere in the ship and it's maintained despite the hole, but it is not breathable by humans."

"Wasn't planning on taking my helmet off," Erik noted.

Osei nodded to another of his troops. He jogged toward the hole.

"This is a good place for our first set of explosives," Erik mentioned to Captain Osei.

The captain nodded. "Agreed. I also think we should have someone guard our exit."

"Yeah." Erik slowly surveyed the room, disgust all over his face. "That's a good idea."

Jia peered at a web. "I'll never think a space raptor is strange again. Compared to this stuff, the Leems seem human."

There had been so many firsts in the last couple of days. She'd jumped across the Solar System and was now aboard an alien ship. She only hoped she didn't have to experience alien security firsthand.

CHAPTER FORTY-FOUR

Erik convened quietly with Jia and Captain Osei at the edge of the room while two of the soldiers prepared the explosive. They looked so unassuming, the black cylinders, but they'd make a nice light show.

"I think we should stay together as one team," Erik explained. "It's too much of a risk with the repeaters and interference that we'll lose contact otherwise."

Captain Osei nodded. "I've already instructed Gamma Squad to stay here to guard our backs. How far are we going to go through this freak factory?"

"Not sure," Erik admitted. "I think we need to make a basic sweep, then we need to figure out what to do. I'm not ready to leave this ship until we've found those conspiracy bastards. For all we know, they've got some gadget and are beaming info to their bosses."

Erik didn't care if it was an intact Navigator ship. It'd possibly driven men to kill each other, and he suspected that wasn't the worst it was capable of.

If he'd found the rest of the bodies, he would have been

happy for a quick explosive delivery run, followed by a nice remote explosion.

Although he doubted any human could control the vessel, the worry lingered. Everything about the ship defied what he'd heard about the Navigators, but it wasn't as if anyone was an expert on the long-dead race. When a culture could only be judged by what had survived through the eons, it provided a skewed view of the truth.

That'd been proven over and over by Earth archaeology. There was no reason to suspect it wouldn't apply to xenoarchaeology.

Besides, he was less interested in the truth than in making sure the conspiracy didn't gain any advantages.

"Package set up, sir," one of the soldiers called to Captain Osei.

The officer nodded at the now-blinking cylinder. "Your show, Blackwell."

"At the least, we need to verify the death of the other team before we make our final call," Erik replied. He inclined his head toward one of the open doors, unsure if that was what the circular holes represented. "We keep it up, keep sweeping, set up repeaters, and set up explosives. If we get enough repeaters going, Emma might be able to do a halfway-decent drone sweep, but we still need boots on the ground to set up the explosives."

"What I've already seen is fascinating," Emma transmitted. "I don't know if you fleshbags fully appreciate the historical importance of your mission."

"I'll worry about the history once we make sure the conspiracy doesn't find a jump drive in the back of this thing and pop over to Earth to lay waste to it with some ultimate alien death ray," Erik replied. "I wonder how they even knew about this thing."

"They paid close attention to astronomy journals?" Jia offered with a slight shrug.

"But no one else noticed, and if what we were told was true, people have been watching this comet for a while."

"It's been bothering me, too." Jia furrowed her brow. "It's almost like they knew where to look, but I can't figure out how they would. Being powerful assholes doesn't mean they're psychic."

Erik frowned. "Maybe they got lucky. When we track the rest of them down, we can ask."

The team proceeded in a staggered formation through the closest exit. The tunnels leading to the ship might not have been big enough to accommodate the exos, but they would have been easy to use in the huge rooms and wide passageways.

Erik quashed a brief thought about going back for the exos. His team would have the same problem as the conspiracy team; they'd have to drill into the comet, and making a tunnel that would accommodate the exos would take a long time with the equipment they had on board. They needed to secure the ship as quickly as possible.

The exit led to a wide, curving passage lined on all surfaces, including the roof, with the same rod-like structures as in the chamber. The team quickly arrived at another chamber with towering veined mounds in the center. Thick droplets of orange fluid dripped from the mounds into a small pool surrounding them. The pool slowly drained into vents in the floor.

Had it been doing that for thousands of years?

Erik was glad he had the helmet on. Something told him the stench would have been unbearable.

"What the hell is that?" Captain Osei asked, matching Erik's next thought.

"I don't think I want to know the answer," Erik answered. "For all we know, we're in their bathroom."

Jia shook her head. "This isn't right. None of this resembles what we've seen from Navigator tech. I keep trying to tell myself that maybe they went off in a different direction, but what little hints of ergonomics information we can glean from their artifacts suggests a form larger than humans, somewhere in the neighborhood of our shape."

"You're thinking too much like a human," Emma commented, her voice thick with amusement. "I'm sure the Zitark version of you would make the same mistake."

Uninterested in the xenoarchaeology, Captain Osei circled his finger in the air and pointed near the mound to indicate where he wanted the explosives set up. Two soldiers jogged that way to perform that task while Corporal Milton set up a repeater.

Jia frowned. "I'm just saying this ship doesn't match what we've seen of the Navigators."

"And perhaps the Navigators didn't have Purists," Emma replied. "They might have decided they were tired of their evolutionary form."

"I suppose. Scientists could spend a hundred years studying this thing and probably learn something new every day." Jia eyed the explosives. "Assuming it's still around."

"We're taking this ship out unless we're dead certain

we've secured it from both asshole humans and ancient security systems," Erik replied. "Though I don't know what they plan to do. We'd have to ferry scientists out here. I doubt we're going to figure out how to fly this thing anytime soon. For now, we'll record what we see and figure out what to do once we've explored the entire ship."

Jia let out a breath she didn't realize she'd been holding as they stepped into a new corridor.

An hour had passed as they explored the ship, moving from chamber to chamber and laying down more repeaters and explosives. Despite the inherent oddness of the biological technology underlying its design, a vague sense of familiarity began to grow.

Structures repeated themselves in different rooms.

There was a pattern to the disgusting madness. The ship was strange, but it had obviously been designed by intelligent beings.

Jia made her own mental designations of different rooms: control rooms, storage, processing, and resource collection. She had no idea if her labels were correct, but they felt right.

It wasn't an outlandish idea. If a sailor from the fifteen century were dropped aboard the *Argo*, he would quickly understand the layout despite the technological differences, though the differences between humans centuries ago and in the current age were far smaller than the differences between humans and the Navigators.

Was Emma right about Jia being presumptuous?

Perhaps, but the only way to know was if they studied the ship.

The lack of solid doors nagged Jia. She could imagine a ship built around advanced biological technology manned by a race with a radically different body plan than most in the Local Neighborhood, but something about the lack of sealed doors poked at the suspicious and paranoid part of her brain that had served her so well for the last couple of years.

Jia needed more data for a better understanding, but that was a fanciful desire aboard the ancient ship of an extinct race.

It was obvious Erik and Osei wanted to blow the thing up, and she couldn't say she thought their instincts were wrong. There were many days she was convinced humanity would have been better off sticking to the Solar System.

Part of her wanted to argue Erik and Captain Osei out of setting up the explosives, but they were right. If the vessel fell into the wrong hands, it had the potential to be apocalyptic.

It'd become obvious that the ship was roughly circular and huge, around two kilometers in diameter, and they'd explored a good chunk of one quadrant and were making their way toward the center. If there was another level, they didn't know how to get to it, and no one was keen on trying to blow a hole in the floor.

Emma had sent drones into the areas with repeaters to keep an eye on things and explore. The team had all the repeaters, so she couldn't lay down any more. The mysterious signal was still transmitting, but otherwise, the ship appeared inactive. Gamma squad, led by Lieutenant Zhang, hadn't reported anything unusual at the tunnel's entrance.

They passed into an empty circular chamber that had exits on every side. It was the first room on the ship that didn't contain at least one ground-floor structure.

It didn't lack the ubiquitous stalactite-like ceiling formations, and unlike in the other rooms, a web of coiled vine-like ropes connected them. The vines were thicker than the ones connecting the ground shapes in the previous room.

"This must be the center of the ship," Jia commented. "But it's kind of a big room just to be a glorified hallway."

Erik craned his neck upward. "For all we know, they built it based on alien feng shui principles."

Jia chuckled. "That's very much true."

Captain Osei pointed at different sections of the room. "I want quadruple explosive and repeater coverage near the exits."

Soldiers scurried to complete their orders.

"There is an issue," Emma transmitted, her tone worried. She restricted the communication to Erik, Captain Osei, and Jia.

Jia frowned. "What's going on? You spot the other team?"

"No, they haven't traveled through any of the rooms where I'm maintaining drone coverage," Emma explained. "But I'm now detecting changes with both the *Argo's* sensors and the drones. Thermal differences and x-ray spikes, among others. Considerable increases across the spectrum."

Jia's stomach tightened and she rubbed the bracelet. "Will our defenses hold?"

"These aren't related to the brain-affecting field if that's what you're asking. I've never encountered a Navigator ship, so I can't say for certain, but my best guess is that it's powering up. If your hypothesis is correct that the mind-control field is part of a security system, it's not unreasonable to assume that more direct defenses might be employed."

Captain Osei gritted his teeth. "Damn it." He motioned for his people to come to him. "Everyone not setting something that goes boom on me. We might have trouble soon."

"Why would it suddenly turn on?" Erik flipped off his rifle safety. "Those conspiracy bastards must have found the bridge, and we have no idea where it is. Shit, we don't even know if they have a hidden elevator we missed."

Jia checked her weapons as she replied, "We don't even know if this ship *has* a bridge."

"What we do know is that we've got a quarter of this freak factory rigged with L-48." Captain Osei nodded toward a sergeant who was priming one of the cylinders. "I doubt this thing is so strong from the inside that losing a quarter of it won't be enough to finish it off, and those conspiracy assholes with it."

"You're saying we bug out and remote-blow it?" Erik asked.

"Yes." Captain Osei frowned. "Even if the L-48 doesn't end them, we can finish them off with the *Argo* and the *Bifröst*. A couple of salvos will open up that tunnel wide enough that we can pound whatever's left."

Erik shook his head. "We need to account for every

single one of those bastards, and we need to be sure, and that means having L-48 coverage over the entire ship. I don't mind sending this thing to hell if we're sure, but we don't know. It could be modular and drop pieces, or have shields that bounce our best weapons off." He traced a long shape with his hand. "We've both seen plenty of Fleet ships take a huge pounding and still limp home. If we take out the conspiracy bastards, we'll have more time to make sure this thing is done. If they fly away with it, we're screwed. This might be our only chance, so we have to do it right."

"What if it's a self-destruct system?" Corporal Milton asked.

"Stow that shit, Corporal," barked Captain Osei. "This ship didn't sit around for thousands of years just to blow itself up now."

Emma chuckled. "There is a certain logic to that. It's not un-persuasive."

"It is for me." Erik turned slowly, surveying the room for any changes. "But something's different now, and we need to—"

"Contact!" bellowed a sergeant. "Eight o'clock!"

The team spun in that direction, their weapons at the ready. The shadowy outline of five human forms walked with an uneven gait from an exit across the room. The new arrivals emerged from the darkness and elicited gasps from some of the soldiers and curses from the others.

The new arrivals' pressure suit design and general body plan suggested they belonged to the crew of the captured conspiracy ship, but they lacked helmets, and strange bulbous growths covered most of their heads. They now had a second pair of dark arms ending in four-fingered claws.

Swollen stomachs pressed against the suits. Their gloves had been torn through on their original limbs by claws. Their now-green teeth were fused together and glistening with some unknown fluid.

Jia hissed in disgust. "I think we know what happened to the team."

"That's only half of them," Erik commented as he selected burst fire. "But maybe they meant to do that."

Corporal Milton gagged. "You're saying they purposely came and turned themselves into that?"

"We don't know. Just throwing it out there." Erik pointed his rifle at one of the mutants. "Surrender!"

The mutants stopped their advance.

Jia blinked. "Is that going to work?"

"I doubt they expected squads of soldiers to show up." Erik grinned.

A mutant turned toward Erik and opened his mouth. The words that came out were unintelligible. There was something vaguely familiar about the speech, but it didn't come close to English or Mandarin.

"Anyone have any idea what he's saying?" Erik asked.

The soldiers all shook their heads but kept their rifles trained on the immobile mutants.

"Emma?" Jia asked. "What are they saying?"

"I don't know." Emma sounded surprised. "My initial analysis suggests they aren't speaking any known human language, but the phonemes are within the range of human capability and match sounds in extant human languages."

The mutant continued speaking, his claws twitching, his tone becoming more animated.

"On your knees and puts all your claws above your heads," Erik barked and gestured with his rifle. "I don't know if this was part of your master plan, or you just drank out of the wrong fountain that hadn't been cleaned in ten thousand years, but we're taking control of this ship. If you don't want to die, you will surrender. Any hostile action will be met by us putting a bunch of bullets in you. Now, are you going to be reasonable, or are you going to force us to kill you?"

The mutant gave a short, curt response in his unknown language before the whole group charged, screeching.

"Of course that'd be too easy," Jia mumbled.

CHAPTER FORTY-FIVE

"Take them down," Erik shouted.

He fired a burst into the chatty mutant, strangely satisfied by the spray of red blood that erupted from the target's chest. The enemy weren't Navigators.

They were the twisted humans his team had traveled across the Solar System to find. He could beat anything that was mostly human.

If it bled, it would eventually die.

Jia and the other soldiers opened fire, and their massive barrage cut through the advancing mutants. The enemies staggered back, now covered in wounds. Unlike Erik's team, it was obvious from the bloody holes that the enemy pressure suits weren't designed to take small arms fire.

That made sense. They'd likely never expected to have to deal with other humans, but it also meant the fight had been over for them before it'd even started. The enemy must have been relying on shock value.

Their claws looked nasty. If they'd ambushed Erik's team, they might have been able to damage their pressure suits past the point of self-sealing, but their arrogance had cost them.

The five mutants collapsed to the ground, twitching and bleeding. One rolled onto his back, gurgling and coughing up blood. The original speaker continued talking in the same unknown language, seemingly not bothered despite the half-dozen new and large holes in his body.

Erik didn't need to understand the words to understand the tone. The bastard was mocking him. He'd credit the man for having balls, but the mutation had probably taken them away.

A mutant jumped to his feet. The concentrated team barrage blew his leg off, but he continued forward, masterfully and ridiculously hopping on one foot despite his wounds. Another barrage sent him back to the ground.

Erik's nostrils flared. No matter how tough the mutants were, they were massively outnumbered. If they could talk, they'd obviously kept their intelligence, and the smart thing to do was stay on the ground.

Facing death bravely was one thing, but charging into a fight they couldn't win was pointless. The mutation might have messed up their self-preservation instincts.

Captain Osei grunted. "If they wanted to be monsters, why bother with this alien shit? Why not just use genetic engineering themselves?"

"We don't know that—" Jia began.

The rest of the mutants leapt into the air in different directions, all emitting a sound that was unmistakable despite the odd hollowness: laughter. They snagged the vines with one set of their arms and quickly climbed hand over hand, like monkeys straight from the bowels of hell, their unsettling laughter continuing.

The team fired, clipping some of the enemies, but not downing them. Unlike before, the mutants now appeared more focused on evasion than pointlessly charging the soldiers.

The legless enemy rolled onto his stomach and charged forward, crawling with surprising speed using his four angled arms. He jumped from the side to side, bullets barely missing him, but keeping him from advancing.

The break in tight formation forced the separation of the squads' fields of fire. The soldiers, Erik, and Jia all fired at whatever monster was closest to them, but now that they were on the ceiling, they could take advantage of the protruding stalactites for cover. That might have been their intent all along.

Erik's burst bounced off one of the stalactites, leaving a small dent and seeping orange fluid for a brief second before the wound sealed itself. The exposed wounds on the mutants were half-closed.

"Oh, great." Erik gritted his teeth. "They regenerate."

This wasn't going to be as easy as he'd hoped. Even the damned crawler's severed leg was closing over.

"Then let's nail the most vulnerable part," Jia suggested as she put her words into actions.

Wearing a satisfied look, she aimed carefully and fired three times into the head of the approaching crawler.

He jerked and twitched before jumping backward. Despite the gaping wound in his head, he continued to circle the team on the ground, drawing fire and letting out an unsettling cross between a cackle and a death rattle.

"Now I'm annoyed," Jia muttered, taking another shot.

Captain Osei nailed a mutant mid-jump on the ceiling. The enemy fell to the ground with a loud thump, leaving it an easy target for nearby soldiers.

They concentrated their attacks near the head, blasting out huge chunks of the skull and neck, but it scrambled back to its feet and bounded away despite the damage.

The crawler took two bursts that made it stumble. The team's bullets ripped through it, but some of the earlier wounds were already beginning to close, including dark green and black patches growing slowly to cover the head and major leg wounds.

"Why won't they die?" snarled Captain Osei. "We're blowing off limbs and taking out their brains. How do you kill something that keeps living even after you blow its brains out?"

His hand jerked toward a grenade on his belt. To Erik's relief, the captain stopped before he could call out an objection. They were flanked in three dimensions by the regenerating mutants. Tossing grenades around at this point would end in team casualties.

Between the Ascended Brotherhood and the *yaoguai*, Erik had gotten used to bizarre enemies. The important thing was to maintain discipline and attention to tactical detail.

The latter flooded Erik's thoughts as he ejected a magazine and reloaded. He'd been so focused on the laying down shots, he'd almost missed the obvious. Winning a battle wasn't just about hurting the enemy. It was also about understanding the enemy's tactics.

Erik narrowly missed a climber with a quick burst.

"They're not trying to close on us. They could be trying to run down our ammo and work our nerves. If that's the case, it means they don't think they can beat us.

Unfortunately, given the looks on some of the soldiers' faces, the plan was working.

"Keep it up!" Captain Osei bellowed. "We didn't come all this way just to get taken down by rejects from the UTC's Ugliest Assholes contest!"

Jia focused on the crawler, her brow set in grim determination. Wounds adorned the crawler's chest, arms, and head, but he remained spry. If anything, he seemed to be moving faster now that he was using his two sets of arms.

Erik's theory was challenged when the crawler charged a soldier, but the enemy skittered back after taking two rounds in the shoulder.

Everything that lived had a weak spot. There were no perfect lifeforms, and even if there were, they wouldn't be made over the course of hours from random humans who'd stopped by an ancient ship that had to be running on minimal power.

"Emma, let us know if you see anybody else," Erik ordered, worried the enemy might be stalling to send in more dangerous reinforcements.

Jia tracked the crawler with her rifle. He was taking more of a pounding than many of them but remained fast enough to avoid many of the attacks.

If Erik couldn't rely on anatomy, he would rely on deductive reasoning. He jerked his head around, looking at the wounds on the enemies. They covered most of their body, but he'd noticed none of them had been hit in one location.

Erik aimed at one of the overhead mutants and took a shot. His rifle cracked, and the burst ripped the monster. He screeched and fell, flailing as he landed with a loud thud. Unlike before, he didn't return to his feet. With another weaker screech, he twitched and thrashed. There was no laughter.

"Lower abdomen," Erik shouted. "*That's* their weak spot."

Everyone stopped their indiscriminate fire and aimed their next shots. Not everyone could land a direct hit against fast-moving targets, but having three squads, Jia, and Erik in the room made it inevitable. The other mutants fell in rapid succession, the crawler lasting longer than others, if only because of the difficulty of hitting his abdomen given his orientation.

With calm precision, the soldiers approached the twitching mutants.

They aimed as squads into their abdomens and blew them apart with concentrated fire. The speech might have sounded human, but the death screeches were anything but.

The wounded enemies thrashed and twitched, their slow regeneration no longer in evidence before they stopped moving and slumped.

Erik let out a breath. "That's what you cocky bastards get for underestimating us."

Jia let out a sigh of relief. The soldiers exchanged looks, some taking the opportunity to load fresh magazines in case of another ambush.

Erik shouldered his rifle, walked over to one of the corpses, and pushed it over with his boot. He knelt to inspect the abdomen. Heavy rifle fire had mutilated most of it, but small, leathery black tendrils remained spread throughout the exposed internal organs, all running to a small dark deflated mass bleeding orange, at least what remained of it.

"There's something in here," he called back. "I have no idea what."

Jia headed over to inspect the body. She tilted her head, her expression calm and analytical as if she looked into strange human mutants' perforated bodies every day.

"It's almost like a parasite," she murmured. She gestured at the next closest body. "Check the abdomens and see if you can find something like that in the others."

Erik moved over to the nearest remains and stared at it. "Yeah. Not much left, but definitely something in here."

Soldiers looked into the other bodies and nodded at Jia. Corporal Milton edged toward the corpse but didn't dare crouch next to it.

"Is this what's going to happen to us?" he asked. "We're going to end up with some alien thing in our intestines?"

The other soldiers exchanged worried looks. One man crossed himself.

"We don't know that," Captain Osei insisted.

Jia stood. "Actually, we do."

Erik didn't frown at her. Jia could be blunt, but if she was about to say something, it would be based on the best knowledge available to her.

The captain glared at her. "Are you trying to panic my men?"

"No, Captain. If anything, the opposite." Jia motioned to the tendrils. "The team on the ship wasn't mutated, and

Emma's verified a lack of contamination. We haven't autopsied the bodies, but I'm presuming if they'd started mutating, Emma would have let us know."

"If I was feeling generous," Emma offered. "But, yes, I have total drone coverage of the bodies aboard the captured ship. They are just lying there dead, with no strange mutations or evidence of any physiological changes."

Jia gestured at the bodies. "The parasites aren't that small, and not a single one of these people still had a helmet on. If I had to guess, I'd say they probably pulled it off because of the signal and then the parasite entered." She opened her mouth and pointed down her throat. "Maybe through here."

Several soldiers grimaced. One woman gagged.

Jia knocked on the side of her helmet with her knuckles. "We've got a defense against the signal, and now we know as long as we shoot the parasites, we can finish these mutants off quickly. We've got total tactical control of the situation."

The tension slowly bled off the captain's face. "Okay, I see what you're saying. You think this is all part of the security system? The ship turns invaders against themselves?"

"It could be." Jia shrugged. "It could be that the parasites had nothing to do with the Navigators' plans. Maybe they went to a restaurant that undercooked their meat. Everything I'm saying is heavily based in guesswork about a race that died out before we even had fire."

"Undercooked meat?" Captain Osei smirked. "So they

ended up in a comet floating to Earth with mutating parasites and death signals?"

"Stranger things have happened." Jia shrugged.

"I think if that was true," Osei looked at a few of the bodies, "it'd be the strangest thing that ever happened."

Erik smiled at Jia, remembering something from the fight. "Hey, that one guy was hopping for a while."

Jia shrugged in confusion. "We blew his leg off. Hopping was inevitable."

"These things aren't quite zombies, but they are sort of zombies, and he was hopping." Erik shook his hand back and forth. "Just saying, that almost counts as *jiangshi*."

Captain Osei looked at the two of them. "What are you two talking about?"

"Ignore him," Jia ground out. "He's being obnoxious about stupid stuff from Earth." She pointed at Erik. "They weren't dressed appropriately to be *jiangshi*. What's next? Only do training scenarios that involve fuzzy kittens?"

"That would lead to us getting attacked by packs of fire-breathing kittens." Erik grinned. "Don't worry, I was joking." Erik looked at the captain. "Mostly. But before I throw Emma into a black hole like I promised, she can translate that language for us. Or is it totally alien?"

"I'm working on the translation, Erik," Emma replied. "I'm finding patterns that suggest it might be human, but I need time. Whatever form of communication it is doesn't match any of the languages I know, and my language base includes one spoken only by twenty people on a small Pacific island."

"They spoke to us for a reason. They must have thought we'd have some chance of understanding."

Captain Osei's brow wrinkled in thought. "Will it help if we know what they were saying? They probably were just bragging about how they were going to kill us."

"If they can talk, they're not mindless," Jia replied. "And they were talking for a reason. We might be able to get out of here without any more fights, and we also might be able to figure out what's going on."

Erik shook his head. "Osei's right. It doesn't change the plan. If we didn't think we needed to blow this thing halfway across the galaxy before, we do now. Since Emma and Gamma Squad are watching our backs, we need to sweep through the ship and lay down explosives as quickly as possible, then we're leaving and vaporizing this ship and every parasite and weird-ass murder-field generator on board."

Captain Osei nodded with a satisfied look.

Erik turned to Jia. "Agreed?"

Jia offered him a firm nod. "Some things are better lost to history."

CHAPTER FORTY-SIX

Now less interested in exploration and more in dropping explosive charges, the team cleared the next quarter of the ship far faster than they had the first quarter.

Fighting parasitic creatures that inhabited human corpses, Jia thought, encouraged them all at a primal level.

There was little chatter as they proceeded from room to room with zero opposition.

They weren't there to take in the sights of the bizarre ship. If all went well, they'd make sure no one ever could.

Jia was feeling confident they could set everything they needed to annihilate the Navigator ship in less time than it had taken for their initial inspection. The remaining crew from the conspiracy ship remained unaccounted for, but everyone expected they'd run into them sooner or later.

Horror was a funny thing, and training did a lot to blunt its effects. In the coming weeks, perhaps they would have time to reflect on what had been done to the people aboard the captured ship and those who had boarded the alien vessel.

But for now, they were nothing more than an enemy who needed to be put down.

Jia couldn't work up much concern. What little belief she had in the potential restraint of the conspiracy had gone away on Venus when they ran into the hybrid agent.

The conspiracy members weren't brave men and women plumbing the depths of forbidden knowledge to save humanity. They were disgusting, morally bankrupt monsters who had greedily pushed too fast and too far.

Now their outer forms reflected their inner truths.

Sophia Vand wasn't enough. The conspiracy had to be stopped. It needed to be burned down, root and branch.

You bastards made the mistake of not finishing off Erik at Molino, Jia thought. *Now you have both of us to worry about.*

Erik, Jia, and the soldiers passed into a new wide and long chamber. Pulsating columns ran from the floor to the ceiling, the light glowing brighter in them than the walls and the ceiling.

Smaller mounds similar to ones they'd seen in other rooms surrounded the columns.

"It's fortunate you have me with you," Emma announced, more than a hint of satisfaction flavoring her tone. "Because you would be hard-pressed to gain the same benefits in the same period of time from even a dedicated specialist, but I bring true creativity with massive analytical speed."

"Care to explain why you're being so smug?" Erik asked. "Smugger than usual? Or is it Fleshbags Should Appreciate Their AI Masters Day?"

"I can translate the language, more or less," Emma

replied. "Once I realized its fundamental nature, it became a trivial exercise."

Captain Osei's brow lifted in surprise. "You translated an alien language that quickly?"

Emma laughed. "While I do appreciate you being appreciative of my capabilities, it's important that I be honest so you can better understand both my potential and my limits. My achievement is impressive, but no, I didn't translate an alien language, which was why I could do this so quickly."

"I don't understand. If you didn't translate it, how can you understand it?"

"Because I translated a *human* language," Emma replied. "That is to say, those unfortunately parasitized gentlemen were speaking a language from Earth. A dead one, mind you, but a human language that evolved from and was used by human beings. Well, technically still *is* being used by human beings, as long as you count those who have been transformed by alien technology."

"The Navigators speak some obscure language?" Erik asked, sounding annoyed. "Is this just about screwing with us? If they were threatening us, it'd make more sense to use a language we could understand."

"I can't be sure that sort of thought process had anything to do with it." Emma chuckled. "I can't be a hundred percent certain because of my lack of access to OmniNet resources, but I'm more than confident that the language they are speaking is a form of proto-Afro-Asiatic."

"Huh?" Captain Osei cocked his head. "I haven't heard of that language."

"Of course you haven't." Emma's voice indicated she was waving a hand dismissively. "Because you are not a linguistic scholar, and it's not something most people would concern themselves because no human being has spoken any form of the language on Earth for an estimated twenty thousand years."

Corporal Milton looked from the column he was inspecting toward the captain, his eyes wide. "Did she just say twenty *thousand* years? As in, before we had cities?"

"Yes, that would be an accurate statement."

Jia blinked, letting it settle over her. She didn't understand the implications, and it'd never occurred to her that the odd speech might be something like that. Something percolated in the back of her mind, like two puzzle pieces desperate to fit together.

Erik frowned. "I hate to sound like a recording on replay all the time, but I don't get it. Why would they use a language from that long ago? Why not use something more modern? What's the game here?"

Jia's breath caught as the pieces finally connected. "Because that was the only reference they had." Her eyes widened. "You're right, Erik. There's no reason to try to communicate with us in a language we don't understand, and it's not like those crew members would know a very dead language. Those parasites must not have access to the memories of the host, but if whatever's controlling them visited Earth in the distant past, they might have access to ancient language samples."

"You're telling me the Navigators aren't dead, and they've visited Earth in the recent past, relatively speaking?" Captain Osei asked, sounding dubious. "And they're controlling people through those things we shot in their stomachs?"

"Why not?" Jia shrugged. "The Leems visited Earth, so why not the Navigators? I'm not saying the ancient astronaut theories are true, but it's not insane that the Navigators popped by."

"But they're all dead," he countered. "And they have been for a while."

Jia shook her head. "We assume they're dead because of what we found." She motioned around the chamber. "And now we've found proof that shows that they must have survived longer than we thought."

Erik grunted. "So, what did they say?"

Emma cleared her throat. "Perhaps I should send it only to you, Jia, and the captain first. It has disturbing implications."

"Of course it does." Erik scoffed. "I didn't think they were inviting us over for beignets and roast duck."

"It's fine." Captain Osei's nostrils flared. "My soldiers are professionals. They don't need to be coddled, and this isn't a situation where I want to waste time repeating information."

"Very well," Emma replied. "Note I have made some minor edits for stylistic delivery, but I do believe this captures the general tenor of what was intended by their statements."

Erik circled his hand in the air. "Get on with it. We've still got five more of those things crawling around somewhere."

Emma's first hologram of the mission appeared, her normal redheaded appearance but with a flowing Roman stola. Jia suspected it was the AI's way of trying to be dramatic.

"You," Emma began, "the inferior beings, have come upon this, a vessel of the Gods Who Hunt, the true Hunters, and have walked into your doom. We congratulate you for crawling up from your primitive huts and developing sticks you call weapons and touching the stars. You carry the stink of the toys of our prey, and we know you used their ways to come to this ship. You have ripped space apart like your precious gods, crawling and scratching for more. Know that you will die like the gods whose toys you use, destroyed by this, the memory of us."

Corporal Milton swallowed. "Yeah, that's freaky."

Silence followed. Jia finally spoke up.

"I'm beginning to think this isn't a Navigator ship," Jia suggested.

Captain Osei turned his head toward her. "Huh? You're saying this is Orlox because of all the biotech?"

Jia shook her head. "No, you're not understanding me." She pointed at a column. "Whoever or whatever is controlling *this* ship isn't Navigator tech, and it's not Orlox. It's something different and older. If I'm interpreting Emma's translation correctly, this was a different ancient race, but they seem to know we used Navigator tech to get here." She frowned at the column. "I'm beginning to wonder if this explains where the Navigators went. I think these Hunters killed them. They obviously visited Earth in the distant past."

Erik growled. "You're saying those parasites are the Hunters?"

"I don't think so." Jia gestured at bar-like structures

along the walls. "Everything here is scaled for something much larger than humans, and there's no way this ship was designed for anything remotely humanoid, regardless of size. If those parasites were the Hunters, I think the ship would be laid out a lot differently." She nodded at Erik. "I think you called it earlier. This is the security system. It might even be automated. That might be what they are getting at with the memory comment."

"Then there's no Hunters left on the ship?" Corporal Milton asked.

Several other soldiers nodded their eager interest in his question. Being brave and well-trained only amounted to so much when facing any enemy beyond imagination and known capabilities. Taking down grotesque humans fell into the realm of normal possibilities.

"I think if there were, they would be smart enough to not let us set up explosives on half their ship," Jia answered.

Erik snorted. "Or they're just arrogant assholes who think we can't do anything to them. You heard the big speech. They did everything but say, 'Ours are bigger than yours.' Well, screw them. We'll blow some new holes in these Hunters' ship and show them that humanity has a lot better spears than we did twenty thousand years ago."

Captain Osei looked around the chamber. "But no one else has come at us. I'm sure they've got those five other bastards in reserve, and we know how to beat them now. I also don't get how they'd be smart enough to know we're humans from Earth, but not get that we wouldn't speak an ancient language."

Jia nodded. "I don't think there is a living Hunter on this ship. I think they have something like their version of a limited AI running a standard defensive program. It might be analyzing our language, but Emma only could translate so quickly because she already had data about the language."

"That's true," Emma offered.

Jia continued, "Everything from allowing boarding to letting us explore the ship when it's clear we're not under the influence of the mind-control field doesn't seem like something an alien would allow. It's bad tactics." She unslung her rifle and lowered it into her hands. "The good news—I think—is we have a chance. I believe the system does not have access to its total resources. Otherwise, it wouldn't be relying on recycled human mutants to throw at us."

Corporal Milton stared at her. "Let me get this straight. We board this ship we think is a Navigator vessel, only to find out it belongs to some other race, and they might have been tough enough to take out the Navigators?"

"I should note," Emma interrupted with a smile, "that we don't know they wiped out the Navigators. Bluster doesn't have to be accepted at face value simply because it comes from an advanced alien race. They could be, as you fleshbags put it, 'working your nerves.'"

"But it'd explain where the Navigators went," Jia countered with a thoughtful look. "It'd also explain why humanity has only found limited Navigator artifacts rather than troves suggesting a galaxy-spanning civilization. It might be that all the artifacts we and the other races found were from refugees."

"It doesn't matter," Erik muttered, his speech clipped. "This ship can screw with people's minds and infest people with parasites that make them slaves of the ship or whatever asshole Hunter is hiding in a closet somewhere. I don't care if it's operating on reserve mode. We need to take it out before it figures how to power itself back up." His gaze dipped to his rifle and back to Jia. "The UTC higher-ups can figure out if they want to change the history books after we send this ship to join the rest of the Navigators and Hunters in history."

"There's a problem," Emma reported, her hologram vanishing. "Mutants just attacked one of the repeaters and drones in a room between here and the exit. The attack proves they have additional forces. I'm detecting increases in emissions and signal interference as well."

A hologram appeared, showing three mutants pouncing on a repeater. Two were obviously derived from the human crew of the captured conspiracy vessel, but the third was something else—a much larger humanoid. The mutations and additional arms were similar to the humans', but the original bulky body approached three meters in height. It lacked clothing, but its entire body had been almost entirely covered with the dark green and black patches of the other mutants, this time thicker with an oily layer over a bony material.

Corporal Milton shivered. "I bet that big guy was a Navigator."

"Maybe." Jia stared at the image, both fascinated and horrified by the implications.

"Gamma Squad, report," barked Captain Osei. "The AI is reporting enemy contact between our position and yours. Are you under attack?"

"No contact, sir," replied Lieutenant Zhang. "We

thought we heard something and were just about to call you about that. Should we meet with you?"

"No, hold your position. We don't want those things making it onto any of our ships."

"Another set of repeaters and drones is under attack," Emma reported, sounding annoyed. "The mutant stock doesn't appear to be either human or potential Navigator. They are much smaller. Both forces emerged from different rooms."

Jia took a deep breath and tried not to laugh. Having to deal with a horrific alien menagerie struck her as the expected outcome of a mission to a mysterious comet at the edge of the Solar System.

They'd been unlucky.

The other crew had obviously stirred something long-dormant, but now it was an open question how long it'd take the Hunter ship to activate its full systems.

Jia glanced at Erik. She wasn't going to die here. He wasn't going to die here either. They both still had things to handle, and there were certain things she would tell him when this was all over.

Erik inclined his head toward the explosives in the room. "I think we're going to have to gamble that the explosives we've set up are enough to take this ship out."

"But they're knocking out the repeaters," Captain Osei replied. "They will be going after the explosives next."

"Not if they're attracted to specific types of transmissions," Jia suggested. "That might be why they're leaving the explosives alone. They might not recognize what they are. They've seen us use guns, but not L-48."

"But without the repeaters, we won't be able to set them off remotely."

"We won't. We'll sweep back the way we came at double time. We'll activate timers on as many as we can with a generous margin and get the hell out of here." Erik scowled. "I'm not becoming a pet for these Hunter bastards, and I'm not letting this ship continue to float anywhere *near* Earth."

CHAPTER FORTY-SEVEN

"Timer set!" bellowed a sergeant. He looked satisfied with himself.

The team had backtracked two rooms and hadn't encountered any new enemies, but harsh screeches and bangs echoed in the distance. It had become clear there was no way they'd escape without engaging the enemy reinforcements.

Erik didn't want to admit to the soldiers or Jia that he was worried.

They'd equipped and staffed the mission based on the idea they would be fighting humans, not mutants. Now that the ship was flinging mutants built out of species they hadn't ever encountered at them, he couldn't be sure about anything.

Emma's hologram presented a mutant that was much better armored and farther converted than the human stock they'd fought. If *yaoguai* derived from UTC tech could present a hassle, he couldn't imagine what the Hunters might bring to the fight.

"Emma, make sure Raphael and Cutter know what's going on," Erik ordered. "It might come down to using the biggest guns to finish this ship off."

"I've been keeping them apprised, and they've closed the distance, but I'll give them specific situational details," Emma replied. "Should I put them through?"

"No. We don't need to be distracted with relaying information to them."

Captain Osei gestured urgently. "Next room! Pick it up unless you want to go up with this ship!"

The team jogged toward the next room, everyone's faces locked in intense focus. They didn't have time for fear or worry to overwhelm them. They had a job to do that involved saving their own lives and protecting the UTC.

"I've lost more drones," Emma transmitted, her voice now more difficult to make out because of the drop in the audio. "I'm having trouble overcoming the increased local interference. Incidentally, I can now account for the remaining five humans. There are also some more exotic, smaller creatures that have appeared. I'm doing my best to dodge with my drones, but those parasitized predators are rather insistent on destruction. Annoying and rude behavior from those fleshbags."

"More proof they know exactly what they're doing," Erik replied. "Or at least whoever's in control does. Are they still not going after the explosives?"

"Not yet. They are exclusively targeting my drones and repeaters."

"Definitely not mindless," Jia observed with a deep

scowl. "But they have their limits. This timer plan might work."

"I hope so," Erik replied. "And I hope they'll get a couple of seconds to regret it when we blow the charges and it rips this ancient piece of crap apart."

They arrived in the next room, and a soldier hurried over to set the timer on the explosive. Erik and Captain Osei were decreasing the times the closer they moved toward the entrance and synchronizing them for simultaneous explosion.

There was a margin for error, but not enough if they got pinned down.

Both men understood the implications. Erik didn't plan to die, but he also needed to make sure the Hunter ship was destroyed, and his best shot involved blowing it from the inside.

The increased activity had him concerned. What kind of weapons did a ship that large carry?

"Contact!" shouted a soldier. "Six o'clock!"

Five parasitized humans loped out of a passageway, flanked by two of the taller hosts.

Erik wasn't sure if they were Navigators or some other unfortunate race. In any other circumstance, that might have been a huge revelation, but the xenoarchaeology was the last of his worries, with the minutes ticking down and more parasitized mutants undoubtedly converging on their position.

It wouldn't be any better to die at the hands of a Navigator than a human.

"Open fire!" ordered Captain Osei.

This time the troops didn't need to experiment or waste ammunition. Each squad fired at their closest mutant target. Everyone aimed for the abdomen and fired almost as one, a massive volley of bursts from the high-powered rifles. The angry swarm of bullets ripped into the advancing enemies.

The enemies collapsed to the ground in a shower of blood, most of their midsections gone. One man's body had been all but sheared from his legs by the assault. The taller humanoid hosts staggered back, green and orange blood pouring from their wounds. They rushed away from one another, loping across the ground using a combination of both sets of arms and their legs. One gripped the bars on the wall to climb up.

One of the creatures shouted in a low, deep voice.

"They're saying you'll never escape," Emma translated, sending the transmission only to Captain Osei, Erik, and Jia.

"Yeah. Whatever." Erik nailed one of the mutants in the head. It stumbled backward but didn't drop. He followed up with another burst to both sides of the chest. The mutant pitched forward and landed hard on the ground.

The observant soldiers altered their aim and opened fire, soon downing the giants. The one climbing was the last to die, losing his grip and crashing to the ground. He bounced hard before his head lolled to the side.

"It's more stalling shit," Erik muttered.

"They're trying to bring more reinforcements," insisted Captain Osei.

"At least we know now there's no way the conspiracy guys were ever going to gain control of this shit. Emma, how we doing?" After five seconds of silence, he tried again. "Emma? Can you hear me?"

Jia gave him a worried look. "They're awfully insistent on taking out those repeaters, and she was having trouble as it was."

"We don't have time to mess around with this. If they aren't relying only on humans, we can't predict how many they can throw at us. For all we know, they have a huge storage room filled with hosts they've collected from all over the galaxy."

Captain Osei frowned. "Gamma Squad, status report." His pained combination of worry and a scowl deepened on his face. "Damn it."

"It could just be the repeaters," Jia suggested. "They hadn't been attacked yet."

"Could be." Erik inclined his head toward the exit. "Let's only set the timers on explosives in half the rooms."

A soldier shook his head. "But sir, L-48's not going to go off just because another explosion hits it."

"I know that, but Gamma Squad might need us, and we can't let them stall us for too long. We'll have to gamble that half the explosives we set will be good enough to wound this ship and give us enough time to dig through with our ships and blow the hell out of what's left. L-48's not a toy, either."

"What if we don't get out fast enough?" Corporal Milton muttered sarcastically.

"Then the obvious happens," Captain Osei replied.

Erik let out a bitter chuckle. "Yeah, the Hunters aren't the only ones who'll be history. We've got time, but not a lot. Let's move."

The arming and withdrawal process had become an exact science, and the hard running had them panting but closing in on Gamma Squad and the entrance. If they skipped the rest of the explosives, they could get back to the original chamber in under ten minutes by Erik's estimate.

After the team entered the latest chamber, Erik stopped and swept the area with his gun, his eyes narrowed. The room had previously contained tall mounds feeding into a pool, but the mounds lay open, their outer sides flat on the ground like peeled leaves, exposing an orange-fluid-covered inside.

The conspicuous absence of anything inside convinced Erik he'd found the source of some of the mutants.

Erik jerked his gun at shifting shadows. A horde of creatures clung to the roof, each the size of a large dog, with long, sharply jointed legs. Hardened prickly shells covered most of their bodies, and while they lacked arms and any obvious eyes, the layered mandibles protruding from the small mouths dripping bright orange fluid looked like they could deliver plenty of pain.

He wasn't sure if they represented some poor race parasitized in the distant past or a combat creation of the Hunters.

"Gren—" Captain Osei began.

The monsters rained to the ground screeching, and the soldiers opened fire. With the enemy in their midst, the opportunity to use grenades had vanished.

Bullets bounced off the creature's exteriors, leaving

small dents and cracks but not stopping them. Erik jumped out of the way of a falling monster and fired at one of its legs. Two bursts managed to sever it, but that only slowed the monster.

It rounded on Erik and charged him, snapping with its mandibles. He spun to avoid the attack and took out another leg with a controlled shot. These days, he was used to weird things trying to murder him.

Jia fired directly into the mouth of one of the following monsters. It crashed into the ground and fell onto its back, its legs curling up.

Soldiers cried out as the monsters rushed at them, barreling into some and knocking them to the ground. Their mandibles sliced into the pressure suits, accomplishing with ease what would normally take a high-powered rifle round.

Erik's current opponent rolled onto its side, kicking with its legs. He shoved his rifle into the mouth and pulled the trigger. Orange fluid splattered from inside, and the creature collapsed to the floor.

Jia leapt over a dead enemy and shot at one of the creatures overwhelming one of the soldiers. Her bullets narrowly missed the mouth and bounced off the armored hide right above. She strode forward, taking careful, deliberate shots until one pierced the mouth. The monster fell off the soldier it'd been attacking, and she finished it off with a follow-up shot.

Another soldier was less fortunate. A trio of creatures converged on him and ripped into his suit, their mandibles sinking deep into his leg, chest, and neck. He gave a strangled scream and thrashed.

Captain Osei let out a bellow of rage and barreled toward the man, emptying a magazine in a stream of bullets that managed to land rounds in two of the monsters' mouths. Erik finished off the third attacker, but the massive damage to the soldier's suit, along with the blood everywhere, wasn't promising.

The wounded soldier continued to thrash, paling, his veins darkening. Captain Osei dropped to his knees and yanked out a med patch, the battle still raging around him.

Erik pulled out an AP magazine and slapped it into his rifle. His next burst barely made a dent in a creature's shell, and he growled in frustration.

A creature jumped for the wounded soldier, but Erik's and Jia's combined bursts hit it square in the mouth, knocking it out of the air and leaving it twitching and dying.

The captain slapped on two med patches before yanking a tiny silver canister out and moving it close to the holes in the pressure suit. Fine silver mist sprayed out and covered the holes. The wounded soldier stopped screaming and moved. His veins turned solid black, and his eyes rheumy.

Erik murmured a quick command to bring up the life signs for the soldier, Corporal Galn, on his smart lenses. The soldier's heart had stopped. Erik ignored his frustration, instead concentrating on keeping the monsters from overwhelming the captain.

Jia spun toward another wounded and overwhelmed soldier and rushed toward his attackers, firing several bursts to draw the enemy's attention. The monsters split their forces, leaving them easy prey for the soldiers on one side and Jia on the other.

Bursts and shots grew less frequent as the bodies of the monsters began to pile up. Soldiers exchanged magazines while their comrades continued to fire.

Whatever intelligence the previous mutants had shown wasn't obvious in the latest batch of enemies. That was only a small relief, given the team's casualties.

Captain Osei stood and shook his head. "There's nothing we can do for Galn now," he grimly offered, his jaw set tightly. "I think those things injected something into him. Some kind of poison."

"Is he going to become like those other guys?" asked Corporal Milton.

"We don't know that," Jia replied.

Erik stared at the man. "We need to continue our strategic withdrawal, and we need to make sure this ship goes down."

Captain Osei surveyed the rest of his soldiers. Some had suffered suit damage, but the suits had fixed the holes, or the soldiers had applied their own sealants.

"Blackwell's right," he commented. "We don't want to be on this ship when the L-48 goes off."

"Let's make a straight run for the boarding tube," Erik suggested. "We can't afford to be in too many more fights like this. It'll bleed off too much time, especially since the AP rounds are useless."

Captain Osei stared down at his dead soldier, offering Erik an almost imperceptible nod. "Just promise me, Blackwell, that no matter what happens, this ship gets destroyed. I know you're not military, and I also know you work with ID, but you're not their bitch. I don't know what orders they've given you about this ship."

"This ship is going to hell one way or another." Erik nodded, finding it hard not to remember his dead soldiers on Molino. The conspiracy had sent its people to this Hunter ship. Somehow they knew about it and were prepared to sacrifice countless lives for it.

Navigator or even Hunter artifacts, he thought. *I think I know what they didn't want us to see on Molino. Those bastards.*

CHAPTER FORTY-EIGHT

"Now the Lady's just screwing with us," Erik muttered.

The team was only three rooms away from the entrance now, but none of the other rooms they'd encountered had included huge monsters ripping themselves out of the walls. They were a diverse group of flitter-sized masses of legs and claws, barbs and mandibles, and bony plates.

Erik was having trouble processing what he was seeing. The creatures weren't merely larger versions of the earlier ambushers, but a seemingly random combination of limbs and parts. There was no way they were all derived from the same species.

One new threat scuttled about on four barbed legs. Another twitched forward on five razor-pointed tentacles. A third monstrosity was roughly bipedal, with three barbed-tipped arms swinging. The last looked like some sort of armored starfish demon who had crawled up from hell to take damned souls back with him.

Erik was beginning to think the *yaoguai* and Ascended

Brotherhood he'd fought in the past were mundane compared to the creatures before him.

The soldiers' rifles came alive, with everyone playing to experience and targeting the mouths, at least in the cases where they could see them, but the latest foes were living tanks. The bullets passed into them, but the massive creatures only spat out orange blood and screeched in response.

The starfish's exterior absorbed the bullets with no apparent damage, but it writhed up, briefly exposing a mouth ringed with teeth. Jia and other soldiers tried to down it, but it wasn't any more effective than their earlier barrage. It whipped out with an arm and almost crushed a man.

During a brief discussion in a hallway, Jia mentioned wondering before why none of the doors had closed. The security system or insane Hunter running the defenses might not think it was useful.

Besides, the proper application of explosives could get a team through any barrier.

Erik was half-convinced the system wanted them to have hope, just to crush it. Sadism wasn't limited to the human race. He flung his rifle over his shoulder and reached for the laser rifle latched to his carryaid.

"Back up!" Captain Osei bellowed. "Frag grenades! Throw at will."

Like a practiced synchronized swimming team, the soldiers pulled and primed the grenades in complete unison. They pitched them at a high arc, aiming for the rear of the monsters.

The grenades exploded in a shower of flame and shrapnel. Smoldering chunks of armor or flesh lay on the ground, covered with orange blood, exposing small target opportunities. The monsters screeched and lumbered toward the soldiers, who spread out to avoid the enemy.

The three-armed monster backhanded a soldier and sent him flying into a wall with a crunch. The poor sergeant grunted and fell to the ground, groaning.

Erik brought up his laser rifle and aimed for the head. "Eat this, you freak."

The invisible beam carved a hole through the monster's head and into the wall behind him. Stumbling, the monster fell on its side before a second shot tunneled through its neck.

A tentacle from another monster stabbed a soldier through the head. The monster tossed his body to the side.

The soldiers concentrated fire at the wounds opened by the grenade volley. They blasted more chunks out of the behemoths, but it didn't slow them.

"Plasmas to the rear target!" Captain Osei shouted while ducking a tentacle. He backpedaled and emptied a magazine into the horror attacking him to not much effect. "You're not surviving this, you bastard."

The other soldiers kept their cool, despite their losses and sprinting around the room to duck behind the mounds and columns to avoid the monsters.

Grabbing their plasma grenades, the soldiers hurled them toward a four-legged monster farther back. White-blue explosions lit up the room, scorching and blasting away the wall and the back of the creature.

Captain Osei spun out of the way of the tentacle monster's next attack. It batted his rifle out of his hands, but the weapon dragged along the ground, still connected by a line to his belt. He snatched up his rifle and sprinted out of the reach of the creature.

The monster's wounded comrade thrashed, but squads circled it and unloaded their magazines into the exposed innards. Dozens of bullets ripped through the inside and found their mark, some vital organ or nerve cluster deep inside. With a final screech, it dropped to the ground.

"Cover me, Erik," Jia shouted. "I've got an idea."

"Is it a good one?" he yelled back.

"No, but I'm doing it anyway."

"Of course you are." He sighed.

Jia ran toward the starfish, keeping out of range while taking potshots. Her bullets weren't doing much, so she moved closer. Hoping to end the risk to his partner, Erik fired his laser rifle toward its center, burning a hole, but the starfish barely reacted.

The starfish reared again, exposing its mouth. With a flick of her wrist, Jia yanked, primed, and tossed a plasma grenade into the monster's mouth. The explosion blasted its charred limbs off and left nothing but a half-vaporized husk in the center. The arms twitched for seconds before going inert.

Ignoring Osei and the other soldiers, the tentacled monster spun and pounced at Jia. Erik fired another shot and seared off a tentacle, draining the last of his energy cell.

With a massive thud, the creature landed and sliced at Jia with a tentacle. She tried to go for her rifle, but it cut into her glove. She stumbled backward, gritting her teeth, the holes in the blood-stained suit already beginning to close as she fell to the ground. The monster stabbed again.

Erik yanked the energy cell out of his laser rifle and tossed it to the ground. He pulled another one from the carryaid and twisted it on as rapidly as he could.

The soldiers continued pelting the creature, but although it jerked when a bullet struck an orange-stained wound from their initial attack, it didn't go down. Tentacle after tentacle stabbed at Jia's chest and head as if the monster considered her a greater threat than anyone else in that room.

That wasn't a bad calculation, and the current foes were displaying better tactics than the four-legged ceiling creatures from before.

The kind of opponent who would run at a monster to all but shove a grenade in its mouth wasn't to be taken lightly, but neither was the opponent who was holding a heavy laser rifle.

The monster seemed to recognize its error, or perhaps satisfied with the multiple wounds it had inflicted, it squirmed quickly toward Erik. He narrowed his eyes and aimed high in the central body stalk of the grotesque organic weapon now charging him.

A ladder of holes appeared as he emptied his new cell. Erik's shot had removed most of the central portion of the creature's body. The monster collapsed to the ground in front of him, becoming stone-still.

"Jia!" Erik called, his heart pounding.

He cursed himself. It wasn't that he regretted Jia coming on a dangerous mission. There was no one he would rather have guarding his back, but there was something he wished she knew about how he felt. It would have to wait, *but not much longer.*

Erik was tired of hiding from himself.

"It sliced and stabbed me and it hurts, but I don't think I was poisoned," Jia called, wincing. "My suit integrity is okay, and I've applied a med patch."

Captain Osei pointed at two soldiers and then the downed, groaning sergeant. "You two pick him up." He turned toward the dead soldier and shook his head. "Damn it, Cardiz."

"Is he going to turn into one of those things?" asked Corporal Milton. This time at least, he seemed to be asking a question as opposed to freaking out, but his questions were getting on Jia's nerves.

"Stow that shit, Milton. I'm not leaving anyone else behind, and if he turns into something else, I'll take him out myself."

The corporal nodded and stepped back.

Jia patted down her suit to manually verify the seals and gingerly stood.

Erik inclined his head toward the exit. "We're almost there."

Captain Osei pulled Cardiz's body off the ground. "If we're almost there, we can at least honor some of our dead."

Erik slid the laser rifle back on his carryaid and walked over to the captain. He held out his arms. "I've got a hardware arm. It'll be easier for me."

"Thanks." Captain Osei gave a shallow nod and handed over the body. "Now let's move, soldiers! These men didn't give their lives so we can all get blown up."

He led the way as everyone charged toward the boarding tunnel. The seconds blurred together with no more attacks until they arrived at the initial chamber.

Lieutenant Zhang and what was left of Gamma Squad were spread out near the now dented door, red and orange blood covering their suits and the discoloration typical of seals obvious all over. Small flat drones hovered near the exits. Piles of dead mutants and monsters lay on the ground among the bodies of three soldiers. The charred remains of a starfish clogged a nearby exit.

Captain Osei hurried over to Zhang. "Damn it."

The lieutenant nodded, his mien dark. "We've been trying to contact you, but our transmissions weren't making it. Emma says everything's still clear on the other end."

Erik was glad they had contact again.

"Yes, but the interference has increased considerably," Emma offered. "There was little I could do with all my repeaters and drones destroyed in the other rooms. I considered opening fire to distract the enemies I presumed were attacking you when I lost connection, but I didn't want to risk damaging a part of the ship in which you were present."

"It's fine." Erik looked over his shoulder. "Open the door, and let's get the hell out of here."

The door slid open. Soldiers hurried over to collect the fallen bodies of their comrades.

Emma sighed, the sound weary and long. "The latent interference is now preventing me from effective sensor usage, but they haven't done anything to control sound, and they are rather loud. There are a large number of enemies approaching this location."

"We don't have time to hold these bastards off." Erik nodded toward the dent. "The timers are counting down, but I'm not sure if the door will hold."

Lieutenant Zhang stepped forward. "We just need to hold them until you evacuate to the *Argo*, right?"

"It's suicide," Jia stated.

"If those things flood the tunnels, we're all dead anyway." Lieutenant Zhang gave her a lopsided smile. "I volunteer, but I'm not ordering anyone else."

The rest of the Gamma Squad survivors moved closer to him. Captain Osei and Corporal Milton did as well.

"The rest of you sorry bastards get to the *Argo*," the captain barked.

Erik frowned. "You don't have to do this."

"I do," the captain replied. "But you're wasting time trying to talk me out of it. If we get lucky and we thin the herd, we'll pull back, but you get my people to safety, Blackwell, and then you blow the living shit out of this horror show." He shook his head, his jaw clenched tightly. "There were people trying to get this shit on purpose, Blackwell. Not freak aliens, but human beings, and the UTC needs you to help track those bastards down before they get lucky the next time and figure out how to safely get their hands on this." He rounded on a nearby soldier. "I told you idiots to go through the tunnel," he shouted. "Now move! We've got enough volunteers for this piss detail today."

The remaining soldiers reluctantly jogged into the tunnel, taking their fallen.

Erik saluted Captain Osei. "We'll wait as long as we can."

The other man gave him a toothy grin and saluted back. "Don't wait for too long. We don't have much time left on those explosives."

After a nod to Jia, Erik ran toward the tunnel. Jia cast one lingering gaze around the room before following. Monsters screeched in the distance.

They were out of time in more ways than one.

CHAPTER FORTY-NINE

Jia's heart thundered as they continued the evacuation through the long boarding tube and onto the captured ship and then back over to the *Argo*.

After shedding her carryaid, she continued toward the cockpit, Erik close behind. The soldiers spread out to tend to their wounded and lay their dead down for later respect.

"Captain Osei's squad has made contact with the enemy," Emma reported, her voice subdued. "There is a mix of small and larger enemies. They are holding their own, thanks to judicious explosive usage."

"Prepare to retract the tunnel and seal the ship on my order," Erik ordered as he stepped into the cockpit. He pulled off his helmet and connected it to a hook in the wall. "Send a warning to everybody to get ready. I don't want someone dying because they knocked their heads when we accelerate."

Jia dropped into a seat and removed her helmet. She strapped into her seat. "Preparing for hard burn." Her gaze dipped to the sensors. "The jumpship is close."

"Blackwell," came Cutter's voice over the comm. "Holochick filled us in. We wait, let your explosives go boom, and then we blow away whatever's left, right? If there *is* anything left."

"Yeah. That's the plan." Erik settled into his seat with a frown. "We're just trying to give Osei some time."

"Do you want me to unload everything we've got?" Cutter asked.

"Everything," Erik ground out. "I don't want anything left when we're done, but the L-48 should do most of the work for us. I'm hoping it'll at least make sure that damned ship doesn't power up any more than it already has."

"Only Captain Osei and Lieutenant Zhang remain alive," Emma offered dispassionately. "Shall I seal the *Argo*?"

"Not yet," Erik replied, his hands curling into fists. "We need to give him a chance to escape."

"Unless you altered things when I lost contact, I esti- mate you have about four minutes left before the explo- sives go off," Emma replied. "It's highly unlikely he can move through the tunnel and the other ship and arr—"

"You seal at one minute," Erik interrupted. "Not a damned second sooner. Understood?"

"That might be insufficient time to avoid damage, depending on the size of secondary explosions. I would recomm—"

"One minute," Erik shouted.

"Understood," Emma replied timidly.

Jia's hands flew over controls. She didn't want to leave the escape to Emma. She owed it to the men who had died, and the men they might have to leave behind to be personally involved.

The enormity of the situation weighed on her.

This wasn't some skirmish over political control on the frontier, or even good men taking on ideologically misguided terrorists.

A horrible enemy had been sleeping in the Solar System for thousands of years, and now soldiers were giving their lives to protect their species from something powerful enough to prey on the Navigators.

"Is everyone secured?" she asked.

"All survivors are secured," Emma replied. "Erik, I've lost my feeds to the alien ship. My remaining drones were destroyed, but before I lost my feed, Lieutenant Zhang was dead, and Captain Osei had suffered grievous wounds and extensive damage to his pressure suit. The enemy is now in the boarding tube."

Erik gritted his teeth. "Seal the ship."

"Making all due preparations," Emma offered apologetically. "And I'm sorry."

"Not your fault."

Jia stared at a data window, waiting for full retraction and sealing before pulsing the side thrusters and spinning the *Argo* around. "Initiating hard burn!"

Even the *Argo's* superior grav compensators couldn't block the push against her seat as the engines screamed to life and pushed it away from the other ships. She stared at the sensor display as the marker indicating the comet grew distant and the symbol depicting the jumpship grew closer.

"One minute until estimated explosion," Emma reported.

"Do you think it'll be enough?" Jia asked. "We didn't cover the entire ship."

Erik shook his head. "We wouldn't need that much on a human ship. I just wanted to be sure. We placed enough L-48 to do a decent number on a tower. For all their weird-ass biological shit, their monsters died when we started using heavy guns. I'm sure there will be pieces left over, but that's where we can clean up with the jumpship."

Jia took slow, careful breaths, keeping up the thrust.

"Thirty seconds," Emma offered. "Twenty-nine, twenty-eight…"

It was absurd. Her overzealous sense of justice had set her on a path that led to a new, hostile alien race. If men hadn't just died, she would have laughed at the ridiculousness of it all.

Now, she just couldn't.

"Ten, nine, eight…"

"When we get a chance to catch our breaths," Jia murmured, "we need to talk about something."

"Seven, six, five…"

"Fuck that," Erik replied. "I already know what you want to say. I love you."

"Five, four, three…" Emma counted.

"I love you, too," Jia murmured and brought up the rear feed.

"Two, *one*…"

It was time to see if it was all worth it.

CHAPTER FIFTY

The explosion rippled out from the side connected to the boarding tube, blasting ice and rock in every direction and consuming the conspiracy ship.

It was eerily beautiful—the beginning of its death at the hands of both ancient ice and modern fire.

Jia was impressed. When Captain Osei and Erik had discussed the L-48, she'd anticipated it damaging the Hunter ship but not being visible from outside.

A secondary explosion burst from the conspiracy ship. The force of the blast launched a huge chunk of the comet away, revealing the dark body of the disk-like ship. The flying debris obscured the direct view, but it didn't hide the gaping hole in the Hunter ship. It was as if the comet was an outer body, and the ship the heart.

The humans' effort had torn out the dark heart of the vengeful waking god.

It was insane. Erik and Jia had been outgunned many times in their short career together, but taking on the Hunters went beyond that. The two of them had been stone-age warriors with spears trying to charge a machine-gun nest.

Jia shook her head. She *couldn't* think that way.

They'd just blown a hole in the Hunter ship using a combination of human explosives and sacrificing a human ship. As impressive as the Hunter biotechnology was, the team had won fights against their monstrous creations.

The Hunters were more advanced, yes, but humans *did* win. A god who could bleed was a god who could die, let alone a half-forgotten remnant, long-buried and comfortable with death if not for the arrogance of the conspiracy.

"Was it enough?" Jia asked, gaze shifting between the obscured camera feed and the sensors. "And did you know the chain explosion would work like that?"

"We got lucky," Erik admitted. "They must have had a lot of ordnance on board their ship. L-48 is nice. A ship full of torpedoes is better."

Jia allowed hope to well up inside her until she reviewed the sensors once more.

Rapidly building emission readings across the spectra didn't bode well for a total defeat of the enemy. Other than the impressive explosion of the conspiracy ship, there'd be no subsequent explosions, no evidence the Hunters had a room filled with missiles or torpedoes waiting to explode.

It was time to go. Jia spun the *Argo* around, fired the thrusters to line them up with the *Bifröst,* and prepared for whatever insanity came next. The fight wasn't over.

"What are you seeing, Cutter?" Erik asked, sensing Jia's focus on piloting.

"I don't think we killed it. It's a lot more active than before." Cutter groaned. "I think we pissed them off. I don't know about the wisdom of spitting in the eye of an ancient, powerful..." he waved his hands around, "race thing."

Erik let out a mocking laugh. "We're long past that decision. I think we were the second we stepped aboard that ship, but certainly after we started shooting things and tossing grenades."

Jia frowned as her eyes narrowed. Something was happening in the feed, but she couldn't make it out. With a quick flick of her fingers, she magnified the image. She didn't know enough about the enemy to interpret what they might be doing from sensor readings alone.

Grievous wounds in a vessel would normally doom it, but the ship began to seal itself like it had a gigantic version of the spray the boarding party had used. That in and of itself wasn't shocking, given that the *Argo*'s hull and armor possessed similar properties, but the darkened, irregular outer hull wasn't the only new structure emerging. Rounded organic columns, similar to what they'd seen inside along with bulbous fleshy stalks, emerged from the hull.

That wasn't unsettling; it was the speed of the growth that managed to send Jia's already pounding heart into overdrive. She didn't know a ship in the galaxy that could regenerate that fast. Even advanced Orlox biological technology couldn't shrug off such a massive amount of damage with such quick repair.

The bleeding god didn't care because the wound was not a threat.

"I'm detecting a massive energy surge," Emma reported. "It might be best to dock the *Argo* so I can establish reliable, direct control of the other ship and prepare for our departure."

"Not yet," Erik ordered. "And we're not leaving before we finish off the Hunter ship. Redirect the grav shields to our exposed side and power all weapons. Minimize power to non-essential systems. Lanara, make sure we don't blow ourselves up during all this. If we're going to die, I want to make the enemy work for it."

"If we do blow up, it'll be your fault, Blackwell," the engineer responded. She sounded out of breath. "And I'll find some way—preferably horrible—to haunt you."

"I'll be dead, too."

"That'll make it twice as annoying."

A bright flash filled the feed, along with a notable spike in x- and gamma-ray emissions. The entire outer shell of the comet shattered as if struck by an invisible giant swinging a hammer of the gods.

Jia didn't want to gasp, but her desire didn't stop it from coming out. She'd never seen *anything* like this technology outside of bad science fiction movies.

The excitement continued.

Seconds later, the shell blasted away in all directions to free the ship from its long imprisonment. Somehow, despite being smaller than the cometary shell that had imprisoned it, seeing the circular mass hanging in space made it loom larger.

"Well, that's...something," Erik muttered.

"So much for L-48," Jia grumbled.

Clusters of glowing red dots spread over the surface of the ship. If they looked like dots at this distance, they must have been huge up close. Jia didn't have time to think too deeply about them since they spread everywhere until a diffuse energy field clung to the vessel's hull, if that was the appropriate word.

Could a ship have skin or an exoskeleton? Jia's vocabulary failed her. She would hate to be taken out by what vaguely resembled a gigantic space microbe.

"We should light them up," Erik suggested.

"If we try to waste them now, what's left of the comet is going to take the hit," Cutter complained. "We'll be spending more time melting ice than hurting them. I think it's time to show it our ass and live to fight another day. We might as well take advantage of the comet."

"Didn't you hear me earlier?" Erik growled. "We're *not* leaving. If the L-48 didn't do the job, we're going to do it. The guns on our ships aren't for show, Cutter."

"Let's plow the snow," Jia suggested with a nod at Erik.

Running wasn't their style. It was time to teach the Hunters that quintessential human emotion: *fear*.

The surviving remnants of the comet hurtled through space, including toward the two ships. Jia marveled at what was effectively a large scatter-missile. Any concern about being pelted disappeared as the point-defense laser turrets on the *Argo* and *Bifröst* came alive.

They blasted the fast-moving chunks into smaller pieces manageable by the grav shields, responsible for nothing more than minor tremors through the ship as they bounced off.

"Come on," Jia whispered.

The turrets continued to annihilate the comet chunks, but the Hunter ship didn't move.

"We've yet to receive any significant damage," Emma reported. "Grav emitters and hull are holding."

"We might not have finished the ship off," Jia began, "but that doesn't mean we didn't wound it."

"Yeah. I'll take it, especially since I think we busted up their most important system." Erik brought up the manual controls for the rest of the *Argo's* weapons.

"What's that?" Jia asked.

"Their weapons," Erik replied. "They're not taking a shot, which means we still have a chance. It looks like all their fancy ancient repair gear didn't bring back anything they could use to defend themselves. Fixing a single hole, even a big one, isn't the same as dealing with a massive, constant barrage of attacks."

"Most of the debris field coming our way has passed," Jia replied, calm returning to her voice.

"Cutter, get ready to fire," Erik ordered. "In thirty seconds, we'll both shower death on that bastard until he's in as many pieces as the comet. Then we'll blast those pieces into dust."

Cutter whistled, the sound extra-annoying over the comm. "Damn. You *do* understand what we're about to try?"

"Stop a dangerous alien ship from escaping into the Solar System?" Jia asked. "After fighting our way off it through dangerous alien creatures and parasitized beings, including some who might have been Navigators?"

The *Argo* shook. The small surviving chunks of the debris field bounced off the grav shield, leaving a diffused cloud hanging in space near the ship. Jia angled the ship for maximum coverage from the turrets.

"No!" Cutter yelled. "This is the real deal: a battle between humanity and an alien race. I've done a lot of crazy runs for Alina over the years, but I *never* thought I'd end up in this situation."

"Humanity's had skirmishes with aliens before." Erik let out a bitter chuckle. "I would have preferred to fight the damned lizards. The L-48 would have finished *them*."

"We can do this," Cutter replied. "And we'll be awesome. These guys are a lot tougher than the Zitarks. Once we beat these guys, all the government needs to do is tell everyone about it, and none of the other races will ever screw with humans. Go, Humanity!"

Jia shook her head, surprised Cutter could be so cavalier and excited about facing off against a gargantuan living ship from a race that might have destroyed the Navigators. She'd thought he was more interested in running, but she'd witnessed that before.

The man didn't want to fight but could find strange reserves of bravery when his back was otherwise against a wall.

Her heart continued its insane gallop. She admired his courage, but if he'd seen what they had inside, he might be more concerned, even sitting behind the controls of a ship brimming with weapons.

"We're mostly clear of the debris," Emma reported. "No significant damage was sustained."

"Huh." Erik chuckled. "Still no guns from our Hunter ship. Too bad for them. They shouldn't have brought giant starfishes to a space battle. Time to send those bastards back into history."

Jia held her breath. Cutter was right; what they were

about to do was historic. Her distant descendants might read about it, or they might be annihilated, and no one would ever know the truth.

That would neatly solve the issue of worrying about her descendants and whether she might make a good mother.

The *Argo* fired first. Erik rapid-fired the torpedo launchers, quickly emptying the stores before unleashing the anti-ship laser turrets and Lanara's newly installed plasma turret. She noticed he looked sterner than normal.

This wasn't a battle they could assume they would win.

The *Bifröst*'s turrets joined the fray. Her laser and plasma cannons fired next, but the longer recharge cycle kept them from being near-continuous like the turrets. Torpedoes and missiles spat from the larger ship, forming a swarm heading toward the Hunter ship.

Jia held her breath as the camera and sensor displays lit up with dozens of small contacts, each representing the culmination of humanity's thousands of years of weapons development. They were massive explosives that could easily destroy a lesser ship, but no human vessel had fought such a large ship.

Bright plasma discharges joined the invisible laser beams to strike first while the missiles and torpedoes continued their flight. Jia let out the breath she'd held, waiting for some indication of damage and seeing none.

The next phase would be critical. The enemy ship was far too large to hope to dodge the angry swarm of explosives, but it was hard to believe they didn't possess or have an equivalent to point-defense lasers. The function of the stalks, columns, and bumps on the surface remained unclear.

Nothing fired. If they possessed the relevant defenses, thousands of years of stasis or the L-48 had knocked them off-line.

She could hope.

While the human ships continued streaming energy weapons to little visible effect, the missiles and torpedoes continued their inexorable approach with enough death inside to level a mountain.

The projectiles delivered by the *Argo* were all high-powered single warheads, but many from their jumpship contained scatter warheads and split apart at the last moment. What had already been an overwhelming swarm became an all-encompassing field of obliteration difficult to distinguish on the sensors.

"Survive this, you monsters," Jia muttered as they finished their trip.

The explosions overlapped, joining one another to form an expansive red-orange cloud of doom. It grew large enough to obscure the mammoth alien vessel. If the Hunter ship had done anything to stop the missiles and torpedoes, they might have had a chance.

Jia smiled triumphantly. The barrage they had laid down would have shredded an entire fleet of human ships.

Erik didn't stop his attack. He had emptied their torpedo launchers, but he continued firing the laser and plasma turrets into the explosion.

That made sense to Jia. The armor or shields protecting the Hunter ship might have absorbed the earlier attacks, but the explosions had to have stripped away those defenses and exposed the weaker inside.

"Cut off the plasma turrets, Blackwell," Lanara shouted. "We're risking blowing our power conduits at this rate."

"It's okay," Erik replied, ceasing fire with the plasma turrets but maintaining his laser fire. "The missiles and torpedoes all hit the bastard anyway."

Jia was entranced by the bright blast now covering the ship. All technology had its limits. The Hunters might be more advanced than humans, but they weren't gods. Plenty of human civilizations had found that technologically inferior societies could put up a good fight.

Humans were good at many things, including killing. The Hunters should have known better than to pick a fight with a race who had gone from swords and spears to rockets in spacecraft in short centuries.

The explosion began to dim.

Jia's smile collapsed as the explosion ebbed. "No! It's impossible. It can't be."

The Hunter ship floated untouched in space, the red energy field the same intensity. Jia couldn't accept it. The combined barrage delivered by the human ships would have destroyed significant chunks of Neo SoCal, but they might as well have been throwing stone-tipped spears at a six-foot metal wall for all the good their attack had done.

"Uh..." Cutter transmitted. "What now?" he looked around to confirm what he was positive was the truth. "I'm out of missiles and torpedoes."

The jumpship's cannons and turrets continued firing, but contrary to Jia's theory, the Hunter ship didn't seem any more bothered by them now than before being struck by the barrage of missiles and torpedoes.

Erik let out a frustrated bellow. "Those damned bastards should just die already."

"I don't mean to sound like a chickenshit after what I said earlier," replied Cutter, audibly swallowing over the line, "but based on what Holochick told me, those dudes are tougher than the Navigators. I was all pumped, but it's obvious now they're out of our league. How the hell do we beat people who are stronger than the Navigators? This might be a good time to show them our asses. Discretion is the better part of valor and all that."

"We have to stop that ship," Jia insisted, her voice stern. "We don't know how they travel. If it's got anything like our jump drive, we're screwed. No, humanity's screwed. They could jump right to Earth."

"But it doesn't even have guns," Cutter complained.

"They don't need guns," Erik muttered, his jaw clenched. "And that's assuming they don't repair them in a couple of days. Even without them, they can go to Sedna and infect everyone, then the outer colonies, or like Jia said, go straight to Earth and land in Neo SoCal so they can make millions of parasites. The UTC has all the colonies, but one out of every two humans lives on Earth. If it falls, humanity's done. The UTC will collapse, and what the Hunters don't finish off, the Zitarks will."

"But we can't win!" Cutter argued. "We threw everything we had at them, and it didn't even scratch them. This isn't a fight anymore. This is us awaiting execution. What do you plan to do, Blackwell?"

"Ram them," Erik declared, his voice calm. "It's the only option we have left. If we run, we're dooming thousands, if not billions, to die."

"Oh, man," Cutter grumbled, wiping his face. "How did I know you were going to say that?"

Jia turned to Erik and shook her head. "I get what you're saying, but it's not a viable strategy. Even taking into account the kinetic energy we could create with a decent run-up, if our missiles and torpedoes didn't scratch it, we wouldn't accomplish anything without something like years of constant acceleration. I don't think they're going to sit around and wait that long."

"I refuse to give up," Erik replied, his face blank. "Those soldiers didn't die for nothing, and I'm not going to run when a damned alien ship full of monsters is in my home system." He growled, "Lanara, isn't there something you can do? Turn us into a bomb, like Vand did with her ship?"

Lanara didn't answer for a couple seconds, and when she did, her voice was noticeably more subdued than normal. "It's like Lin said, Blackwell. I can turn us into a bomb, but it's not going to be worse than what we just delivered."

"Somebody give me an idea that works then!" Erik slammed a fist into a bulkhead in frustration. "We *have* to win. We've got the best AI in the UTC and a state-of-the-art ship. This is our home system, and the piece of Hunter crap sat in a freezer for thousands of years. They haven't even fired on us."

Jia wondered if that represented contempt more than a technological limitation.

"I-I…" Raphael sputtered. He let out a nervous titter. "If you're thinking about ships as bombs, I've got an idea. Get the *Argo* back here and dock. I'll need Emma's help, and I can't guarantee it'll work, and you know how much I respect you all, but I'm going to need to go radio-silent for the next few minutes as I begin setting it up. Remember, no guarantees."

"A chance is better than nothing," Erik replied. "Do what you need to, and I'll talk to you when I get over to the *Bifröst*." He switched the comm broadcast to everyone aboard the *Argo*. "We're going to return to the jumpship. Once we arrive, everyone head over there and strap in. I'm going to level with you. Our first attack didn't go well, but Raphael has an idea he's working on. I'm not sure, but this might come down to turning the *Argo* into a bomb, so haul ass the second we dock."

Jia stared at the camera feed, calm settling over her. The red glow was brighter than before, but she didn't worry. They had a chance.

Humanity wasn't defeated...*yet*.

CHAPTER FIFTY-ONE

Erik stomped through the doors to the bridge of the jumpship, Jia right behind. He'd wanted to go check on the soldiers, but they were big boys and girls and knew what they needed to do. For now, he needed to concentrate on winning against the enemy ship, and that would come down to whatever plan Raphael had cooked up.

Despite being larger than the cockpit of the *Argo* and having more seats, the bridge of the jumpship didn't look much different.

In some ways, it was inferior. The chairs weren't as comfortable as those aboard the smaller ship, and the increased number of seats and consoles made it a tighter area for individual crew members despite the overall larger area.

Erik understood. The military had focused on pure utility for the bridge of the experimental jumpship. After all, they hadn't been sure it wouldn't explode on the first jump.

The risk of participating in the propulsion test almost seemed quaint now that they were facing off against a monster-sized ship that had shrugged off their best weapons like they were nothing.

The Lady wouldn't abandon Erik, not yet. If she wanted him to die, she would have let him die on Molino or taken him out during the jump.

Fear was only useful in that it kept one from blindly throwing their life away. If Raphael's plan didn't work, Erik had to find a new one.

"If we can't ram the ship," Erik glanced at Jia, "We will have to get our exos on and go back inside."

She gazed at him as her brain worked through what he'd said, then delivered a quick nod.

Erik turned back and continued his thoughts.

Blowing it up from the outside might not work, but they'd already proven they could hurt it from the inside. They just needed more coverage.

Since the Hunter ship still lacked weapons, they could potentially drill inside or use local explosives to force their way in. They'd have to face off against the mutants again, but this time, they would bring their exos.

Cutter kept licking his lips in his seat near the front of the bridge but didn't bother to look at the new arrivals. Raphael hunched over in a chair surrounded by data windows, murmuring quietly under his breath, the occasional number slipping out. It reminded Erik of Lanara.

Erik walked past him to an IO port in a command console and inserted Emma.

The AI had warned him on the way up that she would

go quiet after a brief examination of the *Bifröst*'s systems. She didn't bother to explain what Raphael had in mind, only told Erik to get her to the bridge and insert her for "maximum efficiency if you want to live" and requested that Lanara head to the engine room of the jumpship to prepare for both manual assistance in power rerouting and grav emitter manipulation.

Erik trusted his people, virtual or otherwise. He was good at many things, but he wasn't an engineer or a scientist. He was a master of the art of killing enemies, and now it was time to let the others do what they could.

I bet the military never thought the ship would get this kind of workout so soon, Erik thought.

He dropped into a seat near Raphael in the back and strapped into his harness. His fingers tapped on the console as he brought up his own data windows, including camera feeds of the Hunter ship.

The enemy remained stationary, the energy field surrounding the ship continuing to grow brighter. That had to mean something, but no one had said anything. The others were distracted, but if it were easily interpretable, Jia would explain.

Erik had his own theory. It had to be a powerful shield, something operating on different principles than the basic grav shields human ships used. That was the only explanation for how the Hunter could have shrugged off the apocalyptic onslaught they'd just delivered.

The theory continued under the assumption that Raphael was a bright guy and a military scientist who understood battlefield needs. He must have figured out some way to disrupt the shield, and if all he wanted was a few minutes to himself to set it up, Erik was more than happy to give it to him—as long as it ended with the Hunter ship destroyed.

Raphael jerked his head up and gave Erik a wild-eyed stare. "First of all, Erik and Jia, I want to be totally honest with you because I couldn't live with myself if we did anything without you understanding everything."

"No one's asking you to be anything but that," Erik replied. "We don't have time for bullshit right now. Just lay it on us and tell us what we need to do."

Jia nodded her agreement, her attention glued to her data windows, including numerous secondary sensor displays. She would speak up if she noticed anything unusual.

"The thing is, I've got an idea, and I've got the basics for it laid down," Raphael continued unsteadily. "But I can't guarantee it'll work. I *think* it will work, and I'm not just saying that because it's you two."

Erik snorted. "There are no guarantees in life and especially no guarantees in combat. If that's what's worrying you, drop it. We're dealing with something none of us was prepared for. We're long past the phase of workshopping ideas through committees for cost/benefit analysis."

"It's, uh, bigger than that." Raphael swallowed and bit his lip. "It's not just that it might not work. Even if it *does* work, there is still a good chance we'll die."

"Can I vote no on the dying part?" Cutter asked. "Because I'm not cool with that."

"Shut up." Jia glared at him. "This isn't a democracy."

"Jia's right," Erik added with a nod. "Dying's not high on

my list of things to do anytime soon, but I'm far less worried about whether we'll die than if whatever Raphael has planned will take that Hunter ship with us. We have to think about what's best for the Solar System and the UTC, not what's best for us."

"Still not fond of the dying part of the plan," Cutter mumbled.

Raphael took in several deep breaths and slowly let them out. "If I can pull it off, I'm pretty sure it'll take out the Hunter ship, 'cause what I have planned would take out a small moon or a large city."

Erik grinned, hope flooding back in and pushing away his doubts. "That ship's big, but it's a lot smaller than a moon. I like your plan already. Not so much the dying part, but the killing the Hunters part."

Jia watched Raphael for a moment. He had placed his hands like he was going to slap someone, talking to himself.

Seriously brainy individuals exhibited odd characteristics when they were stressed.

"Okay. Time to man up like the Obsidian Detective and woman up like Lady Justice." Raphael slapped his cheeks. "You can do this. I can do this. *We* can do this."

She winced; he *had* slapped someone.

"We need to know what you're going to do," Jia offered quietly. "So we can set up an appropriate follow-up plan. We trust you, Raphael, but we have no idea what's going on."

"Sure, sure, sure. That makes sense. Um, do you want the technical version or the laymen's version?"

Erik grimaced. "Give me the kids' version. I don't want to spend the next hour asking questions."

"The jump drive's kind of like a portable HTP," Raphael explained, tracing a circle in the air with his hands. "It's less that we're jumping from point to point and more like we're opening a gate and shoving it over the ship, then going out the other side. It's obviously a lot more complicated in terms of the physics, but that's the laymen's version."

Erik nodded slowly. "I follow you so far, but how does that affect your plan? Remember, this isn't about getting away. We can't just run. If we gather the Fleet, they might be able to take that thing out, but it would take too long, and we could lose a couple of planets by then, potentially including Earth. I am interested in the part where you said this was about blowing up small moons."

Raphael waved his hands in front of him. "No, I'm not talking about running. I get that we need to take that thing out." He squared his shoulders and puffed up his chest. "I know you would never run to save yourself when other people are in danger. This is an attack plan."

Jia's brows slowly lifted. "I don't understand. How is it an attack? What does the jump drive have to do with blowing up the ship?"

"You going to try to slice them in half with a hyperspace gate?" Cutter suggested.

The pilot's suggestion surprised Erik. He wasn't sure if something like that was possible. It wasn't something the military had ever suggested as a viable tactic.

Raphael shook his head. "No. Something like that wouldn't work. If I..." He sighed. "The simple version is, the gate the jump drive generates would collapse instantly and do nothing to the enemy ship, but there *is* a way we can use it. We can do something with this drive that is normally impossible because it'd require building an entire HTP. It's been considered theoretical until now, but I know the ID and DD have been combing astronomy data, looking for evidence that the Leems have done it."

Jia gasped. "You're going to nest hyperspace gates? But if you do that—"

"It'll create a forced hyperspace leakage into normal space without the normal inverted field barriers that prevent significant overlap and start baryonic and gravitational disruption," Raphael explained, grim-faced. "A cut in space. The wound will quickly seal itself, but not before releasing more energy in a relatively contained area than any weapon humanity's ever thought about producing." The uncertainty left his face. "We're lucky that we can even try this. We might be able to jump anywhere with the drive, but this trick isn't as forgiving. It's only possible because we're so far away from a significant gravity well. I've done some quick calculations, and like I said earlier, I'm pretty sure I could destroy a moon with this, or at least take a major chunk out of it."

"Good." Erik focused on the Hunter ship in the feed. "They aren't gods, and let's hope they haven't ever had someone come up with this idea before. I'd like to see them become a large number of tiny particles."

Cutter waved his arms. "Sure, but what about *us*? Remember the part where he mentioned us dying earlier? I know it's a noble thing to die protecting people, but I'm not that noble. I'd prefer to kill the enemy *and* survive."

"Yes." Raphael offered a sheepish grin. "That's where things get a little dicey."

"Define dicey," Jia replied.

"Here goes." Raphael nodded firmly, his gaze flicking between Erik and Jia. "I'm ninety-ninety percent certain I can pull this off. Obviously, Emma will be doing the heavy lifting of directing the nested jumps. I've got most of the systems set up, and Lanara's setting things up on her end, but I'm not certain we can survive. We'll be awfully close to the hyperspace leak."

"Can't we just fly away and then do it?" suggested Cutter. "Why do we have to be close? I can live without getting a great view of the ship being destroyed."

Raphael's shoulders slumped. "We have to be relatively close to pull it off. It's a limitation of the fundamental nature of how our jump drive works. There's nothing I can do about it. Give me billions of credits and a couple of decades and I could maybe make something longer-range, but as far as things in the next few minutes, this is it. We've got to stay close to kill the ship."

"But you can guarantee the explosion at ninety-ninety percent?" Erik asked.

"Yes, but I can't—"

"I only care about the *explosion*," Erik interrupted curtly. "If it doesn't go off, we're not going to die from it, so that doesn't matter much." He nodded at Cutter. "You didn't see what was in there. We can't let that thing get out of here, no matter what. I'm not here to die, but I'm not here to let that thing get away, either."

Cutter pointed to a radar display. "If it's stuck out this far, it might take a year or two to get to Earth and months before even something like Sedna. That'll give the Fleet plenty of time to gather an armada. Two ships might not be enough, but a hundred?" He clapped. "Boom!"

Erik shook his head. "We can't assume the ship doesn't have better propulsion tech, something like a jump drive. They might not be able to use it right away, but if we leave them alone, they can continue repairing their ship. We might have only days, not months. Shit, considering what we've seen, we might only have hours, Cutter." He gestured to a data window with an image of the Hunter ship. "Even if we leave, the only thing we can do with days to work is jump back with this ship, and we're back to the same thing. If our cannons and missiles won't scratch it, it's not like coming back with slightly better-tuned weapons will do much. Jia and I spoke about boarding it again, but if we go back for reinforcements, when we come back, they might have anti-ship defenses ready."

"I always knew I was going to die young." Cutter averted his eyes. "I didn't think I'd die in a hyperspace leak explosion thing, though. I guess if you're going to die, you might as well do it in a spectacular way."

Raphael managed a weak smile. "Our deaths aren't assured. I'd estimate we've got better than even odds of surviving. With good piloting, the odds go up."

"Good piloting?" Cutter's brow lifted. "Okay, this sounds like a part where I can help. I'm liking this plan a lot better now."

Erik nodded to Jia. "I'm not trying to die here and take you with us. I'm trying to stop something beyond our tech, and Raphael's got the only option short of us trying to fight our way back in."

"I know," she answered. "And I agree with your call. I trust Raphael, Emma, Lanara, and Cutter."

"Damn." Cutter clucked his tongue. "When you say it like that, it makes me feel like a badass."

"Raphael, do it," Erik ordered, turning to the image on his screen. "Obliterate the ship."

Raphael nodded quickly. "We need five to ten more minutes. Lanara's making some modifications, and Emma's finishing her calculations. They're hurrying as much as they can, but there are only so many shortcuts we can take."

"That's fine. It's not like we're under attack."

"Damn it." Cutter jerked his head down toward a data window. "Oh, this isn't good. You shouldn't tempt fate, Blackwell."

"What's wrong?" Erik asked, his voice tight.

Fate could screw off. The Hunters were going down.

"Something's happening with the other ship," Jia explained with a sigh. She pointed to different data windows containing numbers and graphs Erik could barely interpret. "All sorts of increased readings. This isn't good."

"This entire situation isn't good," Erik replied. "But can you be a little more specific about what 'not good' means?"

Raphael summoned a new data window and tilted his head, murmuring something under his breath. "I think we're running out of time. Some of the readings we're getting off that ship are similar to what we'd see in a jump drive. I think they're powering up for a jump. I don't know why it's taking so long, but there's a lot we don't know about them."

"You keep working on your plan." Erik nodded to Cutter. "And go ahead and give me weapons control."

"Why?" Cutter looked at Erik like he'd lost his mind. "We unloaded everything we had, and it didn't do crap. It did less than crap. You think they're suddenly going to drop their shields?"

"I might not know crap about hyperspace physics, but I'm willing to bet if we're pounding that thing with weapons, we can delay its jump. Fields are like that."

"Firing a bunch of weapons will prevent us from doing what we need to do, too," Raphael interjected.

Erik tapped at a virtual display to link all the weapons together for a combined volley. He'd need to stretch this out, and they were too far out to mess with drones. "Does your setup mean we can't shoot at all? This plan doesn't do any good if they jump away."

"I suppose not." Raphael shrugged. "We can do all the preparations, but you probably won't be able to shoot during the last minute or so. Besides messing with some of the fields, we'll need the power."

"Fine. You, Lanara, and Emma continue to get ready." Erik tapped a control. "I'll keep him busy until it's time."

Erik fired turrets and cannons simultaneously. It was all but impossible to miss, given the size of the target ship and its lack of relative motion. As before, the beams and pulses struck the ship but didn't penetrate the outer defenses.

"That doing anything to stop the energy?" Erik asked.

Raphael smiled. "From what I can see, yes. There's no way they'll be able to stabilize for a jump with these readings."

Erik attacked once more. Satisfaction filled him despite the lack of damage. Stalling was something he could do.

A lack of return fire meant it was now a race, one he intended to win.

"How tough are you, you bastard?" he muttered.

CHAPTER FIFTY-TWO

Jia kept reminding herself that no matter how powerful the Hunter ship was, it'd been sitting barely active in ice for thousands of years.

Quick repairs might be impressive given the scale of time, but the enemy was not operating at full capacity.

Any small malfunction might give the humans an opportunity to carry out their plan.

The *Bifröst* wasn't a mouse taking on an elephant. She was a venomous snake nipping at the ankles of a wounded jackal. With speed and agility, she could bring down the larger prey. Just because something was hard didn't mean it wouldn't work.

Raphael's plan didn't worry Jia. They would win. They weren't a ragtag band of misfits, even if they might look that way from the outside. The man currently designing a dangerous if limited-use weapon was one of the best in his field. Being a goofy fanboy didn't make him an idiot.

Lanara's acerbic personality was matched by her skill as an engineer. Emma had earned her right to be arrogant, her skills having been displayed on countless occasions during her time with Erik and Jia.

Cutter was a damned good pilot.

There was no other team in the UTC who could pull off what they were about to do, which was why it had to work —for both them and the human race.

Plasma shots exploded against the outside of the Hunter ship, still doing no visible damage. It was more like a fireworks show than a battle.

Jia tried to imagine how much damage they would have delivered had they been firing on a colony or a city. The contrast between that and the lack of damage to the Hunter ship was awe-inspiring.

Erik didn't continually fire the weapons, instead firing impressive-looking but mostly ineffective volleys every couple of seconds. They were a mouse poking the elephant in the eye until it charged and fell into the spiked pit.

Did whatever or whoever was controlling the ship understand what the humans were up to? Did they have any clue about the pain and destruction the jumpship was about to summon?

Jia sure hoped they didn't. She wanted their final moments to be filled with shock and horror.

The Hunters had made one big mistake. They had dared to look down on humans as an inferior race. Today, the team on the bridge and in the engine room would prove to whatever intelligence was running the alien ship that humanity wasn't to be taken lightly.

Cutter was right. This was effectively the first battle of a galactic war, and the human crew would win it through a combination of ingenuity and trust in one another.

And if they died, it wasn't like she'd be around to worry. Despite the situation, Jia smiled at the thought.

The parasitized humans had implied that they knew the humans were using Navigator technology. Jia allowed herself to be outraged on behalf of the ancient race. For all she knew, they could have also been bastards, but at least they'd inadvertently gifted humanity with advances, and now one of those advances would help destroy their ancient enemy.

Jia frowned at a sensor display. "Wait, something's happening with the other ship, more localized than before. I think they're tired of us taking potshots. Cutter, evade!"

"Oh, shit!" Cutter yelled and pulsed all the lateral thrusters.

Two bright red lines of energy spread around the perimeter of the Hunter ship and met in the middle. With a bright flash, shimmering scarlet pulses burst from the ship and sped toward the jumpship.

So much for the enemy's weapons being offline.

Cutter's anticipation and reflexes saved the *Bifröst*. The attacks narrowly missed, the pulses continuing past into space.

"Emma, please reinforce the shields," Erik commanded.

The movement of the ship and the limited arc of the cannons made it hard to line up every weapon, but he swiveled the turrets to focus on the source of the last attack and opened fire. If attacks could disrupt the jump, they might be able to do the same with the weapons.

"Emma needs to concentrate on the calculations," shouted Raphael, his face red. He grimaced. "Sorry, but what she's doing is different than a normal jump. Keep us alive, but keep Emma and Lanara out of it until we pull it off."

"Understood," Erik replied.

Jia saw a huge grin take over Cutter's face as he dipped the ship. The huge vessel might not be the *Argo*, but the enemy's attacks were proving scattershot and clumsy.

At least someone was having a good time under fire.

She smiled, realizing something important. "I don't think their targeting system, however it functions, is working right. You can do it. You can keep protecting us."

"You have a limited window to maneuver," Raphael explained to Cutter, sweat dripping down his face. He tapped a data window, and two lines appeared on one of the radar displays. "If you're closer than the front line, we'll die in the shockwave. If you're farther back, we won't be able to open it, and I assume the Hunters will end up finishing us off."

"I can do this all year," Cutter offered cheerfully.

His smile was infectious. *We* will *do this*, she thought

The Hunter ship released another barrage, and another hard lateral burn paired with a dive saved the jumpship. With most of the power to the grav compensators routed elsewhere, the abrupt movement challenged Jia's stomach.

They might survive the battle, but she was glad she hadn't had much to eat.

"Can't I just back up and then thrust forward when it's time?" Cutter asked. "I am awesome, so I can keep doing this, but I have no problem with doing the easier thing if it's possible, right?"

All the earlier fear was gone from his face, replaced by unmistakable excitement. Fight had won over flight.

Jia looked at her screens. "The delays continue to suggest the weapons aren't fully repaired." It might take them minutes to fix them or days, but it didn't matter because Raphael's plan would be ready before that.

"It'll throw off my calculations and calibration if we pull too far back," Raphael shouted. "Keep in the zone and let us finish them." He ripped his attention away from Cutter and returned to his data windows. His fingers flew over two separate keyboards, and he stuck the tip of his tongue out of the corner of his mouth.

Jia focused on the secondary controls. She was doing her best to offer dynamic power routing in the absence of Emma's and Lanara's attention—any small thing that would allow Cutter to concentrate on dodging attacks.

Cutter's continued manipulation of the large ship was impressive, and she took note of how he made use of timing and specific thrusters to pull off maneuvers she wouldn't have thought possible. She might be naturally talented, but he was talented *and* had years of experience.

A third barrage erupted from the Hunter ship. Cutter's stomach-churning maneuvers dodged most of the pulses, but a blast clipped the side. The *Bifröst* lurched and shook. Alarms sounded, and new windows popped up in front of Cutter and Jia. Thruster damage, fire, and a loss of hull integrity joined the loss of two turrets on the damage report.

Jia grimaced. "Just keep flying. I'll handle everything else."

Cutter's nod was almost imperceptible. He didn't divert his eyes from the vital displays and windows in front of him.

Jia's quick commands evacuated the oxygen from the fire-ravaged compartment and dropped emergency bulkheads. The glancing blow had vaporized an outer compartment like it was nothing, but fortunately, it was nowhere near the crew quarters, the soldiers, or the cargo bay.

"We can't take many more hits like that," she offered, licking her lips. "And if they hit us dead on, it's going to blow a major chunk of the ship away."

Raphael wiped sweat off his brow. "Almost there. Just keep us alive."

Erik shifted to continuous fire concentrated on the source of the enemy's counterattack. The invisible lasers and bright plasma blasts pelted the center of the Hunter ship.

Seeing no obvious damage, Jia wasn't sure if their attack accomplished much. Her intense focus on backing up Cutter blurred the seconds together before the next enemy attack. This time Cutter managed to evade the entire attack.

Jia took slow, even breaths as she monitored system damage. The Hunter ship let loose another deadly barrage.

Cutter shouted triumphantly as he made the thrusters dance. "That's right, assholes. I'm Cutter Durn, and I'm the best damned pilot in the entire galaxy. There's no way you can take me do—"

The *Bifröst* shuddered, and bright light blinded Jia. Shrill alarms sounded. Sparks flew everywhere, and heat ate at her face. An acrid stench filled her nostrils.

Jia's head throbbed. Something hot and moist slid down the side of her head. She opened her aching eyes and gasped. She was looking straight out a jagged hole in the bridge. Pieces of the ship floated in the distance.

Small fires had broken out in the front of the bridge.

Her heart thundered, and even the faint shimmer of the emergency oxygen field wasn't enough to keep it in check. If they hadn't been strapped in, they would have been knocked out of the ship. She touched the side of her head and brought her hand forward.

She was bleeding.

"Cutter, get into the back, and I'll start the emergency bulkhead sequence," Jia shouted. "One more hit up here and we'll lose the field and the oxygen, but at least that'll put the fire out."

She turned her head toward Cutter. Massive burns covered most of his face and upper body. His head hung loosely to the side. His eyes remained wide open and staring into the distance. Large metal fragments had pierced his abdomen, chest, and heart.

He wasn't breathing.

Bile rising in the back of her throat, Jia craned her neck to look into the back. Raphael was pale with a painful-looking cut on his cheek, but obviously conscious, based on his fevered typing. Erik looked more annoyed than wounded, but two small pieces of sharp shrapnel lay in his lap near scratches in his suit. If he hadn't been wearing it, they might have gutted him.

Erik shook his head at Cutter's body, frowning. "I've lost fire control. Get back here, Jia, and take control. Based on their previous pace, we've got fifteen or twenty seconds at most before the next shot. He worked his ass off to save us. Don't waste his work."

Jia wanted to ask if Erik didn't care about Cutter, but that wasn't fair. They'd both seen good people die during their time together. There was always a price for hunting evil, and today, it'd been high.

She unstrapped her harness and flipped over the seat, the reduced gravity making it surprisingly easy. She jumped and half-floated into a seat farther back and pulled herself down. After strapping herself in, she summoned primary virtual controls with a couple of quick commands and hand gestures and activated an emergency bulkhead.

With a whoosh, the bulkhead dropped and separated the front half of the bridge from the back half, protecting them with more than a single oxygen field, but also leaving Cutter's body on the other side.

Jia pushed the death out of her head.

Survival.

That was all she could concentrate on, or they would all end up like Cutter, and millions of other people would suffer and die.

The Hunter ship fired again, this time with a smaller number of shots. It didn't matter if it represented contempt or weakness. Jia would take every advantage offered.

Jia managed to avoid all but one shot, which sheared another turret off the ship. They'd hit about twenty percent of the thrusters.

She understood the enemy ship's motivation when they fired another smaller barrage more rapidly than before. Careful dodging saved the damaged jumpship, but Jia didn't know how long she could continue to evade, given the state of their ship.

"We're done," Raphael shouted. "*Now* you can run!"

"Die, you monsters!" Jia yelled as she started turning the ship.

Jia didn't know what to expect. She'd seen footage of hyperspace gates opening, but the process was different than how their current vessel beat the limits of FTL.

A tiny but unbelievably bright dot appeared in the center of the ship, as if a heart was shining from the inside. Jia's brain had just begun to register what she was seeing when the dot exploded into a storm of kaleidoscopic particles. A devastating blast wave of pure white energy ripped from the center of the ship and expanded in all directions.

It was less an explosion than an erasure.

The wave ate the Hunter ship from the inside out, the pieces breaking into other pieces, and colorful arcs of energy leapt across the ship, leaving clouds the only memory of the once-mighty Hunter ship.

The *Bifröst*'s thrusters pushed the ship away. The wave continued closing on them and threatened to overwhelm the fleeing jumpship. Jia didn't know what to do except continue fleeing at top speed.

She roared her defiance as they continued to accelerate. The wave struck the ship, sending it into a spin, and then dissipated. The rest continued spreading, weakening as it moved through space.

More alarms sounded, along with more damage reports. There were so many hull breaches, it was like someone had fired a ship-sized shotgun into the back of the vessel. They'd lost more thrusters, and there was a breach in the cargo bay, but not severe enough that emergency seals and bulkheads couldn't handle it.

Without a word, Emma took that over for Jia.

There was no time to fear. No time to worry. There was only time to survive.

It didn't matter if Jia had reduced power and fewer thrusters. Dying at this point would be an insult to the men who'd already given their lives. It'd prove the Hunters right about humanity.

Jia canceled out the spin with counterthrust and decelerated. She took ragged breaths and blinked to clear her eyes as she consulted the damage reports before looking at the feed and what remained of the working sensor displays.

The Hunter ship was gone, with only a loose cloud of debris marking its previous position. They hadn't just ripped it to pieces, they'd obliterated the enemy.

"Anyone else hurt, Emma?" Jia croaked. She winced at the throbbing in the side of her head.

"There are minor injuries among the uniformed boys and girls," Emma replied somberly. "Mr. Durn was the only fatality. There is, of course, massive damage to the ship. The jump drive is mercifully intact, but I wouldn't recommend attempting to do that before spending some time engaged in repairs."

"I-it worked." Raphael wiped away tears. "I can't believe it."

"Yeah." Erik nodded. "Believe it. We won."

Jia stared at the nondescript gray emergency bulkhead, picturing the man's body on the other side. "But not without losses."

He looked in the same direction. "Yeah. Not without losses."

CHAPTER FIFTY-THREE

May 22, 2230, Edge of Solar System, Cargo Bay of the Bifröst

Standing in the cargo bay, Erik regretted not having anything nicer to wear, but none of the surviving soldiers had brought along their dress uniforms.

Everyone still alive on the ship stood in the cargo bay, watching him expectantly. Lanara, Raphael, and Emma had been working for the last couple of days to repair the ship. Raphael was now confident they could jump back.

The scars of the battle were obvious in the cargo bay, including emergency patches placed over the seals from the battle and damaged exos and vehicles.

Erik would have preferred to have their ceremony in a different room, but this was the best place to accommodate all of the people aboard. The designers of the jumpship had never considered that someone might want to give an in-person speech to everybody aboard.

Not that the Fleet was much better about that. Typically, big speeches on Fleet ships were held in fighter bays.

Erik had spent a lot of time considering what Alina and the government brass might be thinking since the battle. They had no easy way of instantly verifying the jump had been successful, let alone the mission.

But Alina and the military wouldn't have sent them across the Solar System with an expensive experimental drive if they'd expected them to fail. Erik's and Jia's previous successes were the reason they'd ended up with the ship.

Erik hadn't bothered sending a message back to Penglai. The ship could jump back to the base before it would even arrive. Any assets tasked to observe the target location would see the battle, but only after days of delay as the light made its way across the Solar System.

The fantastic propulsion advances achieved through reverse-engineering Navigator technology hadn't been matched by advances in communication, other than sending messages through HTPs, but that still didn't allow the transmissions to be FTL once in-system.

But there was something more important Erik wanted to take care of before they jumped back, something he owed.

After a brief discussion, the team had decided to keep the bodies aboard so they could be returned to their families. Not everyone wanted a space burial, but the dead deserved some words—not only Cutter and the fallen soldiers recovered from the Hunter ship but also those who hadn't made it back, including Captain Osei and Corporal Milton.

Erik straightened his back and focused on the crowd inside the cargo bay. "This isn't going to be a big formal ceremony, and I don't have the knowledge or authority for proper ceremonies for everyone's background. I figure everyone will get that from the Army when we get back to Earth, but I also think those who gave their lives deserved to be acknowledged right here, right now in the shadow of the battle against an enemy none of us could ever have anticipated or even imagined."

The gathered soldiers nodded. Lanara stood somberly off to the side near a sniffling Raphael. Jia offered Erik a comforting smile. Emma was no doubt listening, but she chose not to manifest holographically.

He was no stranger to death, which was why he understood how important rituals like this were. If this was a battle in war, it'd be considered an outstanding win, with a small number of assault infantry and a pilot traded for an entire enemy capital ship.

That thought didn't comfort him.

"Every man and woman who puts on the uniform understands what it means and the risk it entails." Erik raised his voice. "But this isn't just about all the soldiers who sacrificed their lives on that Hunter ship. This is also about Cutter Durn, whose skills kept us from dying. You all know how much damage this ship took, but at least we're still here, breathing and *able* to grieve."

Murmurs of appreciation spread through the small crowd, along with nodding acknowledgments. Erik and Jia had already passed on everything that had happened to the surviving soldiers. They deserved to have the big picture after being so close to death.

"We should remember what they sacrificed their lives

for, and what we accomplished in these last few days." Erik frowned. "Which was nothing sort of a miracle."

The soldiers watched with rapt attention.

"This wasn't just an anti-insurgent raid or a handful of idiot terrorists, or even a border skirmish against space raptors who don't know how to mind their own business," Erik continued. "We faced off against deadly and dangerous technology from a race who had space travel before we had civilization—the most dangerous race in the galaxy."

He swept the crowd with his gaze. "We took our hits and lost good people, but we stayed true to our training and loyalty and one another. We beat the Hunters back and protected not only our lives but also our home planet and our species. We can't choose how we'll die, but we do choose how we live, and if we make the right choices, when we die, it won't be a waste. Just like it wasn't for Captain Osei and your fellow soldiers."

Erik waited, letting his words sink into the crowd. Some of the soldiers looked angry, others sad. He understood their feelings. He'd been there countless times, let alone after Molino. After a while, losing people became familiar.

He could only hope it never became easier.

"And it's certainly not a waste to lay down your life to defend humanity from all enemies, human and inhuman," Erik continued. "Now, let us remember those we have lost."

Thirty minutes later, Erik leaned against the cargo bay wall, one leg up. The soldiers chatted quietly among themselves. Most had come over to thank him for his leadership and words. There was no pattern. Some of the younger soldiers seemed unfazed, while grizzled NCOs came off as shellshocked.

Jia walked up to Erik with a soft smile. "This mission was different."

"That's one way to put it," he agreed.

"The conspiracy miscalculated," Jia continued. "In many ways. If we hadn't been here, that ship would have been able to repair itself, and we both know how that would have ended."

"You don't need to talk me down, Jia." Erik nodded at the soldiers. "People die in battle, and now we know about the Hunters."

She glanced over her shoulder at the soldiers beyond. "Do you think there are more ships like that one out there?"

Erik shrugged. "Who knows? I suspect we will find out the hard way."

CHAPTER FIFTY-FOUR

"No, no, no," Julia howled as she read the report. She balled up her fists and pounded them so hard on her table that her plate and bowl of soup rattled. Some of the contents spilled over the lip of the bowl.

Impossible.

The word flooded her mind. Minor failures were acceptable, but such a complete reversal on one of her most important plans was unfathomable. This wasn't a minor low-level operation, but a key component of her long-term strategy.

Julia took pride in her patience. It was hard to be a member of the Core and not be patient. When she'd set up the mission to send her agents to the comet, she'd known that in the best-case scenario, it would take years to see results. It'd never occurred to her that she'd have nothing to show for it.

Not even a single artifact.

Complete, utter failure. The word shame wasn't

adequate for how she felt, but the incandescent rage helped dull the former.

With a scream, Julia stood and swept her arm across the oak table, knocking her wine glass to the floor. She curled her hands into tight fists until the pain of her nails digging into her palms grounded her back in reality. She stood there, nostrils flared as she sucked in breaths and imagined the deadly revenge she would wreak on everyone who had interfered with her plans.

How had so many things gone wrong?

Her analysts were still putting together what had happened at the edge of the Solar System, based on a small number of coded transmissions from her and limited long-range observational data.

The worst part of the situation was that Sophia was laughing at her from beyond the grave. It was obvious the dead Core founder had been fully aware of the Hunter ship and sent her own people.

Julia's team was able to destroy them, but there was evidence of a third ship and a massive explosion.

But how did Sophia know to send a ship of her own? Julia had learned of the ship through the application of her own artifacts in combination with a mixture of careful xenoarchaeology information of questionable provenance that came from other races. It'd taken unusual cunning, money, patience, and extraordinary resources.

She didn't understand how Sophia could have learned about the comet without Julia's agents becoming aware of it.

The ship her people had destroyed had clearly identified themselves as Sophia's agents, but that still didn't explain the interference at the undersea resort.

She had her proof. There was someone else in the Core who was a threat.

The government's dogs were now sniffing around more than she would have liked, and she suspected they were the third ship. There was only one explanation for how a third ship could have arrived, which was frustrating in its implications.

"They've gotten that damned drive to work," Julia spat, chest heaving.

The Core had made a critical error by attempting to seize the drive rather than obliterating the entire facility. She didn't mourn the loss of the Ascended Brotherhood, but if they'd destroyed the research facility, it would have set the jump drive project back decades.

They might not have been able to recover from the loss. While it was by no means certain the government's project would succeed, the Core had coveted the jump drive and the AI navigator for their unique potential.

The raid hadn't seemed like a major failure at the time, but no one had anticipated that the government could go so quickly from lab prototype to ship jumping across the Solar System.

That was how people lost conflicts. Small mistakes compounded into irreversible critical failures. A step in the wrong direction made it impossible to escape fate.

Julia sank back into her chair, ignoring the spilled wine on the floor, her rage providing a cathartic clarity. Even the Navigators and Hunters hadn't had time-travel technology. There was nothing that could be done about the past. The only important consideration was how best to handle the future.

The key to the future was her survival.

She stared through her window, fixating on the snow-capped mountains. They were ancient, eternal compared to humanity, but even they changed, shaped by the relentless forces of the elements. It was an important reminder. Nothing could escape outside influences.

The Core had to be like the mountains. They needed to take the long-term view, and as the first among the Core, she would lead them in that.

If the jump drive had been key to disrupting her operation, she would need to think how best to counter it. It's very nature provided at least some defense.

"The drive is experimental and has barely been tested," Julia murmured. "It has to be unstable or limited in range. Jumping to the edge of the Solar System is one thing, but even jumping to Alpha Proxima involves far greater risk."

Her greatest gambit had failed, but that didn't mean she was defeated. A defensive position might be warranted.

It was time to leave Earth for a while. The more distance she could put between her and Blackwell and Lin, the less risk she'd personally take. Earth was important to her plans, but not the only part. It was time to pay closer attention to her other projects.

Julia would lose some power in the Core, but so be it. She'd trade a temporary loss of influence for survival. If she were careful, she could even figure out who her greatest enemy in the Core was.

"You can't have me, Last Soldier and Warrior Princess." Julia grabbed her wrist to still her shaking hand. "Do you hear me? I'm not Sophia. She lost perspective and became static. I will adapt to the situation at hand."

The window was closing, but she still had time. She would survive and prosper no matter the sacrifice, whether it be the rest of the Core or an entire world.

CHAPTER FIFTY-FIVE

Jia stared at the main pilot's seat in the cockpit of the *Argo*, her heart heavy.

She hadn't known Cutter for very long, but those hours she'd spent next to him in the copilot's seat had led her to consider him a friend. For all her natural talent, he'd taught her a lot about flying. Even in those last few minutes, she'd picked up techniques on how to maneuver the jumpship in emergency situations.

Erik's ceremony on the jumpship had helped push Cutter's death toward the back of her mind, and she had occupied herself on the long trip back to Earth with piloting simulations. Now that she was back on Earth, there was nowhere to run from her memories and thoughts.

But that didn't have to be a bad thing. She could use it to fuel something better and more positive.

Jia ran her hand over the back of the seat and smiled. "I'll do my best to become the top pilot in the galaxy. It might sound arrogant, but I'm already halfway there."

Her PNIU chimed with a call from Erik. She tapped the PNIU to accept it.

"Jia," Erik offered, "we're ready. We're just waiting for you."

"I'll be right there," she replied, casting one last look at the space.

Jia made her way out of the cockpit and to the galley of the *Argo*. The ship hadn't escaped unscathed during the battle, and the occasional loose panel was a reminder that not everything had been fixed.

Lanara's immediate efforts in the aftermath in the battle had been focused on the jumpship, and though she'd spent time on the smaller vessel on their return to Earth, she'd spent more time hiding in the engine room than doing much work.

The *Bifröst* was currently undergoing repairs at Penglai, despite Alina's concern about too much military control. Having a genius engineer and a brilliant AI could do wonders to support the vessel without an entire team, but Lanara and Emma couldn't make up for the large-scale resources necessary to repair the jumpship after suffering such heavy damage.

Raphael had remained at Penglai to double-check the jump drive.

Jia had been concerned at first about parking the ship in a military base, especially given the modestly long trip from Earth required to get to Penglai, but the more she thought about it, the less she worried. The mission and tests had proven the ship worked, and the destruction of the Hunter vessel had reinforced that, but without Emma, the jump drive was almost useless.

It would have been nice for the ship to be stored at a closer location, such as a LaGrange Point, but that would have to wait for the future when the ship hadn't been half-melted by alien attacks.

Jia arrived in the galley. Erik, Alina, and Malcolm sat at a table. Emma was there as well, in a simple white dress rather than one of her elaborate costumes. She'd done that less in the last week.

Perhaps it was her way of mourning.

Malcolm had done his part to clean up for Erik and Jia while they were off Earth, and although Erik had explained what had happened on the mission, the technician kept glancing at Alina and rubbing his wrists as if afraid she was going to gun him down to keep the government's secrets.

Jia couldn't blame him. A conspiracy of humans was frightening, but not the nightmare fuel of an ancient alien race that could turn you into a monster and flew around in kilometers-wide spaceships.

Or maybe Malcolm's reaction was more fundamental: *fear*.

He could be worried that what had happened to Cutter would happen to him. Jia wouldn't have blamed him if he didn't want to be involved anymore, despite his self-professed reasoning that it was unlikely they would run into the Hunters again.

Jia took a seat after offering everyone a polite nod. "Lanara's not joining us?"

Alina shook her head. "She's in a bad mood."

"Isn't she always?" Malcolm asked.

"She might not always show it, but she cares about people in her own way," Alina offered quietly. "She'd worked on and off with Cutter for a couple of years, and she just needs to be given time and space to work through what she's feeling."

"Oh." Malcolm looked down. "Sorry. I didn't mean to be a dick about it."

"No problem." Alina looked thoughtful. "Dying in a battle against an advanced alien race is the closest any of us will come to dying in an epic battle against ancient gods. It's tragic, but honorable at the same time. I'll probably end up assassinated by some corrupt crony of the conspiracy when my back is turned while eating a French fry."

"I'd prefer to die in bed surrounded by my grandkids," Malcolm replied. He shrugged. "If I have to die."

Erik cleared his throat. "Not to be a meeting purist, but we aren't here to talk about that."

Alina nodded. "You're right, we aren't. I know we could have done some of this over the comm on your way back from Penglai, but I thought, given everything that's happened, we should do it face to face." She turned to Malcolm. "I wanted to make sure you're still interested in helping Erik and Jia. It's unlikely the next mission will involve the Hunters or the Navigators, but this mission proves that anything could happen out there." The smile she offered turned ice-cold. "You stay with them and you'll get a chance to be a hero, but at the same time, your chances of dying old and happy and surrounded by grand-kids go down. That's what it means to work in the shadows."

Malcolm swallowed. "I understand, and I'm still in."

"Good. We need all the reliable people we can get." Alina turned to Erik. "Now let's get down to why we're here. Slaying gods, fake or otherwise, gets people talking, Perseus. Important people."

"Meaning what?" Erik folded his arms. "You can't seriously be saying I made too much noise."

"Yes, I am, but not in the way you're probably thinking. There are a lot of conversations going on, major ones." Alina gestured to the ceiling. "Not everyone above my paygrade agrees with your call. The military in particular is irritated about the loss of potentially harvestable offensive and defensive technology."

"Bullshit," Erik coughed. "That Hunter tech wasn't anything like we use or even the Navigators used. There was no way they were going to be able to do crap with that."

"They don't agree."

Jia scoffed. "What, you're saying that the government would have preferred we let some rapidly-repairing ancient and advanced hostile alien ship run free in the Solar System? Did they bother to read about how the thing was going somewhere? If we got lucky—and that was a big if, considering the taunts about us being humans—it would have left. But it was far more likely it was going to jump to Earth and remind us why we're supposed to be afraid of the Hunters."

"To be clear, Jia's statement isn't based on a potential misperception," Emma offered with a withering glare at Alina. "It was almost certain that the ship was preparing an attempt at FTL travel, and the delay between minimal activity and being able to absorb full attacks from two heavily-armed ships was very brief. It wouldn't have been surprising if it was back to full operation within days, if not hours. I know fleshbags don't always value their lives, but it would have been a massacre, even if they'd gathered every ship in the inner Solar System."

Alina raised a mollifying hand. "I'm simply passing along what they said. Personally, I agree with your call. From what I've read, we don't want any part of that disgusting technology." She gestured at her chest and then Jia. "We're on the same side, protecting humanity, and this new discovery, these Hunters, represent the gravest long-term threat to us." She sighed. "I'm telling you all of this, not because anyone's going to come after you. I don't even think there will be a problem with the jumpship being at the base as long as you keep Emma with you, but I just want you to understand the mindset of the other people watching this."

"What is the mindset?" Erik asked with a look of disgust.

"They appreciate the little information they can glean from what Emma and the surviving PNIUs recorded during the mission, but there's a faction who thinks we're far more likely to go to war with a Local Neighborhood race than run into another Hunter ship, and they believe we've thrown away a game-changing tool. Based on the Hunter ship's attempt at communication using a dead language, they feel there's little evidence of any significant recent activity, so they are operating under the impression there would have been minimal risk to any of the colonies or Earth.

"Minimal risk?" Jia threw her head back and laughed. "They wanted to risk the lives of billions of people in our home system to get a leg up on a war that hasn't even happened yet? We wouldn't need the Zitarks to invade if we'd let that ship get away. The Zitarks could try their hand at taking over the mutant-infested planets left behind." She motioned around the room wildly, her face contorted in fury. "*That* was their takeaway? If they really care, they should be telling the scientific community. 'We've discovered a new ancient race who had obviously been on Earth and interacted with humans. Researchers need to re-evaluate their previous discoveries and theories.' There might be Hunter artifacts sitting out there that people don't understand because they've been trying to apply a Navigator paradigm to their examinations."

"I don't care about all of that," Erik offered. "The government can kiss my ass. I made the right call, and I'd make it again."

"I know." Alina's brow creased. She stared at the table for a moment before looking up. "You should know the general public isn't going to be told about the incident. Despite half the government thinking this was a fluke, the other half is worried about panic, and both groups are worried about having to explain how a human ship took out such a powerful alien. For now, I think it's best if you keep the truth to yourself. We don't need more enemies. Despite the political ramifications, this is being viewed as a successful operation overall, even by some of the people who question destroying the ship."

"Shouldn't we be doing the opposite of keeping a low profile on this?" Jia asked. She gestured to Alina. "I'm talking about the human race, not Erik and me. Not only should we be telling the public, but we should also be reaching out to the other races. If we're lucky, that was the only Hunter ship left, but we're still not sure if there were Hunters aboard, or if we were just facing a leftover AI. If a fully-operational ship wakes up in a populated system with a full Hunter crew, it might require a massive combined fleet to take it out. For all we know, this could be the thing that unites the Local Neighborhood races.

Alina raised a brow. "There's been some talk about that kind of thing too, but I doubt it'll go anywhere. Again, everyone's worried about short-term versus long-term. They're already quietly covering up the ship's destruction by suggesting there was a long-running weapons test that went poorly."

"If the Hunters killed the Navigators, they're a threat to the entire galaxy." Jia cut through the air with her hand. "What good does it do to worry about the short-term if you have no long-term?"

"All true, Jia." Alina sighed with a rare look of defeat. "But before we can even hope to risk trying to use this as a bridge to the other races, we need to get our house in order. Because there's at least one group of humans who conveniently knew where to look for a Hunter ship and who have no qualms about killing people or turning them into twisted shells of themselves."

Erik's expression darkened. "That's been bothering me. Did the conspiracy know it was a Hunter ship, or did they think it was a Navigator ship? Do we have any way of figuring that out?"

"We don't know, and no, we don't." Alina offered him

an apologetic look. "We've got the data from the rod you recovered on the sub, and we've got data Emma was able to pull from the conspiracy ship before it blew to hell. At a minimum, that gives us more investigation leads, including digging deeper into the Vand Foundation, but there are still a lot of unanswered questions." Alina's smile returned, unnerving Jia. "But it's almost certain now, based on what we've seen and the second ship being there, that there is an internal struggle within the conspiracy. We might not know enough about them to use that directly to our advantage yet, but it at least means they'll be distracted, so we'll have more opportunities to probe and dismantle their operations. I don't mind winning with constant but small slices."

Malcolm blew out a breath and tugged on his collar. "I don't want to sound like a total psycho, and I know I wasn't there, but what if the Hunters aren't gone, and they somehow manipulated the conspiracy to send people there to wake them up?"

Jia's stomach tightened. There was a certain logic to that, but being logically consistent wasn't the same thing as being true. She suspected that if ancient aliens were behind the conspiracy, many aspects would be different.

Alina gave Malcolm an appraising look. "I'd be lying if I said the thought or at least one similar hadn't occurred to me, but I suspect if there was some member of an ancient alien race around, they would have found a way to go to that ship themselves rather than send humans."

Erik chuckled. "Maybe Garth was right, and they're hiding as platypuses until it's time to take over." He shrugged when everyone gave him a surprised look. "Not saying I believe it, but a week ago, I would have thought it was crazy to find an ancient alien ship sitting in a comet. But I'm not that worried about the Hunters."

"Why is that?"

"If they show up again, we can just double-gate them." Erik slammed his fist into his palm. "In this case, it's the humans running around with Zeus' lightning bolt."

Emma rolled her eyes. "You weren't paying much attention when Raphael explained it, were you?"

"I paid attention to the part where it could kill the enemy and we'd have to be close to do it." Erik frowned. "What's the problem?"

"What we did was incredibly dangerous, and there's no guarantee we can do it again without destroying ourselves. In addition, we were also fortunate that we were in a specific position in the system where we could do it. If that Hunter ship had been closer to Earth, we wouldn't have been able to layer the gates like we did, and the ship would either have escaped or destroyed us." Emma frowned. "Therefore, it's *not* an ultimate weapon, Erik, unless all our battles are fought at the farthest edges of every system, and I think that's an unlikely scenario."

"Then we need more and better weapons," Erik grumbled. He looked at Alina. "On both ships."

Alina nodded. "I'll see what I can do. For now, good job. I understand how frustrating it can be saving people and not having anybody ever know about it, but I know, and I appreciate what you've done. And I'm not the only one. Don't let my warning earlier make you think everyone in the government is out to get you."

Erik waved a hand. "Not important to me. We stopped

those asshole aliens, and we screwed with the conspiracy. That's a double win. I just want you to find us a new mission, so we can keep it up." He offered her a feral grin. "Maybe we can lure the conspiracy to the edge of the system and double-gate them."

CHAPTER FIFTY-SIX

Comfortable, so comfortable.

Jia lifted her beer to her lips as she nestled her head on Erik's chest. They lazed together on his couch. There had been some discussion of a training date, but taking a couple of days off not worrying about either a cancerous conspiracy or homicidal ancient aliens was well-deserved.

Erik knew that if either of them ran themselves ragged, they wouldn't last. Also, the conspiracy might have taken a hit, but they were still out there.

Other thoughts, buried and delayed while they were in survival mode, resurfaced, some good and some stabbing deep into his soul. It was time to stop stalling.

Erik blew out a breath. "There are things we need to talk about."

Jia sat up. She took a sip before setting the beer on Erik's coffee table and offering him a soft smile. "We could have talked about things for a week on that ship."

"But we were both coming to terms with what happened," Erik replied with a shrug. "But now we don't have a mission or Alina hanging over us. I figure there are fewer distractions."

"Okay." Jia's voice was soft. "I don't have a problem with talking. Let's do it."

"I think we both realize what must have happened on Molino now."

Jia looked into his eyes. "Alien artifacts. That must have been what they were hiding. The government would have forced them to turn them over, and even if they smuggled them out, they would have been logged and left a trail for someone to follow. They needed to cover their tracks, even if it made them look suspicious as hell."

Erik gave a slight nod. "It's the only thing that fits. The only thing worth killing my entire unit over. The only question I have is whether those artifacts were from the Navigators or the Hunters."

"Does it make a difference?" Jia asked. "Either could potentially unlock powerful technologies."

Erik shook his head. "I suppose it doesn't make a difference, but I'm wondering now if they knew there were artifacts on Molino before the colony was established."

Jia furrowed her brow as she considered the question. "I don't think so. I can't explain how they stumbled onto the Hunter ship, but if they had an easy method for finding artifacts, I think we would have seen more evidence of it. I think they're keeping an eye out, but that's not the same thing as being able to pinpoint things easily."

"Evidence?" Erik let out a dark chuckle. "You mean like full-conversion Tin Men immune to cybernetic psychosis syndrome? Or Leem-human hybrids who are tougher and faster than either race?"

"That's not the same thing. Those are just iterations on existing technology."

"So is the jump drive." Erik shrugged. "I'm just saying, these people are not just steps ahead of us, but steps ahead of the entire Intelligence Directorate. But it doesn't matter."

Jia's eyebrows lifted. "It doesn't?"

"Yeah. I've got a simple solution to the problem."

"And what's that?"

Erik's smile turned lupine. "We take them all out. We've made major inroads against them, and I'm sure Alina and the rest of the ID are sifting through the data and finding new targets. And now we have the jumpship. They've got to fix it and further calibrate the drive, but it means there's nowhere in the galaxy they can hide."

He lay his head on the back of the couch and his muscles loosened. It felt like it'd been years since he could relax like this after all the danger.

Men had died, but that wasn't new. He would honor their sacrifices the same way he was honoring the Knights Errant: by hunting down the people directly or indirectly responsible and making them pay.

A comfortable silence spread between Erik and Jia. She returned to resting her head on his chest but left her beer on the table. He almost laughed, remembering how a single beer used to be too much for her, along with a single use of her stun pistol, but now he couldn't imagine anyone else at his side in battle or in a bar.

"That's not what I thought we were going to talk about," Jia murmured.

"Oh?" Erik kissed the top of her head. "What did you think we were going to talk about?"

"The truth about us," she replied. "It came out during the mission, then we both pretended it didn't happen. It's not like us to be cowards."

"I don't know if that was pretending or cowardice." Erik sighed. "We had a lot of shit to take care of, and everything has its time and place."

Jia lifted and shook her head before settling it back in its comfortable spot. "That's an excuse we both keep telling ourselves. That there will always be a better time, but there's always something that's going to be happening. I was tired of waiting for you to get the hint, but I don't have to because I know how you feel." She turned her head and kissed him. "I love you, Erik."

"I know, and I love you, Jia." He eyed her. "I kind of mentioned it."

"Sure, when you were worried about us dying." Jia shook a finger. "Don't even try mentioning the conspiracy."

Erik pulled Jia up and turned her until he was looking into her eyes. "I could get you killed."

"I could die falling in the shower, and it's not like you're dragging me along." Jia smirked. "I would think by now you get that I don't do *anything* I don't want to do, and there's no man out there who can force me to go against what I think is right. Just ask our first captain."

Erik laughed. "That's true." He stroked her cheek. "You make me think…"

She wasn't so patient this time. "*What?*"

"That there's something else after the conspiracy. A future other than just revenge."

Jia leaned closer and gave him another light kiss. "Is that so wrong? Having a future?"

"No," Erik breathed. "It's not. It's just not something I thought I could have after Molino."

"You didn't die on that moon, Erik," Jia patted his chest. "It's okay to want to live. I'm going to be at your side and there with you in the future. For now, we can concentrate on taking out the conspiracy, or whatever occasional ancient alien race shows up and threatens us."

Erik laughed at her knowing smile. "Fair enough." He nodded in the direction of his bedroom. "I know something else that could get our minds off the conspiracy."

Jia ruffled his hair. "Sure, use *them* as an excuse when you want some." She sat up, grabbing his hand to pull him up. "I'm also not shy about doing things I want to do."

THE STORY CONTINUES WITH
DESPERATE MEASURES

Pre-order Desperate Measure for Delivery on October 2, 2020

AUTHOR NOTES - MICHAEL ANDERLE

AUGUST 9, 2020

Thank you for not only reading this book but through these *Author Notes* as well!

Where do we go from here?

I have to admit, I'm getting a little lost between what I just finished (editing the final draft of Book 09) and what is releasing (in this case, book 08.) Sometimes, I want to integrate the two stories and talk about something that I just finished, assuming you have read that story, when in reality, you are finishing the previous book.

But I am concerned that the book previous to this might have happened two books ago, and it will prove the suggestion that I've lost my mind.

Because it's only a suggestion until I do something to prove the suggestion is right.

I hope you enjoyed this story. We are getting closer and closer to the answers to who did what to whom, what power do they hold, and will the group or groups responsible get away with it, or will Jia or Erik deliver them a final goodbye?

What will Erik do with Emma to help save her? Will they have to give everything back to the military (including Emma), or is that little concern that in the end, they will be too dangerous because of what they know to be allowed to live?

If they know too much, can the military do anything or make it quiet enough with Emma around?

Strange are the thoughts of an AI.

Being forewarned is forearmed. While I don't personally believe those at the top will do anything catastrophically stupid, I don't have the final book laid out, so I can't be sure.

I'm a cynic. I absolutely believe that the inclination to be stupid in thoughts and deeds escapes no one. We all upon occasion fight the negative, selfish proclivity to do without consideration for the repercussions.

Which, generally speaking, isn't a big deal for you or me. However, when you are high up and entrusted with power, a slip-up might have magnified results.

I'm pretty sure I know two people who would bring the superior firepower to argue their case if need be.

LOCAL NEWS

So, I have a desk (or two) again!

During COVID, I have been working out of a home office in our condo on the Strip. After grieving through the changing of what I knew to be reality for fifty years, I dealt with working in a small space.

While one of my walls was all glass to see outside, that didn't allow too much because the blinds needed to be closed, or I had an office that might as well have been an Easy Bake™ Oven.

So, I kept the blinds closed, no seeing outside.

My wife and I had plans to move eventually. The condo was never our "forever home," but more our home for right now.

In late May, early June I decided I would push to find out if we could move up the timeframe on switching homes from the condo to something that allowed me to see outside.

Fortunately, Judith was amenable to my desire to look around.

We moved close to mid-July, and three weeks later, I have a desk I can use to type these *Author Notes*. Previously, I was working off of a nice set of table and chairs (outdoor furniture) the previous owners left with us.

That was the good part. The bad part is we are in the hot part of the Las Vegas / Henderson summer. Temperatures during the afternoon are between 108-112 on average.

I drank a LOT of water.

I didn't work much past noon or one before I packed up my stuff and moved inside. I like my routine, and for three additional weeks, I've had no routine. I am looking forward to trying to create a routine here in Henderson that will last me for years to come.

Book 09 has been finished and sent to Dreamscape, our Audio partners. Now, I need to write the author notes for that book...soonish.

Because it's not happening this morning, Mr. Campbell,

no matter how nicely you asked. I have a strong need for breakfast ;-)

Ad Aeternitatem,

Michael Anderle

BOOKS BY MICHAEL ANDERLE

For a complete list of books by Michael Anderle, please visit:

www.lmbpn.com/ma-books/

CONNECT WITH MICHAEL ANDERLE

Website:
http://www.lmbpn.com

Email List:
http://lmbpn.com/email/

Facebook Here:
https://www.facebook.com/groups/lmbpn.opusx/